BANSHEE

LINDSAY RUMBOLD

Published by Resolute Books
www.resolutebooks.co.uk

To Dave and Young Mr R.

You'll have a long wait for the film version…

RAF Martinford, 449 Squadron, 1964

Officer Commanding: Wg Cdr Edwin Merrick

Crew of Vulcan XL433:
Pilot, Flight Commander: Sqn Ldr Charles Hesketh-Shaw
Co-Pilot: Flt Lt Trevor Marshall
Navigator (Radar), Head of Navigation: Sqn Ldr Ted Radcliffe
Navigator (Plotter): Flt Lt Reg Mitchell
Air Electronics Officer: Flt Lt Chris Perkins

Crew of Vulcan XL447:
Pilot: Flt Lt Tony Brookes
Co-Pilot: Flt Lt John Miller
Navigator (Radar): Flt Lt Dave Gregory
Navigator (Plotter): Flt Lt Bob White
Air Electronics Officer: Flt Lt Neil McGoldrick

Crew of Vulcan XM568:
Pilot: Flt Lt Fraser Campbell
Co-Pilot: Fg Off Brian Grice
Navigator (Radar): Flt Lt Jim Farrell
Navigator (Plotter): Flt Lt Ken Markham
Air Electronics Officer: Flt Lt Mike Duffy

Engineering & Ground Crew:

Senior Engineering Officer (SEngO): Sqn Ldr Percy Burroughs

Avionics Integration Junior Engineering Officer (JEngO): Flt Lt Gordon Thompson

Avionics Integration Senior Non-Commissioned Officer (SNCO): Flt Sgt Bob Hunt

Vulcan XL433 Crew Chief: Ch Tech Kendall

Vulcan XL447 Crew Chief: Ch Tech Morton

Vulcan XM568 Crew Chief: Ch Tech Andrews

Fli-Tek Engineering Management:

George Watson

Jeff Kelly

"A murderer is less to fear. The traitor is the plague."
Marcus Tullius Cicero, 106BC – 46BC

Tuesday 11 October 2022

YELLOW EARTHMOVERS, SPLASHED grubby brown, clanked under fitful autumn sunshine. Caterpillar tracks criss-crossed a muddy corner that once was grass but would soon be a brand-new wind tunnel facility. Shattered echoes of clattering thud-thud-thuds bounced back in all directions from the new marketing block under construction less than half a mile away.

The site was a maze. 1950s buildings mingled with others in a layout that might have made sense when this place was RAF Martinford, but not now it housed Braxton Sports Cars rather than aircraft.

A mud-splattered excavator stretched its wide-toothed bucket towards its next chunk of earth. As it dug in, metal scraped and ground across something unexpectedly hard. The machine hesitated, then revved harder, fighting to move whatever was stuck. The ground trembled. Something gave way with a mighty *CRACK*.

What had seemed solid ground was suddenly something else.

Crumbled concrete stuck out of a heap of earth; harsh, sharp edged, scarred from the excavator's bites. Rusty reinforcing bars glowed orange against the dirty beige.

Urgent shouts rang out. The excavator reversed, halted, then grumbled in idle. Workmen in glaring yellow high-vis vests stood around, shocked expressions on their faces. Several took off their hard hats and scratched their heads, confused.

Puzzled curses mingled with voices raised in debate over the rumbling machines.

''S concrete.'

'Not supposed to be concrete here. Supposed to be just soil.'

'Yeah? What's that, then? Scotch mist?'

'It just moved as I—'

'Looks like a bunker.'

'Don't be stupid—'

'What the—'

One of the workmen, shovel in hand, kicked away clumps of mud in front of the bitten-off corner. He scraped the surface to reveal yet more concrete, this time like a floor – and something else. A manhole cover.

'Hey,' he shouted, 'is this an access panel?'

Another man, with FOREMAN printed in big black letters on the back of his once yellow hi-vis, scratched his forehead under the brim of his battered hard hat. He reached into his pocket and unfolded his copy of the site plans. He scowled at the paper, then at the ground. 'Nothing on here about that,' he growled. 'Right, stop everything!' With that, he stomped off, muttering to himself as he pulled his mobile phone out of a pocket.

The workman who had kicked away the earth looked around. 'Got a crowbar?'

'Whatcha doing?' asked another.

'Gonna have a look.'

'You serious?'

The man nodded. He pointed at the idling JCB. 'If that's not made a dent in it, can't be that bad under there, can it?'

Someone handed him a crowbar. 'Rather you than me, pal. I won't tell Health and Safety if you don't.'

After a few false starts, the metal lifted. A dark, dank, concrete-lined chamber sank into the ground. A rusty ladder, bolted to one wall, headed straight down.

Men clustered around the edge and peered in. One used his phone as a torch, but it didn't illuminate much beyond a grubby surface that had to be a floor, maybe ten feet down, peppered with dirt and debris.

After a bit of debate, one of them lashed his smartphone to the end of a shovel handle, set it recording, and pushed that down the hole. All the video revealed was a dark passageway, with what looked like a room beyond it; gloomy, forbidding, and empty. Nothing looked like it was about to collapse.

'Stuff this,' said the man who'd opened the chamber. 'I'm gonna have a look.'

Before anyone could argue, he shinned down the rusty but surprisingly sturdy ladder and fished his phone out. Might as well record the occasion, he told himself.

Clumps of dirt and bits of broken concrete dotted the dark passageway's slimy floor. Every careful step of his boots made a soft sucking sound that echoed off the silent walls. The cool air smelled of damp earth, and something else; slightly musty, but he couldn't place it. At one side was a half-height opening, like a window. His light revealed a room, dull and empty, its dirty wet floor covered in more chunks of rubble.

Ahead, a couple of steps led down into blackness.

He hesitated. What was he thinking he'd find? Maybe he shouldn't have been re-watching *The Walking Dead* over the weekend. Down here was still and soundless; he could barely hear anything from the surface. Even his own breath was loud. His heartbeat thudded in his ears.

The passageway ended in a brick wall, with a doorway to his right.

He shone the torch into the gloom.

It was another room.

Stacks of paper clustered against cracked concrete walls green with age and damp. He peered closer; dark mould speckled the mottled, damp sheets. Cables still hung on the walls. A light bulb, caked with grime, dangled forlornly from the ceiling.

Curious, he stepped inside. His boots squelched on a layer of mud. That odd, fusty smell grew stronger.

Around him, rotting cardboard folders and more soggy heaps of paper were scattered on the ground, as if they'd been hurriedly dumped.

Something else lay on the floor in front of him, just visible in the edge of the torch beam. He turned the camera and light onto it.

He cursed and fumbled the phone.

A skeleton sprawled in the corner against the crumbling wall. It still inhabited the remnants of a stained suit, shirt, and tie.

He stared at it in disbelief for several seconds. His body, deciding it had had enough of being down there, edged him out of the room then up towards the rectangle of light that beckoned him back to the surface.

As his boots clanged on the ladder, one of the others shouted down, 'D'you find anything?'

There was only one thing he could say. 'I think we better call the police.'

Wednesday 12 October 2022

'AH, Farnsworth, could I have a word, please?'

'Sir?' Flight Lieutenant Alex Farnsworth stopped in his tracks and put the cafetière and his mug down on the kitchenette worktop. This wasn't about him fetching his own mid-morning coffee, was it? Truth be told, he just needed to get his bum out of his chair.

Squadron Leader Burden – not especially tall, but broad, and running to chubby – filled the doorway. He peered over the top of his gold-rimmed glasses; such a schoolmasterly gesture that Alex momentarily felt twelve years old again.

'The MOD had a call from Warwickshire Police last night.' Burden rapped his fingers on the doorframe. 'A body was discovered at a former RAF base yesterday. Hidden in a bunker no-one knew was there until a digger unearthed it.'

Alex blinked. 'What?'

Burden's expression hinted he'd had the exact same reaction. 'I know. Sounds crazy.'

'Just a bit.' Alex chanced a sip of coffee. 'Where?'

'Braxton Sports Cars at Martinford in Warwickshire. Formerly RAF Martinford. Which closed in 1979.'

Alex frowned. 'Then it's more likely to be linked to them, not us. Isn't it?'

'You'd think so, however…' Burden took a deep breath. 'From what the police have said, the body's surrounded by RAF documents. I say body. Skeleton's more accurate.'

'In that case, isn't this a job for Operation Nightingale?' asked Alex. Operation Nightingale, and the Defence Archaeology Group, undertook various field archaeology projects such as excavating crashed WW2 aircraft.

Burden gave a humourless smile. 'Something's got to have been in the ground over seventy years before it counts as archaeology. And the police think this is more recent than that.'

'Oh.' Alex pulled a face. This was beginning to sound complicated.

'While others in what's currently Special Investigation Branch will be liaising with Warwickshire,' continued the squadron leader, 'we want you to examine the scene and review what's in there.'

Alex tried to hide his grimace. Oh, great. A clean-up operation? This felt like giving the new boy all the fun jobs…

Burden raised an eyebrow. 'We need to figure out who this person was, what they were doing, and just what paperwork's in there with them.'

Alex nodded. 'Sir.' Just what he wanted to be doing: poring over what would probably turn out to be illegible scraps or, perhaps the best-case scenario, someone's hidden mess bill.

Burden cleared his throat in a manner that suggested he knew exactly what Alex hadn't said. 'DI Parkins will see you at the Warwickshire Justice Centre in Leamington Spa at 0900 tomorrow.'

Thursday 13 October 2022

O900 IN LEAMINGTON meant an early start from Halton. Alex suppressed a yawn and fidgeted in the Vauxhall Insignia's passenger seat. A morning spent on the A41 and M40 was no-one's idea of a good time.

The man driving, Flight Sergeant Andy Woods, was one of the unit's senior NCOs. Yesterday afternoon, Burden had pointed Alex towards him as an experienced investigator, and someone who could help him learn the ropes. Alex gladly accepted: he was still settling into this role and privately reckoned he needed all the help he could get. Even Woods acknowledged yesterday this case could be tricky, though his slight smile told Alex he relished the challenge.

'Traffic,' Woods grunted. He was taller and chunkier than Alex, though probably around the same age, also mid-thirties. A cricked nose and cauliflower ears hinted he played rugby. 'Who agreed this time?'

'The boss, I assume,' muttered Alex. 'It wasn't me.'

There was an awkward pause. Woods kept his eyes on the road. They were still travelling out of Aylesbury. 'You, er, you're new to us, aren't you, sir?'

Alex nodded. 'Transferred from Intel at Waddington a few weeks ago.' He didn't really want to go into more details than that at the moment. 'Fancied a change.'

Woods absorbed this with a nod.

'Sorry you got lumped with babysitting me,' added Alex.

Woods risked a chuckle. 'I've been here since the year dot, pretty much, so I get all the good jobs.' He glanced over. There was no mistaking the curiosity in his expression. 'This sounds like it could be interesting, though. It's not the sort of thing we usually get.'

Ahead, past the car dealerships, Alex spotted a set of distinctive golden arches by the roadside. On cue, his stomach rumbled. 'Do we have time for second breakfast?'

Woods grinned. 'You're the one in charge, sir. If you say we do, we do.'

A quick circuit around the drive-through resulted in a pair of double Bacon and Egg McMuffin meals with hot drinks. Alex bought them – as it was his idea, it was only fair. Woods hoovered up his food with remarkable speed, and they were back on the road within five minutes. Alex was still finishing off his hash brown.

'Thanks, sir.' Woods almost managed to hide a burp.

'Sometimes it has to be done.'

Woods chuckled. 'That's what my kids would say. D'you have any?'

'Um. No. Not yet.' Alex coughed. Another subject he'd rather not go near just yet. 'How old are yours?'

'Six-year-old girl, four-year-old boy. My missus has her hands full with them.' Woods grinned broadly. 'Wouldn't swap them for the world, apart from at seven o'clock on a Saturday when I'd like a lie in.'

Alex laughed.

Now the ice had been broken, the journey along the A41, M40, and eventually the A452 into Leamington itself passed comfortably, if slowly.

Much to Woods' irritation, there wasn't any visitor parking at the Warwickshire Justice Centre itself. He had to squeeze into a space along the road outside. Alex smothered a groan at seeing they'd have to pay for parking, too.

Finally, they eyed the steps up to the building. Its bright, white, modern angles felt at odds with the faded Regency glamour surrounding it.

'Shall we?' said Alex. Woods nodded. They headed towards the building.

The main doors slid open to reveal a clinical waiting area. A couple of rows of hard metal seats sat in front of a screened-off desk. A thin, smartly dressed woman in her mid-forties, her dark brown hair in a short bob, stood up as they entered. Her footsteps echoed on the grey lino floor as she walked towards them. She radiated an air of competence and calmness. 'Thank you for coming,' she said. 'I'm DI Michelle Parkins.'

After the flurry of introductions, Parkins walked them through the building. 'I must say,' she began, 'thank you very much for your help. Braxton haven't been able to tell us much at all. You'd think they'd know what was under their own site.'

Woods tsked in sympathy.

'How can we help?' asked Alex. He'd spent a large part of the journey wondering exactly what they could do, here. In spite of Woods' open curiosity, he was far too cynical to believe he, as the "new boy", would get something particularly interesting.

Parkins ushered them into a room. 'I'll show you. Please, take a seat.'

The three of them settled around a table. A projector beamed a rectangle of blue light onto a white wall. Parkins plugged in the laptop sitting by it: the picture flickered, then resolved.

Woods pulled out a notebook and pen.

Parkins steepled her hands on the table. 'At 1537 hours on Tuesday fourth of October, we received a 999 call from Braxton's Design and Development Centre at Martinford reporting the finding of a body. An excavator removed some earth and dislodged a concrete block. That revealed a manhole cover. That led to a previously unknown underground room, which contained skeletal human remains.'

Woods scribbled this down.

Parkins pushed a button on the computer. A rectangular hole in the ground, debris scattered all around, appeared on the wall. 'This is the manhole,' she said. 'One of the builders opened it and decided to go for an explore. He found… this.'

The image changed to that of an underground room.

Walls green with age and damp glimmered in the harsh camera flash. Papers, piled everywhere and stacked high, appeared to be turning into mulch at the bottom. Grubby clothes rested on the floor in the far corner, as if what was left of a suit was having a rest.

Woods whistled, not quite under his breath.

Alex stared, dumbfounded. Even though this was what Burden described, seeing it was something else.

Parkins cleared her throat. 'This is as it was, just after the builders discovered it.'

'Why were they digging there?' asked Alex.

'The building contractor's ground clearance crew were flattening the area before digging foundations. The site's earmarked for new buildings,' said Parkins.

'And this was completely unknown?' asked Woods.

Parkins nodded. 'The contractors cleared the site a bit more and uncovered a set of stairs, also hidden by a concrete slab. It appears the lot was then buried under earth. Lots of it.'

'Deliberately concealed,' murmured Alex. That was the only logical conclusion.

Parkins continued, 'This is what we saw when we got down there.'

The screen changed. Human remains sprawled against the grubby concrete. A skull stared sightlessly. Despite the dirt and staining, what remained of the knotted tie that peeked under the bony chin was still flamboyantly patterned in a bold monochrome paisley.

Alex couldn't help himself. 'What a tie.'

'Beautiful, isn't it?' commented Parkins, deadpan.

Woods coughed. 'Have you been able to recover them?'

'We weren't able to remove him until late last night, but we hope to do what we can of a post-mortem in the next few days. The pathologist should have at least an interim report within the next few weeks.' Parkins paused, thinking. 'We might be able to identify him through dental records. We're waiting to see if we can obtain a reasonable DNA sample, but... I doubt we will.'

Alex studied the remains on the screen. He couldn't disagree with that assessment.

Parkins leant forward. 'We're in the process of clearing the room and sweeping for evidence. There's a huge amount of paperwork in there. Some of it's beyond rescue, but an awful lot still needs dealing with, and what we've seen so far seems to be RAF.'

'We can help however you need. Obviously, we'll need clearance from you once the scene's been recorded.' Deep in thought, Alex rubbed his chin. Depending on the date and contents of the papers, there was a chance they could still technically be restricted and not cleared for public dissemination. That could make things even more awkward.

'We'd appreciate your help recovering the papers, for a start. Some are a bit worse for wear. We'll also need your help to review them, to see if they can help us,' said Parkins.

Woods sucked his teeth. 'I can speak to the RAF museum conservators' team. And our Air Historical Branch. They might have some advice.'

Alex smiled. 'Good idea. Please do.'

Woods made another note on his pad, then looked back at Parkins. 'What have you done with the site?'

'Currently, it has one of our crime scene tents over it. We've implemented cordons as per standard procedures. Unfortunately, the scene's close to one of the main roads through the site, so we've had to close the road and effectively cut Braxton in two. Due to the, ah, access issues, all we've removed and recorded so far is the body.'

'What's Braxton's response been?' asked Alex.

'Overall?' Parkins shrugged in an exaggerated gesture. 'They don't seem to know anything. They didn't know the room was there. They don't know if there are more underground rooms or tunnels. They don't know when the room dates to. Their surveyors don't seem to know anything, either.' She sighed. 'We're due to see the CEO, Greg Hardiman, this afternoon. We currently have open access to the site while crime scene recording is ongoing.'

Alex exchanged a glance with Woods: maybe he'd been right, after all. 'If everything other than the body is still in there, we can develop the recovery plan between us this afternoon.'

'Of course.' A corner of Parkins' mouth twitched up. 'Perhaps between us, we can refresh the company's memory.'

PARKINS NEATLY PARKED the marked Vauxhall Astra in a visitor space in front of Braxton's main building; gate security had waved them straight through. Another member of CID, DS Richard Kinnear, joined them for the visit.

The three-storey-high, glass-fronted L shape shimmered in the autumn sunlight. Manicured, dark green shrubberies ran down the front of both sides. A tall revolving glass door spun lazily in the corner, wide enough for them all to enter at once without feeling squeezed.

Directly behind the revolving door was a wooden-floored, airy atrium that spanned the building's full height. Braxton's latest model, the Dreadnought GT, gleamed nearby, spotlit on a slowly revolving pedestal. Alex admired the muscular, low-slung sports car, resplendent in metallic battleship grey: unfortunately, the only way he'd afford one of these would be if he won the lottery.

Opposite the car, a smartly dressed receptionist controlled visitor access to the building from a sweeping oak desk. Alarm flickered in her eyes at the sight of RAF uniforms, barely camouflaged by the welcoming smile forced across her face.

Parkins did the talking and introductions. They all signed in. The receptionist buzzed open the glass barrier and led them across to the right, to a large oval conference room that overlooked the car park and gardens. A rectangular oak effect table and several black leather and stainless-steel framed office chairs occupied the immaculate charcoal carpet. Judging by the new carpet smell and the unmarked pale grey walls, these rooms had recently been redecorated.

'Mr Hardiman will be with you shortly,' she said. 'Can I get you any drinks?'

While the receptionist took their drinks orders and bustled off, Alex chose a corner seat just behind the door that gave him a view across the car park through the floor-to-ceiling tinted window. Curious, he ran a finger along the table's oak-coloured grain; it was plastic.

Kinnear sat heavily in a seat opposite Alex, and it creaked. 'You'd think with the cost of their cars, they'd spend a bit more on the furniture,' he muttered.

Woods fidgeted in his chair next to Alex; that, too, groaned under his weight.

Before anyone could respond, a man flung the door wide open and walked in, his footfalls soft on the carpet. 'Good afternoon, I'm Greg Hardiman.'

The heavy door swung closed behind him, almost knocking over the woman who'd tried to follow him in while balancing a tray filled with mugs and biscuits. Alex stretched and grabbed the handle just in time to stop the door slamming shut in her face.

Hardiman half-turned to Alex, frowning, but Parkins was already on her feet. 'Mr Hardiman, thank you for seeing us. I left a message—'

Alex stood and hauled the door open wider. The young woman flushed and held the tray out, as if in protection. Alex smiled at her and said softly, 'Can I take that?'

'Thank you,' she whispered. She carefully handed him the tray, shot a brief, wrinkle-nosed glare at the oblivious Hardiman, then retreated. Alex let the door gently close behind her. He slid the tray onto the table.

'As you know,' continued Parkins, 'we believe the underground works and the body date to when this was RAF Martinford, and so we informed the MOD. They've passed it to the air force. This is Flight Lieutenant Farnsworth, and Flight Sergeant Woods, RAF Police Special Investigation Branch.'

Alex pushed a smile onto his face. 'Good to meet you, Mr Hardiman.'

'Likewise, uh, Flight Lieutenant.' Hardiman shook hands; the man's palm was clammy. A smile scuttled across Hardiman's face.

While everyone else sat, Hardiman handed out the drinks but didn't offer the biscuits around. Finally, he settled into a chair. His stylish shirt and tie, chic glasses, and swept back dark hair seemed calculated to make him look younger than he was. Tell-tale grey glittered at his hairline. While Parkins explained the findings so far, Hardiman's eyes switched back and forth between Woods and Alex. Worry creased his brow.

'I can ask one of my team to print off a map,' said Hardiman. 'Perhaps you'd like to see where this, er, find is in relation to everything else here.'

Parkins glanced at Alex, who nodded. If nothing else, it would be interesting.

'Do you have any RAF maps?' asked Parkins.

Hardiman gave Alex an uneasy look. 'Um, no. We moved in blind, as it were. I believe when the company bought this site, surveyors mapped what was above ground. Some buildings were reused, but others were demolished long before I came here.'

'How long has Braxton been here?' asked Alex.

'Since 1984,' said Hardiman.

Alex frowned, considering. Not that he wanted to rule anything out prematurely, but it was unlikely Braxton had anything to do with the bunker or its contents. He shared a look with Parkins; she seemed to be thinking the same.

'It can't hurt to have a look,' she said.

Hardiman excused himself. Within a few minutes, he returned with a roll of paper. He spread it across the fake oak and repositioned a couple of the coffee mugs to hold the corners down.

They studied the map. Black lines showed the roads and current building layout; a box, drawn in pink highlighter, marked the bunker's location. It sat perhaps half a mile southeast from the hangars, in an area of mostly undeveloped land. On one side it was bounded by one of the minor roads through the site, and on the other by Stratford Road, the main public road alongside Braxton.

Hardiman lifted his eyes from the map and looked at Alex. 'You don't think there's anything else under here, do you?'

Alex shrugged. 'I don't know. I'm not an expert on airfield architecture.'

'The survey teams are just looking around that bunker,' said Hardiman. 'Should we do the whole site?'

'It's your site; do as you think best,' said Alex. That sounded far harsher than he intended. He cleared his throat. 'Obviously, it depends where you're considering development.'

Hardiman scowled. 'We're running behind with the building works as it is.'

Alex stared at the map. Even after so long, RAF Martinford still influenced Braxton's site layout. Judging by the shape, the runway and taxiways were the basis for the test track, and the three hangars reused as workshops with little in the way of external modifications. Presumably, the technical and administrative areas were reused by Braxton: he'd noticed on their drive through the site that several buildings had a 1950s air about them.

One thing about the road layout struck him. 'Was Martinford a second world war airfield?'

'I think so.' Woods studied the map. He gestured to the site main road layout; three straights, laid out in an 'A' pattern, with one of the straights parallel to the main straight of the test track. 'These could've been the original runways. Or at least, where they were.'

'Could this date to then?' asked Hardiman. 'If it's that old—'

'I'm afraid we're not able to confirm anything yet,' said Parkins.

Hardiman blinked rapidly, his mouth opening and closing a few times. 'So... is it murder, then?'

'Until we have evidence otherwise, we treat all incidents like this as suspicious,' said Parkins smoothly.

It would be hard to find a scenario that looked more suspicious – not that Alex would tell Hardiman that. 'The criminal investigation will take priority,' he said.

Hardiman sniffed. 'Do you have a timescale?'

Parkins cleared her throat. 'Before we can make any kind of judgement, we need to see exactly what we're dealing with. Please show us the site, Mr Hardiman.'

A LARGE WHITE rectangular crime scene tent sat over a hole in the ground like a grim gazebo. Access to it was blocked by a series of tapes tied to metal poles stabbed into the ground, creating an inner and outer cordon. Vehicles clustered on the road by the outer cordon. A white VW Transporter van, doors wide open and its interior packed with plastic boxes, was parked next to a white Transit and a blue and yellow Battenberg-patterned Ford Focus estate.

Off to one side, some distance away, two men towed what looked like a low rectangular box on wheels in a straight line across the stripped earth, marking their path as they went: they were geophysical surveying.

People clustered around the hole in the ground within the tent and inner cordon. A few were clothed from head to toe in white protective overalls.

'Will you need the road to be closed much longer?' demanded Hardiman.

'Difficult to say,' said Parkins. 'The road will need to be closed at least until the scene is recorded.'

'The closure may need to be extended, depending on what's revealed once that's complete,' added Alex.

Hardiman huffed but didn't say anything.

Alex looked at Parkins questioningly, and she nodded, a trace of a smile on her lips. 'Thank you, Mr Hardiman,' she said. 'Please will you wait here while I show our RAF colleagues what was found?'

Hardiman nodded, lips pursed in a suppressed scowl.

Parkins and Kinnear ushered Woods and Alex through the cordons.

Since the discovery of the bunker, more earth had been removed to reveal the concrete bunker roof and a second rectangular metal manhole cover, which hid a simple set of concrete steps down. Jagged concrete and clumps of earth still dotted the ground. The steps, and the original access found by the workmen, were isolated by orange plastic free-standing barriers, just as if they were roadworks.

Alex looked around. Piles of earth dotted the mud and scrubland around them: the excavators and bulldozers lined up some distance away, silent and still, waiting to restart work. Clearly, this part of the site had lain undisturbed for many years. No wonder Braxton hadn't expected to find anything here: he wouldn't have, either.

One of the white-overalled bodies pushed its hood down, revealing a woman with short brown hair. She headed towards them purposefully. 'Hello, inspector.' She smiled at Parkins, then nodded at Alex. 'I'm glad you've brought some air force assistance. You might find this interesting.'

Stained papers lay limply in a series of clear plastic evidence bags, flat on the table.

Woods stepped closer and silently bent over, reading what he could see of the bags' contents. He blinked, taken aback, then peered closer.

After a few moments, he looked back up, his face twisted in utter bewilderment. 'They're ops records.'

'What?' Alex frowned. He inspected the bags Woods pointed at. Sure enough, one page was headed OPERATIONS RECORD BOOK, RAF

Form 540. '449 Squadron,' he read aloud. '1964.' What on earth was a squadron ORB doing in there? Baffled, he met Woods' confused gaze.

The investigator looked questioningly at Alex.

'It appears to be a log of everyday squadron flying activities,' said Alex.

'Which could make our man either later or contemporary,' murmured Parkins.

'And raises a lot more questions.' Woods exchanged a glance with the investigator, then moved closer to the table again, brows furrowed and lips pursed. 'I can see some '700s there as well.'

Alex scanned the bags: Woods was correct. F700s were one of many forms used for aircraft maintenance records: they should have travelled with the relevant airframes or been destroyed. Not shoved in a bunker. Woods was right about this being interesting, after all. Perplexed, he rubbed his chin. 'They shouldn't be there,' he said, half to himself.

Parkins said drily, 'I assume this isn't standard RAF practice?'

'Not in the slightest.' Alex stared off into the distance, deep in thought. 'Which makes me wonder exactly what happened here.'

'You and me both.'

Tuesday 14 July 1964

GORDON SHUFFLED THE paperwork spread across his desk. Oh, the fun of being a junior engineering officer, or JEngO…

Four Bristol Olympus 201 engines howled as a Vulcan took off. The thunderous roar resonated through the building; his morning cup of tea shuddered on his desk. A perk, or disadvantage, depending on your opinion, of having an office by the corner of Hangar 3, the closest hangar to the runway. Familiar though the sound was, he paused to listen. One of these days, he'd manage to identify each aircraft by her engine noise alone.

Well, there was one clue. It had to be one of the Operational Conversion Unit aircraft, the only other flying unit based here at RAF Martinford. He smiled to himself.

That memo from his boss caught his eye again: Sqn Ldr Burroughs, otherwise known as SEngO, wanted an avionics integration update on the three Vulcan B.2s allocated to A-Flight – which was, in fact, the only flight – of 449 Squadron.

With an internal shrug, he flicked through the various sheets piled by each of the three aircrafts' serial numbers.

There was a tap on his door. It swung open before he could speak.

'Mr Thompson, are you decent?' Fraser strolled in. He surveyed the paperwork with a grin.

'Mr Campbell. I've always thought of myself as a pretty decent chap. What about you?' Gordon pushed his seat back from his desk and regarded Fraser, head on one side. 'Anything else you want to feed back about '68? The boss wants to know how his star planes are settling in.'

Fraser was the captain of Vulcan XM568's crew: he'd flown her back on Friday after yet another round of electrical system tweaks and an upgraded Banshee installation. She was currently undergoing some ground-based checks before the longer-range testing was due to begin, either tomorrow or Thursday, depending on the weather.

Fraser shook his head. 'No. I think I said everything the other day.' An eyebrow briefly raised. His hazel eyes sparkled with mischief as he sat in Gordon's spare chair. 'Tony's itching to check out his.'

Gordon rolled his eyes. Tony would be, of that he had no doubt. 'I bet. Well, H-S didn't have much to say about her after flying her back the other day, so…' H-S, or Sqn Ldr Hesketh-Shaw, was 449 Squadron's flight commander and the pilot of XL433.

'Short, mid-level flight this afternoon at two o'clock, we were briefed.'

'What, on '47?'

Fraser nodded. 'Surprised H-S didn't take that honour for himself.'

''33 had an issue with the bomb bay temperature getting close to limits, so we've had a look at all the ducting. Part of what he's checking later,' said Gordon. It wasn't a big issue as such, but Gordon never liked to leave something unfixed.

It did mean that Flt Lt Tony Brookes' crew, and XL447, would have the honour of the first real test sortie with the latest version of Banshee installed. She was meant to be flying this afternoon to start ticking items off the long list of tests.

Gordon caught Fraser's pout; Fraser hated not being first with anything. Not that he'd admit it.

'You get to go up for the first full installation test,' he reminded. 'Settling checks OK?'

'So far,' said Gordon. 'There's not much clearance in the bomb bay with the drum tanks in, though.' Fli-Tek, as Banshee's designers, must have worked hard to ensure the system would fit in XM568's bomb bay, sandwiched between two auxiliary fuel tanks mounted either side of it.

Fraser nodded. 'Surprised they didn't just use the saddle tanks.'

'Capacity.' Two types of auxiliary fuel tanks could be bolted into the Vulcan's bomb bay. The drum tanks were slightly larger, and shaped as their name suggested; the saddle tanks were sculpted to clear a Blue Steel missile, the RAF's primary weapon.

'Because obviously, I'll get the chance to fly to Moscow and back via Leningrad,' said Fraser, his words heavy with sarcasm. 'Two for the price of one.'

'I thought you were going to head for the Med.'

'That was with the normal bucket of sunshine. This, though...' Fraser trailed off.

'You could maybe make Libya.'

'Oh, great,' groaned Fraser. 'Eternity stuck in El Adem.'

'Well. When you put it like that...' El Adem wasn't the most inviting place in the world. Gordon scratched his moustache. On the whole, he tried not to think about such things.

Fraser pulled his chair closer to Gordon's desk and gave him a conspiratorial look. 'I wondered if you wanted to be our sixth crewman for the first flight,' he asked. 'You're hot on the electronics side of things, and Mike was saying he'd welcome a second pair of eyes.'

'I'd love to. So long as H-S and my boss clear it.' It was six years since he'd been in a flying Vulcan, but his short stint as aircrew, as an air electronics officer or AEO, had been the best, and most useful, of his life. Mike was Fraser's AEO. Then caution kicked in. 'Why?'

Fraser shot him a look, but grinned. 'You always think there's a catch.'

'There usually is.'

Fraser pursed his lips. 'I just feel like her being so well-behaved on the flight down was too good to be true. OK, we didn't have any fuel in the drum tanks, and we didn't press any new buttons, but...'

'We're testing the tanks now, and you can come and check the rest later or tomorrow. Chief Andrews has already been fussing over her, so...' Gordon spread his hands. 'I'm not guaranteeing anything, but so far, so good.'

'Well, the invitation stands.'

'I've flown with you before, so I know what I'm letting myself in for.'

'Of course. I'm the perfect pilot.'

Gordon chuckled. 'I'll ask Brian what he thinks to that.'

'I think you forget, I flew with you, too,' Fraser reminded him.

'I promise not to press any buttons or throw up on anything, provided you promise not to do any aerobatics.'

Fraser laughed. 'Where's the fun in that?'

'That's not part of the test plan.'

Fraser rolled his eyes, but a trace of a smile still played on his lips. 'And I thought this test flying would be fun and exciting.'

'The excitement's from something else,' muttered Gordon. After all, he'd witnessed part of Banshee's ground testing a few months ago; that was plenty exciting.

Fraser glanced at the clock over his shoulder, then stood. 'Speaking of which, we're in the simulator today. Even though we're borrowing one of the OCU's.'

'Have fun. You around later?'

Fraser shook his head. 'I'm seeing Sophie this evening.'

Gordon raised an eyebrow and smirked.

Fraser grinned back. 'I'd invite you along, but three's a crowd, you see.'

'That's all right. I wouldn't want to give you too much competition.' Not that he would be: Fraser, barely thirty, was some years younger, and Gordon had no illusions about his own attractiveness. Besides, beautiful and lovely though Sophie was, she adored Fraser.

'I believe you. Millions wouldn't.'

'Yeah, yeah.' Gordon looked at his paperwork and sighed.

Fraser grimaced at the piles. 'Rather you than me.' With that, he turned and headed for the door.

'That's right,' called Gordon, 'you get on with the fun bits.'

'Don't worry. I will.' Fraser gave a sarcastic wave then shut the door behind him.

Gordon reached for his now-cold tea and winced as he took a sip. Much as he was looking forward to being airborne, if Fraser and the chaps wanted him in the cockpit with them, they had to be concerned about Banshee and all the modifications.

Right now, he wasn't sure he could blame them.

WHAT FELT LIKE hours later, Gordon frowned at the clock then double-checked his watch; both matched. By now, Tony should be preparing to take XL447 up for her mid-level flight, but he'd not heard the hangar doors open. Just what was he playing at? Didn't he know they had a programme to stick to?

The crews were meant to verify several key things on the next few flights, regardless of aircraft used. Interference with navigation and radars was one; electrical generation and charging performance another; the ability of the Vulcan's battery back-up, ram-air turbine and Auxiliary Airborne Power Plant to function—

Footsteps stomped down the corridor outside. Voices echoed. Some childish urge made him creep to his door, wait till the footsteps were right outside, then yank it open.

Tony took a startled step back. Behind him, his taller and leaner co-pilot, Flt Lt John Miller, bit back a laugh.

'Tony, John,' said Gordon cheerily. 'Fancy seeing you here.'

Tony's mouth moved like a goldfish's. After a few seconds, he managed, 'Gordon. I was coming to see you.'

Gordon kept looking at Tony, ignoring John's theatrical eye roll. 'Oh, right?'

'She's not right. Chief Morton's saying she is, but—'

'Shall we go and have a look?' Gordon gestured for Tony to lead the way. As Tony strode off, Gordon caught John's eye; John spread his hands and shook his head.

Tony marched straight across the hangar towards XL447, her vertical stabiliser pointing high, like a shark's fin.

Gordon frowned at the mucky grey-green camouflaged Vulcan. Her black radome nose gave her a cartoonish look. 449 Squadron's Vulcans were among the first aircraft to be painted in the new, low-level colours; the air carried a faint scent of pear drops from their fresh coating of cellulose. Some loved the new scheme, along with the challenge of flying practically on the floor, but he wasn't so keen. Anti-flash white highlighted the purity, grace, and simplicity of the Vulcan's lines; camouflage, by definition, didn't. That said, blotched as she was, she was still a beautiful, sleek craft.

Tony's voice broke into Gordon's thoughts. 'They've shut the bomb bay. We need to look inside the bomb bay.'

'47's glossy, pale underside shone in the reflected work lights. From the outside, there was little to differentiate her from a standard Vulcan B.2.

'What's the problem?' asked Gordon. *Give me strength*, he found himself thinking. 'Explain here, and—'

'I need to show you.' Tony marched off towards a cluster of techs, waving his hands and shouting.

John groaned and muttered something under his breath.

'Can I have a clue?' said Gordon.

'He's not happy about the Banshee install,' said John.

'Neither am I, to be honest, but it's within bounds. We ran ground checks this morning and everything was within tolerance.' Gordon sighed and absent-mindedly rubbed his moustache. Some of the wiring routing and joins did look a bit Heath Robinson, but they were physically and electrically sound, which was what mattered; this was a prototype, after all. 'Yeah, it's not neat in places, but it works.'

Gordon glanced around the aircraft. XL447's cockpit door and ladder were down, and the wiring to give her ground electrical power trailed across the floor. He walked over to the bottom of the ladder and peered up into the blackness of the Vulcan's cramped cockpit. 'Anyone up there?'

'West, sir. Double checking Banshee's instrument lighting as requested.'

'OK. Can you open the bomb bay doors for us, please?'

'No problem.'

Gordon walked under the wing to see Tony stomping towards him, followed by Crew Chief Morton, the man who made sure his ground crew kept '47 maintained and airworthy. Morton's face was like thunder; he caught Gordon's eye and shook his head.

Before Tony could speak, the bomb bay doors splayed open with a mechanical hum.

Gordon stared at the revealed mechanism. How on earth could you compare the destructive power unleashed by a Blue Steel missile, or even the wartime Grand Slam Lancasters carried, with what this Vulcan cradled within… It was a different world.

Tony ducked underneath without another word. Chief Morton frowned at John, who shook his head with a sigh, pointed at Tony, then folded his arms.

Gordon gestured at Chief Morton; they both ducked underneath to join Tony.

'Right, what's going on?' said Gordon.

Hands on hips, Tony glared at the fuseboard up against the forward pressure bulkhead, right at the front of the Vulcan's cavernous bomb bay. Various chinagraph pencil scribbles covered the additional panels wedged in, labelling new fuses, wires, and routings. Though the bomb bay wasn't exactly small, the Banshee device packed the central third of it: a tangle of wires and tubes around a series of metal boxes with a flat panel held underneath. Additional brownish patches underneath her wingtips betrayed the location of other, new, antennas. 'Wasn't this meant to have the fore and aft internal fuel tanks?'

'What are you planning on doing, touring Siberia?' Gordon couldn't help his sarcasm. Chief Morton smirked briefly.

Tony huffed and waved at the aircraft. 'Can you get the tanks in if Banshee's in?'

'We want to keep an eye on the install to see how the mountings hold up during manoeuvres. We can't see all the mountings if the tanks are in place,' said Gordon, as patiently as he could.

'But Fraser's—'

'XM568 has different tests allocated.'

Tony scowled at the floor, jaw working, but didn't speak.

'As does H-S's, XL433,' reminded Gordon. 'He's out with her on Tango dispersal doing ground running checks and preliminary power stabilisation before a low-level transit check tomorrow.'

'Which is what we were told in the briefing,' muttered John pointedly.

'And, as you can see, '68 is sitting over there because we're doing the settling checks on the tanks prior to sending her up.' Gordon pointed to where XM568 sat at the back, then exchanged a glance with John. 'Fraser and Brian are in the flight sim this afternoon.'

Tony swallowed. For the first time, he seemed to realise just how much of a fuss he was kicking up; he avoided Chief Morton's raised eyebrow stare and looked at the floor. Pink tinted his cheeks.

'West's up there double checking all the new bells and whistles, so cockpit wise everything will be fully functional.' Gordon nodded at Chief Morton. 'Obviously, if something's not right, come back and report it, but as far as we're aware, she's as she should be.'

John cleared his throat. 'So, we can crack on with pre-flight checks once she's wheeled out?'

'By all means,' said Chief Morton. 'Let's get her out, shall we?'

He headed to the ladder and shouted up at West, and Gordon gestured to John and Tony to get out of the way.

Tony refused to meet Gordon's gaze; he ran a hand over his brylcreemed but still wavy hair.

Over Tony's shoulder, John mouthed "told him"; Gordon nodded.

'I don't know how the boss is getting on,' said Gordon, 'but I can assure you I'll be keeping a close eye on '47.' *And the others*, he added in his head. 'If you take her up for the flight as briefed, we'll review afterwards. Any snags, I'm sure Chief Morton can sort them in a jiffy. OK?'

'As you say,' said Tony levelly.

John bit his lip to stop himself sniggering and exchanged a meaningful raised-eyebrow glance with Gordon.

Abruptly, the hangar doors rattled open; daylight streamed through the widening gap. Without another word, Tony stalked off towards the exit.

Once he was safely out of earshot, John blew out a long, irritated breath. 'How much trouble d'you think I'd be in if I, say, ran him over with the Landy?'

'Can't say, but I think the boys in here would stand you drinks for a while.' Gordon sucked his teeth. 'I know I would.'

John chuckled. 'Don't tempt me. Really, don't.'

'Is he always like that?'

'Pernickety? Not usually.' John turned and looked at XM568. 'I think he's just feeling a bit… under pressure.'

He knew exactly what John meant: Fraser and his crew were a rare breed, rated Select Star; objectively and repeatedly one of the best performing crews in the whole of Bomber Command. And Fraser wasn't backward in coming forward about that fact. 'There are ways of dealing with it, though. Pissing off your ground crew isn't one of them.'

John nodded. 'I'd better go and get on with my checks, else everything'll be my fault in the debrief.'

'Good luck.' Gordon patted John on the shoulder. 'Rather you than me.'

⮔

A FEW HOURS later that afternoon, Gordon peered around one of the aircraftsmen's shoulders at XM568. 'How's she looking?'

'She's looking good. Fuel tank wise, at least.'

Gordon opened his mouth to say more, but a door slammed. He glanced across the hangar to see someone in a rumpled blue flight suit stomping towards his office.

'Oh… 'scuse me…' he muttered, then hurried over. He got to the corridor just as whoever it was flung his office door open: it banged hard off the stops.

'Oi, careful!' shouted Gordon.

'Don't you dare tell me to be careful!' The man whirled around and jabbed a finger in Gordon's face: it was Tony, flushed, dishevelled, and furious. 'That… that bucket of junk!' he yelled. 'You said it was fine!'

Gordon held up his hands. 'OK. Come in, sit down—'

'It nearly bloody killed us!'

'Wha—'

'This whole project is a…' Tony stopped, panting for breath. He scraped a hand across his forehead and through his hair; despite the Brylcreem, it was all over the place.

'Come in,' repeated Gordon quietly, 'sit down, and tell me all about it.'

'I'll be filing an SOR,' snapped Tony.

Gordon blinked. An SOR, or Special Occurrence Report, was a formal way of reporting any issues that affected aircraft airworthiness and safety. On the one hand, such issues needed to be logged and dealt with, but on the other, it was a lot of paperwork. Even more than he was currently dealing with.

'That's your prerogative,' he said, keeping his voice level. 'Are you going to make me wait till you've submitted it to tell me what this is all about?'

Tony took a deep breath, but before he could speak, Hunt appeared behind Tony in the corridor and cleared his throat. Flt Sgt Bob Hunt was Gordon's right-hand man.

'Ah, Bob,' said Gordon. 'Get us a couple of cups of tea, will you, please? NATO standard.'

With that, he guided the now subdued Tony into his office, virtually plonked him in a chair, then took his own seat. 'Now. What happened?'

Tony drew in a shuddering breath. He pushed his chair right up to Gordon's desk, straight across from him, rested his elbows on the wood, and met Gordon's eyes. In his own was the look of a man who'd been faced with one of his deepest, darkest fears; Gordon fought the urge to look away.

'We flew the mid-level transit and activation check over Orkney.'

Gordon nodded; he remembered the briefing, too.

''47 passed all the pre-flight checks. Chief Morton told us Banshee was operational. In fact, you—'

There was a knock on the door: Hunt eased in, carrying two steaming mugs of tea, both strong, with milk and two sugars. Over Tony's head, he gave Gordon a sympathetic glance, but he set the mugs on the table without saying a word.

'Thanks,' said Gordon. Hunt nodded in acknowledgement, then closed the door behind him.

'We said everything was airworthy,' prompted Gordon. He pushed a mug towards Tony and grabbed his own.

Tony shot him a brief glare, then nodded. 'Flight up to Orkney – everything was fine. Until Neil pushed the button.'

'What happened?'

'Our Vulcan turned into a rather large and heavy uncontrollable glider.'

'Fuck.' The involuntary swearword hissed out between Gordon's teeth.

Satisfied at this reaction, Tony sat back. He waved his hands to emphasise his words. 'We lost everything – and I mean, everything. Main power, alternators, battery back-up, the works. I thought the B.2 wasn't supposed to suffer this.'

'Me too,' admitted Gordon. A large part of the B.2 upgrade had been a complete reworking of the electrics and power generation systems, following a few failures and aircraft losses on Vulcan B.1s. Given Vulcans relied on electricity to run the powered flight controls, any loss or interruption of the power supply was a major issue.

After a few seconds, Tony carried on. 'We started at seven thousand feet. By the time we'd got the dog running, we were below two and a half.'

Gordon blew out a long, slow breath. The dog was a slang name for the Auxiliary Airborne Power Plant or AAPP, which was a gas turbine supplied by Rover, the car company. That was meant to provide emergency generating power if the electrics failed when airborne. Tony didn't need reminding it shouldn't have taken that long to activate it.

'We lost flight controls, everything. If… if I'd trimmed her any differently…' Tony's jaw tightened, and he glared at the wall behind Gordon's head.

'You got the AAPP running,' reminded Gordon gently. 'Then…?'

'Neil managed to get the alternators back online. The battery back-up was completely shot, but control wise, she felt fine once we got power back.' Tony swallowed. 'It all went. Everything. No throttles, no elevons, no rudder… I almost blew the door manually to give them a chance.'

At two thousand feet below a plunging Vulcan, that might not have been much of a chance. Not that Tony needed reminding; the shock still radiated off him.

Gordon sipped his tea. Blimey. Where did he start with this? He tried to think. 'First of all, yes, you need to do that SOR. You've debriefed, haven't you?'

Tony nodded. He picked up his tea and stared into it.

'You didn't call a Mayday?' said Gordon.

'How could I? Nothing worked!'

'When you recovered power—'

'When we recovered power, I climbed us as high and as fast as I dared,' snapped Tony. 'Neil told ATC we'd had some electrical issues but were evaluating – when everything seemed to be OK, we elected to return here.' At this, he gave Gordon a wary look. 'You know we've been told not to divert to other airfields unless absolutely necessary?'

Gordon blinked. 'Fraser said something about it…'

'It's an order from the Wingco himself.' Tony sipped some tea, then set his mug down with a deliberate clink. 'Unless life is at stake or there's a threat from the aircraft to the country below, we are forbidden from landing anywhere other than here. And even then, I got the impression they'd rather we wiped ourselves out than be forced to stand guard around our tin triangle till the cavalry arrive.' He scowled. 'Was that what he said?'

Gordon nodded. Fraser hadn't been quite so scathing, but the gist was the same.

Tony raised an eyebrow, as if surprised, then glanced down. He sighed, the noise making it sound as if he was running out of steam.

'You file the SOR,' said Gordon. 'We need to find out what went wrong, because I don't want it happening again. Full stop.'

ONCE TONY LEFT, Gordon pondered what had happened. Of course, he knew what Banshee was meant to do to its surroundings, but supposedly months of work had gone in to make sure this kind of thing wouldn't happen. What about all the ground trials they'd done at Malvern? Or the work at Boscombe Down? Surely Avro – well, Hawker Siddeley he supposed they were, now – had worked with Fli-Tek at Woodford? They had to have; how else would they have got such a neat installation in the bomb bay, between the drum tanks?

Besides, XL433 sailed through her ground checks earlier. In fact, Sqn Ldr Hesketh-Shaw had wanted her to be ready to fly tomorrow. Even so, Gordon would ask Hunt and Chief Kendall, XL433's crew chief, to get the erks, or aircraftsmen, to scrutinise every inch of her. Again.

XL447 would have to be grounded until they had some answers; for that, Fli-Tek would have to come and examine Banshee, too.

With a sigh, he reached for his phone. Time to spread the bad news.

Thursday 16 July 1964

TEA IN HAND, Gordon nudged open his office door. Time to start Thursday. Fli-Tek were due in later to examine XL447's Banshee system. She'd undergone several different functional checks yesterday, courtesy of various teams of technicians; piles of test results sat off to one side, where Hunt had dropped them earlier. Perhaps unsurprisingly, though XL433 had cleared all her ground tests, Sqn Ldr Hesketh-Shaw hadn't taken her up for her flight yesterday.

Then Gordon saw the folder, right in front of his chair. He groaned. He knew exactly what that was.

The start of Tony's SOR about XL447.

Despite the extra work he could've done without, he couldn't help but smirk; maybe Fli-Tek would actually answer some of their questions about Banshee now. He doubted it, but still…

He set his mug down, plonked himself in his chair, and began to read.

Tony hadn't minced his words; he'd written almost exactly what he'd reported to Gordon the other day. For once, Gordon couldn't blame him. Had they been lower, things could have been very, very different.

There was a knock on the door. Gordon shut the folder. 'Come in.'

Fraser peered around the door. 'Is it safe?'

'Safe as anything round here.' Gordon sighed and pushed the folder to one side, and Fraser's eyes followed it. 'You heard, then?'

Fraser shut the door behind him, then sat down. 'Tony told us yesterday,' he said in a low voice. 'He wanted us all to know. In fact, he pretty much demanded H-S stop all flying till we know what happened.'

Gordon involuntarily raised his eyebrows. That wouldn't have gone down well. 'I think we're all hoping we'll get some answers.'

'Tell me about it.' Fraser glanced away. His brow lowered for a moment before he looked back at Gordon. 'Has anything cropped up on the boss's?'

'Not that I've had reported. Ground tests are all looking as per spec, so far.' Gordon coughed. There was one other thing on his mind. 'What's worrying me is West and the chaps are telling me it looks like there are differences in installation between H-S's, yours, and Tony's Vulcans.'

'But we're using '33 for the baseline running tests to clear the others.'

'Exactly.'

The two men shared a look.

Gordon reached across for his tea; he swigged some of the tepid liquid and fought back a grimace. One day he'd finish a cup while it was still warm. 'And if Watson spots us with the bomb bay doors open,' he continued, 'we get him interfering and telling us not to look without permission.'

Fraser scowled. 'That man.'

'Well, with this, the ball's in our court. He's due in later to "help", but we'll see how much use he actually is. Tony isn't going to let it be brushed under the carpet, and neither am I.'

'Don't expect much,' warned Fraser.

Gordon drained his mug; it clinked as he set it back down. 'You've never said. What's the story with you two?' George Watson and Fraser got on like a house on fire: plenty of sparks and interesting to watch from a safe distance. Neither camouflaged his dislike of the other.

Fraser leant forward. 'Old man Turnbull – you remember him, don't you? – used to fly Canberras and did a bit of test flying in the fifties. You know, altitude and distance records? Anyway, when I asked him about it all, he mentioned there was a certain contractor who could never, ever give a straight answer. Even if he promised you something, chances were you'd get the exact opposite. He reported some handling concerns with one particular mod, and when he got a copy of the official report, Watson had twisted his words to make sure it sounded like there were no issues whatsoever. He was furious, but by then, of course, it was too late.'

'Is that all?'

'What do you mean, *all*?' Fraser scowled. 'The man's… well—'

'That was a fair few years ago,' interrupted Gordon. 'Things might have changed.'

'I doubt it. The leopard doesn't change his spots,' muttered Fraser. 'What else could he have lied about?'

Gordon opened his mouth to reply, then stopped. After all, Watson had assured him all three aircraft would have an identical Banshee installation.

Fraser raised an eyebrow knowingly but didn't speak.

Gordon conceded defeat. 'All right. But I'm still not sure he's as black as you're painting him.'

Fraser gave Gordon a serious look. 'I hope – for all our sakes – you're right.'

GORDON GLANCED AT his clock. It was almost time for the big meeting.

He grabbed his notes, then pushed himself away from his desk and headed towards the hangar. XL447 had been manoeuvred to the back of it, the other two Vulcans crammed in around her. Under the work lights she gleamed, seemingly innocent.

He withheld a sigh. This was the most frustrating part of the whole project: he had to wait for Watson and his men to arrive and inspect the Banshee system, and its installation in the Vulcan, in detail. Neither he nor his team were supposed even to touch any part of that system. Quite why Fli-Tek had to be so protective of their bit of kit, who knew, but if this was going to be the pattern for the rest of the project, everything was going to take three times as long as it should.

The sound of faint footsteps echoed towards him. A uniformed Hesketh-Shaw, slender and sandy-haired, ushered another figure in a suit through the gap between aircraft: he was roughly the same height, but rounder, with thinning dark hair spread across his head. George Watson.

He perambulated his way towards XL447. There really was no other way to describe the man's leisurely, rolling gait. Should the four-minute-warning siren sound, Watson would probably still amble his way, too unfit to move any faster. Still, he might provide shelter for others if the balloon did go up.

The buttons on Watson's shirt strained to control his expanding gut, which flowed over his trousers like it was trying to make a break for the floor. Sweat rose on his brow; he coughed, dragged a white handkerchief from a pocket, and dabbed at his forehead. He stopped by XL447, pink, shiny, and slightly out of breath.

Hesketh-Shaw caught Gordon's eye and nodded. 'Good morning. You've met Mr Watson before, haven't you?'

Gordon nodded. 'Yes, sir. I was present at some of the RRE trials last year.' Repressing a shudder, he shook Watson's clammy hand. RRE was the Radar Research Establishment, based at Malvern in Worcestershire; some of Banshee's feasibility studies had taken place there. 'Welcome to Hangar 3.'

'Thank you.' Watson paused and gathered his breath. 'Flight Lieutenant Brookes talked me through the issues witnessed in flight a few days ago.'

'I see,' said Gordon. He glanced at Hesketh-Shaw, but the man said nothing.

Watson cleared his throat. 'Have you found any problems with the jet?'

'Since she landed, we've found a minor discontinuity in the battery back-up circuits.' Gordon looked squarely at Watson. 'Circuits that were fully functional when she left.' And certainly nothing that should've caused what Tony reported.

'Are you sure there wasn't any kind of pre-existing issue?' asked Watson.

Hesketh-Shaw spoke. 'I flew this aircraft down from Woodford. Most everything performed as expected. Avro gave it a clean bill of health.'

'Oh. Er. Well...' Watson fumbled for his hanky and patted his forehead again. He shoved the damp fabric back into a trouser pocket.

'You've seen the SOR?' asked Gordon.

The moment of silence stretched slightly too long.

Hesketh-Shaw met Gordon's gaze, but his expression was unreadable.

'Obviously, this is highly sensitive,' said Watson, filling the silence. 'We have to consider how widely information may be disseminated – and what's wise.'

Gordon withheld a grumble. What did Watson think was going to happen? That he'd stick Tony's report on the station noticeboard? No-one gossiped like aircrew, anyway; he didn't doubt every 449 Squadron crewman already knew all about what happened. 'Nevertheless,' he said, 'we've had a serious problem that needs investigating, from all sides.'

Hesketh-Shaw opened his mouth, but Watson spoke first. 'We're aware of that, and yes, we need to examine the aircraft and the systems.' He drew himself up and gave Hesketh-Shaw a serious look. 'Shall we start?'

At Gordon's nod, West attached ground power and then shinned up the cockpit ladder to open XL447's bomb bay. The doors powered open with a mechanical hum.

Almost immediately, Watson disappeared underneath. Hesketh-Shaw gestured to Gordon to follow.

'Oh, yes, this is set-up A,' murmured Watson. 'Without the long-range tanks.'

''33 and '68 have the tanks,' said Gordon. 'Neither of those has started flight tests yet.'

'But '33's been ground running without any issues?' Watson stared, wide-eyed, around the interior of the bomb bay.

Hesketh-Shaw frowned. 'Yes and no. We had an issue with the bomb bay maintaining operating temperatures on the return flight. Mr Thompson's team rectified a ventilation issue. Since then, it's passed all ground tests so far.'

Though his gaze was fixed on the Banshee unit, Watson's hands tangled around themselves like he was washing his hands in invisible water. His brow furrowed and his lips moved. 'From the flight profile Brookes gave,' he said eventually, 'this damage shouldn't be present.' He pointed to where traces of white paint gleamed on the corners of the middle panel framework. Barely visible were matching dents and chipped paint on the interior of the bomb bay doors.

'Avro did have some doubts regarding clearances,' said Gordon.

Watson sniffed, irritated. 'We adjusted the mounting positions as much as possible.'

'We've looked at all the fatigue gauges.' Gordon stuck his hands on his hips. 'There's no indication Brookes flew outside the permitted envelope.'

Watson didn't turn around.

Hesketh-Shaw peered closer. 'Would this small contact result in what Brookes experienced?'

Watson baulked. 'It… well, it shouldn't.' At last, he turned to look at Gordon. 'Have you checked the RAT?'

'Yes, but we can do it again if you like.' Gordon nodded towards his office. 'Or I can show you the test results. It's absolutely fine.' The RAT, or Ram Air Turbine, was intended to provide emergency electricity generation until the AAPP started, or the aircraft sorted itself out.

Hesketh-Shaw observed Gordon, then shook his head. 'That won't be necessary.'

Both Hesketh-Shaw and Gordon looked at Watson: he blinked rapidly, avoiding their gazes.

'We dragged her out yesterday and functionally checked the AAPP,' said Gordon. 'We followed all procedures, and everything passed. I can show you the paperwork if you like.'

Watson peered intently inside the bomb bay. 'There shouldn't be any interactions if everything was fitted properly.' He gestured up at the forward bulkhead – the same one that had given Tony cause for concern.

'Wasn't this fitted by your company while this Vulcan was at Woodford?' said Hesketh-Shaw mildly.

Watson's mouth moved; his chins wobbled. 'Er… well… yes,' he mumbled. Abruptly, he pulled himself upright. 'May I have the assistance of your team to run some diagnostics? I brought some test kit with me.'

WHILE WATSON WENT to retrieve the test equipment, Gordon called West down from the cockpit. He then found Hunt and asked him to round up a couple of the others to assist if required.

By the time he'd done that, Watson stood by XL447, flanked either side by two large, black suitcases.

'The squadron leader said he'd come back to review later,' said Watson.

Gordon nodded and gestured to Hunt. 'Sergeant Hunt here will help you as much as he can. You've got three techs at your disposal as well.' He paused. Curiosity might have killed the cat, but he had to know what was happening. These were his aircraft, after all. He glanced at Hunt and couldn't resist a sly wink. 'I'll stay and supervise.'

Hunt's mouth twitched in a half-smile.

'Oh. Er,' began Watson.

'We're only here to help,' said Hunt firmly.

A couple of aircraftsmen dragged out one of the raised safety platforms. Watson complained and faffed, huffed and puffed, but eventually managed to set up his oscilloscope and test equipment.

Much to Gordon's surprise after Fraser's bout of doom and gloom, Watson happily talked them through what he was doing and what he was verifying while he was off the ground and buried in the bomb bay. Basically, he was checking the power circuitry that connected Banshee to the aircraft was fully functional, and that all fuses, interlocks and protections were intact.

After much shuffling, grunting, and groaning as Watson awkwardly moved in the confined space, he declared all was as intended, bar the discontinuity Gordon had already uncovered.

'I don't understand,' said Watson. He eased his way down the ladder, leant against it, and mopped his forehead. Damp patches shaded under his armpits. 'I can't see anything out of order,' he panted. 'Other than that discontinuity. Though one of the protectors failed.'

Gordon frowned at XL447. Really? 'So…'

'That… well… that shouldn't have happened anyway, but that should only occur post triggering.' Watson frowned. 'That doesn't explain…' He ran a hand over his thinning hair. 'Everything else on that aircraft is within spec. The PGU test cycle shows that's in line with what we fitted to her, so…'

Gordon exchanged a glance with Hunt. 'PGU?'

'Pulse Generator Unit. I mean, yes, it's on the upper limits, but it's within the specs we supplied to Hawker Siddeley.'

'Which means?'

'Hawker Siddeley, well Avro as they were, are the Vulcan experts,' said Watson primly.

'But they're reliant on your information,' said Gordon.

Watson glared at him.

'We can't keep taking this aircraft back to Woodford,' said Gordon. 'You know how late this programme's running, and they're busy trialling Blue Steel modifications as well.'

'This will make Blue Steel obsolete,' said Watson.

Gordon thought, but didn't say, *you hope*. Instead, he said, 'We all know how closely the Air Ministry are monitoring this programme. Especially with how TSR2 is delayed too.' He took a deep breath. 'What can we check, here, to help?'

Watson frowned. 'Are you a Vulcan expert?'

Gordon felt Hunt's stare. 'Well, I've been engineering avionics and suchlike on them for eight years, since they entered service. Including my tour as aircrew. I might not be an expert, but I know more than most.'

Watson blinked, as if affronted. 'Oh.' He shook himself.

'What do you recommend with the test programme?' Gordon held back a frustrated sigh; he needed a clear *go* or *no go* decision.

'That discontinuity. Could it be due to a pre-existing issue?'

Gordon pulled a face. His gut told him it wasn't, but without hard evidence either way… 'It could,' he said, as noncommittally as possible. 'Then again—'

'Perhaps switch this airframe to ground running to see if the issue recurs?'

Gordon had to admit that was an idea. 'We can discuss that—'

'Excellent.' Watson rubbed his hands together. 'I think I've done all I can here.'

FRASER GLARED AT Gordon. He put his beer on the mess bar, then folded his arms. 'Watson said WHAT?'

The noise level in the officers' mess dipped. It quickly recovered; chatter once again filled the air, swirling with the cigarette smoke.

Gordon winced. So much for coming in for a quiet drink this evening; perhaps he should've said no. But he needed to bounce what happened this afternoon off someone. 'Even my boss conceded it was an idea. What was I supposed to do?'

Fraser shook his head in disgust. 'Your trouble is you're too reasonable sometimes.'

'I was there as he ran the tests. He talked me through them—'

'Were you watching?'

'Yes,' insisted Gordon.

'Did you understand what he was doing?'

'I thought I did.'

Fraser eyed him dubiously for a few seconds, then drank some beer.

Gordon sighed. 'He was pushing to send the bloody thing back to Woodford. Again.'

'Again?'

Gordon nodded.

'Oh, for—'

'I know. I think Avro's are sick of the sight of them.' Gordon stared into the amber liquid of his pint, thinking. 'All I got out of him was one of the circuit protectors failed. Which it shouldn't have. But none of us could find any other problem.'

'Or you couldn't find a problem with '47 – and he wouldn't admit to a problem with Banshee.'

Gordon nodded. That had occurred to him. He picked up his drink.

Fraser raised an eyebrow.

'Anyway,' said Gordon, 'I now have to explain to H-S and SEngO why we're going to have to change the test plan.'

'That'll go down well.'

'At least Tony won't have to worry about bailing out if she throws an electronic tantrum again.'

Fraser stifled a snigger.

'Bob and the boys are tearing her to bits to find the root cause of that discontinuity. Maybe that was what blew the protector.' Gordon knew he was trying to convince himself as much as Fraser, here.

'Did you actually get a straight answer out of Watson about that?' Fraser's expression showed he knew exactly what the answer was, but he had the decency not to look smug when Gordon shook his head.

There was one thing Gordon had to ask. 'Still want me in the air with you?'

Fraser met his gaze, all humour gone from his face. 'If you're still willing?'

'Oh, yes,' said Gordon. He finished his pint. 'I'm going to find out what's happening with these aircraft if it's the last thing I do.'

Friday 14 October 2022

'Ponsonby. Thank you for coming promptly. I appreciate you have a busy schedule.' Cavendish gestured at the spare seat in front of his elegant walnut desk.

Quentin Ponsonby lowered his slim frame into the soft leather. The call from Cavendish's PA had come just as he settled into his office that morning; one didn't just tell Cavendish to wait. 'I understand we have a sensitive issue.'

Cavendish nodded. Just past middle-aged with thinning brown hair, he wore a sober but smart grey suit and what appeared at first glance to be an old school tie. However, his eyes belied that first, almost mundane, impression; they were dark, hard, and calculating.

He leant forward and steepled his hands under his chin, his usual expression of deep thought. 'Are you aware of what is already being referred to as "the body in the bunker" at Braxton, formerly RAF Martinford?'

'I heard something in the news. Though I must confess it seems rather odd.' Quentin paused. 'And I don't understand quite why we should—'

'—be involved?' interrupted Cavendish. 'Yes, I thought so too. However, it seems more may have happened at Martinford than we first thought.'

'How so?'

Cavendish sat back, his chair creaking. 'There is a suspicion that certain activities undertaken at RAF Martinford should, even now, still be classified Top Secret. UK eyes only at that.'

Quentin blinked. That was unexpected. 'I see.'

'The MOD, via the Joint Intelligence Committee, have asked us to keep an eye on things. Informally.'

'I presume at the moment the investigation is still with Warwickshire Police?'

'Yes, although they've requested RAF Police Special Investigation Branch assistance. RAF files are certainly present, but as yet, their scope and sensitivity are undetermined.'

Despite himself, Quentin's curiosity was piqued. 'You wish for me to monitor the situation?'

'Yes. I trust you'll use your discretion and judgement.'

Quentin smiled. 'Of course. Do we know the nature of these activities?'

'That has not been revealed. We're to treat everything with the utmost delicacy.'

Intriguing. Quentin took off his glasses and rubbed the bridge of his nose. 'Have the RAF allocated an officer to run the operation?'

'Yes. A former intelligence man, it seems.'

'Am I to liaise with this officer?'

'Yes and no.'

Quentin laughed drily and slipped his glasses back on. It was going to be one of those situations.

'As far as the RAF are concerned, yes. As far as we are concerned...' Cavendish smirked.

'Am I to, ah, guide and advise?'

'Indeed.'

Quentin smiled. He knew what he had to do. 'To whom do I report?'

'Me.'

'I shall, of course, do my best.'

Cavendish shifted in his seat and quirked an eyebrow. 'I trust you can offer our service friends plenty of assistance.'

Quentin returned the smirk; whether it would be the assistance desired was another matter. 'Of course.'

Perhaps this new assignment in London wasn't the boring dead end he'd feared it might be.

ALEX SUPPRESSED A yawn and stared at the text on his screen. It seemed like the only noises in the whole building were his breathing and the occasional asthmatic whirr of his laptop's cooling fan.

Some hours ago, Redfern had sent through a list of files to help his and Woods' research. Ignoring everything else, he dived straight in.

Given the scene revealed at Braxton, he couldn't reach any conclusion other than the body and the papers were meant never to be seen again.

The police were tackling the removal process at Martinford itself, but he'd tasked Woods and the rest of his team to find any needles of information within the haystacks of official archives. While at least one document dated to 1964, he didn't want to take that date for granted just yet. Later, or earlier, files could well be hiding in the stacks.

Why? He kept circling back to that question. Why conceal this death? Why hide the papers like that? Especially when at first glance, the contents were run-of-the-mill: a Form 540, Operational Records Book, was simply a log of squadron flying activities, recording which aircraft and crews flew when and where. Nothing exotic. Or incriminating. It didn't make sense.

He sighed and reached for his now-cold coffee.

As Woods said, RAF Martinford started life as a World War Two Bomber Command Operational Training Unit, or OTU, built in 1940 to train mostly Canadian and New Zealand air force crews to fly the Vickers Wellington twin-engine bomber.

Interesting though that was, their man was more recent than that.

After the war, Martinford was wound down and almost forgotten until the V-bombers – the Vickers Valiant, Handley-Page Victor, and Avro Vulcan – were on the horizon. The wartime base was flattened, completely rebuilt and enlarged; wholly new married quarters were built on newly acquired neighbouring land.

Alex recalled the rows of brown brick terraces and semi-detached houses that lined the side of the road for some distance before Braxton's main entrance; the site must still use the original gatehouse and route in. It made sense. Why build a new entrance when a perfectly serviceable one existed?

In 1956, the revamped RAF Martinford became one of the first V-bomber bases, housing a Valiant Operational Conversion Unit. Within a couple of years, a Victor OCU also took up residence. The Valiants were replaced by Vulcans in 1960; the Victors left in 1963, but the Vulcans stayed till 1971.

A few years later, the site was closed and downgraded to care and maintenance, before being bought by the local council in 1979. The married quarters then became council housing and part of a new village, renamed Martinford Grange; the remainder of the site was undeveloped until Braxton bought it in 1984.

Odd to think the site had been civilian for as long as it was RAF.

Alex scanned the list of units based at Martinford. Satisfyingly, 449 Squadron was there: a test and evaluation unit, using Vulcan B.2s, which moved in as a new unit in early 1964. It disbanded towards the end of September 1964 and didn't reform elsewhere.

Odd. New squadrons could be formed, but such a short life was highly unusual. 449 Squadron must have had a very specific task.

Intrigued, Alex flicked through the files. Whatever 449 Squadron tested and evaluated, it wasn't recorded, at least in these publicly accessible documents. Perhaps Woods' team would uncover more once the police gave the go-ahead. After all, if a plain ORB had been hidden, what else was in there?

He sighed. Chewing over these so-far unanswerable questions was a heck of a way to spend his Friday evening.

Out of curiosity, he looked up aircraft incidents in the post-war years. Unsurprisingly, there were several training prangs during the 1950s and 1960s; mostly minor incidents, which damaged pride more than the aircraft concerned.

Then he came to an incident that made him pause.

A Vulcan had crashed.

The text gave only the bare minimum of information:

> *4 August 1964. Vulcan B.2 XM568 (449 Sqn) lost; damaged beyond repair.*

Alex scanned the papers again.

*11 September 1964. 449 Sqn disbanded. Vulcan B.2s
XL433 and XL447 taken off charge and scrapped.*

Could it be coincidence that a 449 Squadron aircraft suffered the worst accident linked to Martinford?

Interesting that the remaining Vulcans were simply scrapped.

He swallowed the last, bitter dregs of cold coffee and pondered. If the type was being retired or removed from service, that would be understandable, but it was unusual, if not beyond the realms of possibility, for fully functional and serviceable airframes to be scrapped. Unless, of course, they were involved in some incident he hadn't yet come across. But still, repair or reallocation as a training or instructional unit was more likely.

That said, the Royal Navy took over the nuclear deterrent mantle with the advent of Polaris and nuclear submarines during the late 1960s. With the demise of 449 Squadron and the impending transfer of the UK's nuclear deterrent to the Royal Navy, the Vulcans may simply have been surplus to requirements. Particularly as 449 Squadron didn't re-form elsewhere.

Three aircraft was a small allocation for a Squadron, though. It was barely a Flight.

Tired, he rubbed his eyes then glanced at his watch. No wonder the place was quiet; it was well after 1700.

What he needed was dinner. To relax, unwind, and allow his mind to digest what he'd read.

His choices? Whatever was left over in the mess, with maybe a read of a crumpled newspaper if he was lucky; or back home, with a book or TV for company and a chicken chow mein he'd batch-cooked last weekend.

Four weeks after moving into his new house, he still had a few things to unpack and sort through. In particular, his books were waiting until he got some shelving to replace what he'd let Anna keep. When they separated last April, he'd boxed up as much as he could of his non-essential possessions and shoved them into storage. Sorting everything out, now he knew he'd be living somewhere more than a few months, was a strange mixture of depressing and cathartic. He'd feel better for it, but…

It was one reason he just kept working. *Well,* he could imagine his boss saying, *Alex has got awful taste in women, but when the chips are down, you can't get him off the case.* He allowed himself a smile, but it faded.

He didn't miss Anna – that would be like missing having Covid. He missed what he'd hoped their life might have been.

No point dwelling on it, though.

He shut down his laptop and headed out.

ALEX PUSHED OPEN his front door. It may be dark and silent, but to him, it was a welcome, quiet sanctuary.

One thing he and Anna had talked about, in the beginning, was buying their own home. Covid, and lockdowns, had put paid to that…

She was a nurse; once it became clear how serious the pandemic was, she'd been sent to work away in Manchester for months. They'd both agreed, given the seriousness of the situation and the risks of infection, that it would be best if she stayed up there and he stayed away.

That had been the start of the end.

Still, putting the offer in on this house by himself, once his transfer was confirmed, felt like a victory.

Smiling to himself, he flicked the lights on and walked through the narrow hall to the kitchen diner. Flattened cardboard boxes left over from the move piled up in the corner by the French doors: they'd go to the tip at some point this weekend. He'd tried, and failed, to fit them in the recycling bin.

Truth be told, he'd have preferred something other than a small new build on yet another anonymous estate, but it was well-equipped, didn't need much decorating, and it had a garage and a drive.

He slipped a decaf Americano pod into the sleek black Nespresso machine, which nestled by the brushed chrome kettle and toaster his younger sister, Beth, had bought him as a housewarming gift.

That reminded him. He fished out his personal mobile and checked the family WhatsApp while the machine churned away: nothing untoward, just the usual chitchat between his parents and Beth. His parents lived in Cornwall now, Beth was an engineer for BAE Systems at Barrow-in-Furness in Cumbria, and he was here in Buckinghamshire.

A message pinged up from Beth, just to him: *Free for a FaceTime?*

He typed back a yes. He was rifling through the fridge for his dinner when the familiar trill sang. 'Evening,' he said.

Her smiling face peered back through the rectangle of his phone screen. 'Hello hello. Haven't heard much from you the last few weeks. Just wanted to check you were still alive.'

He laughed. 'Yeah. I've been busy, so…' He tried, and failed, to keep the phone steady.

'What *are* you doing?' Even technology didn't hide her mildly frustrated amusement at his struggles.

'Trying to retrieve the food I batch cooked at the weekend.'

'Ooh. Get you,' she said.

'Well,' he sighed. 'Not like I've a huge amount else to do.'

She pulled a face. 'How's the new job going?'

He paused, tub of food in one hand and phone in the other. Aside from the Martinford investigation, how did he feel about it? Truthfully, he wasn't feeling the urge to socialise much with his new colleagues yet: it felt like everyone was either young, single, and partying, or married with families, like Woods. He felt like he occupied some weird niche in the middle. 'I… it's OK. I'm still settling in.'

Beth scowled. 'You've not heard anything from she who must not be named, have you?' That meant Anna. The two of them had never seen eye to eye. In hindsight, he should have paid more attention to that. Concern creased her brow when he didn't immediately respond. 'Have you?'

He shook his head. 'Not a thing. In any case, this is as fresh a start as I'm going to get, unless I leave, change my name, and move to Greenland.' He popped the lid off the tub of chicken chow mein and put it in the microwave. A thought struck him. 'While you're here…' he aimed his phone towards the toaster and kettle, '… thanks for these.'

'Yay! Knew they'd look good.' There was no mistaking her satisfaction. 'D'you like them?'

'Yeah.' And he genuinely did.

'So, you wouldn't complain at matching items for Christmas, then?'

He laughed. 'No. I take it from that you've bought them already.'

There was a pause. She fidgeted. 'They were in the sale.'

'Nice to know how much you value me.'

'You're priceless.'

'Without price, then.'

The retort had been automatic, but she gave him a meaningful look.

It hit him that he'd never made those sorts of comments about himself until Anna. And the aftermath. Thank goodness for friends and family.

Beth cleared her throat. 'Have you heard much from Sam recently?'

That stopped him dead. 'No. Last I heard, she was seeing someone new.'

Beth nodded. She clearly wanted to say something else but couldn't work out how.

He decided to say it for her. 'She's allowed to. It's a good four years since – since Dan died.' Dan Kaminski had been one of his intelligence colleagues, alongside Steve Rimmer, whom he also needed to catch up with at some point. They'd worked alongside each other on multiple deployments around the world, not to mention when they returned to the UK. They'd quickly forged a solid friendship, often centred on banter, motorbikes, and their mutual dislike of football.

During February 2018, Dan started complaining of headaches and blurred vision. The next month, he suffered a devastating seizure out of the blue. By July that year, he was dead. Killed by an aggressive, malignant brain tumour.

Sam was Dan's widow; Freddie, who had to be at least five now, had been a babe in arms when Dan died. Alex had stayed in touch to begin with, but then…

He sighed. Sam was also a school acquaintance of Beth's. Not that they were close, but they seemed to chat every now and again.

'She messaged me the other week.' Beth looked down. 'So I brought her up to date. She says well done.'

'Hmm.' Alex wasn't sure what to say to that.

'Sam reckoned she didn't think you'd be that bothered.' Beth laughed. 'Just shows she didn't know you at all, doesn't it?'

'Neither of us knew the other.' Alex stared down at the worktop, unable to look at the screen. Those months after Dan's death were a blur. Not that every death out there wasn't a blow, but this was more personal. More of a reminder that a future wasn't guaranteed.

Anna was a friend of an acquaintance he bumped into in the pub one evening, not long after Dan's funeral. In the beginning at least, she was beautiful, charming, funny, and intelligent… and he'd fallen head over heels.

Looking back, he wasn't thinking straight. He should have pressed pause on life and regrouped. Instead, he'd jumped into things with wild abandon, determined to make every moment count and say *yes* to everything he could. *One life, live it*, Anna would say. *No regrets.*

Talk about a lesson learned. Plus plenty he regretted.

Beth coughed awkwardly. 'Anyway, I said I'd tell you to drop her a message and let her know how you're doing.'

He smiled. 'I will. Anyway. Enough about me. What's going on with you?'

'Well…' While she updated him with the latest on her house purchase with her boyfriend, Ross, Alex pulled his food out of the microwave and started eating.

As she talked, the living room door opened behind her; Ross walked in, spotted Alex, smiled and waved. Beth smiled and waved over her shoulder. 'Hiya, love.'

Alex swallowed a mouthful of chicken. 'Hi, Ross.'

In the background, Ross called, 'Hi.'

'I need to finish my dinner,' said Alex, 'and I suspect you guys need some.'

'Yes please,' shouted Ross, unseen. Beth laughed.

'So, talk soon?'

'Yep,' said Beth. 'See you later.'

'Bye.'

Saturday 15 October 2022

FOOTBALL BLARED IN the background; the big screen on the wall flickered as players, dressed in red or white depending on their teams, jogged across a lurid green pitch.

Alex shrugged to himself. This might be an essential Saturday afternoon ritual for many people, but its lure escaped him. Even growing up, he'd never been that bothered about the sport.

Mark Fletcher arrived, carrying two pints. 'Glad you could make it. It's been a while.'

'Hasn't it?' Alex took his pint of Bombardier and nodded a thanks. Mark texted a few days ago, asking if he was free for their semi-regular Saturday afternoon pint. Covid interrupted for a while, as it did almost everything else, but they restarted as soon as restrictions eased. It would take more than a pandemic to disrupt permanently the ritual they'd had in place ever since they'd served alongside each other during various detachments. When they first met, Alex had been in charge of intelligence briefings to aircrew; Mark had been a Hercules pilot. These days, Mark flew civilian airliners and was getting used to life outside the RAF with his young family.

'Claire's mum's around this weekend, so she's got some help with Indi and Josh.' Mark grinned. 'Grandma trumps daddy every time.' Five-year-old Indi, or India, loved all shiny things with wheels and engines, while six-month-old Josh was already trying to pull himself up to chase after her. Between them, the couple longingly reminisced about restful sleep. 'Anyway. Never mind the new house, how's the motorbike hunt going?'

Alex chuckled. He absent-mindedly ran his finger along the edge of his soggy beermat. 'I've finally bought one.'

Mark gave him a mock round of applause. 'About time. Did you go for the RR in the end?'

Alex sniggered. Fast and gorgeous though it was, the BMW S1000RR sports bike was built for men younger than him with a lesser concept of their own mortality. He tried, but failed, to keep his face straight. 'I went full middle-aged wannabe.'

'Oh, mate. Not a '1200 GS. Please tell me you didn't buy the matching suit?'

Alex took a leisurely sip of his pint. 'Says the man who bought Rossi replica leathers to go with his R1. And it's a GS Adventure, thank you very much.' The BMW R1200 GS Adventure was a big, upright motorbike capable of crossing deserts and mud tracks as easily as speeding down the M25. Maybe it was childish to have bought it, but what the hell. Anna loathed the idea of him being on two wheels and pushed him to sell his last motorbike, so buying one now the dust had settled from their divorce felt natural. A step towards reclaiming who he was.

Mark laughed. 'Go hard or go home, eh?'

For a while, they watched the football match on the big screen. Alex wasn't bothered about the game, but Mark was, and he knew Mark didn't get much chance to sit and watch it uninterrupted these days.

'You should come over on it,' said Mark after a while. 'Indi would love it.'

'Sounds good.'

Some noise from the flickering screen made them look across; some overpaid supposed athlete was grievously injured just from his opponent brushing past. Alex sighed, bemused by the Oscar-winning performance; did they make such a fuss if someone bumped into them on the street?

Mark went to drink his pint and noticed Alex's was still half full. 'Going steady?'

Alex nodded. 'Trying to keep a clear head at the moment. I've got a mystery on my hands.' He gave Mark an edited summary of what had been discovered at Martinford.

Mark pondered. 'I heard about that. Funny business.'

Alex picked up his pint. 'You're not wrong.'

Mark glanced across at the TV: it was half-time, and the pundits were busy pontificating. 'My old man used to be connected with the intelligence services. Have you ever heard of the Mitrokhin Archives?'

Alex paused. It sounded familiar, but he couldn't place it. It half sounded like some '80s synth-pop band. He resisted the urge to ask what their hit single had been. 'No?'

'Ah. Vasili Mitrokhin was a KGB archivist who defected to the West in the early nineties. He brought with him copies of KGB internal files relating to all kinds of Soviet intelligence operations throughout the world, from the 1930s to the 1980s.'

'Such as?'

'Reports on the Cambridge Five. You know, Kim Philby, Donald Maclean, Guy Burgess, and that lot?' Mark finished his pint. 'But more than that. His files named agents, said what they did, where they lived, what their targets were, even what KGB heads thought of them. Some we didn't know about until he revealed them – Melita Norwood being one. You remember? That old lady, "the spy who came in from the Co-op", some years ago?'

'Sounds familiar.' Alex drank some more.

'Anyway,' said Mark, 'my dad's decided, now he's retired, he wants to research a bit more of what went on here in the Cold War. Mitrokhin's files show the KGB had agents within the establishment and various defence programmes in both the US and the UK throughout the Cold War. And we still don't know who some of them were.'

'Really?'

Mark nodded. 'He mentioned one to me because the file said the KGB suspected he was a double agent. But he and his controller disappeared without a trace – or at least, they ignored all attempts to restore contact.'

'When was that?'

'Early to mid-sixties, I think.' Mark stared reflectively into his empty pint glass. 'The reason I'm mentioning it is he said the suspected double agent was apparently an RAF officer.'

'Has he looked at our own files?'

'That's it. He's asked. They're still restricted.'

Alex opened his mouth, frowned, then shut it again. In lieu of a response, he finished his own pint.

Mark leant forward conspiratorially and dropped his voice. 'And he said something about it being linked to RAF bombers.'

Alex blew out a long breath. When he replied, his voice was barely above a whisper. 'Martinford was a Vulcan base in the sixties.'

The two men stared at each other for some time.

Alex stood. 'My round. Same again?'

When he returned with two more pints, Mark continued, 'There's also some top-secret project linked with it. The KGB codenamed it "PEREGRUZKA".'

'What does that mean?'

'It translates to something like "overload" or "overcharge", I think. Pretty much everything had odd codenames in those days, though. Want me to see if I can get you copies of what dad's got?'

Alex considered. 'Please. At worst, it'll be interesting reading.'

'The one thing dad said comes across in this file is that the Soviets were very, very scared of whatever PEREGRUZKA was.'

Quentin spotted his old friend across the restaurant and made a beeline for his table. This was an evening, and a dinner, he'd anticipated all week. 'Valentin. Long time no see.'

'Quentin, good to see you, old friend. It has been long time.' Valentin stood and gave Quentin his customary bear-hug welcome. 'Five years, yes?'

'At least.' It had to be something like that since they'd last met in person, but Valentin Aleksandrovich Zhilin had hardly changed. Tall, and still in excellent physical shape, he wore his usual casual suit and open-necked white shirt. Only the smattering of grey that sparkled in his thick black hair and the faint lines around his eyes hinted at the passage of time.

Valentin released him, and they sat at the table. An open bottle of red wine and two large, half-filled glasses stood invitingly before them.

Valentin scrutinised him, as if inspecting a second-hand car. 'You look tired. Worried. You have lost weight, yes?'

Quentin forced a smile. 'Oh. It's nothing. I'm fine. You, on the other hand, look like life has been good.'

Valentin grinned broadly and held up his right hand; a diamond-studded platinum band encircled his ring finger. 'Very good. Been married three years now. We are expecting our first child. A son, I hope. Next March. Katya is glowing.'

'Congratulations.' Quentin smiled, genuinely pleased, and offered his hand across the table; Valentin shook it heartily. 'No wonder you look well. The love of a good woman, eh?'

'Yes, yes. She is… very good woman. I am lucky man.' Valentin laughed. 'You?'

'Hah. Almost married to the job.' Quentin made no attempt to hide his bitterness. 'For what good that does.'

Valentin regarded him, eyebrow raised, over the rim of his wine glass, but didn't speak. Instead, he sipped his wine.

Quentin added, 'Sorry. Things have been… difficult.'

Valentin leant forward and lowered his voice. 'You do not look well, my friend.'

Quentin avoided his friend's gaze. Instead, he picked up his glass and drank deeply. As expected, Valentin still had excellent taste in wine. He forced himself to savour the mouthful. With a sigh, he slid the glass back onto the table. 'I'm fine. Nothing that can't be solved soon. I hope.'

'It is not your health?' asked Valentin. Concern flickered across his brow.

'No. My health is, well, as good as anything.' Quentin stroked the long stem of the wine glass, thinking how to respond.

'Is it your work?'

'Just life.' This time, Quentin didn't bother pretending. He simply downed what liquid was left.

Valentin refilled Quentin's glass without a word before topping up his own from the already almost empty bottle. He gave Quentin a sympathetic look. 'This evening is on me. Call it apology for not visiting.' He gestured to the waiter for another bottle.

Quentin snorted. 'My troubles aren't your fault, Val. Not at all. But thanks for this. I mean it.'

'Can I help?' Valentin smiled – rather wolfishly, Quentin thought. 'Tell Brother Valya your problems?'

'I'd rather forget them. For tonight, at least.' Quentin forced a smile. 'We've got five years to catch up on.'

A broad grin split Valentin's face. 'We do.'

As food arrived, and another bottle of wine was emptied, Quentin reminisced. He and Valentin had met at Trinity College, Oxford, way back in the hazy days of the mid 1990s: he read Philosophy, Politics and Economics, while Valentin, taking advantage of the thawed Cold War, read Economics and Management. Given their range of shared interests – women and wine being two – it didn't take long for them to become firm friends, bolstered by their first jobs being in London; Valentin landed a role with an investment bank, while Quentin dipped his toes into the murky waters of the Civil Service.

Nine years ago, Valentin had news that his father, Aleksandr, was not well back in Moscow, so he'd returned to do his family duty. Shortly after that, Aleksandr passed away, leaving his engineering consultancy firm to Valentin.

Tired of Russia, Valentin sold the business and moved to London in 2018 to set up a new consultancy, specifically to take advantage of the UK's pool of talent and wider commercial opportunities. It had been hard, and 2022 had been a difficult year, he admitted. Valentin had done his best to try and distance himself from his homeland's disastrous "special operation" in Ukraine, even highlighting the fact he'd become a British citizen, but the reputational damage was done.

Beyond an occasional email and rare social media update, he just hadn't had the chance to stay in closer contact – for which he apologised profusely.

Quentin thought, through the rosy haze of a bottle of wine, that he hadn't exactly tried to keep in touch with anyone, either. Partly because of the demands of his job, and partly because there were few people he had the time for. Life was simpler if he was unencumbered.

For the last ten years, he'd held various liaison roles at the British Embassy in Washington. Six months ago, he'd been encouraged, for want of a better term, to return to London. He was having to slip back into old haunts, reacquaint himself with old friends.

As food came and went, they ate, talked, and drank, covering such diverse subjects as Chelsea football club, horse racing, and Selfridges.

Then Valentin said something that blew the warm fuzz of alcohol away. 'I hear rumours you are stuck.'

Quentin held himself still. 'What do you mean?' he managed.

Valentin gave him a look. 'We visited these places together, long time ago, you and I. We made good profit.' He rubbed his fingers together in the universal sign for money.

'You quit while you're ahead,' said Quentin dully.

'Get ahead with the next win, yes?' Valentin finished his glass; when he upended the bottle to refill it, only a dribble of wine came out. He frowned and waved for another bottle.

Quentin stared at the table. It seemed to be the only thing that wasn't spinning around him, and that wasn't all down to the alcohol. 'That's what I thought.'

They sat in silence as the waiter brought another bottle. Valentin greedily tipped it into his glass, spilling a little. He pointed it at Quentin, who shrugged; one glass more would make no difference now.

'It isn't that bad,' said Quentin.

Valentin quirked an eyebrow but didn't respond.

That aside, it would've been nice had his new job come with a pay rise. Quentin pushed the thought away. His was a plum job, and he had the skills for it. It was a passport to higher, better things. Just because he'd made some… unwise investments, it didn't mean he required subsidies, like some badly run farm. He prided himself on not being completely motivated by financial rewards. Yet there was no denying that a little extra cash would help things flow just that bit smoother right now.

Was it just the wine, or was Valentin once again giving him that appraising look?

Quentin gathered himself. If he'd been sober, he might have thought to ask where Valentin had got his information. Instead, he replied, 'I'm flattered you worry about me.'

'I would not want you to suffer,' said Valentin. He waved his glass in the air. 'Perhaps I can help.'

Quentin laughed. 'Some tips, perhaps?'

Valentin grinned. 'If so, my friend, I would not work for a living.'

'Wouldn't we all?'

Valentin leant forward and gestured Quentin closer. A blast of wine-breath enveloped him. 'I can help you, maybe. If you help me. We both get rich.'

Dulled by the wine, Quentin frowned. 'If you need my help, Val, then yes. What can I do?'

A slow, greasy smile spread across Valentin's face. 'Thank you. Not much, yet, but… I will let you know.'

Friday 17 July 1964

FOR THE FIRST time in too many years, now he came to think of it, Gordon pulled on a flight suit. Anticipation tingled through his veins.

Not only had his boss cleared it, so had Hesketh-Shaw and the Wingco. Apparently, the view from Command was they'd welcome a bit more engineering input. If that gave him a chance to be airborne, he was more than happy to oblige.

The only downside? He had to be passenger in an aircraft Fraser captained. He grinned.

XM568 BASKED ON the dispersal. Sun glinted off her canopy; her bright yellow access ladder dangled underneath her open cockpit door. Off to one side at her rear, underneath the shady spread of her delta wing, squatted the Palouste: a mobile ground power unit, ready to coax the Vulcan's four Bristol Olympus 301 turbines into howling life.

A lazy breeze brushed him, heavy with the scent of jet fuel. He inhaled deeply, smiling; there was nothing like that smell in the morning. For a moment, it was as if he'd travelled back in time, and he was an AEO again. The fuel bowser responsible lumbered away with a diesel grumble.

Faint jet noise filtered down from the skies above. He glanced up, shading his eyes, but could barely make out contrails against the cloud-dappled blue.

Ahead, two figures circled her: Brian and Fraser, finishing their pre-flight walk around. Others stood around the Palouste, ready to start it up. Chief Andrews looked across at Gordon and nodded.

Gordon returned the nod. Underneath the excitement, adrenaline twisted his stomach. His part of the briefing was simple, if not exactly small: keep note of everything related to Banshee, compare it to specification, and note any aircraft behaviour out of the ordinary. Not that the rest of the crew wouldn't be doing that, of course, but as he didn't have an official job to do as well, in theory that meant he could give Banshee his full attention.

Watson's weasel words from yesterday ran across his mind. Much as he told himself Fraser was being unreasonable, looking at '68 it was hard to wipe that sliver of doubt from his mind.

Footsteps thudded on the concrete behind him: the rest of Fraser's crew, walking up to their aircraft.

Time to get inside.

That distinct Vulcan scent greeted him as he climbed up the narrow ladder into the cramped darkness of XM568's cockpit: a hard-to-describe blend of rubber, leather, metal, oil, and warm electronics. Nostalgia stirred; maybe he'd missed this more than he thought.

Up top, Fraser and Brian sat shoulder to shoulder in the narrow section of the nose the pilots called home, with only a small crescent of windows to peer out of. In front, each pilot had a fighter-like control stick. Between them lay a movable set of panels with the fuelling controls, the four throttle levers sitting at the top, nearest her nose.

Momentarily disconcerting as it was to be in a cockpit and see Fraser in the left-hand seat, not the co-pilot's one on the right, there was no mistaking his confidence: he continued his checks with the ease of a man who'd done them thousands of times. Gordon smiled to himself.

A thick, black, rolled-up curtain divided the cockpit between the two pilots and the remaining crew.

Below the pilots, at the back, sat the navigator radar, navigator plotter, and air electronics officer in their rear-facing metal seats. Their stations, bristling with buttons and dials, glowed dully, each man already working his way through his pre-flight checklists. As he listened, Gordon fancied he could still make a half-decent stab at the AEO's list.

Funny how something could stay buried in your mind for years, until something nudged it out.

Gordon plugged his headset into the intercom and plonked himself on one of the small ledges either side of the door that doubled as jump seats, beneath the pilots but just behind the rear crew.

In the V-Force, only the pilots got the luxury of ejector seats: everyone else got a parachute, which doubled as a seat cushion. Gordon felt his own underneath him. Perhaps he should've refreshed his parachute drill. Oh well, too late now. Besides, if things did go that wrong...

At the signal from Chief Andrews, he pulled up the ladder and stowed it in the nose, in the vacant visual bomb-aimer's compartment. That was an anachronism these days: a mile here or there with a nuclear bomb wouldn't make much difference.

The door shut, sealing him and the others in darkness.

HE STARED AT the haphazard mess of papers spread across his desk. He knew he should clear it away. Indeed, he could hear his wife's voice, telling him a tidy desk equalled a tidy mind and that he'd feel better for clearing out the clutter. Even though it was his office, and if that was how his desk was, it was no-one's business apart from his...

The thought trailed guiltily away.

Deep inside, part of him quailed. How had he ended up in this mess? Familiar fear squeezed his guts; nausea swirled. Resigned, he pushed it aside. The time for worrying about all this had long passed. It was far too late to think about that.

Look at it this way, he told himself, *you do have a reason to tidy your desk.* He tried not to think too hard about exactly why.

Half an hour later, cold sweat poured off his brow. He'd finished. Even his shirt was clammy with perspiration.

Paperwork was now in orderly rows and piles, rather than the heaps it had been. To all intents and purposes, it looked like he'd just tidied up.

The fact he'd used a tiny camera to photograph choice documents, reports, specifications, and drawings...

He closed his eyes and shuddered.

In the beginning, it had been, if not a game, then a way of keeping score. A little secret, a frisson of danger; from the outside, he was a respectable man, wearing respectable suits, driving a respectable car. No-one would ever suspect him, such a pillar of the community. But he knew the truth.

Of course, he hadn't started on this course intentionally. It had taken him years to fall this low, he thought with a bitter smile. He should have known better than to trust women bearing drinks and requesting his company.

Oh, if only things had been different…

Tears prickled behind his eyes. Embarrassed, he pinched at his eyelids.

Of course, the woman was obliging. Very obliging, in fact. Incredibly so.

Which made being presented with surprisingly good quality pictures of them both all the more shameful. After all, said the man showing him the pictures, no-one would want a man in his position to be seen doing *that*…

So, he'd acquiesced. At that time, he wasn't doing anything too critical – and initially, they just wanted snippets. Titbits of information. Nothing too hard to acquire. Nothing especially dangerous. In return for his reports, he was sent regular, untraceable, payments of cash: nothing large enough to arouse suspicion, but enough to buy himself a nice car, a nice flat, nice clothes.

Eventually, though, their demands grew. So did the risks. And the rewards.

Banshee.

The most complex, expensive, and sensitive defence programme since the development of the atomic bomb. Critical to the defence of the United Kingdom. Even the Americans didn't know about it: this was purely British. Intended to remain secret, even to their allies, until it was fully operational. The system that would re-establish Britain as a nation to be reckoned with.

He screwed his eyes closed and tried to shut out the clamour of his conscience.

In the beginning, he'd been powered by anger and greed as much as fear. He didn't think communism was as bad as was made out by the Yanks, and certainly the capitalist West had done him few favours. But, as Banshee developed and proved more feasible, his misgivings grew. Just what was he doing? Sometimes, he told himself he was doing the world a favour. Preventing an arms race by making sure the other side was even. Sometimes, usually in the dead of night, his conscience hissed he was hastening the end of the world, betraying those who put their faith in him. Betraying them as surely as that scarlet woman betrayed him.

Maybe he should just hand himself in. Information on a spy ring would be valuable, after all. He might get a lesser sentence. He tried not to think that treason was still punishable, in theory, with the death penalty. Then again, would he prefer death to dishonour? He was but one cog in a mysterious machine. Perhaps death was the least bad option.

Not for the first time, he wondered about ending it all, but his mind shied away.

Too much of a coward even for that, his conscience sneered.

Instead, on autopilot, he reached into a desk drawer and found his hidden bottle of comfort. His almost empty bottle of comfort. Or mother's ruin, as his long-loved wife would have said.

Carefully avoiding thinking, he unscrewed the top and downed what was left.

FRASER TRIMMED XM568 for straight and level flight. Despite the extra weight of all the shielding, fuel tanks, and Banshee itself, she still flew with power, precision, and grace. The giant bat was ridiculously agile for such a large machine, and surprisingly stealthy: something every Vulcan pilot used to his advantage during any joint exercise with the Americans, much to their annoyance. She was far more manoeuvrable at speed and altitude than any fighter – even including the Lightning. Fraser smiled underneath his mask.

Ken's voice crackled over the intercom; as nav plotter, he was in charge of navigating the aircraft. 'Fifty miles to target... now. Flying time to target, five minutes.'

'Roger,' said Fraser.

'Banshee primed,' reported Jim. As nav radar, he deployed what weapons the Vulcan carried.

'All protections functional,' Mike, the AEO, stated, then he repeated the briefing's notes. 'All ECM off. We're to carry on to target with no evasive measures.'

Fraser frowned. He still wasn't convinced about the sensibility of testing even an ultra-low-power version of Banshee over any part of Britain. Especially as activation of any of the Vulcan's electronic countermeasures, or ECM, over mainland UK was strictly forbidden without prior government approval; the equipment blacked out all television and radio signals, and more, in the aircraft's vicinity. He was surprised they'd got permission to do this, even if Watson insisted this was the only way to check the deployment mechanism didn't interfere with anything in flight.

The only area where he fully agreed with his superiors and Watson was that final trials, with all ECM activated and Banshee at full power, would be conducted in Australia later this year or early next year, as far from civilisation as they could possibly go.

However, for this first part... he sighed. Orders were orders.

Besides, he reminded himself for the umpteenth time, the flight profile for this test over the remote ranges of northern Scotland was simple; drop to low-level, as the V-Force now flew, but instead of popping up again to bombing height, remain low until Banshee was discharged, then climb to high altitude and return to Martinford.

That is, unless whatever issue struck Tony's Vulcan affected them, too.

Jim interrupted his thoughts. 'Target marker on visual.'

'Banshee charged,' said Mike.

'At altitude,' said Brian, his young co-pilot.

Fraser watched the dials and nodded. 'On schedule?'

'Yes, skip,' replied Ken.

Fraser cast a glance across at Brian; nerves showed in the set of his eyes, but his gaze was level and steady. Then again, they were about to trigger an experimental weapon for the first time since it had been installed, Tony's flight notwithstanding.

'Skip, course and altitude corrections coming up,' said Ken.

Fraser eased the throttles back, following the course given. XM568 pitched slightly nose-up; he adjusted the elevons to keep her level.

'Discharge in five seconds,' said Jim.

Fraser counted in his head and reached zero just as Jim reported, 'Banshee discharged.'

A high-pitched electronic scream pierced his ears through the headset. Fraser cursed. Instinctively, he pulled the Vulcan into her climbing escape manoeuvre—

The big delta hesitated, her engines idling down, her controls slack—

Abruptly, the stick tightened; as if by magic, she followed his input, turned, and soared. Her engines howled, spooling up to full throttle several seconds slower than usual.

Out of the corner of his eye, he caught a glimpse of Brian, wide-eyed, his shoulders sinking in an unmistakeable sigh of relief.

You and me both, he thought. 'AEO, what happened?'

Seconds passed before Mike replied, voice clipped, 'Lost primary electrical and battery back-up power for about a second. Checking all systems.'

'Roger.' Fraser scanned the dials in front of him: all looked normal. XM568 climbed steadily, as if nothing had happened. Brian busily checked his own dials and gauges; he nodded when Fraser looked across. 'Everything appears to be functioning up here. Keep an eye on her, will you?'

Fraser watched '68's controls for a few more moments. Nothing appeared out of the ordinary; she seemed her usual, responsive self. He shot a sideways glance at Brian. Judging by the look on his face, he needed something to take his mind off things. They'd already reached cruising altitude for the trip back. 'Brian, want to bring this lady home?'

Brian blinked. 'I could do with the handling experience.'

'Then you have control.'

'I have control,' Brian echoed.

Fraser loosened his belts and fidgeted. This wasn't a long flight, by any means, but he'd happily take the chance to move a little. The Vulcan's seats weren't exactly luxurious.

'Skip,' said Mike, 'I've not been able to raise the ranges to confirm our results.'

'Nothing at all?' Fraser stopped mid-stretch.

'Not even static. I've raised ATC, so it isn't us.' Mike sounded a little defensive.

Fraser considered. 'That's OK, Mike. No doubt the results will be waiting for us when we land. Course, Ken?' He knew roughly where he was; he just wanted to make sure his crew did, too.

'Still on course.' Ken reported on a couple of landmarks that Fraser could see – good, that meant at least the Vulcan's navigation systems functioned. 'Expected time back at Martinford is 1713 zulu.'

'Just in time for tea,' muttered Jim.

Fraser remembered his passenger. Gordon had been uncharacteristically silent. He prodded, 'Flash, what happened?'

There was a pause. Abruptly, Fraser realised none of his current crew had heard Gordon called that before; only the rest of his first aircrew used to call him that, all those years ago. Gordon had always been "Flash" in the air, after the comic book character. He'd slipped back into it without thinking. He prayed Gordon wouldn't retort with what had been his own OCU nickname: "Soup". He'd worked hard to leave that behind. Maybe some still used it, behind his back, but his reputation was such that no-one would use it to his face.

Though Gordon would. He grimaced.

'Oh, thanks,' came Gordon's voice, heavy with sarcasm. 'Just when I'd stopped hearing that. You owe me a drink for this.'

Before he could speak, Gordon carried on. 'I was watching the generator panels when Jim hit the button. I need to review the manuals, but—'

'What do you mean, you need to review the manuals—' began Mike.

Gordon interrupted, voice flat. 'What I saw means this tin triangle shouldn't be flying. Something happened, but I'm damned if I know what. Or why we're still in the air.'

A shiver passed down Fraser's spine.

Someone started to speak, but Fraser cut them off. This was no time to speculate. 'We'll go through it at the debrief.' *Let's get home*, he added to himself. He wanted to think about this when he was safely back on *terra firma*.

AN HOUR OR so after the debrief finished, Gordon banged on Fraser's door in the officers' mess. Being the unmarried men of the crews, they were the only ones either not renting outside the base or in married quarters.

Fraser opened the door and ushered Gordon into the small, yet neat room. He sat on the narrow bed and looked up, unmistakeable fire in his eyes.

'Well, that went well,' he muttered.

'Didn't it?' Gordon sat in the old and tatty visitor's chair by the window: it creaked under him as he relaxed back.

The debrief had been fraught, to say the least.

The lack of response from the ranges wasn't due to an issue with XM568. In fact, XM568 was quarantined, pending inspection.

Not only did Banshee knock out the marker on the target, but it also blew the range's main comms board. And most of the power circuitry at the nearby base.

When Hesketh-Shaw questioned Mike and Jim's version of events, Gordon stepped in and backed them up, as well as adding a few choice criticisms and questions of his own. XM568 should not have suffered such a power interruption. Clearly, she had. Even now, he could see the dials spinning in his mind's eye. He shuddered.

'So much for all the electrical upgrades.' Fraser gave Gordon a sidelong glance. 'Did you see Watson's face drop when you mentioned XA908?'

'Uh huh.' Vulcan B.1 XA908 suffered a complete electrical failure flying over Michigan in 1958; the battery back-up, which was supposed to last twenty minutes, barely lasted five. Without power, the crew were passengers as she plunged to the ground. None of them escaped.

'Notice how he didn't have any answers for us.'

Gordon grunted. 'And how he mumbled some nonsense about system integration issues.'

'We followed the flight plan,' continued Fraser, 'we did everything we were asked, with the aircraft we were given. Watson told us it would be fine. You were there; it wasn't.'

'I know, old chap.' Gordon sucked his teeth. Fraser didn't need to elaborate. At that height, with no power, they'd have been helpless as the Vulcan plummeted. What was perhaps worse was he genuinely had no idea how XM568 recovered and restarted flying. What he'd said on the flight back was the truth: for a split second, he hadn't expected to be here tonight. Yet she'd behaved herself impeccably on the way back.

Fraser scowled. 'The worst bit is, it's starting to look like Tony isn't such a whinging old woman after all.'

'No, he's still a whinger. Just ask Chief Morton.'

Fraser snorted. 'How he got selected for this, I'll never know.'

'It's not what you know, it's who you know.' Gordon idly inspected his fingernails. 'John reckons his wife's pally with the Wingco's.'

'Hmm. Wouldn't surprise me. Heard John muttering about some dinner party he and Miranda weren't invited to. Nor me. Brookes is quite the social climber.'

'Yeah. But we know our place.'

'Well, you know yours.'

'Yeah, cleaning your mess up.'

To Gordon's surprise, Fraser didn't rise to the bait. Instead, he bit his lip and frowned at the floor.

Just as Gordon was about to speak, Fraser looked up, suddenly determined. 'Come on. I can't be bothered with the mess tonight, and I need to stretch the old girl's legs. Let's get out of here.'

FRASER'S AUSTIN-HEALEY 3000 shone in the summer evening sun, a graceful, sleek shape detailed in glossy red and brilliant chrome. He wasted no time in lowering the car's black soft-top.

'You're going to mess my hair up,' said Gordon.

'What, your moustache?' retorted Fraser.

Gordon heaved an internal sigh of relief at the smile that edged onto Fraser's face. Fraser had a tendency to take things a bit too seriously for his own good sometimes. He brushed his fingers through the 'tache. 'Just 'cause you can't grow one.'

'I can. I just choose not to.' Fraser smirked. 'You need one to hide your face.'

'Nah, I don't want to give you too much competition. Are we going, or what?'

They lowered themselves into the low-slung sports car. Fraser carefully adjusted the choke and fired up the 3-litre straight six: it coughed, then purred into life.

'You're a lucky, lucky man,' said Gordon. 'She sounds amazing.'

'Doesn't she?' Fraser checked the temperature and oil pressure gauges, then tickled the throttle. The engine growled: both of them grinned like schoolboys at the wonderful noise. 'Smooth as silk.'

Fraser drove the Austin-Healey much like he flew, with precision and care. He was even careful not to work the engine hard until it was fully warmed up. Gordon doubted Tony would do that.

To shut out his thoughts, Gordon closed his eyes and savoured the Healey's purr over wind noise as they wound their way through the lanes.

'Falling asleep, old man? Today's trip too tiring for you?' Fraser called. He brought the car to a stop at a junction.

Gordon bit back a swearword and contented himself with a hand gesture. Fraser laughed.

'Where're we going, anyway?' asked Gordon.

Fraser shrugged. Though the road was clear, he didn't move off. 'I… I was thinking of popping by Sophie's. D'you mind?'

Gordon raised an eyebrow. Not that he did, but there was one thing he had to point out. 'Well, no, but I thought we were going to the pub?'

'We are. Just…'

'You're not going to claim she's on the way, are you?'

Fraser glowered at him. Gordon closed his mouth. Obviously, today's sortie played on Fraser's mind, too.

Without another word, Fraser drove on.

After maybe twenty minutes or so, they pulled up outside a neat, suburban semi-detached 1930s house, somewhere in north Leamington. Fraser keyed off then hopped out. 'I'll be back in a mo.'

Just as he reached the door, Sophie opened it, surprise and delight on her face. Her simple duck-egg-blue shift dress, and the black Alice band that held back her brown hair, emphasised her beauty rather than made her look plain. 'I thought I heard you,' she exclaimed, beaming. Fraser pulled her close and kissed her cheek.

Not wanting to intrude, Gordon inspected the Healey's red leather dash and the grain of the wooden steering wheel. He glanced up and met Sophie's gaze over Fraser's shoulder. A faint blush tinted her cheeks, but she gave him a shy smile; he wondered if his smile in return was just as bashful.

'Fraser, you shouldn't make your friends wait!' she chided, leading Fraser back towards the car.

'He's not really a friend,' retorted Fraser with a grin, 'he just promised me a drink.'

'And he promised to take me to the pub,' said Gordon.

Though Sophie shook her head, as if annoyed, there was no hiding her amusement at their bickering. 'You're very patient with him, Gordon, I must say.'

Fraser scoffed. 'Him? Patient with me?'

Sophie shushed him by placing a finger on his lips; he gave her a big-eyed innocent look, trying to elicit sympathy. Much as she tried to keep a serious face, her mouth moved, betraying the grin underneath.

'And I think you're patient with both of us,' said Gordon.

Fraser shot him a surprised look, but Sophie laughed. Fraser took her hand and gently kissed it.

'I wasn't expecting to see you till tomorrow,' she said.

Fraser glanced down at the pavement, coughed, then pushed a winning smile onto his face. 'We were just passing, so I thought I'd say hello as it's been over twenty-four hours since I last saw you. Can't stop for long.' A thought seemed to strike him. 'I… need to refuel the Healey before our date tomorrow, you see.'

'Oh! So where are we going?'

Fraser momentarily looked blank, then winked. 'It's a surprise.' He kissed her again. 'Sorry it's such a flying visit. I… I just couldn't resist.'

She giggled and flung her arms around him; he squeezed her close and murmured something in her ear Gordon couldn't hear.

'It's all right,' said Gordon pointedly. 'Carry on. I'll just stay here.' He made a show of rummaging in the Healey's door cavity and groaned theatrically. 'You could've left me a book to read.'

Fraser sighed, but Sophie chuckled.

'Miss Baxter,' said Fraser, 'I'm afraid I need to depart.' He pulled a funny face at Gordon; Gordon rolled his eyes.

'In which case, Mr Campbell,' she said, matching his mock-formality, 'I will say goodbye.' She kissed Fraser, who finally released her.

To Gordon's surprise, she darted lightly to his side of the car. 'Goodbye, Mr Thompson.'

'Goodbye,' he managed.

Her bright blue eyes sparkled with humour; she grinned, and for a moment leant so close, he wondered if she was going to kiss his cheek, too. 'Don't let him drag you all over the countryside.'

Gordon couldn't help a laugh. 'Don't worry,' he said, 'I won't.'

Saturday 18 July 1964

UNDERNEATH GORDON, THE Bonnie grumbled and complained. One cylinder didn't want to keep firing.

He scanned the road ahead; luckily, there was a lay-by not too far away. So much for a nice morning ride to Warwick and back...

After yesterday's drama, he thought a bit of tinkering, followed by a trip out on the motorbike, would help clear his head. However, things seemed determined not to go as planned.

Despite the new spark plugs he'd fitted earlier that Saturday, his Bonneville still wasn't reliably running on both cylinders. She coughed, spluttered, and refused to cooperate for long. Was it the points? The magneto? Whatever it was, both he and the Triumph needed a break. He shrugged off his thick leather jacket and took off his white, open-face helmet. Though it wasn't particularly sunny, it was fairly warm, so the breeze was welcome.

Hopefully Fraser was having a much nicer day out with Sophie: he'd recalled just in time that Stratford-upon-Avon was just down the road, and therefore the perfect destination for a countryside drive then a riverside walk and a spot of lunch. They had a loose agreement that he'd meet them there, possibly mid-afternoon.

Gordon usually enjoyed getting his hands dirty: it allowed his mind to process things while his hands toiled. He kind of missed working hands-on with aircraft, though he didn't miss the pressure of it. Much as he'd liked being airborne – both yesterday, and when he did his stint as aircrew – truthfully, it wasn't for him. Not permanently.

A pale green early Vauxhall Victor puttered slowly past. It creaked to a stop a few yards further down the lay-by. All its chrome trim glittered despite the dull day, though rust nibbled the corners of the doors. Across the rear bench seat, two young children squabbled, arms waving. The woman in the front passenger seat, her neat peroxide hair almost covered by a bright floral scarf, gave him a nervous smile over her shoulder. Her red lipstick was faded from repeated pulls at the almost-gone cigarette between her manicured fingers.

The driver got out. 'Excuse… oh. Gordon.' It was Tony.

Both men stared at each other, taken aback. Almost unrecognisable off duty, Tony wore smart beige trousers. A brown checked tank top covered the best part of a white short-sleeved shirt.

'Tony.' Gordon nodded at him and then the woman he presumed must be his wife. 'Mrs Brookes.'

After a couple of moments, Tony seemed to shake himself. 'Darling, this is the, er, Gordon I was telling you about.'

Oh. Right. Gordon raised an eyebrow, surprised. Mrs Brookes frowned at Tony, then gave Gordon a funny look. Shouting from the back of the car stopped her before she could speak; she spun around and hissed something at the children. Gordon wasn't an expert, but it looked like there was a boy, maybe aged seven or eight, and a girl a couple of years younger. The boy had a shock of thick brown hair that fluffed around his ears. The girl had obviously inherited Tony's curls, though they were a bit more tamed; her hair fell in tight, dark ringlets around her face.

'Anyway. Are you OK there?' Tony gestured at the Bonneville and walked towards him. 'Can we help?'

Gordon paused, genuinely surprised at how pleasant Tony was being. 'Thanks for asking. She's not running well. I changed the plugs before this run. I was just letting her cool down a bit before I dive in to check the points and the magneto. I should be able to fix her then.'

'Ah.' Tony nodded. He shoved his hands in his pockets. He seemed unsure what to say next – but not in a hurry to leave, either.

Even from where he stood, Gordon could hear the kids complaining in the car. 'Out for a family drive?' he asked.

Tony winced. 'That's the plan. Debbie – my youngest – wants to go to Warwick to see the castle. And Dennis wants to have a picnic by the river at St Nick's Park.'

'Unless she behaves, she's not going anywhere!' shouted Mrs Brookes into the back of the car. All that did was kick off more loud protests from the dark-haired girl.

Tony closed his eyes for a moment, a muscle in his jaw twitching. Despite the shouting, he didn't move. He eyed the motorbike. 'You've got the right idea, there,' he muttered morosely. 'Can't fit kids on that. Or the wife.' Then he raised his voice, 'Just coming, darling.'

'Thanks for stopping,' said Gordon. 'It's much appreciated.' He chuckled. 'If I'm still here when you come back, I'll gladly take you up on the offer.'

Tony gave a rare, genuine smile and then climbed back into the car. It coughed, spluttered, but eventually caught on the third try. Through the wrap-around rear screen, Gordon could see Mrs Brookes waving her hands, while small heads bobbed around in the back.

Given how old the children looked, Tony must have married very young; he was younger than Fraser, if Gordon remembered correctly. Married quarters were usually in short supply, even for officers. And it wasn't like the pay was that great either. Fraser's inheritance – rather than his flying wage – paid for his big Healey.

No wonder Tony was desperate to dot every *i* and cross every *t*; promotion would help pay his bills and get them a much-needed bigger house, no doubt.

A prod told him the Bonnie was now cool enough to work on. He rolled up his sleeves and set to work. Fortunately, he'd dismantled and fettled her enough times that most of it he could do on autopilot.

What was it Fraser had said? That Mrs Brookes was very friendly with the Wingco's wife? Well, officers' wives did form a bit of a social club. Aircrew wives stuck together, that was for sure. He supposed it was that common experience of having their men fly off, often at short notice for indeterminate periods.

Ah ha. Gordon spotted the problem and kicked himself for not having spotted it earlier; one of the HT leads' ends was loose and refused to fasten properly. At least now he knew, he could limp it to Leamington and get a spare set.

A memory struck him: 'The Gordon I told you about,' Tony had said. That raised two questions. One, just what exactly had he said to his wife? And two, should he have said anything, given the utter secrecy surrounding Banshee? They weren't to discuss it with anyone not on 449 Sqn, not even the OCU staff. What details could Mrs Brookes accidentally let slip to the wrong ears?

THE WELL-WRAPPED packet in his pocket felt like a stone. Strategic sticky tape sealed it against air, water, and prying eyes.

Unusually for him, he'd taken the train rather than driven; he didn't know Birmingham well, and while there was a certain logic to making sure his movements were erratic, getting lost was not what he wanted to happen.

Adrenaline tingled through his veins, almost but not quite pushing away the fear and self-loathing that swirled permanently, nauseously, in his gut. Much as his mind told him to calm down and relax, that no-one paid him any attention, he still cast a surreptitious glance around as he climbed off the train.

New Street Station was in a state of flux: demolition and rebuilding both going on at once. As he threaded his way out, it was hard to miss that wherever he looked, comforting, familiar Victorian brick would soon be replaced by sharp, brutalist concrete. A few black, bulky steam engines still puffed their sooty way, hauling trucks, but several rounded diesel trains chugged through, pulling passenger carriages.

Modernisation, progress, was key. It was impossible not to feel Britain was on the move, heading to a bright, shiny, technologically advanced future.

His conscience sneered that he was helping the other side to modernise, too. Never mind that progress could be one of the keys to security, eh?

Ignoring it, he wandered through the city centre, making a show of looking at menswear in a few different stores before he headed to his true destination.

Lewis's was a huge department store, spread over several floors. People thronged through it, spending their Saturday eyeing the goods on show. Conscious of needing to look casual, indeed natural, he explored the food hall first. He treated himself to a bag of broken biscuits. After all, if they were just for him, what did it matter?

Then he headed to the escalators, towards his target.

His instructions were simple: leave his package, containing the protected camera, in the cistern of the first toilet on the left in the men's facilities. But he didn't want to rush there.

Instead, he inspected new suits in menswear. Some of his current ones felt a bit snug…

You're getting fat, his mind taunted. Living on biscuits, dripping sandwiches, and chips and beer. Not to mention the spirits. What would Maureen say?

Maureen wouldn't say anything, he reminded himself bitterly. She died twelve years ago.

How had it been that long?

Long enough for him to sink pretty low. Even without this weight dragging him down further.

He closed his eyes and tried to gather his thoughts.

Instead, they mocked: *And you wonder why that tart who trapped you never came back. Why would she? What would anyone want with you?*

I have information, he silently protested to himself. This delivery would give him a pretty substantial payment; the Soviets weren't backward in coming forward. For communists, they had no problem paying for information they wanted, and they wanted Banshee to a degree that frightened him, if he thought about it too long.

Especially given all the issues they were experiencing. Campbell's sortie yesterday, on top of what happened when Brookes took his aircraft airborne, was deeply, deeply worrying. In more ways than one. Hawker Siddeley, the conglomerate that included Avro, were pressing for answers. Answers he didn't have. They were pushing the boundaries here, everyone knew that, but somehow, they still expected him to understand every single quirk and nuance of every moment of every test. He wished he did.

Did that shiny new Rover make up for this? That fancy suit?

He squared his shoulders and headed to the men's room.

Task complete, he meandered around menswear for another ten minutes or so, as instructed, trying to work out if anyone had followed him in or out. He couldn't tell.

Then, his final job of the day.

A telephone box was his next port of call. He dialled a number from memory and recited the lines he'd been told to say to indicate a drop had been made with no problems.

'I visited Aunt Mabel. We had afternoon tea.'

Then, he scurried back to New Street and the train home.

His pockets might be lighter, but his conscience wasn't.

Wednesday 26 October 2022

ALEX CLIMBED OUT of his car and headed towards the Warwickshire Justice Centre for the first of his day's meetings. He suppressed a yawn. It had been a long and busy drive from Halton through rush hour; no chance of a second breakfast this time. Woods had spent the last couple of weeks liaising with the police, Braxton, and the Air Historical Branch as they worked their way through the bunker's contents. Much as the drive over had been annoying and slow, it was worth it to see what Parkins had called him about last night.

Despite the normality, even banality of the last couple of weeks, Braxton and Martinford still lurked in his subconscious. Instinct whispered that this find was far more than a simple body. He'd even gone so far as to start looking up books and other historical sources to shed even a chink of light on 449 Squadron. Hardly a trace of it remained: that both intrigued and irritated him, as well as those further up the chain.

At last, he'd have something to chew on.

Almost as soon as he arrived, he was ushered through reception into a meeting room, where DI Parkins waited. 'Thank you for coming,' she said. 'I thought you'd appreciate the heads-up on the preliminary post-mortem results.'

Alex nodded. 'We do. Thank you.'

Parkins smiled wryly. 'I'm afraid our post-mortem places our gentleman's death squarely in our – and your – jurisdiction.'

Alex leant forward in his chair. Frankly, he'd have been surprised if that wasn't the case. 'You have a date?'

Parkins rocked a hand. 'Well, an indication. The suit came from a tailor on Savile Row – Hardy Amies. You can still buy a suit from them today. If you've got the money, that is. We sent them photographs, and they estimate it dates to the first half of the 1960s.' She handed a sheaf of papers to Alex. 'All our analyses, and the results so far, are in there. He was a white male, European, aged between thirty-five and fifty. He was approximately 172 to 177 centimetres tall, or five foot six to five foot eight if you prefer imperial. He was heavy for his height, judging by the size of his suit.'

Alex flicked through the report. He'd study it in more detail later. 'Have you found cause of death?'

'The pathologist believes cause of death was a gunshot wound to the head, and it's unlikely to be self-inflicted. There are no signs of blunt force trauma. Not enough soft tissue survived in a good enough condition to do anything other than basic toxicology tests, and I doubt we'll get anything useable from those.' Parkins tapped the table. 'During our sweep of where the body was found, spent ammunition was recovered. A single cartridge.'

Definitely murder, then. Not a surprise, but confirmation was helpful. 'Were you able to identify the weapon?'

Parkins took a deep breath. She gave Alex a look he couldn't quite read. 'Our ballistics expert is certain the cartridge belongs to a nine-millimetre calibre handgun. Most likely a Browning.'

Alex blinked. That was an unexpected twist. 'A Browning?'

'Yes. It matches the injuries sustained by the victim. Again, the information is in the report.' Parkins stared at him, head on one side. 'I understand RAF personnel are issued with Brownings.'

'Were. The MOD recently replaced them with SIG Sauers and Glocks. Still nine-millimetre.' Alex rubbed his chin. He wasn't foolish enough to think the type of handgun was a coincidence. 'Interesting. You haven't found the weapon?'

Parkins shook her head. 'No.'

'What are your next steps?'

'As a starting point, we'll examine missing persons reports from the time to see if anyone matches our gentleman's description. We've got dental x-rays, so we can match with dental records if required. We intend to cover from 1960 to 1970.'

'If he was military, his disappearance should have been noted,' said Alex. 'I'll kick off a search of our archives for the same period.'

'Thank you. In the meantime, I'll ask our forensic facial reconstruction artist to create a likeness of our mystery man. Flight Sergeant Woods said you'd be happy to help fund that, and the DNA sampling. Unless you have any objections?'

'No, please do.' If nothing else, Alex was curious to see the man's face. 'If we can assist with anything else, please, let us know.'

Parkins smiled, relieved. 'Thank you. The coroner will be officially opening an inquest in the next day or so. It's hard to see this as anything other than murder.'

Alex returned the smile. 'I agree.' He hesitated. This was where he was treading on unfamiliar ground. 'I understand your team have collated the papers and objects found in the bunker.'

'We haven't finished yet. There's a tremendous amount. Literally several vans full.' Parkins shifted in her seat and leant across the table. 'We're in touch with your conservators, but…' She spread her hands and ducked her head in apology. 'As a cold case, even though it's suspicious, we can't devote much resource to it. First indications are maybe half of what was recovered is unsalvageable, but that still leaves us with a lot. And of course,' she added with a self-deprecating chuckle, 'to us civilians, a lot of it's gobbledegook anyway. I imagine we'll transfer it all to you at some point.'

'We can help. Alongside your team, of course, or under supervision as required.'

Parkins eyed him. 'Is there something about this case that means I should bump this up my priority list?'

Alex paused, considering his words. He didn't like to pull rank, but he could hardly say nothing. 'Well. Shall we say our man has raised more questions than we have answers at the moment, and some of the questions imply rather awkward answers?'

'Mm. That could explain the call my boss had yesterday from someone in MI5, then,' she said, slowly.

What? Alex frowned, taken aback. 'Excuse me?'

Parkins blanched. 'Oh. I… I thought you knew.'

Alex shook his head, trying to process the news. If their roles were reversed, he'd no doubt have thought the same. 'Probably a fair assumption, but no.'

'Hmm.' Parkins shrugged. 'He asked for the current status, and for us to keep him up to date on our progress. He asked if we should find any, ah, documents of interest, that we forward them to him. He wasn't particularly forthcoming about what that would mean, though.'

Alex rubbed his forehead. His thoughts whirled. Just what can of worms had Braxton opened? Why were MI5 interested in this? Did his boss know about this? He sighed. All things to consider later. 'Did you get a name?'

'Something Ponsonby, I believe.' Parkins caught his expression; sympathy softened her face, and she smiled. 'I'll speak to our guys and see when we can arrange you access to the evidence here. Woods has really helped our team out during the last few days.'

'Thank you.' Alex breathed an internal sigh of relief. 'I hope between us we can make some sense of this.'

AFTER LEAVING PARKINS, Alex stopped at a drive-through coffee place on the way out of Leamington, ordered a coffee and sandwich, then parked up for an early lunch in the Insignia. He messaged Woods, letting him know he'd be at Braxton in an hour, and then settled down to read the preliminary post-mortem report in more detail. It wasn't the sort of thing to read in full public view in a cafe.

A surprising amount remained of the suit. It looked luxurious: lighter brown pinstripes lined the dark grey-brown, finely woven wool. While the remnants of the once-white shirt were nothing more exotic than cotton, the richly patterned grey-black paisley tie was sumptuous woven silk. The man's all-leather dark brown brogues were worn, but not excessively so.

All that had been found was a grey silk handkerchief square in the top jacket pocket. Wear patterns hinted the left-hand internal breast pocket often held a wallet, but no wallet was present.

The man wore no jewellery, just an analogue watch on his right wrist. Alex flicked through the report until he found a picture. The passage of time hadn't been kind to it: though the metal case looked solid, the golden finish had corroded, revealing pitted base metal underneath. The wristband, which he guessed was once something treated to look like brown leather, was tattered and stained. Presumably, the by-products of decomposition hadn't helped.

The cracked and cloudy face hadn't photographed well: he could make out the hour and minute hands and faint numerals, brassy against the grubby cream, but that was about it. The foggy glass – well, Perspex, probably – obscured all other text beyond a vague impression of letters somewhere in the middle and at the bottom.

He looked at the clothing again. The suit trousers were straight legged, while the jacket was single-breasted with a not especially wide lapel; the shirt was plain, with only a larger collar differentiating it from a modern equivalent. As for the tie… that alone dated it to the 1960s. Otherwise, this was a fairly conservative, business-like outfit.

So why would someone wearing such a suit be shot dead in a bunker on an active RAF base?

Considering, he sipped his coffee and took a bite of his sandwich.

Officers and airmen inside the base would have had their uniforms. Of course, they'd have civilian clothes too, but these looked a cut above what an average serviceman would've been able to afford. Swap it to today, and they looked a step beyond what he'd be willing to spend, too.

The watch didn't fit. He wasn't an expert, but it didn't look like an expensive timepiece. It was no Rolex or Breitling. It was also not the type of watch aircrew wore; they preferred easy to read, precision dials.

His instincts told him their body, therefore, was not aircrew, RAF, or even a member of any UK armed force.

He picked up the report again and searched for the ballistics section. The pathologist recorded cause of death as a single gunshot wound. The bullet entered through the left eye socket and exited through the rear of the skull, on a slight downward trajectory that meant it was unlikely the wound was self-inflicted.

A single spent cartridge, a 9x19mm parabellum round, was recovered amongst brick debris and papers; the deformation and location were consistent with it having passed through the man's skull, bounced off the wall and come to rest. No weapon had yet been found.

All of this indicated the man was shot in that room, around the same time or after the papers were deposited.

The police ballistics expert believed the weapon used was a Browning Hi-Power 9mm. Exactly the weapon used by serving members of the RAF during the 1960s. Certainly, the ammunition was the right type.

Not aircrew or ground crew, but shot with one of their weapons, using their ammunition.

Alex groaned to himself.

This was not going to be a simple, clean, or easy investigation.

BRAXTON SECURITY, NOW used to various uniformed bodies visiting daily, simply waved Alex through the gatehouse onto the site itself.

Even now, two weeks since the bunker was discovered, the tent still stood proudly over the hole, the cordons unchanged from his last visit. About the only difference was that fewer vehicles were parked up: only a Police Transit Connect van, and a plain white VW Transporter.

Somewhere close by, an engine barked into life and settled into a pleasing, rough-edged burble that had to be a V8. It revved and got closer, the noise sharpening into a deep, metallic snarl. Unable to repress his inner petrolhead, he looked. A small, two-seat coupé, maybe the size of a Jaguar F-Type, approached the nearby roundabout. The black and white swirled plastic wrap camouflage did little to hide its petite curves from prying eyes. That would be the new model that had been pictured in Autocar a couple of weeks ago, then.

It roared as the driver shifted down a gear or two. Tyres briefly squeaked in protest as it circled the roundabout then headed down towards the site's second exit with gusto. That distinctive, rasping growl echoed into the distance.

'Ah, sir, good afternoon.' Woods walked out of the tent.

'Good afternoon.' Alex smiled; Woods nodded in acknowledgement. They both knew he'd been eyeing up the prototype sports car. 'Have you had much trouble?'

Woods shook his head. 'Not really. We've had a few try and nosy past the cordons, but nothing unexpected. A couple got upset about the road and footpath closures and gave the police some grief, but it's funny how an RAF uniform seems to calm people down and help them listen to reason.'

Alex grinned. 'Good. Much disturbance from the vehicles?'

Woods chuckled. 'Only that.' He gestured in the direction the coupé went. 'Makes a nice soundtrack, if you ask me. You should hear them out on the test track at full chat.'

Alex could imagine. 'Nice.'

Woods cleared his throat. 'Ready to see what we've been doing?'

Alex nodded.

As they headed into the trailer that passed for a mobile office, Woods updated him on the ground survey teams sent in on behalf of the police and Braxton; so far, they'd found no trace of further underground works in the vicinity of the bunker.

Of course, Alex thought with a smile, absence of evidence wasn't evidence of absence.

Woods summarised the bunker clearing process. Removal was painstaking: before each layer of documents could be moved by the police forensics team, it was photographed and its location recorded and sketched in detail. Only when that was complete could it be transferred to clear plastic bags, labelled for traceability, then boxed ready for transport. Woods' clipboard was several A4 sheets thick with an index listing files, bag IDs, and locations. Parkins hadn't been wrong about the sheer volume of paper. Even with Woods' meticulous notes, sorting through it all would be quite some task.

Woods gestured to the inner cordon. Various items of lifting equipment were nearby, but it seemed the main flow of traffic used the original entrance and stairs. 'I believe it'll be another two days before we've got everything out. Obviously, the closer we get to where the body was, the more, uh, challenging recovery is.'

Alex nodded. That wasn't a surprise. Frankly, he didn't envy whoever was doing that.

'The police are still going through it all, but we've recovered enough that… well…' Woods shuffled through his scribbled notes. 'So far, we've got a cross section of paperwork from 449 Squadron, Electronic Warfare Test and Evaluation. We've got logbooks, maintenance records; all sorts.'

'Electronic Warfare?' asked Alex, intrigued.

'Yeah. That bit's missing out of official records,' added Woods. 'It looks like they were performing some sort of trials.'

'When?' asked Alex.

'What we've recovered so far dates to 1964. That said, we've still got some left to remove.'

'And what you've recovered relates only to 449 Squadron?' asked Alex.

Woods nodded. 'We've got references to some aircraft, as well – Vulcan B.2s – and a few names, which we can start tracing.'

Alex rubbed his chin, thoughtful. 'From the official records I've seen, not much else is recorded about 449 Squadron.'

Woods rifled through his notes and frowned. 'Yeah. We've not found anything concrete, either in our records or at the National Archives. The odd thing is there's plenty about the Vulcan OCU, which was based here, but…'

'Nothing much about this 449 Squadron.'

'No mention of Electronic Warfare, either. Or what they were doing.'

Alex's brow creased, and he withheld a sigh. Curious as all this was, there went his hopes that there'd be a quick answer to at least some of their questions. 'I've just come from the police station. DI Parkins gave me the preliminary post-mortem results.'

Woods raised an eyebrow expectantly.

Alex continued, 'It looks like our man died sometime during the 1960s.'

Woods pursed his lips. 'Well.'

'And it appears his pockets were emptied, and he was shot in the head with a nine-millimetre Browning.'

'Murder, then?' Woods stared out into space for several seconds before drawing a slow breath. 'Nothing we've recovered so far refers to any missing airmen or aircrew.'

'From what he was wearing,' said Alex, 'I don't think he was either.'

HARDIMAN USHERED ALEX into a seat. 'Please, sit, Flight Lieutenant.'

'Thank you.' Alex lowered himself into the chair as Hardiman took his seat behind the desk.

Hardiman's office, on the top floor of Braxton's shiny new Product Development Centre, was rather nice; much larger than Alex's own and certainly better furnished. A long, thin window ran the length of the walls at ceiling height, allowing in light but not the view; underneath it were various images of Braxton's race cars in motion. Conceptual, stylised drawings of road-going Braxton models dotted the cream walls.

'What can you tell me?' asked Hardiman.

'I'm afraid the road closure must remain in place for at least the next 48 hours to complete clearing the bunker.' Before Hardiman's scowl turned into a reply, Alex continued, 'The good news is the ground survey teams have completed their search of the surrounding area, and it appears clear of further underground structures.'

'That's a relief,' muttered Hardiman. He looked up. 'Site services have had a few, uh, complaints about access across site—'

'I can only apologise for the inconvenience,' said Alex, 'but the police, with our assistance, are investigating a death. I'm sure we'd all rather our presence was not required, but as we are, we have a duty to investigate thoroughly.'

Hardiman's brow lowered. 'Have you any news on the body?'

Alex contemplated how to respond. After all, DI Parkins and her team were responsible for the criminal side of things. 'Warwickshire Police should be releasing an update soon. I expect some kind of investigation will be opened.'

'Oh.' Hardiman glanced down at his desk. He bit his lips into a thin line, then gave Alex a nervous look. 'Right.'

'However,' said Alex, 'once the bunker is cleared, we shouldn't need to return to your site.'

'So… it's not linked to us?'

Alex couldn't help a smile at the nervousness in Hardiman's voice. 'Not unless there's something you haven't told us.'

Hardiman winced. 'Oh, no. No. You can trust me on that.'

BACK AT HIS car, Alex checked his phone: Redfern had left him a message, requesting an update. Once he'd connected his phone to the car's Bluetooth, he dialled Sqn Ldr Burden's office and headed back to the motorway.

Redfern answered. 'Ah, the boss was just wondering if we'd hear from you.'

Alex grimaced. That wasn't quite the response he'd hoped for. Obviously, Braxton's mystery played on people's minds. 'I've got the preliminary post-mortem results. Can I speak to him directly, please?'

'One moment.'

It was, in fact, two minutes by the Insignia's clock before Burden came on the line.

Alex didn't beat about the bush and filled Burden in on the post-mortem results.

Silence buzzed for several moments, distorted through the Insignia's hands-free system.

Eventually, Burden spoke. 'Hmm. Interesting.'

'You could say that.' Alex cleared his throat. 'May I suggest our PR officers discuss with the police the feasibility of releasing something as an update. I don't believe we should reveal everything—'

'From what you've said, we know nothing.'

Alex replied, not missing a beat, 'I'm sure PR can say nothing using many words.'

Burden gave a short, sharp laugh. 'I suspect you're right.'

'DI Parkins requested it when she handed me the report. As she's been more than helpful so far, I'd like to return the favour.'

'Very well.'

'I'm returning from Braxton now,' said Alex. 'Woods confirmed what's been recovered so far only mentions 449 Squadron and dates to 1964.'

'What about our official records?'

Despite being alone in the car, Alex smiled, without humour. 'We've a few gaps in our archives there.'

'I see,' said Burden slowly.

'It'll be another 48 hours or so until the bunker is completely emptied,' said Alex. 'DI Parkins will let me know when we can go to review—'

'When will we know what these documents are?'

'So far, it looks like we've got a cross section of everyday admin. The key question is why.' Alex took a deep breath. 'Another question is, why did MI5 call the police about this case?'

All Alex could hear for a few seconds was the droning of the Insignia's tyres on the tarmac.

'What?' Burden sounded just as shocked as he'd been.

Alex repeated what Parkins had told him.

Burden muttered something unintelligible. 'I wasn't aware of that.'

'Neither was I.'

'Well. I shall make enquiries, as they say.' Burden sniffed. 'At the very least, we should've been informed. Anything else?'

'Not yet. A lot of the recovered papers need conservation, before either the police or us can study them properly.'

'Why can't people die neatly?' Burden murmured, half under his breath.

'I suppose as far as the killer was concerned, this was neat,' Alex said. 'No trace of anything above ground.'

'True.' Burden paused. 'So, no idea when we'll have any answers?'

'Woods is doing his best. We're waiting to hear from the conservators. It'll be a few days at least.'

'That's not fast enough.'

Alex swallowed, trying to loosen the tension in his jaw. What could he do, change the laws of physics? Involuntarily, his hands clenched the steering wheel. 'A lot of the papers have suffered from being underground alongside the body. We can't read what we can't see. I'll speak with Woods and see what we can do to speed things up.'

'Whatever assistance you need, call me.' Burden coughed. 'We need answers.'

Thursday 27 October 2022

BACK AT HIS desk the next morning, Alex scanned Woods' emailed update and sighed. There was a frustrating lack of progress. So far, initial searches hadn't revealed any missing RAF personnel, at any point within the 1960s, from Martinford or—

His phone rang. Cursing the interruption, he picked it up. 'Farnsworth.'

'Morning.' It was Redfern. 'The boss was wondering if you were free just now. He's got a visitor curious about your current case.'

'Oh.' Alex recalled his conversations with DI Parkins. Might this be MI5? 'I should be able to pop down.'

'Great. We'll see you in a few minutes.'

Alex made his way to Burden's office, some way down the corridor from his. He knocked on the door, then let himself in at the call.

'Ah, Farnsworth. Do sit down.' Burden, seated at his desk, gestured to the unfamiliar man sitting in one of the visitor's chairs. 'This is Quentin Ponsonby, who is—'

'Attached to the security services.' Ponsonby stood and extended his hand: the firmness of his grip and the steely glint in his eyes took Alex by surprise. 'We've been made aware of your investigation.'

'I see.' Alex sat. Tall and slender, Ponsonby wore a sharply tailored dark grey suit, crisp white shirt, and a thin, subtly patterned navy tie. His jacket moved as he sat down, revealing a vivid purple lining. His greying hair, coiffed upwards in the style of a much younger man, added to the impression that, viewed from the back, he'd look half his age. From the front, though, it was a different matter. Grey designer stubble dappled his sharp chin and hollow cheeks. Thick, black-rimmed angular glasses did not flatter his harsh, taut face.

Suddenly, Alex realised his scrutiny was being returned, and Ponsonby wasn't impressed with what he saw.

'Can you tell us a bit more about your role here, Mr Ponsonby?' prodded Burden.

'Given the highly unusual nature of the find at Braxton, we'd just… like to keep an eye on things.'

Before Alex could speak, Burden gave him a warning look then turned back to Ponsonby. 'What would you like to know?'

Ponsonby half smiled. 'I expect we'd all like to know the same things, Squadron Leader. To understand just what has happened.' He glanced at Alex.

'I understand you've spoken to the police,' said Alex.

Ponsonby chuckled. 'Superintendent Griffiths did tell me you were discussing the case yesterday.'

Burden's eyes narrowed momentarily. 'As you're here, Alex, you may as well tell all of us what you currently know.'

Alex ran through the few things they knew about the body. 'I'm afraid to say his death is being considered suspicious.'

Burden raised his eyebrows as if to say he'd be surprised at any other conclusion.

'Cause of death?' Ponsonby leant forward, scowling.

This would be awkward. Alex hesitated. He glanced at Burden, who shrugged.

Alex ran a hand through his hair. 'A single gunshot wound to the head. In the forensic experts' opinion, it wasn't self-inflicted. The weapon used was a nine-millimetre Browning. I don't think it's a coincidence that it's the sort of weapon aircrews could be issued with at the time.'

'I see.' Ponsonby absorbed this. 'Any clues from the paperwork discovered alongside?'

'So far, it looks like all the paperwork is linked to a single squadron – 449 Squadron,' said Alex. 'It also looks like almost everything about this squadron was buried with the body; very little's in our official records.'

'Hmm.' Ponsonby exhaled. 'Irregular.'

'Well.' Burden took his glasses off and frowned into the middle distance. 'That's… different.'

'To say the least,' said Alex. 'Especially as what documents we've been able to see so far seem ordinary.'

Burden slipped his glasses back on.

'Ordinary?' Ponsonby and Burden exchanged a look.

'Just the usual paperwork any flying unit generates,' said Alex. 'Ops records, aircraft maintenance logs, that kind of thing. Nothing particularly unusual, yet. We haven't found anything so far that can explain why we've got such a drastic variation from procedure here.' As if a dead body wasn't variation enough.

'Peculiar.' Ponsonby paused. 'Have you been able to find any more information about this squadron, what was it?'

'449 Squadron? Not much more, no.' Alex sighed. 'From what we can work out, they were testing something, but what, we don't know. They were formed specifically for whatever it was. And when they disbanded, they didn't reform elsewhere.'

'Any hints as to what they were trialling?'

Alex sucked his teeth. 'Nothing concrete, no. I hope we get more details as we go through.'

'It's all rather… ah…' Ponsonby waved a hand in the air.

'Isn't it?' Even though Ponsonby hadn't exactly said anything, Alex knew what he meant, and he had to agree. 'Which means I have to ask, Mr Ponsonby, is anything present in your archives that would give us some more hints as to just what was going on here?' Not to mention explain why MI5 were interested in what happened some decades ago. Mark's words from the weekend ran through his mind. Could it really be linked to this mysterious PEREGRUZKA? Could there have been a KGB agent at Martinford? It was almost unthinkable.

'You must admit,' said Ponsonby, 'these are highly unusual circumstances.'

'Yes,' began Burden, 'but—'

'People are murdered in all kinds of ways,' interjected Alex, 'but not all of them attract the interest of MI5.' Not to mention how Ponsonby had completely avoided answering his question.

'I'm just wishing to… keep an eye on things. Informally, as it were.' Ponsonby looked at Burden. 'We could also offer you and the police assistance, for example, with document analysis.'

Burden blinked. 'We have our own conservators, thank you.'

'We've considerable expertise in document analysis.'

'I'm sure you do,' said Burden.

'Still, we'd like to offer assistance,' persisted Ponsonby. 'If you send the files—'

'I'm afraid that's not possible,' said Alex.

Ponsonby snorted. 'Do your team have the expertise and the tools they need?'

Alex laughed drily. 'That's irrelevant.'

'Excuse me?' Ponsonby looked at Alex.

'This is a criminal case,' said Alex. 'Until we're told otherwise, everything recovered is under police control, as it's evidence.'

Ponsonby's faint growl of frustration spoke volumes. He briefly clenched a fist before deliberately flattening his hand on his lap.

Alex said, 'The files relate to Martinford as an active RAF base. Specialist officers and our own Air Historical Branch are offering the police plenty of assistance in conserving the documents until their full extent is understood.'

'Are you sure they can cope with all that paperwork?' Despite the apparent air of concern, and carefully blank face, Ponsonby's voice carried a hint of scorn.

'Given the Air Historical Branch deal with everything the RAF has ever printed, yes.' Alex didn't hide his amusement. 'Have you seen how much paperwork it takes to get an aircraft flying? Let alone take one to war?'

'But—'

'This is clearly a criminal matter at what was, at the time, an active station, and I'm liaising with the police on behalf of the Royal Air Force. I'm more than happy to provide information as we get it, but…' Alex sighed. 'Like you, I have to wait.'

Ponsonby's mouth moved in what, if he'd been a child, Alex would've called a sulk. 'I see. You will keep me informed?'

Alex met Burden's gaze, wanting to know himself. Would they?

Burden nodded, imperceptibly. 'Of course we will.'

'Thank you, gentlemen.' Ponsonby glanced at his watch, then stood peremptorily. 'I'm afraid I have another engagement. I'll speak with you soon.'

With that, he strode out of the room, the door clicking shut behind him.

Burden raised an eyebrow and met Alex's nonplussed gaze. After a few seconds, he leant back in his chair and stared at the ceiling.

'Interesting,' said Alex. That was an understatement.

'Yes.' Burden still stared at the plain white above him. 'It's been a while since I've dealt with a gentleman like that.' Burden pronounced "gentleman" in such a way that Alex heard "arsehole".

Alex chuckled; he had to agree. 'I wonder if he was the one who called Warwickshire Police.'

'More than likely.'

'Something must be going on here.' Alex drummed his fingers on his knee, thinking. 'Assuming Mr Ponsonby is being upfront about being part of the Security Service, that's the domestic side.'

Burden nodded. 'Then there has to be something that makes them think whatever Braxton uncovered is, or was, a threat.'

Alex took a deep breath. 'What I didn't say earlier is that a lot of the paperwork states that 449 Squadron was an Electronic Warfare Test and Evaluation Squadron.'

'Electronic Warfare?' Burden straightened up, curiosity in his eyes.

Alex nodded. 'We don't yet know what they were testing. What EW equipment did Vulcans have?'

'Defensive ECM, I believe. Radar warning receivers, signal jammers, that kind of thing,' mused Burden. 'I can't think why they'd need a specialist squadron to test that by then, though.'

'It's hard to see what else could be involved,' said Alex. 'Or even why anyone would be interested after so long.'

If Alex remembered correctly, these days the RAF had two Electronic Warfare facilities – the test range at RAF Spadeadam in the wilds of Cumbria, and the tri-service Army, Navy and Air Force Defence Electronic Warfare Centre, part of the Air Warfare Centre based at RAF

Waddington. How that compared with the situation in the 1960s, though, he had no idea.

'Is Woods still with the police?' said Burden.

'Yes. They're hoping to get the last of the papers out by tomorrow.' Alex glanced up, trying to remember. 'He's making what notes he can, but…'

'The Staish gave me the go-ahead to authorise more help for the police, be that feet on the ground or funding to get things done elsewhere.'

'So he's curious about Martinford, too?' Alex grinned. Staish was shorthand for the station commander, the group captain in charge of the whole base, in this case, Group Captain Rob Hendry. Alex hadn't met the man much, but Burden knew him fairly well; the two often played golf.

Burden chuckled. 'Or curious about why MI5 are curious.'

'I think we all are.'

BACK IN HIS office, Ponsonby growled under his breath. The achingly slow drive back to London, crawling his Audi along the busy M1, had done nothing to improve his mood. It was hard to view that morning's meeting as anything other than a waste of time.

Not that he was surprised by the RAF's refusal to release the files or smooth the path to the police, but he'd hoped – against hope, perhaps – they'd roll over and play ball. But no, they wanted to keep it all to themselves and play wholly by the book. In other circumstances, Quentin may have admired that dedication.

Strictly speaking, he needed hard evidence of a threat linking this investigation to something in the present. Something clear and unequivocal that no-one, not even the RAF, could argue with…

Clearly there was *something*, given that Cavendish was unwilling to spill the beans about it.

Quentin drummed his fingers on his desk. How did they expect him to do this when no-one would tell him anything? For a split second, he longed to be back in Washington. Then he'd know whom to call to influence matters.

But he wasn't. He was at a desk in London, shuffling papers.

He forced himself to unclench his fists.

Even he had to conclude that what he'd considered but trifling peccadilloes, others saw as lapses and indiscretions. Certainly, he'd been unwise, but still…

He stared, unseeing, at the ceiling.

Surely Farnsworth had to have an Achilles heel; something he could use as leverage. Every man had a weakness.

With that thought, he scrolled through his emails till he found the background files he'd requested.

Up until last year, Flt Lt Alexander Thomas Farnsworth, RAF Police, Special Investigations Branch, had been in intelligence, Operations Support. Amongst other places, he'd served on multiple detachments to Afghanistan.

Afghanistan. Of course.

He thought he'd recognised the name.

During the early days of his tenure in Washington, some years ago, there'd been a contretemps regarding intelligence sharing and resulting military actions in Afghanistan. RAF and USAF intelligence had clashed regarding interpretations of a particular set of images and information; the result was a "heated exchange of views" that led to the American officer concerned having to be dissuaded from filing a formal complaint against the RAF officer. However, plenty of informal criticism flowed both ways through diplomatic channels, until the USAF were forced to admit the RAF were correct.

The only other interesting thing on file was that Farnsworth was divorced as of March this year: a short marriage, which had lasted just over a year before he filed on the grounds of his wife's adultery. She hadn't contested, and everything went through cleanly. As of then, it appeared he'd been living almost a hermit's life.

Quentin – once divorced, when young, and twice shy ever since – could have understood more if it had been the other way around. He'd long ago realised he wasn't made for monogamy of the formal, wedded sort. A woman who could catch his mind as well as his eye was a rare delicacy to be savoured; to pass up such opportunities when they presented themselves was absurd.

Perhaps the erstwhile Mrs Farnsworth was similar. Perhaps Farnsworth himself wasn't up to scratch; or, possibly, he enjoyed a more diverse lifestyle, as some would say these days. Quentin allowed himself a momentary smirk. Such thoughts were, of course, conjecture.

Either way, he now had a measure of the man.

Just as Alex was about to leave the office that evening, his phone rang. He pulled a face at the clock but answered regardless.

It was DI Parkins. 'I was expecting to leave a message,' she began, with an apologetic half-laugh.

'Sometimes the job just demands the hours,' Alex replied.

There was a muffled sniff of agreement, then a contemplative pause. Occasionally, Alex felt the wheels of his RAF life crushed everything in their path. Not that he had a packed social calendar at the moment. He shook himself just as Parkins cleared her throat.

'Our missing persons search in Warwickshire hasn't thrown up any likely candidates in our probable timeframe.'

'None at all?' To be fair, he'd have been surprised had they found an answer so easily.

'No. What about your search?'

'Nothing yet,' said Alex. 'Though we're still reviewing the archives.'

'I'd hope if someone disappeared from a base, someone else would miss them elsewhere,' said Parkins.

An analogous situation sprang instantly to mind. 'Yes, me too. Missing airman Corrie McKeague is a case in point. Different circumstances and a different time, of course, but...'

'We're about to open the search nationwide. For our mystery man.'

Alex blinked. So far, he'd assumed the man would be part of, or at least local to, RAF Martinford, but that was far too simplistic. 'Good idea. We'll search elsewhere, too.'

'I appreciate the term "needle in a haystack" might apply,' said Parkins, with a glimmer of humour.

'As you said, though, someone ought to have missed him, somewhere.'

Parkins was silent for a moment. 'I hope so.'

They drew the conversation to a close, and Alex hung up. An unpleasant thought circled his mind: who'd miss him?

For several moments he stared, unseeing, into the distance. His parents; his sister; the friends who'd survived the divorce, maybe? Not that he was in contact with everyone, all the time. The first sign he'd disappeared could well be the fact he didn't turn up for work.

With that cheery thought, he slung on his coat and left.

After a dinner retrieved from his freezer, Alex picked up his personal mobile. There was a text from Mark: he'd spoken to his dad, who'd suggested meeting up at Mark's house Saturday lunchtime. Then they could have dinner afterwards, and he'd be free to stop over for a proper catch up. Would that work?

Alex replied that it would, and would Claire mind if he brought the motorbike?

Mark thought if it kept India out of Claire's hair for a bit, she wouldn't mind in the slightest.

Alex grinned to himself. An opportunity to stretch the GS's legs, spend the weekend with some friends he hadn't properly caught up with for some time, plus the chance to find out a bit more about this mysterious top-secret project. Even if it didn't link to Martinford, it would be fun, to say the least.

'Ah, Ponsonby, what do you have for me?' Cavendish leant forward and steepled his hands on the rich leather top of his walnut desk.

Ponsonby dropped into the leather chair. Quickly, he summarised the little he knew.

'The RAF are keeping their cards close to their chests with this,' he finished. 'Flight Lieutenant Farnsworth is particularly unwilling to share information.'

'Group Captain Hendry called me earlier. Shortly followed by Detective Superintendent Griffiths. Both regarding our case.' Cavendish fixed Quentin with a hard, dark stare; despite his avuncular appearance, Cavendish was not a man to mess with. 'It falls under criminal jurisdiction. Due process must be followed.'

Quentin hid his discomfort under a forced smile. 'I must apologise. I haven't been back in this country long.'

'I appreciate one can get used to other countries' methods,' said Cavendish smoothly, 'however, here I would like you to consider at least the appearance of following procedures, lest we be faced with accusations of perverting the course of justice.'

By Cavendish's standards, this was a royal dressing down. Quentin swallowed but managed to reply, 'I merely offered assistance to deal with the recovered documents.'

Cavendish lifted his chin and pursed his lips, as if considering his response. Eventually, he said, 'I've been handed an impossible challenge: to find out who this man was, without telling anyone what we know so far.' He gave Quentin an assessing look. 'This must go no further.'

'Not even the RAF?'

Cavendish sniffed. 'They'll find out soon enough. I'm afraid the discrepancy between 449 Squadron's official records, and those found under Martinford, is entirely deliberate.'

Quentin raised an eyebrow.

Cavendish continued, '449 Squadron was formed for one specific task: to further the UK's strategic offensive capability. Once this task was complete, 449 Squadron was disbanded and effectively airbrushed from the records to protect the work done.'

'So...'

'Braxton's error risks more than they know.'

'And the body?'

Cavendish hesitated. Uncharacteristic uncertainty shaded his eyes. 'This is the issue.'

Quentin waited.

Cavendish cleared his throat. 'The calculated obfuscation of 449 Squadron and their task means the situation is genuinely unclear.'

'In other words, we don't know exactly what's under Braxton, or who this man could be.' Quentin frowned into the distance.

'The precise nature of the project has also been, shall we say, lost in the mists of time, but one thing is clear.' With that, Cavendish leant forward and lowered his voice. 'This was intended to neutralise Soviet defences. Not damage, not even delay, but wipe them out completely.'

Friday 28 October 2022

ALEX PARKED UP outside the Warwickshire Justice Centre and made his way in. Woods had called first thing this morning, asking him to visit as soon as possible; he and the archivists had untangled some of the many threads of Martinford's paper trail.

The trouble was, this morning, he was supposed to update his boss, but he'd left his apologies with Redfern and jumped straight into the car regardless. He genuinely couldn't wait to hear what they'd found. Woods sounded like a boy who'd just unwrapped a longed-for toy on Christmas morning. That had to be worth yet another drive to Leamington.

Woods fidgeted with excitement when Alex walked into reception. 'Sir.'

'Good morning,' said Alex, smiling. 'So, we have something?'

'Oh, yes.' Woods grinned.

'Really?'

Woods gestured to Alex to follow him along the corridor; their footsteps echoed hard on the lino. 'Definitely. We've found something big.'

'How big?'

Woods waved his hands, like a man demonstrating how big the fish that got away was, but he didn't speak. When they got to an unremarkable door, Woods knocked.

After a few moments, the door was opened by a small, bird-like woman who scrutinised them over her glasses. Her slight, pale frame was almost swamped by a thick burgundy woollen dress, and dark hair pulled into a sharp bun added to her severe air. She nodded in recognition at Woods. 'Morning. Good to see you both. Come in.'

They trailed her into a large, windowless room. The musty scent of old paper drifted in the air. Fluorescent lights dangled in long strips from the ceiling, their buzz just on the edge of hearing. Though the room could hardly be described as tidy, there was an underlying order to the papers stacked neatly on the long benches. Each heap seemed to be tagged with something.

Alex glanced at the woman; her manner reminded him of a headmistress. After weaving between the benches, she stopped at one end of the farmost one. 'Thank you for coming,' she said. Her cheeks flushed a little: she was younger than her bearing suggested. 'I'm Leah Ball, forensics, with a side speciality in document analysis. Have you had any hints about what we've found?'

'No. He's left it to be a surprise.'

Woods had the grace to shuffle his feet when she gave him a bit of a glare.

Alex grinned. 'Can we start?'

She nodded. 'As far as we can tell right now, the recovered papers cover the day-to-day operations of 449 Squadron, Electronic Warfare Test and Evaluation, between approximately February and August 1964. And when I say operations, I mean, we've got almost everything here.' She gestured to particular piles as she carried on. 'Forms for aircraft flights, aircraft maintenance, crew training…'

Alex surveyed the stacks. The obvious logic and clarity in her approach was reassuring. 'So, you've sorted the papers by type?'

'Subject. And date. Where we can, yes. Most recent is at the top. I think we've saved roughly half what was in there. The rest is with your recommended conservators to see if they can salvage anything else.'

'Have you got enough to work out what was happening?' asked Alex.

'Well, we can make an educated guess,' she said, eyes bright.

In his peripheral vision, Woods seemed to tremble with excitement.

Impatience stirred, but Alex managed to ask calmly, 'And that is?'

She took a deep breath. 'It looks like 449 Squadron was evaluating a new type of weapon. We've got a report that says preliminary trials were performed at the Radar Research Establishment at Malvern during 1962 and 1963. It appears this squadron's role was to perform flight trials in this country and check it was integrated system-wise with Vulcan bombers.'

Alex held up a hand. 'Wait a moment. What do you mean, new type of weapon?'

Ball hesitated. She exchanged a look with Woods. 'We're not sure yet. The only thing we can tell for sure is it was top, top secret.' She pointed to one stack of papers. Writ large across the top sheet, in bold black letters against the aged cream, was TOP SECRET – UK EYES ONLY.

Alex frowned, trying to think. 'Can you find out what it was?'

'We're going through the documents to see what we can find.' Uncertainty flickered in her eyes.

Woods cleared his throat. 'All we know for definite is it was going to be an offensive weapon in its own right. Not just a jammer or radar. The weird thing is, very little of this is corroborated by other records. It's like 449 Squadron was just buried.'

'Please, don't worry about that,' said Alex. 'Just tell me what you find here.'

'This weapon had a codename,' said Woods. 'One I've never heard of.'

'What was it?'

'Banshee.'

Ball and Woods took him through as much as they'd been able to reconstruct so far of the story of 449 Squadron. They also handed him a list of officers and NCOs explicitly named in the paperwork, with a note or two saying what they did, if documentary evidence backed it up: others in the team were already tracing them and their subsequent careers within the RAF.

Some papers referred to the project with an alphanumeric code of TL.772, but even then, Banshee was used almost interchangeably. Whatever it was, the fact it was being tested at RAF Martinford, a Vulcan OCU deep in Warwickshire, rather than at the RAE in Farnborough or A&AEE at Boscombe Down, hinted at a desire to keep it away from known research establishments. It was clearly highly sensitive.

As far as they could tell, 449 Squadron had been created purely to develop this Banshee. Even squadron was a misnomer, as it had only the one Flight of three aircraft.

Sqn Ldr Charles Hesketh-Shaw headed the Flight, followed in seniority by Flt Lt Fraser Campbell, then Flt Lt Anthony Brookes. Their three Vulcan B.2s were, respectively, XL433, XM568 and XL447: XL433 and XL447 were retrofitted with more powerful Bristol Olympus 301 engines to match XM568.

So far, they'd recovered various aircraft drawings and installation diagrams that seemed to relate to the Banshee system as fitted to each Vulcan. Woods admitted they hadn't had a chance to study them properly yet. All they knew for certain at this point was that it was carried within the bomb bay, and each Vulcan had been specifically modified for this programme. Some papers referred to the Vulcans as B.2.Bs.

'Do we have any technical data on Banshee's design? Anything on what it was, or how it actually worked?' asked Alex.

Woods pulled a face. 'Some. We haven't studied it in any detail yet.'

'Can you give me at least a summary of what you have?'

Ball nodded. 'I'll do that directly.'

She bustled off. Alex stared at the heaps, lost in thought. As if trying to identify their dead body wasn't mystery enough…

'There's one other thing,' said Woods. 'At the moment, we've not been able to trace the flight commander's next move – either in all this, or in our records. Everyone else listed, we've been able to identify and make a start on tracking down, but not him.'

'This Hesketh-Shaw?'

'Yes, sir. It's like he just disappears.' Woods sucked his teeth.

Ball came back with a folder full of papers. 'Here you are.' She glanced at Woods. 'You were talking about the untraceable flight commander?'

Woods nodded. 'He's not recorded missing.'

Odd. Alex tried to tell himself this was probably some admin error or just a gap in their records but couldn't quite convince himself. 'The clothes indicate our body was probably rather large. Larger than I'd expect a Vulcan captain to be.'

'Tall or round?' enquired Ball.

'Round.' Alex paused. 'We still need to look into that, though.'

Woods coughed. 'We've found documents relating to a crash of a 449 Squadron Vulcan in 1964 as well. XM568, by the looks of it. We're yet to work out what story they tell us. Or if there's anything in our existing archives about it.'

Alex frowned at Martinford's paperwork, spread before him. Somehow, he couldn't help thinking it would bear little more than a passing resemblance to anything officially recorded.

'THANK YOU FOR being able to accommodate our last-minute adjustments,' said Sqn Ldr Burden. He gestured Quentin to a chair. 'Please, sit.'

At least the call delaying this morning's update arrived first thing this morning; even if it took his PA all morning to rearrange the rest of his day's meetings, there was no way he wouldn't have travelled for this. Though this was originally meant to be a telephone conference, he'd pushed for it to be face-to-face. Privately, he was surprised the RAF had agreed to two face-to-face meetings with him on consecutive days. 'I take it this means you have some news for us.'

'I sincerely hope so,' murmured Burden. 'Farnsworth is on his way, and—'

There was a brisk knock on the door.

'Come in,' called Burden.

A marginally taller than average figure in blue-grey RAF uniform, carrying a couple of cardboard folders, entered the room: Flt Lt Farnsworth. From a distance, the man seemed older than his face showed: he scanned the room with the wary manner of a cowboy sizing up a saloon. Even the shadow of his peaked cap couldn't camouflage the hint of cynical world-weariness in his steel-blue eyes. Close-cropped dark blonde hair peeked under the sides of his hat.

'Sir,' said Farnsworth. He nodded at Ponsonby.

'Ah, do take a seat.' Sqn Ldr Burden leant forward, curiosity clear in his expression.

Farnsworth sat in the only spare seat, next to Quentin, and took off his cap. 'Thank you.'

'Update us, please,' said Burden.

For a split second, embarrassment shaded Farnsworth's features. 'So far, our body remains unidentified.'

'Not at all?' queried Burden.

'I'm afraid not. A DNA sample is being taken, which will be compared with what's in the national DNA database.' Farnsworth smiled thinly. 'Though this assumes any relatives have a criminal past.'

'Nothing from Missing Persons?' asked Burden.

'No-one of the right age, description, or gender – at least, within the timeframe concerned. Yet.' Farnsworth opened a folder and scanned a sheet. 'Neither have our searches identified any missing airmen or officers, and we've opened the search nationwide. It seems our man appeared out of nowhere.'

Quentin regarded Farnsworth through narrowed eyes. Cavendish's words rang in his ears. Surely the records couldn't be that obscured. 'Is that so?'

Burden raised an eyebrow. 'But that's not possible.'

'I know. Warwickshire Police are exploring every avenue they can.'

Pensive, Burden tapped his chin.

Farnsworth continued, 'Woods' team have scoured the records for every unit based at RAF Martinford for the years 1960 through to 1970.' Farnsworth cleared his throat. 'That said, we've uncovered an irregularity.'

'Irregularity?' asked Quentin.

'Yes. And it concerns the squadron whose archives were found with the body, 449 Squadron. Although the officer commanding the Flight isn't recorded as missing, leaving the service or retiring, we haven't found any onward postings yet.'

'Do you have a name?' asked Burden.

'Squadron Leader Charles Hesketh-Shaw. 449 Squadron's flight commander, and a long-serving Vulcan captain.'

'Could he be our man?' asked Burden.

Farnsworth's brow furrowed. 'I'm not convinced he is, but we need hard evidence to prove one way or the other.'

'What makes you think he isn't?' prodded Quentin. Out of the corner of his eye, he caught Burden rolling his eyes; clearly, he was being pushy again.

Farnsworth's gaze went to his commanding officer; after a pause, he replied, 'Clothing hints our body was a solid, largely built man in life. A Vulcan cockpit isn't roomy, to say the least. I can't imagine someone his size or shape would be able to get into the pilot's seat easily.'

Quentin almost opened his mouth to protest, but Cavendish's earlier warning still stung. Instead, he nodded. If even the RAF weren't convinced he was their man, why stir things up unnecessarily? 'Of course,' he conceded.

'Woods also confirmed to me this morning the paperwork recovered from Braxton concerns the operations of 449 Squadron only, during 1964.' With that, Farnsworth cast another glance at his superior officer.

That meant they must have found something else, but they weren't willing to share it with him just yet, though he had to ask. 'Have you any detail about these operations?'

Burden frowned briefly.

Farnsworth said, 'I'm afraid I can't divulge our findings until we've confirmed—'

Quentin sniffed.

'May I remind you just how many papers were recovered from Braxton?' said Farnsworth.

'You really have nothing more?' Ponsonby prodded.

Burden took off his glasses and tapped the arm of them against the table. Though he stared off into the distance, he gave a barely discernible nod.

Farnsworth hesitated. '449 Squadron seem to have been a specialist squadron, operating Vulcan bombers and developing some sort of new – for then – technology. The exact details are unclear, but we're in the early days of analysing the documents. Whatever it was, was extremely sensitive. The fact none of this was officially recorded…'

Adrenaline tingled through Quentin. So, Cavendish's information was correct. 'What do you think it could be?' he asked.

Farnsworth met Quentin's gaze, but his eyes were like a steel door; they betrayed nothing. 'Why is this so important to you, Mr Ponsonby?'

Burden sharply cleared his throat.

Without missing a beat or breaking eye contact, Farnsworth said, 'I will, of course, forward a summary of our findings as soon as I have one. I trust you received the copy of the preliminary post-mortem?'

'I did, yes.' Quentin refused to look away.

Amusement glimmered in Farnsworth's eyes, though his expression didn't change.

'If this body isn't our missing squadron leader,' said Burden, 'who is he?'

Seemingly despite himself, Farnsworth nodded. 'That's what we'd all like to know.'

QUENTIN HAD ALMOST reached the exit when a voice stopped him.

It was Farnsworth. Quentin hadn't registered earlier that the man's build was stronger than he appeared; his shoulders were substantially broader than Quentin's.

Quentin allowed Farnsworth to catch up with him.

'I think I owe you an apology,' said Farnsworth.

'What for?'

Farnsworth narrowed his eyes and looked Quentin up and down. 'We both know I was a little cautious in volunteering information to you.'

'Tell me. Do you play poker at all?'

Farnsworth blinked but didn't seem shaken by the non-sequitur. 'No.'

'Pity.' Quentin pushed a smile onto his face. 'A face so expressionless would be quite an asset.'

'As is, no doubt, your ability to change the subject.' Again, amusement glinted in Farnsworth's eyes, but this time, a hint of a smile played on his lips.

'Do you think this is a game?' said Ponsonby coolly.

Farnsworth regarded Quentin, head on one side. 'I couldn't say. Who defines the rules?'

'Who says there are rules?' Despite himself, Quentin grinned.

'Spoken like a true diplomat.'

Quentin, taken aback, shook his head slightly. 'I don't know what you mean.'

'Hmm.' The way Farnsworth said it, he knew exactly what that meant. 'Something tells me you know more about RAF Martinford than you wish to say.'

'What makes you think I have any more knowledge than you?'

Farnsworth scanned him; again, that trace of a smile lingered. 'I hope you don't play poker with that face, Mr Ponsonby.'

With that, the man strolled past, out of the building.

Monday 20 July 1964

GORDON SAT AT his desk, staring disconsolately at the piles of things to read, respond to and sign, which didn't seem to have shrunk in the hours since he'd started first thing this morning. If he'd known all this came with promotion, he wasn't sure he'd have gone for it. Still, with command came responsibility: it just seemed that with responsibility came paperwork. Lots of it.

Just as he pulled yet another stack towards him, there was a knock on the door. He sighed.

Hunt edged in. 'Sorry to disturb you, sir, but I know you wanted to know. We've found something on '68.'

Gordon grinned. His men knew him well; they'd got straight into examining the aircraft this morning after Friday's flight. He gave the paperwork one last glance, then stood. 'Good work. Let's have a look.'

He followed Hunt through to the hangar. West, grubby in his overalls, stood by a collection of parts. Gordon recognised how they were laid out – he'd done it himself, in his time – but the parts themselves weren't immediately familiar. 'What've you found?'

West cleared his throat. 'This.' He picked up a spindly tangle of metal.

Gordon racked his brains. 'That's some kind of antenna, isn't it?' He looked at the spread of parts. His gut sank. He didn't know them because they were all components supplied by Fli-Tek. 'Have you taken Banshee to bits?'

'Er… only what we think is the array assembly, sir.'

'You do know only Fli-Tek are supposed to service that?' Gordon kept his voice level.

West's eyes widened. 'Um. It pretty much fell out as we opened the bomb bay, sir.' He added, hurriedly, 'And we were told to tear things down till we found the problem.'

Gordon tried to stop himself grinning. That was exactly the response he'd give to such a question. 'And you have. This is the first one you've looked at, isn't it?'

West fidgeted. 'Well, we had a very good look at '47's...'

'Before or after '68?'

'After, sir,' West mumbled.

'Fli-Tek will ask the same question when they discover we've taken their precious system to bits,' said Gordon. 'They're supposed to be the only ones to work on it.' Personally, he'd have done the same; not that he could admit it, here and now. That was a discussion he'd have to have with Watson, Hesketh-Shaw and Burroughs, his own boss. 'All right. What did you find?'

West held up the battered, crumpled part. 'It looks like this bounced off the Banshee unit itself from the witness marks. But that's not all. We compared it to '47's, and it's different.'

Gordon raised his eyebrows. Interesting. So much for Watson insisting there were no differences in installation between aircraft. As far as he knew, Banshee was supposed to work exactly the same regardless of which aircraft it was on. 'How's it different?'

Hunt cleared his throat. 'Easier if we show you.'

He led Gordon over to where XL447 stood, her bomb bay doors splayed open. West pointed up to what looked like, on closer inspection, a chunkier version of '68's part, folded up against the underside of Banshee itself. 'This is it. We think.'

'Have you found the root cause of that protector failing?'

West shook his head. 'Fli-Tek seem to think it's connected to the break we found in the back-up circuits, but the circuits aren't linked at all. Not if it's been wired up to spec. We've been trying to trace it out, but...'

Gordon's shoulders slumped.

'Fli-Tek are coming in later to replace the protector, anyway,' added West.

'Have you found why we've got that circuit break? And the damage to the bomb bay?'

'If you look right up there, one of the front unit retaining bolts is missing. We found it in bits underneath when we opened her up. One of the rear bolts is bent, and the other was loose, so it wobbled on its mountings.' Hunt gestured at the inside of the aircraft, then at the Banshee unit. 'That smacked into one of the wiring runs, and we've got some witness marks on the port PFCU lines as well as the doors. Probably a good job tank A wasn't in, else that would've got bashed.'

Tank A was the front-most auxiliary fuel tank that could be fitted inside the Vulcan's bomb bay. Much of the aircraft's wiring and hydraulic lines for the powered flight controls ran the length of the fuselage inside the bomb bay; potentially vulnerable, with something big, heavy, and loose in there. 'Well, that could explain what '47's crew experienced. What about '68's hiccup?'

Hunt looked at him. 'You were on that flight, weren't you?'

Gordon nodded. 'It was pretty memorable. You've checked all her alternators and generators?'

'We have. They're fully functional. What we did find was a crack in the shielding around the main busbar.' Without being asked, Hunt headed straight for XM568. 'Now,' he continued, 'I don't know if that's linked to whatever caused that – antenna, possibly? – to break, but we've no witness marks on the inside of the bomb bay, other than a couple of little scuffs where it must have fallen off in flight.'

'She wasn't being thrown around, I can tell you that much.' Gordon heard the vehemence in his voice. He paused and took a deep breath. 'We stuck perfectly to the flight plan; manoeuvres, speeds, heights, everything. Apart from post triggering.'

Hunt hesitated. 'Just what did she do?'

Gordon quickly ran through everything he'd experienced on XM568; even the memory prickled his nerves. As he talked, both Hunt and West were staring at him, West's mouth hanging open.

'That shouldn't have happened,' said Hunt. His face was white.

Gordon felt the tightness in his jaw. 'I know.'

'That cracked shielding might have contributed, but…'

'Keep looking, please.' Gordon hesitated. This looked like Fli-Tek were using them for development. Admittedly, that was part of the programme, but this level of difference between aircraft made him uncomfortable. Especially as no-one had mentioned it. Someone wasn't being straight with them. That rankled. Besides, he owed it to Tony and Fraser to find out just what was going on. 'As far as I'm concerned, you now have permission to take more of Banshee apart on either aircraft if you think there's an issue there. I'll have a chat with the boss and take the flak.'

There was no mistaking the relief that flashed across both West's and Hunt's faces. Gordon smiled. 'Good work. Thank you. Let me know what else you find.'

When he got back to his office, Gordon spotted a scribbled note from Ray, one of his other NCOs: Sqn Ldr Hesketh-Shaw requested his presence in the ops room at 1530. If memory served him right, Fli-Tek representatives were meant to be on base today, theoretically to go through the results of the trials conducted last week.

He glanced at his watch: he had approximately twenty minutes to prepare.

This was going to be fun.

After much internal debate, Gordon decided against taking the fragments from XM568 into the briefing. He did, however, scribble a whole load of notes and questions on a sheet of paper, which he folded up and stuck in his pocket. Then he donned his hat and ventured out.

Somewhere behind him, the earth shook as a Vulcan howled into the sky. He turned to look: he couldn't make her out, but it had to be one of the OCU's aircraft. Both '47 and '68 had bits missing, and '33 was still firmly in the hangar.

Ahead, he made out Tony Brookes and Fraser, walking in together. Judging by Fraser's hand gestures, he was expanding on Friday afternoon's occurrence. Fraser glanced over his shoulder and acknowledged Gordon with a smile.

'Tony. Fraser,' said Gordon.

'You're getting dragged along too?' asked Fraser.

Gordon nodded. 'This about Friday?'

'I should hope so,' retorted Fraser. He shot a sideways look at Tony, whose face was somewhere between uneasy and angry.

'I told—' Tony began.

Gordon nodded. 'My chaps have been busy this morning. We've found some interesting things. On both Vulcans,' he added.

Tony simmered down.

Curious, Fraser tilted his head to one side.

'Tell you in there.' Gordon smiled, but there was no humour in it. 'I don't want to spoil the surprise.'

Inside the ops room, Gordon once again felt the weight of responsibility: as 449 Squadron Avionics Integration JEngO, he bore the responsibility for keeping their Vulcans and Banshee systems in perfect flying order. In spite of everything else thrown at him.

At the front, Sqn Ldr Charles Hesketh-Shaw stood, scanning the room.

Watson sat on a chair nearby, patting his brow with a crumpled handkerchief. His rumpled grey suit looked as if it had been slept in. Next to him sat a slender, slightly younger man also in civilian dress; a neat cream shirt, a striped burnt orange tie tucked into his shirt placket, and crisply ironed black trousers. Even this man seemed to eye Watson with a degree of distaste.

What do you know, George? Gordon wondered exactly what he wasn't telling them. He fingered the folded paper in his pocket.

As the clock struck the half-hour, Hesketh-Shaw cleared his throat. 'Gentlemen. Thank you for coming. You all know Mr Watson of Fli-Tek.' He gestured towards George. Watson glanced up, ducked his head in acknowledgement, and shoved the hanky back in his pocket. Hesketh-Shaw waved at the other man. 'This is Mr Kelly, another technical representative.' Kelly nodded.

Hesketh-Shaw continued, 'I'm sure you all know by now we've had issues with the trial aircraft. Brookes, Campbell, you were in the cockpits concerned, and you both reported flight control issues – specifically, loss of controls. Brookes, you and your crew have, ah, given a comprehensive report on your sortie, which Mr Watson is familiar with. Campbell, explain Friday's occurrence, please.'

Tony, his mid-brown curls neatly brylcreemed in place for a change, raised a cynical eyebrow.

Fraser cleared his throat. 'On Friday seventeenth of July we took XM568 up for the preliminary ultra-low power verification checks over Scotland. When the button was pressed, we suffered a serious disruption to the whole aircraft electrical supply. My AEO almost deployed the RAT, but power restored itself. A good job, seeing as we were at a thousand feet.'

Watson stared, wide-eyed; Kelly blanched, as if hearing it for the first time.

Fraser glanced across at Gordon for confirmation.

Gordon nodded. He repeated everything he'd said in the original debrief.

'The last I heard,' murmured Hesketh-Shaw, 'that area's still without mains power as well.'

Gordon swallowed. That was news to him.

Watson blinked rapidly. 'I… er… had been told, yes.'

Hesketh-Shaw stared at Watson for a few moments, then looked at Gordon. 'Mr Thompson, have your team made progress with the airframes?'

Gordon stood. 'Yes, sir.' He pulled the paper out of his pocket, then looked sidelong at the still-sweating Watson.

'And?' prompted Hesketh-Shaw.

'I'll start with Brookes' Vulcan, XL447.' Gordon pointed to the chalkboard behind Hesketh-Shaw. 'If I could illustrate?'

Hesketh-Shaw shrugged. 'Go on.'

Gordon got up and walked up to the board. He picked up a piece of chalk and sketched an approximate side view of '47's bomb bay. Then he drew a series of dotted lines. 'This is where Banshee should have sat, but here's where it ended up; one of the front mounting bolts was either not fitted or it fell out, and the remaining bolts, especially the rearmost, bent under the weight. My chaps found witness marks on the bomb bay doors and on the aft PFCU runs.'

Watson swallowed. He shot Gordon a nervous look. Kelly peered closer, frowning.

Tony sat back, folded his arms, and radiated an unmistakeable air of "I told you so".

'As yet,' added Gordon, 'we can't say for certain if this contributed either to the open circuit or the protector failing. But it won't have helped.'

Hesketh-Shaw nodded to Tony, then looked at Gordon. 'Do you know what the source of the issue was?'

'This is where it gets interesting,' said Gordon. All watched with interest as he wiped the board clean. 'Now, the issues reported with XM568 were very similar, but the cause was not the same.' He spun on his heel and pointed the chalk at George. 'Mr Watson, do you know of any differences between the Banshee units on our aircraft?'

George's lips moved; he looked around, perplexed. 'I… well… minor differences, perhaps—'

'Minor,' repeated Gordon. 'So, you'd classify the antenna arrays as minor?'

Someone hissed a quickly drawn-in breath, but Gordon kept his eyes on Watson. The man's face rolled from shock to fear to anger in the blink of an eye. Kelly folded his arms; he turned to Watson, too.

'Your team,' said Watson carefully, 'should not have touched that part of the system.'

'As it more or less fell off in their hands, would you like them to have dropped it?' retorted Gordon.

'Mr Watson has a point,' said Hesketh-Shaw. 'Mr Thompson, the agreement is we call in Fli-Tek for any engineering modifications or issues with the Banshee unit itself.'

Gordon braced himself. 'I know, sir. However, the unit was so damaged on XM568—'

Hesketh-Shaw waved his hand. 'A discussion for later. Please, continue.'

Watson flushed; he glared at Gordon.

'The damage led me to authorise my team to remove the unit from XM568 and compare it to XL447's.' That was sort of true. He waited for

Watson to resume eye contact, but the man's gaze flicked anywhere but at him.

'Mr Thompson, that call was not yours to make,' said Hesketh-Shaw.

Gordon sucked in air through his teeth and put on a contrite face. 'I've reason to believe this device affected the airworthiness of both planes. I wouldn't be doing my duty to the crews if I didn't investigate, sir.'

Hesketh-Shaw pursed his lips, brow furrowed as he considered.

Gordon pressed his point. 'You're a pilot yourself. It's my job to give you all a snag-free – well, ideally – Vulcan. You need to trust your aircraft.'

Hesketh-Shaw nodded. He gave Watson a thoughtful look. 'OK. I understand. Though I will be discussing this with Squadron Leader Burroughs.'

Gordon swallowed and nodded. That meant a meeting with hats on with the boss later; the best he'd expected, really. 'Yes, sir.'

'Your findings?' asked Hesketh-Shaw.

Gordon took a deep breath. 'The antenna arrays look superficially similar but are completely different between the two aircraft. '68's part is thinner, smaller, and had been damaged at some point.'

'Damaged?' asked Watson.

Gordon nodded. 'Yes, although my team couldn't find any witness marks on the aircraft itself. Not like on '47.'

Watson frowned.

Before any of them could speak, Gordon referred to his notes and carefully drew two shapes on the board. 'Mr Watson, can you tell what it is yet?'

Someone almost, but not quite, suppressed a snort of laughter.

'I…' Watson hesitated.

When Gordon turned around, Watson stared at the board, perplexed.

'That – the one on the right is version B, wide angle, that was fitted to '568. Version A, narrow beam, that was '447's.' Watson stood and approached Gordon. He held his hand out. 'May I?'

Gordon glanced at Hesketh-Shaw, who shrugged. 'Be my guest.' He dropped the chalk into Watson's hand.

Watson studied the shapes. 'You've drawn these as they are off aircraft?'

'As my team found them, yes.'

Still eyeing the board, Watson bit his lip, deep in thought. 'The iteration of version A, fitted to XL447, is an early one. It's somewhat heavier than our original estimate. We hoped the bolts would take it, but in-flight motions must have strained them.'

Tony's face darkened, but Watson didn't notice. Even Kelly looked a bit dubious.

'Does that explain the effects of the cracked shielding?' asked Hesketh-Shaw.

'Motion in flight—'

'I followed the flight plan given,' snapped Tony. 'Ask my crew.'

Watson blinked a few times, then rubbed his face. 'It may have been an interference effect thanks to the damaged wiring,' he mumbled.

'Pardon?' asked Fraser pointedly.

Watson's jaw clenched. 'It may,' he said, louder, 'have been an interference effect thanks to the damaged wiring. I'll need to take both components back with me for evaluation.'

'Of course,' said Gordon. 'Now, '68 is slightly different—'

'XM568 has version B, which is in a much earlier stage of development.' Watson drew on the board. He planted a pudgy finger on a curve. 'It was crumpled here?'

Gordon pointed to another section. 'And here. No obvious witness marks, either on the component, the other bits of Banshee, or the Vulcan. All we did find was the protection had split around the main busbar.'

Someone whistled under their breath.

Watson paled. 'Really? That… well… er… hmm.'

'I've asked my team to keep looking to see if they can find a cause.'

Hesketh-Shaw stared at the board and rubbed his chin. 'Thompson, I'd like your team to inspect XL433 as soon as practicable.'

'Of course.' Like Gordon couldn't wait to see what they found there, either. He cleared his throat and glanced at the frowning Watson. 'Did you want Fli-Tek—'

'Just get on with it,' said Hesketh-Shaw.

Watson almost glowered, but the shapes on the board distracted him. 'You did follow the flight plans as developed—'

'Yes,' insisted Tony.

'We followed them to the letter,' interjected Fraser sharply. 'In my case, cruise there, drop to a thousand feet, deploy, then turn and climb back home. And before you start, it's only an evolution of the Low Altitude Bombing System. With which I tormented the Americans last year.'

'Don't rub it in,' muttered Tony under his breath.

Fraser continued, 'We're not amateurs. We're among the best bloody crews this country has got. If this system can't cope with us treating it with relative kid gloves, it's not going to cope when it's on aircraft dispersed to some god-awful airfield in the middle of nowhere ready to be shot off at two minutes' notice—'

Hesketh-Shaw held up a hand; Fraser stopped. 'What iteration is fitted to XL433?' asked Hesketh-Shaw.

Watson shook himself and handed the chalk back to Gordon. 'Er. Let me check.'

Kelly scrabbled around inside a briefcase and retrieved a folder, which he handed to Watson.

Watson ruffled through the pages. 'XL433 also has version B, but shielding as per '47. Have you... has it—'

'I'm due to take '33 up tomorrow morning,' said Hesketh-Shaw. 'A duplicate of Campbell's flight.'

Watson stared thoughtfully up at the ceiling for a moment.

'Why are they so different?' asked Gordon.

This time, Kelly spoke. 'We're trialling methods of improving signal distribution and strength. Version B is meant to improve radiated efficiency, while minimising internal heat effects.' He glanced around at the questioning faces and sighed. 'Our designer had some concerns about thermal dissipation, both from being encased close to the charger within the bomb bay and from repeated activations.'

'We've never activated it more than once in flight,' said Fraser.

'And this isn't accounting for any heating effects from activating the ECM,' said Tony. He exchanged a worried glance with Fraser.

'Darwin isn't going to be cold when we're there, either,' added Gordon.

Watson chewed his lip and stared, pensive, at the floor.

Hesketh-Shaw strode forward and wiped the board clean. 'OK. Mr Thompson, you and your men shall inspect XL433 as soon as practicable and feed the results directly to me when finished. Mr Watson, you and Mr Kelly will take the damaged Banshee units back to Fli-Tek and discuss any of the finer points with Mr Thompson's men. Fraser, Tony, we and our co-pilots shall have a discussion here in one hour to thrash out sortie details.' Hesketh-Shaw looked pointedly at Watson. 'Depending on the results of the inspection, I intend to take XL433 up as planned tomorrow. Unless you wish to advise me otherwise?'

Watson shook his head.

'Then that's all for now, gentlemen. Dismissed.'

HUNT WATCHED A group of erks carefully inspect the Banshee central antenna mechanisms on XL447. At Gordon's footsteps, he turned and gave him a questioning look.

Gordon shook his head. He needed to have a think. But first… 'Glad I caught you. H-S has asked us to inspect '33 before his planned flight tomorrow. Can you get some of the chaps to—'

'I'll do it myself,' said Hunt.

'And he wants us to inspect Banshee on it as well.'

Hunt glanced over Gordon's shoulder. 'No Watson?'

Gordon shook his head. 'I think we've set the cat amongst the pigeons.' *About time*, he added in his head. 'Either Mr Watson or Mr Kelly will be here shortly to take the damaged units back to Fli-Tek.'

'Both of them?'

Gordon nodded. 'Make sure they know everything you found. I imagine they'll be here shortly.' He grimaced. This was the bit he wasn't looking forward to. 'And I need to go and have a chat with the boss.'

BAD NEWS TRAVELLED fast. Gordon walked into Burroughs' office just as the man put his phone down. He regarded Gordon with a faintly disapproving look, as if his star pupil had been caught doing something dodgy behind the bike sheds.

'You probably know who that was,' said Burroughs. He gestured to the worn chair in front of his wooden desk. The faint scent of pipe tobacco drifted in the air.

Gordon sat. On autopilot, he went to remove his hat; he hesitated, then lowered his hand. 'Er… yes, sir.'

'I don't have to tell you what it was about. Or what they said. Do I?'

Gordon shook his head.

Burroughs sighed. He leant forward and propped his elbows on the desk. 'What happened?'

'Sir?'

'You told H-S and Fli-Tek the parts fell off. Is that true?'

'Well…'

Burroughs' raised eyebrow stare didn't waver.

'It did off '68,' Gordon admitted. 'The focusing antenna was loose, and the boys said it fell out.'

Burroughs kept staring.

Gordon took a deep breath. 'But it hadn't on '47. It looked so different we took it off to try to understand what was going on.'

'How different?'

'Completely.' Gordon spread his hands. 'It even looks like they use different size bolts.' He shook his head. 'What's worse is I don't know if that antenna being loose on '68 would disrupt her electrics like that. It probably did something, but what, only Fli-Tek are likely to know, and I don't think they'll tell us. And worse again is, it's different to '47. Similar issue, but we couldn't find the same problem. It must have been something else. We found some damage to her PFCU wiring, but I don't honestly know if that should've had that effect.'

Burroughs frowned.

Gordon carried on before he could speak. 'I'm not going to lie, sir; what happened in '68 scared the heebie-jeebies out of me. Her entire electrical system fell over, and if you ask me, it's a miracle it picked itself back up and we got back here. We don't know why it happened. If we don't know that, we can't say it won't happen again. And if it happens again…' he trailed off, suddenly conscious he'd been ranting.

'Fli-Tek are here today, aren't they?'

'Yes. They're coming to take the units off '68 and '47 for evaluation.'

'H-S wants to take '33 up tomorrow. While Fli-Tek are here, have them inspect her alongside our team.' Burroughs studied Gordon. 'Would you be sixth crewman again?'

Gordon swallowed. That was the 64,000-dollar question. Not that he was keen, but… 'If that's what's needed, I will.'

GORDON WALKED BACK to the hangar, deep in thought.

Kelly stood by XL447; he nodded as Gordon passed. One of the techs was busy in the bomb bay. A box full of parts sat on the floor by XM568. They must have finished removing the control units.

Hunt and Watson stood by XL433. Hunt faced the aircraft; Watson spotted Gordon and glowered. 'What are you doing with these aircraft?'

'Excuse me?'

'The damage on '68…' Watson tutted.

'Feel free to look at all her fatigue gauges. She was not being thrown around. Neither is she being shunted around the workshop.' Each aircraft had fatigue gauges that monitored the stresses sustained by the airframe in flight. Gordon folded his arms. 'Anyway. There's a chance I may be a sixth crewman again tomorrow. Have you found out why these power interruptions happened?'

Watson swallowed and gave the glossy grey-green aircraft a nervous look. 'Kelly is looking after '68 and '47.'

'That's nice, but that's not what I asked.' *Give me strength*, thought Gordon.

Footsteps echoed behind him; Kelly approached.

'We'll take the units back and bench test them.' Kelly pointed to the boxes on the floor behind him, each labelled for the different aircraft. 'Beyond the issues already found, nothing jumps out as being obvious on the aircraft themselves.'

'Thank you.' Gordon took a deep breath. 'We'll keep looking.'

'Has ground testing shown anything on this one?' Kelly gestured to XL433.

'No,' said Hunt. 'So far, everything has passed with no issues.'

Gordon cleared his throat. 'We did have to rectify the bomb bay ventilation ducting, last week, once she got here. Something dented one of the pipes. My guess is a clumsy fitter, somewhere along the line. It's been fine since we did that, though.'

Watson stared up at the Vulcan, lost in thought. It was like he didn't see anyone else there.

Kelly shifted on his feet. 'We should have some results on these by the end of the week.'

'Thanks.' Gordon stepped closer and peered up at the Banshee unit. Now he could see the similarities to '68's installation: it was neater than '47, notwithstanding the fixing issue.

Watson twitched and shook himself, but he still refused to look at Gordon. 'We've found nothing here,' he said, eventually. 'She's good to fly tomorrow, if that's what the squadron leader wants.'

'Then that's what I'll tell him.' Gordon nodded at Hunt. 'Let me have your report when it's done, please.'

THAT EVENING, HE pushed his way into the pub. The darts team were playing tonight; lots of unfamiliar faces made the place busier than usual, even in the saloon away from where the game was played. Cigarette smoke and chatter filled the air.

But one face was very familiar indeed: the thin middle-aged man with neat black hair raised a hand in greeting and gestured to the additional pint of Double Diamond that sat in front of a spare chair.

Excellent, on all counts – it was safe to talk, and after the day he'd had, liquid refreshment would be very welcome. He knew this man by the name of Peter, though it was unlikely to be his real name.

He shrugged off his sports jacket and eased himself into the seat.

Peter forced a smile. 'Good to see you.' Worry lined the corners of his eyes.

He hesitated, pint already halfway to his lips. 'Is there a problem?'

Peter nodded, lips pressed together in a thin line. As if to fortify himself, he picked up his own pint and took a sip. He leant forward, casting a glance around. 'You could say that,' he said, so quietly his voice almost blended into the background. 'We've managed to decrypt the last batch of transmissions, using the pads we copied during our search of your friend's flat.'

'And?' He put the pint down.

Peter swallowed. 'You're not alone. You have company.'

For a second, his meaning didn't register. When it did, he went cold, as if he'd been swallowed by an avalanche. He stared, slack jawed, waiting for Peter to continue.

'A second person is sending information about the project. We've codenamed him Dogberry; the others call him Doctor.'

He licked his lips and tried to catch his thoughts. What did this mean for him? Fear needled his spine.

'Doctor made a dead drop this weekend just gone.' Peter watched him. 'It seems, at the moment, your friend is happy you two don't know about each other.'

'I'm due to make a drop in four days.' He picked up his pint and drained about a third of it in one gulp. 'What do we do? Surely we have to stick to our plan. Even if it'll make it clear that one of us isn't playing a straight bat.' What a phrase to use, when discussing espionage: surely the entire practice was dishonest and unsporting.

Peter briefly smiled. He nodded. 'That's the assessment back in the office. Especially as we don't yet know what was delivered. Cassius is going to London shortly to drop it off. We're not sure where he collected it from. It wasn't one of your sites.' Cassius: his "friend" Johnson's codename. Just like his own was Ariel.

'Do we know anything about Dogberry?'

Peter drank some more. 'It appears, although it's not conclusive, he's an engineer. So, we presume he's employed by either Hawker Siddeley or Fli-Tek. Everything sent so far relates only to this project, so we suspect the latter is more likely.'

He cursed, rubbing the back of his neck. Close enough to Banshee – and to him – to endanger it all.

'And he's been sending data for some time. Cassius referred to some of this weekend's drop as corrections and clarifications.'

He blew out a long, slow breath. 'That hints he's been talking to them for a while.'

'It does.'

'If so, I'm not surprised he's sent some corrections. We had some incidents, last week, which unsettled a few.' It unsettled him too, if he was honest. It seemed everything on this project had to be smoke and mirrors: nebulous, hard to grasp, impossible to pin down. Thompson appeared determined to make it tangible and solid – something he was silently thankful for. 'At the moment, it's still full steam ahead. Do you have what I need?'

Peter nodded and smiled. He handed over an A4 manila envelope.

He drained his pint and sighed. A second was very tempting, but it would have to wait until he got back. If nothing else, he probably should show his face in the mess.

'If we receive any information on our new friend, I'll get in touch.' Peter tapped the dark wooden tabletop and fixed him with a steady gaze. 'Do any possibilities come to mind?'

He cast his mind over the engineers and managers he'd met since joining the Banshee project. 'None immediately.' He'd be vigilant now, of course, if only to cover his own back. 'If I do suspect anything, I'll let you know.'

While still seated, he shrugged his jacket back on and picked up the envelope: it felt thicker than usual. Something to study tonight, while his wife slept, blissfully unaware beside him, just in case Johnson wanted to discuss anything. If he was being fed two completely different sets of data, surely that would be sooner rather than later.

Tuesday 21 July 1964

GORDON WALKED UP to the dispersal. XL433 was already out on the pan. Around her, early morning summer mist blurred the countryside, smudging bright greens into pale shadows.

Reminding himself it'd be sunnier up high didn't help that much.

His stomach churned; he'd not felt able to eat much beyond a bowl of cornflakes for breakfast. Nothing like an early morning call, requesting your presence on the next Banshee test flight, to focus the mind.

Walking into the unknown was comparatively easy. Walking into the realm of half-known possibilities, on the other hand…

'H-S said you were joining us,' said Ted.

'Yeah.' For once, he didn't feel like talking. Neither did Ted, it seemed. Hands in flight suit pockets, they stared at the aircraft.

Activity flurried. Ground crew attached the starter, while Hesketh-Shaw and Trevor rattled through the external pre-flight checks.

Hunt and the boys hadn't found anything out of the ordinary; they pre-emptively inspected the problem areas from '68 and '47, and all appeared normal. Gordon swallowed. Neither of those aircraft had had such a detailed inspection pre-flight, so there could have been an issue there. True as it was, that thought made him feel rather too like Watson for comfort: clutching at straws rather than grasping certainties.

H-S's voice interrupted his thoughts. 'We'll be flying no lower than fifteen hundred feet today.'

Gordon turned. As Hesketh-Shaw held out a spare "Bone Dome" to him, he noticed the man's blue flight suit and tie were rumpled. Maybe it was his imagination, but Hesketh-Shaw's face seemed wearier than usual, eyes baggy with tired shadows.

Gordon took the helmet. 'Thanks.' Not that it would give him that much more of a chance to bail out, he reflected, but the thought counted.

By the time he'd wedged it on his head, Hesketh-Shaw had disappeared up the ladder; Trevor was halfway up, and the rest of the crew waited to get onboard.

Time to get this show on the road.

TENSE SILENCE FILLED the Vulcan's lower cockpit while above Trevor and Hesketh-Shaw completed their checks. A rumbling whine grew and grew: the engines, one by one, spooled into life.

In the orange-shaded dimness, Gordon peered at the generator dials and controls on the panel in front of Flt Lt Chris Perkins, the AEO. Dials and gauges twitched and settled. The airframe vibrated gently under his feet, mirroring the steady high-pitched thrum of her engines idling, dull through his helmet.

Everything looked normal. Just as it had on '68.

'All right?' asked Chris. The rear crew's intercom wasn't yet connected to the cockpit.

'Yeah.' Gordon scanned the panel till he found the dial he remembered. 'Keep an eye on that one,' he said.

Chris peered closer. 'Banshee charge status?'

'Yeah.'

'Mike ran through that flight with me,' said Chris. Sympathy showed in the set of his eyes above his oxygen mask. With a gloved hand, he tapped the next dials: engine alternator status. 'He mentioned these as well.'

Gordon nodded. Top of his list, when – if – he landed, was to dig more deeply into how Banshee was wired into the Vulcan. Electronics always struck him as a bit of a dark art, and the more he thought about it, the more apt it seemed. Especially with this project.

Ted coughed. 'I hope H-S promised you some beer for this.'

'I wish.' Sarcasm coloured Gordon's tone. 'I get to enjoy the warm glow of helping.'

ACID BURNED GORDON's throat as his stomach wrenched, and he stifled a burp. Normally, travel sickness never bothered him, but every rolling swoop and crest of the Vulcan, felt rather than seen from his dim perch, stirred his guts. Maybe the air was a bit bouncier today; Friday's flight hadn't felt this rough. Neither had he.

His ears ached, then popped. She was descending.

Adrenaline shot through him: he stood, braced himself against her curved side, and waited. He stared at Banshee's instruments. So far, nothing about their movements looked out of the ordinary. That didn't ease his mind.

Reg interrupted his thoughts. 'Target marker on visual.'

'Banshee charged,' said Chris. Gordon observed the gauge; its needle rested against the 100% marker.

'At altitude,' said Trevor. 'Level at fifteen hundred feet.'

'On time, skip,' said Ted. 'And on course.'

Gordon sensed the airframe slow. That ever-present engine whine dropped just a little.

'Discharge in five seconds,' said Reg.

Gordon counted down in his head. His gaze never left the dials. Five… Four… Three… Two… One.

'Banshee discharged.'

A faint squeal echoed over the intercom. Charge status flicked to zero.

The unmistakeable rumbling crescendo of four Bristol Olympus 301 jet turbines ramping up to full throttle filled his ears and pulsed through his feet; he clung onto the grab handle as she tilted skywards, climbing hard.

This time, Banshee's dials did what he'd expected from the off-aircraft tests: all four engine alternators were working, and Banshee was pulling a reasonable amount to recharge.

Gordon let out a breath he hadn't realised he'd held.

'Thompson.' Hesketh-Shaw's voice crackled over the intercom. 'What's happening?'

'Everything looks good with Banshee.' Words Gordon never thought he'd say, at least not while airborne. 'No faults.'

'No faults with the aircraft,' confirmed Chris.

'Marvellous.' Hesketh-Shaw sounded almost cheerful. 'Let's get back.'

GORDON SAT THROUGH the debrief, but his mind wasn't on it. Not that he wanted a repeat of Fraser's flight, but why had they got away with it? What made XL433 different to her sister aircraft?

'Thompson?' Hesketh-Shaw called. 'Are you with us?'

There was a faint chuckle from the other men in the room.

Gordon winced. 'Sorry.'

'What differences did you see in the back, today?' Hesketh-Shaw's face was neutral, but there was a curious glint in his eyes. Even Ted and Reg leant forward to listen. Trevor put out his cigarette and scratched his head.

'Banshee worked,' said Gordon, flatly. 'That's the first time I've seen it do on an aircraft what I expected from the ground testing. And I don't know why.'

'Talk us through it,' said Hesketh-Shaw.

Gordon referred to his notes, scribbled on his pad during the flight back. 'Before activation, I'd say everything was as spec. It replicated off-aircraft tests; it replicated what I saw on '68. Nothing on any of Banshee's readouts was out of spec that I could see. Activation procedure was exactly the same as on the previous sortie.' He switched his gaze between Hesketh-Shaw, Trevor, Ted, Reg, and Chris. 'You all followed the same steps, same protocol, as did Fraser and everyone last week.'

'Good to know,' said Hesketh-Shaw. His lopsided smile didn't reach his eyes.

Gordon continued. 'Banshee was activated. What I saw this time was what's supposed to happen: charge status went to zero, Banshee generators came online and started to recharge at standard rate. It looked like they were pulling an expected 15% of engine generator output, which is within spec for a climb scenario and on a par with the lab tests.'

'Whereas, with '68…' began Chris.

'Charge status went to zero, but everything else…' Gordon sighed. 'Banshee generator status wasn't stable. That's half of it.' He paused, something occurring to him. 'When we activated Banshee on '68, we got a hell of a shriek over the intercom.'

'We had a bit of one,' said Trevor.

'Nothing like what I heard last time,' retorted Gordon.

'The Banshee's wail,' murmured Hesketh-Shaw, half under his breath.

There was a moment of silence. Gordon stared at the scuffed melamine table. How did he explain what happened next when he didn't understand it himself? ''68's dials bounced around like crazy, until… they didn't.' He rubbed the bridge of his nose. 'I don't know what changed. I don't know why it stopped. And I don't know why today's flight was textbook.'

'Apart from the ground crew's inspection,' said Trevor. 'Went over her with a fine-toothed comb, Chief Kendall said.'

'When do we expect to hear from Fli-Tek about the control units?' asked Chris.

'End of the week.' Gordon rubbed his eyes.

'Hmm.' Hesketh-Shaw drummed his fingers on the table, frowning. He exchanged a glance with Trevor. 'That's the test plan out of the window. We need more flight hours before the end of the month. Next Friday.'

Gordon grimaced. There was no easy or nice way to ask this, so he might as well jump in with both feet. 'Which issue of the test plan are we talking about?'

Someone snorted with suppressed laughter.

Hesketh-Shaw just hid a smile. 'The Wingco wanted us to have two hundred and fifty flying hours and five Banshee low-power activations under our belts by the end of July. We've got maybe a hundred hours, and three. Not to mention only one of those three was textbook.' Hesketh-Shaw frowned over Gordon's head.

'On the flip side,' said Gordon, 'we've managed eighty-five percent of the ground running side of integration testing.' As an afterthought, he added, 'Not that we can test much more with only one Vulcan.' It wasn't like the ground-based testing was that complicated, either: it basically just checked the Vulcan's auxiliary fuel tanks functioned, that the aircraft powered up and down smoothly, and that the rest of her systems functioned.

'What a mess,' murmured Ted.

Trevor tapped his packet of John Player cigarettes on the table. He looked at Gordon. 'What would you do?'

That was simple. 'Stop all Banshee testing until we understand exactly why '33 was fine, and the others weren't. It worries me we don't know what's gone on.' Gordon took a deep breath. 'I'll say that to whoever needs or wants to hear it, too.'

'You might find some don't want to hear it,' murmured Ted.

'It's the truth.' Gordon met Hesketh-Shaw's gaze. The man nodded.

'One can only hope we get some answers when Fli-Tek bring the units back,' said Hesketh-Shaw.

Gordon laughed bitterly. 'I don't think Fli-Tek and answers go together.'

'If it helps,' said Hesketh-Shaw, 'I agree. We should stop all testing until we understand what's happening.' He eyed his crew. 'If any of you disagree, of course…'

Trevor snorted. He took a drag of his fresh cigarette. 'No, I'm quite happy to stay here in one piece, thank you very much.'

Hesketh-Shaw grinned. He stood. 'In that case, I shall go and spread the news.'

Wednesday 22 July 1964

GORDON KNOCKED ON Sqn Ldr Burroughs' door. This morning's meeting wasn't something he was looking forward to. All Banshee aircraft were now grounded, following yesterday's post-flight debrief, and he couldn't imagine his superiors were that happy about it.

'Come in,' called Burroughs.

To Gordon's surprise, Wing Commander Merrick stood behind Burroughs: arms rigid, hands clasped behind his back, head held high. There was no disguising the anger that simmered through Merrick's stance. Burroughs almost seemed to shy away from him; his chair was as far from Merrick as it could go while still under his desk.

'Sir.' Gordon laid a hand on the spare chair, but Burroughs minutely shook his head.

Oh. It was going to be one of those meetings. Gordon winced.

'Thank you for coming,' began Burroughs. He glanced over his shoulder at Merrick. 'We've had an official complaint…'

What? Before Gordon could respond, Merrick slapped an orange cardboard folder down on Burroughs' desk.

'I have a letter here from Fli-Tek. Mr Watson has complained, in the strongest terms and at the highest level, about your handling of the Banshee system.' Merrick flipped open the folder and picked up a typewritten sheet. 'He says, and I quote, "Flight Lieutenant Thompson has ignored all the conventions that had previously been agreed regarding demarcation of responsibilities between the RAF and ourselves.'" He laid the sheet down and looked up at Gordon. 'What do you have to say for yourself?'

Unthinking, Gordon scratched his moustache. 'Well—'

'Do you have any idea of the gravity of this?' Merrick gestured at the folder.

'Sir, Banshee practically fell out—' Gordon began.

'I don't care if it took itself out of the bomb bay and went for tea at the Ritz!' Merrick snapped. 'You and your men are not to touch that system unless a member of Fli-Tek is present. Do you understand?'

'But—'

'No buts.'

Gordon closed his eyes and tried to think. 'You're asking me to do the impossible.'

Merrick bristled. 'Following orders beyond you, is it?'

'If you want me to keep your aircraft airworthy, we need to work around that thing in the bomb bay—'

'*Around* being the operative word.'

'We can't go through it!' retorted Gordon. 'I want to know why it fell off XL447. I want to know why we nearly lost her and XM568, because—'

'Fli-Tek have got the control units and are evaluating, are they not?'

'Yes,' admitted Gordon.

'Then we'll hear from them in due course. I understand XL433's flight went without a hitch.'

Gordon nodded. 'But I don't—'

'Banshee worked perfectly, did it not?'

'On XL433, yes. And so far, the ground testing we've done has gone well.'

'That, at least, is a positive.' Merrick sniffed. He stared at the wall behind Gordon's head. 'We're incurring significant slippage to the flight test programme.'

'Well, yes.' Gordon ploughed on. 'That's because we've had issues. Tony Brookes raised that SOR—'

Burroughs' lips clamped into a line, and his brow furrowed.

Gordon stopped, his gut sinking. *Uh oh.*

Merrick drew himself up: he wasn't a short man, but the air of arrogance and entitlement he carried made him seem even taller. 'That SOR stops here.' He glanced down at Burroughs before meeting Gordon's gaze with an iron-grey coldness, unyielding as a glacier. 'Brookes filed that without any understanding of the wider issues at play. SORs by their nature are public things. Banshee is meant to be secret, gentlemen. Secret things are not written down, nor discussed by every man and his dog.'

Gordon wanted to speak but kept his mouth shut. After all, he'd encouraged Tony to do the SOR in the first place.

'That aside,' continued Merrick, 'I do understand.' Some of the tension leached out of his stance; his tone softened. 'We're under pressure, here. Time and money are both running short.'

Gordon bit his tongue. Again and again, it seemed everyone wanted something good, fast, and cheap, without realising all three at once was impossible. Good and fast was never cheap; good and cheap was never fast; and fast and cheap was rarely good. But there was no point saying that right now.

'I shall inform Mr Watson and Fli-Tek that I've reprimanded you,' said Merrick. 'I would also like you to keep your investigations of the aircraft under the radar, so to speak.'

'Sir?' Gordon blinked. He frowned at Merrick, then Burroughs. Burroughs looked equally bemused.

'The fact these parts have suffered such failures means Fli-Tek themselves know they're on borrowed time.' Merrick coughed. 'I too would like to understand exactly what's happening with our Vulcans. Continue your inspections. But do not, whatever you do, so much as breathe on anything Fli-Tek have installed without one of their men being present. I don't need to remind you what the consequences will be if I hear so much as a whisper from anyone – anyone at all – that you have interfered with the system. Is that clear?'

'Yes, sir.' Gordon held himself together. If it were just Burroughs in the room, he'd be asking how the hell he could be expected to look at the Vulcans and their relevant systems without touching Banshee; it was impossible. Merrick didn't want to understand that.

'We need to keep this project clean.' Merrick glanced down at Burroughs, who stared at his hands, knuckles clenched white on his desk. 'We don't need to add unnecessarily to the administration you already do, do we?'

'Are you asking me to do this off the record, sir?' Gordon knew he was being obtuse, but he needed to hear it.

Merrick's mouth twisted. 'You understand perfectly what I mean.' He looked at his watch. 'Go back to your duties. Keep SEngO here informed.'

GORDON SOMEHOW MANAGED to walk back to his office, fury fizzing through his veins. Every footstep between his boss's office and his own was measured, deliberate. His jaw ached; he clenched his teeth so hard he half expected a tooth to shatter.

How dare they. How. Dare. They.

He was trying to do his job; look after the crews. Technology and politics were both secondary.

Not to Merrick.

Gordon dropped into his chair. Merrick could do one. So could Watson, for that matter.

Something broke through his seething, and he looked up.

Fraser stood in his office doorway, a curious expression on his face. 'Are you all right? You didn't hear anything I just said, did you?'

Gordon shook his head. He wasn't sure he could speak.

Fraser sat down. 'What happened? John said he saw the Wingco over here...' He watched Gordon's face, understanding dawning in his eyes.

Gordon tried to gather his thoughts. At least, any that were vaguely coherent. All he could do was shake his head and move his jaw to try to get rid of the cramp.

'You got Merricked?' said Fraser. He sniffed, incredulous. 'But... I mean—'

'Oh, I got Merricked all right,' Gordon managed. 'Apparently Tony's SOR is getting canned because, oh, I don't know. Who cares? Merrick wants us to have a clean sheet. Nothing to go on official records. Even if it nearly kills two crews.'

Fraser blinked. 'But—'

'Don't but me. I know. Best bit is I've been warned for not following procedures. Fli-Tek – well, we know who, don't we – fussed at him about it.'

Fraser cursed vigorously. 'Banshee fell to pieces in front of you. What on earth were you meant to do?'

'Who knows?' Gordon flung his head back and stared at the ceiling. 'Ever wonder why we bother?'

'Money? Beer? Ladies? Loyalty to Her Majesty?' Fraser stopped when he saw Gordon's expression.

'I'll see you tomorrow,' said Gordon.

Once Fraser left, Gordon stared blankly at the ceiling, waiting for the anger churning his insides to subside.

This didn't sit right with him. Not one bit. The question was, what could he do about it? There was a fine line between disobeying an order and misinterpreting it—

A *rat-a-tat* on his door broke in. With a groan, he sat up and tried to straighten his face. 'Come in.'

Sqn Ldr Burroughs entered. 'Surprised you're still here.'

Gordon shrugged. 'Not many other places to be.'

Burroughs sat down. 'I had a longer chat with the Wingco after you left.' He laced and unlaced his fingers.

'I know I'm speaking out of turn here, but what does he expect me to do? I'm not—'

Burroughs held up a hand; sympathy showed in the set of his eyes. 'I know. I told him that. And you've got my backing.'

Gordon blinked, taken aback.

Before he could say anything else, Burroughs continued, 'I'd say keep doing things by the book, but God knows which book we're referring to right now. It changes depending who's bent Merrick's ear – but you didn't hear that from me,' he added with a wink.

Despite himself, Gordon half smiled.

'You've been around longer than I have,' said Burroughs. He returned Gordon's half-smile, somewhat sheepishly. 'I was still in short trousers when you were bombing up Lancs.'

'I wasn't far out of them myself,' admitted Gordon. He'd joined up a bit before he'd actually reached eighteen; quite a bit before, truth be told.

'Still. You know yourself something isn't right on these things.' Burroughs' mouth moved; he stared somewhere over Gordon's shoulder for a few moments. 'Merrick asked if I thought you and Fraser were exaggerating about the other day. I was crystal clear that if anything, you underplayed things. Especially as the range are still puzzled about why their equipment blew so violently. We haven't said anything. Of course.'

Gordon swallowed. A shiver tickled his spine.

'Keep doing what you're doing, as you've been doing it.' Burroughs stood. 'H-S and the crews are relying on you. If something happens that's likely to ruffle Merrick, just… let me know before he knows. If you can.'

'I will.' Gordon stood too. 'Thank you.'

Burroughs nodded then left, closing the door behind him with a gentle click.

Gordon stared at the light wood. What should he do next?

What he wanted to do was take Banshee off every aircraft, tear them down, inspect every single little thing, and record it all in minute detail…

Abruptly, he pushed away from his desk and marched down the corridor to Hunt's tiny office. For a change, he was sitting at his desk, surrounded by test paperwork. He frowned when Gordon barged in.

'Sorry to interrupt,' said Gordon. 'But I've got an idea. Can you find the crew chiefs for me?'

HALF AN HOUR later, Crew Chiefs Morton, Andrews, and Kendall crowded into Gordon's office; Hunt perched on the edge of the desk. All wore expressions with varying degrees of suspicion and confusion.

'I know you're all busy,' began Gordon, 'so thank you for indulging me.'

'Is this to do with Banshee?' asked Morton.

'When isn't it?' Gordon took a deep breath. What he was about to ask was not likely to go down all that well. 'You all know the issues. '68 and '47 are currently without their Banshee control units, but '33 still has hers.'

'You want us to inspect them?' said Andrews.

Gordon nodded. 'Go through everything you can. And I mean, everything up to where Banshee is bolted or wired in. Every system. Every fuse. Every bolt. Every wire. Write it all down, too.'

Morton and Andrews exchanged a glance but nodded. 'Everything?' asked Morton.

'Everything. Especially anything that interacts with Banshee.'

'What about '33?' asked Kendall. He was her crew chief.

'Obviously we can't do as much, but…' Gordon trailed off, thinking.

Kendall smiled grimly. 'If anything "falls off", I'm sure we can catch it.'

That was the spirit. Gordon breathed an inward sigh of relief. 'I owe you all. The beers will be on me Friday night.'

PILOTS WHO DIDN'T have an aircraft to fly got bored very easily.

Unless their boss happened to be Sqn Ldr Charles Hesketh-Shaw, that is.

Fraser cleared his throat. 'Boss. What are we doing here? Apart from keeping us out of mischief?'

John snorted. Brian rolled his eyes.

Trevor, Hesketh-Shaw's co-pilot, chuckled. 'I doubt we could keep you out of trouble for long.'

Even Hesketh-Shaw half smiled. 'I thought we should discuss the current test plan, and our concerns.' He straightened his back and gave each of them a serious look. 'I'll be honest with you. Even I'm not one hundred percent convinced of the safety of our Vulcans in the air. Watson and Fli-Tek talk a good talk, but…' He gave Fraser a searching look, then Tony. Tony still hadn't smoothed his feathers from '47's mishap; everyone knew he hated any suggestion he wasn't as good as the others.

'I wouldn't trust Watson if he said the sky was blue,' said Fraser. 'I've made my feelings clear to—'

'Everyone,' interjected Tony.

Brian stifled a laugh at Fraser's glare.

'As I was saying—' Fraser restarted.

Hesketh-Shaw interrupted. 'We all know what you think.'

Silence fell.

Fraser bit his lip. That was the nearest to a rebuke he'd ever had from his current commanding officer. Out of the corner of his eye, he caught Tony sneering; he studiously ignored it.

After a moment, Hesketh-Shaw nodded. 'I believe what you were about to say was that our integration JEngO is well aware of yours – and Tony's – reservations.'

Tony looked at Fraser, as if waiting for him to start. For once, Fraser kept his mouth shut.

Tony raised his eyebrows. 'I bloody well ran to his office after our debrief. Got to give him credit, he listened. And he encouraged me to do the SOR. He said we had to stop this happening again and that Fli-Tek owed us answers.'

'Have we had any answers?' asked John.

The room was silent.

Fraser idly fiddled with his pen. He knew full well they hadn't. So did Hesketh-Shaw; he shifted in his seat and ran a hand through his sandy hair.

'What's happening with the SOR?' asked Trevor. He looked between his CO and Tony.

Hesketh-Shaw leant back and stared at the ceiling. His jaw worked.

'It's canned,' said Fraser. He flung his pen across the room. 'I knew—'

'You knew? You know bloody everything!' yelled Tony. He banged his fist on the table. 'F—'

'GENTLEMEN!' Hesketh-Shaw's chair clattered to the floor as he rocketed upright. 'Brookes, put your damn ego to one side, unless you want to go back to Coningsby and QRA tomorrow. Campbell, think on.'

Fraser swallowed. Much as he occasionally enjoyed poking Tony about his insecurities, even he had to concede now wasn't the time.

'Sir.' Resentment simmered in Tony's voice, but when he spoke again, the challenge was crystal clear. 'Shall I tell everyone what's happened to the SOR?'

You could have heard a pin drop. Unconsciously, everyone leant forwards in their seats; all eyes went to Hesketh-Shaw. Deliberately, he righted his chair and sat back down.

'I'm as happy about this as you are,' Hesketh-Shaw ground out. Anger flushed his face. 'The Wingco told me and SEngO it had to be canned and, in his words, dealt with internally. Off the record.'

SEngO was Gordon's boss, Sqn Ldr Burroughs. Fraser didn't know the man well enough to make a judgement, but that coming from Merrick surprised him. Still, he kept his mouth shut.

Brian scratched his head. 'Dealt with internally? What does that mean?'

Fraser pondered. Not surprising that Gordon hadn't been keen to talk; he was stewing over this.

Tony's voice broke into his thoughts. 'Does this mean Thompson is looking after it?'

'Thompson has been warned,' said Hesketh-Shaw.

Fraser couldn't keep his mouth shut any longer. 'Because—'

'Process, gentlemen. Fli-Tek.'

'So, we follow procedures, but only when it suits Merrick?' retorted Fraser.

Though Tony sounded calm, there was a low growl of fury underneath his words. 'What kind of unit is this? We're told we don't pick and choose the rules, but—'

The door opened, quieting the men. Wing Cdr Merrick strode in. 'Am I hearing my name taken in vain?'

Tall, and still lean despite his age, Merrick was a formidable figure; his WW2 Pathfinders reputation still bought him drinks in the mess, even now. His aquiline nose, and a thick shock of now-grey hair, added to his authoritarian air. He closed the door behind him and stared at Hesketh-Shaw, hands on hips.

To give Hesketh-Shaw credit, he stood his ground. 'Sir. We all have deep concerns about the events surrounding Tony's SOR.'

'I can tell. I heard you in my office.' Merrick's gaze lingered on Hesketh-Shaw, then Tony. Tony looked down at the table.

'Why has Gordon – Flight Lieutenant Thompson – been warned?' said Fraser.

Hesketh-Shaw blinked at the apparent change of subject; Merrick merely sighed. 'It's not just about the aircraft.'

Fraser stood. 'This is politics, isn't it, sir? Fli-Tek don't want us finding any inconvenient little issues that will slow down the programme. Am I correct? Well, they ought to know a Vulcan leaving a delta-shaped hole in the countryside won't exactly help this get into service any faster.'

'I have every confidence in you all to handle any issues you find in the air.' Merrick nodded at Fraser and Tony. 'You both brought your Vulcans home safely, did you not?'

'We did,' said Tony. 'But—'

'And you'll be extra vigilant now you know there may be something?'

'Yes,' said Tony. 'But—'

Fraser clenched his fists. Fury bubbled in his veins. Had Merrick even heard him? 'Sir—'

'Sit down, Campbell,' said Merrick. He met Fraser's gaze; there was a steeliness in his grey eyes Fraser hadn't seen before. 'And calm down, before I send you to the MO for a dose of "mother's little helper".'

Reluctantly, Fraser sat.

Hesketh-Shaw folded his arms and glared at Merrick. 'Fraser has a point.'

'Then test at increased altitude, at least until integration have finished their checks.' Merrick scanned the room, his face unreadable. 'Thompson was warned because two Banshee systems were partially dismantled without Fli-Tek observation and approval. The fact those units suffered some sort of structural failure before dismantling… means his warning is informal.' Merrick sighed. For the first time since entering the room, his demeanour softened. 'His team are still investigating, and if I know that man, he'll be as thorough whether it's official or not.'

Without thinking, Fraser nodded. That was Gordon, all right.

Merrick nodded in acknowledgement. 'No-one wants this to be late. Failure is not an option. The Air Ministry are itching for this to be cleared, so development can begin in earnest for TSR2. Our future – the air force, the country, perhaps the whole world – is in the balance. We must do our bit. Whatever it takes.'

HE SUPPRESSED A yawn. The meeting earlier had taken far more out of him than he wanted to admit. None of the crews nor Thompson fully trusted any of the three aircraft. All of them were wary, and rightly so. Yet Command didn't want to listen.

Thompson's fairies, as the avionics techs were nicknamed, were practically tearing each aircraft apart, yet so far, Watson insisted nothing was out of spec for Banshee. Nothing appeared out of spec for the Vulcans, either, but clearly something was causing issues.

When pushed further, Watson fudged and sidestepped – and took surreptitious swigs from his hip flask when he thought no-one was looking.

Something was causing Watson issues, and he suspected it wasn't just Banshee.

This whole programme was enough to give a man an ulcer. Even without… this…

Taking the usual precautions against being followed, he'd arrived at the rendezvous to find no sign of Johnson. The clock on the wall of the Cadena coffee bar told him Johnson was ten minutes late. He sipped his coffee and ignored the flirtatious smile the pretty blonde waitress sent his way.

Given the situation, he wondered idly if this was some sort of test. To see if he became nervous or edgy.

Instead, he settled back in his seat and picked up a newspaper. Unexpected peace and quiet was a gift he rarely got a chance to enjoy.

A headline about Winston Churchill retiring from the House of Commons caught his eye; he stared off into the middle distance, lost in thought. The doughty old warhorse had seen the threat coming from the

East, all right, even when half the student population of Oxbridge thought communism a lofty ideal.

Who would have thought he, of all people, would end up at the sharp edge of this socialist struggle?

Some betrayed for ideals, for morals, for hope of a better world. After all, even he could see that Marxism-Leninism at first seemed to promise a utopian dream of equality for all once the proletariat rose to throw off their chains. They were the clean motives; if ever disloyalty to one's own state for reasons other than money could be considered as pure, unsullied by self-interest.

He snorted. As if anyone ever took a decision without self-interest.

His had been driven by a simple fact: he needed his career.

So, he'd followed the White Rabbit – or, perhaps, Red, in this case – down the rabbit hole.

Even before that, he'd always felt he had a double life. His days were spent practising wreaking incalculable destruction, while weekends were with his wife in almost cosy domesticity…

That was only the first vow he'd broken.

If the road to hell was paved with good intentions, surely the road to redemption was treacherous with potholes.

Sir Walter Scott's words ran across his mind, as much a statement of fact as a rebuke: *oh, what a tangled web we weave, when first we practice to deceive.*

Especially because the first person we deceive is invariably ourselves.

Unconsciously, he rubbed the back of his neck. His eyes went to the clock again, but movement by the window caught his eye.

He froze.

Fraser, wearing a grey lounge suit, peered at the signs hung in the window. His girlfriend, a pretty young woman in a fashionable houndstooth minidress, clung, smiling, to his arm; Sophie was her name, wasn't it? Her pale pink lips moved, but he couldn't tell what she said. Flirtatious, she batted her eyelashes, perfect in their nest of eyeliner.

Fraser laughed and grinned. She pulled him onwards, still smiling.

But not before Fraser glanced inside.

Their eyes met.

Fraser blinked and shook his head a little, taken aback. He made to stop, but his companion tugged his hand.

Instinct screamed at him to look away, look down, look anywhere but at the man who had to have recognised him. The man who earlier had heard him turn down the offer of a drink in the mess with his crew, as his wife was ill.

His wife was perfectly fine, of course. His wife thought he was in the mess…

Their shadows moved onwards in his peripheral vision. Despite himself, he glanced up.

Fraser's gaze zeroed in on his, eyes narrowed under lowered dark brows.

He'd been recognised. Unconsciously, he held his breath; his pulse thudded in his ears.

Sophie let go of Fraser's hand. She seemed to be asking him what was wrong; she, too, peered in.

Fraser frowned but shook his head. He urged her onwards, but not before casting a long, suspicious look back. Finally, they were gone.

He closed his eyes and tried to regulate his breathing. His heart hammered against his chest.

The entire episode lasted seconds, but it felt like hours.

Why had he agreed to meet here, slap bang in the middle of Leamington? He knew it was a risk. Then again, travelling hours away was another risk. That was why he'd pushed for more dead drops: minimal contact, plus he could pick up and drop off information virtually at his own convenience. But no. Johnson wanted one more face-to-face; Peter's superiors wanted one more urgent delivery.

Would Fraser say anything back at Martinford, tomorrow? Going by this morning, it'd be unusual if he didn't. He'd have to brazen it out. Was it better that he'd been on his own—

At long last, Johnson walked in. He waved, his mouth curled in what, from a distance, was a friendly smile. Although he was around average height, his well-tailored navy suit belied the stockiness and solidity of his build.

Johnson sat opposite him. He glanced over his shoulder, in the direction Fraser had gone. 'Sorry I'm late. Was that a friend?'

Blast. 'Just an acquaintance.' As if he'd throw his colleagues to the wolves. Things were bad enough as they were.

The taciturn KGB man's expression didn't change. 'Then we should get down to business, yes?' Johnson put a copy of Autocar from a few weeks ago down on the table; the text declared the green Morris Oxford, sitting in a wood on the front cover, had value as big as the outdoors. 'Here you are. The details you asked for.'

'Excellent. Thank you.' He picked it up; this thicker-than-usual magazine contained his latest payment, plus the details of dead drops from now on. 'Should I check them?'

Johnson shrugged. 'If you like.'

He never failed to wonder at how perfectly North American Johnson sounded: only the slightest hint on certain words, an occasional change in his speech rhythm, suggested there might be more than one accent in there. He almost admired the man's sheer brass neck.

'I'm sure that's not necessary.' He forced a smile and pushed his newspaper across the table: the envelope Peter gave him last night nestled, hidden, between the pages. 'You might find something interesting in here.'

Much as Johnson's expression didn't change, there was no mistaking the triumphant gleam in his eye as he carefully folded the paper and picked it up. 'Thank you. I'm sure I'll enjoy reading this later.'

That wasn't in doubt. Neither was the assessing edge to Johnson's stare. Perhaps it was the interrogation training, done years ago as a junior pilot, practising in case he was ever captured by an enemy; perhaps it was a sense it was better to stay silent and be thought a fool than talk and remove all doubt. Either way, he maintained eye contact and kept his mouth shut.

Johnson nodded, as if in professional recognition. 'I'm afraid I can't stop.' He stood up, carefully clutching the folded paper. An oleaginous smile oozed across his face. 'But I'm sure we'll see each other again soon.'

Unease pushed acid to the back of his throat; he ignored it. 'I'm sure we will.'

Saturday 29 October 2022

ALEX CAREFULLY SLOTTED his BMW R1200GS Adventure on the edge of Mark's tarmac drive. He dismounted and hefted the thing onto its centre stand, then fiddled to fit the disc lock. Even at ten years old, the GSA was hardly a cheap bike, but he still felt like he lowered the tone of the area by being on two wheels.

Mark and Claire had a modern semi-detached house in a picturesque village on the edge of the Cotswolds; Alex vaguely remembered hearing that Claire's family lived in the area.

Claire's white VW Tiguan sat on their drive next to a silver Honda Jazz that had to belong to Mr Fletcher senior; both blocked in by a careworn blue Mk5 VW Golf that was Mark's work hack. He didn't have to see inside the attached garage to know it hid a mustard Triumph Spitfire; Mark's pride and joy since long before Claire came on the scene. Claire opened the door, holding a chubby baby on one hip. A little girl wearing a dinosaur jumper, jeans and with her light brown hair pulled into pigtails, barrelled down the drive as Alex took his helmet off.

'Unca Alex!' shouted India, flinging herself around his leg and squeezing it in a bear hug. Joshua clung to Claire and stared at Alex as if he was the weirdest thing he'd ever seen. Alex smiled and waved a hello. He patted India on the head. She'd grown a good few inches since the last time he'd seen her.

'Hey, Indi.'

India scanned the huge grey and silver beast of a motorbike. She grinned up at Alex, but before she could speak, Claire joined them. 'Hi, Alex.' She kissed him on the cheek: he returned the greeting.

'Hi, Claire. Good to see you. How are you?'

Before Claire could reply, India tugged at her mum's jumper. 'Mummy, can Unca Alex show me his bike? Please please please?'

'It's OK,' said Alex, in response to Claire's mildly harassed expression. 'Mark warned me.'

Relief softened her smile. 'Tea?'

'Oh, yes please.'

While Claire bustled inside, Alex lifted India up onto the BMW's seat and happily talked her through what all the levers and buttons did. He didn't know many five-year-olds, but India struck him as curious and clever; she listened with an intensity that surprised him.

Claire shouted them inside for lunch. India almost flung herself off the bike's high seat; he caught her and turned it into a pretend take-off and landing. She squealed with delight then ran indoors, leaving silence and a strange bittersweet feeling in his gut in her wake. Hindsight was unequivocal that having children with Anna would've been a bad idea, but…

Claire gently stopped him in the doorway. 'I thought you and Mark would be better off with Gerry in the dining room,' she murmured. 'You might have a chance to talk then.'

Touched, Alex smiled. 'Thank you.'

She grinned and waved a hand. 'It's fine. You turning up on the bike made her day. If you want to get changed, the utility room's there.'

Alex hurriedly wriggled out of his textile bike jacket and trousers, glad he'd packed a pair of jeans and trainers. When he found the dining room, Mark and his dad were sitting at a stripped pine table, close to a considerable pile of papers. Heaps of sandwiches, crisps, and a bowl of salad filled the centre of the table next to a pot of tea.

'Ah, Alex.' Mark stood. 'Thought I heard the bike. You've met my dad, Gerry, haven't you?'

'We met at your wedding, yes,' replied Alex.

Gerry Fletcher was a bit shorter than Mark, and rounder, with thinning grey hair, but the resemblance was clear. He shook Alex's hand. 'Yes, it was. You were best man, weren't you?'

'I was.' Mark and Claire's wedding had been three months before his and Anna's; he still remembered holding Indi as a sleeping toddler while

Mark and Claire enjoyed their first dance. Anna had been propping up the bar.

'How's your fiancée, well, wife these days?'

Caught, Alex hesitated. All he could do was be honest. 'Er… I'm afraid I don't know. We split up last year.'

Gerry paused. 'Oh… I'm sorry to hear that.' He shot a glare at Mark, who cringed and mouthed "sorry".

'Don't be,' said Alex. 'It was a lucky escape.'

Mark coughed awkwardly. 'Shall we eat?'

Over tea and sandwiches, Gerry began, 'Did Mark explain what I was doing?'

Alex nodded. 'And he thought it might help me with my investigation. The cupboard of the official RAF archives is a bit bare.'

Gerry pursed his lips. 'I know. I've found that myself. I wonder if this has escaped because it's not directly RAF.'

'That's a bit conspiracy theorist, isn't it?' asked Mark.

Gerry quirked an eyebrow but didn't reply.

Alex wondered whether to tell them the reason there wasn't much in the archives was because it looked like most of the paperwork related directly to Martinford was hidden under it. Then again, there was another, more likely, option. 'It could also be the usual combination of clerical and bureaucratic errors.'

Mark nodded, grudgingly.

Gerry grinned. He passed across a sheaf of papers in a couple of plastic folders. 'I've copied the relevant files for you. Some of the references can be a little oblique, but I believe I've made some sense of it.'

'Thanks.' Alex eyed them; there were more than he'd expected. 'It looks complicated.'

'It is, a little. Have you heard of the term "legal residency"?'

Alex nodded. 'A foreign country's embassy. Often used as a cover for espionage operations?'

'Yes. However, Mitrokhin and other defectors revealed the KGB also had a series of illegal residencies throughout Europe during the whole of the Cold War.'

'Illegal?' Mark frowned.

Gerry smiled, but there was no humour in it. 'Exactly what it says. KGB, and sometimes GRU agents, often living under stolen identities, working under false pretences amongst unaware westerners. Without diplomatic cover. And a particular target was what the KGB termed S and T. Science and technology. Especially defence.'

Mark opened his mouth then shut it again. He gave his father a dubious look.

'I suggest you have a read yourself,' said Gerry. He looked at Alex. 'Should I spare you the history lesson?'

Alex sipped some tea. 'I know Mitrokhin was a KGB archivist.'

'Indeed. He had access to many, though not all, KGB files from the 1950s onwards, which he copied or summarised – often by hand – and brought with him to the West when he defected in 1992. And PEREGRUZKA seems to fall through the cracks a little.' Gerry paused and flicked through his papers with one hand, while absent-mindedly eating a sandwich with the other. 'Ah. Yes.' He fixed Mark with a piercing gaze. 'Perhaps you ought to see how Claire and your mum are getting on with India and Josh, don't you think?'

Mark blinked, taken aback. His brow furrowed, but he stood. 'I suppose I should,' he said pointedly. He gave Alex a look that told him he expected to be filled in on the juicy details later.

Only when Mark had closed the door behind him did Gerry speak again. 'One can't be too careful.' He sighed. 'In all my years in the business, I learned to trust my gut, and my gut says this is still tricky.'

Alex thought back to his encounters with Ponsonby. He had that feeling, too. 'I'm inclined to agree.' He picked up another sandwich.

Gerry refilled their cups and continued. 'PEREGRUZKA first crops up as a project in 1962. The agent in question, an engineering manager who worked at a defence contractor, was codenamed DOCTOR. DOCTOR was tasked with obtaining as many details about the workings of PEREGRUZKA as possible, but it appears to have been a troubled project. At least, DOCTOR regularly sends corrections back. Then, we have a bit of a gap in available records. By 1964, another agent, codenamed GREY, is now working on the project. GREY is explicitly identified as being an RAF officer involved in modifying the RAF strategic bomber fleet to accommodate PEREGRUZKA.' With that, Gerry leant back in his chair.

Alex blew out a long breath. 'Seriously?'

Gerry nodded soberly. 'That's what the file says. Although no detail is recorded about just what PEREGRUZKA was, it appears to have been some kind of weapons system. And although DOCTOR worked for an aerospace engineering firm, its name is also not recorded in Mitrokhin's notes.' Gerry allowed himself a smile. 'By mid-1964, the KGB were deeply suspicious of both DOCTOR and GREY.' Gerry flicked through his notes. 'The Centre – KGB headquarters – had noticed numerous discrepancies in the information supplied to them by the two agents. At this point, things go awry.'

'As if they hadn't already?' Alex ran a hand through his hair. This sounded far too fantastic to be true.

'According to Mitrokhin, the head of this illegal residency was a Colonel Oleg Vladimirovich Kuryakov, codenamed RADOV. Apparently, he was working in England as a radio component salesman under a couple of cover names – the one he seems to have used here was Paul Johnson. Kuryakov arranged a business meeting in Stratford-upon-Avon as cover for a meeting with DOCTOR; he was due to meet GREY a day or so afterwards.'

'When was this?'

'August 1964. Something had occurred that apparently made PEREGRUZKA far less of a viable enterprise, even for the British. Unfortunately, the incident itself falls in one of the gaps.' Gerry regarded his cup, emptied it of tea, then carefully placed it back down. 'Anyway, Kuryakov sent a preliminary report through, promising a fuller one once he'd met DOCTOR, but it never arrived.

'His preliminary report hinted PEREGRUZKA was about to be cancelled, but that they stood a real chance of getting a march on the technology with DOCTOR's continued assistance – though DOCTOR would need to be coerced. He considered DOCTOR unambitious and cowardly, but with a reserve of low cunning.

'Interestingly, the Centre thought DOCTOR was the double agent, but Kuryakov thought it was GREY. Unfortunately, the archives don't tell us either way.'

Caught in the story, Alex leant forward. 'And then what happened?'

Gerry shrugged. 'That's the million-dollar question. All three disappeared from KGB eyes.'

'All of them?' Alex couldn't believe it.

Gerry nodded. 'Kuryakov didn't return to his illegal residency, and neither did any of the KGB's searches find him. Understandably, they didn't file a missing persons report. That would have brought unwelcome attention. GREY and DOCTOR broke contact with the Centre completely. I've been unable to find anything regarding their fate in our own archives, or in Mitrokhin's. All attempts to contact them again failed.'

Alex absorbed this. 'Are there any details about PEREGRUZKA itself?'

Gerry shook his head. 'Not in Mitrokhin's notes. There are hints. One of DOCTOR's reports talks about a potential long-term functional test in Australia and refers back to work conducted at Malvern. So it was more than likely electronic, be it a countermeasure, or new radar, or something.'

Alex considered how to respond. The fact that Kuryakov had arranged a meeting in Stratford-upon-Avon hinted that GREY, whoever he was, could indeed have been stationed at Martinford. Much as he'd like to think this wasn't remotely possible, clearly it was. He didn't want to jump to conclusions, but it would be one heck of a coincidence otherwise.

'I've copied everything I have for you and given you a copy of my own notes.' Gerry regarded Alex with bright eyes. 'I can see you're making connections.'

Alex grinned. 'Indeed. The question is, am I linking to the truth, or just what I hope it is?'

'And don't forget, this is just one aspect of the story.' Gerry returned Alex's smile. 'I'm currently buttering up one of my old friends to see if he can get me, if not access, then at least a summary of some relevant files we have from the time. Given I was in the trade myself – only abroad, of course – it's intriguing that they won't let us see it now. Of course, some bureaucrat will just say "computer says no".'

Wasn't that the truth? Alex sometimes felt a bit young to be a true Luddite, but even he hated this slavish reliance on technology. Whatever happened to thinking for oneself? 'My team are finding similar issues.' He paused. 'However, the body was found alongside what appears to be part of Martinford's operational archive. I've a team going through the recovered papers.'

'That's a clear breach of procedure. To say the least.'

Alex nodded. That was an understatement.

'The implication, then, is there isn't much in RAF archives to find.' Gerry reached for the teapot. Only a dribble came out when he tipped it into Alex's cup; he sighed and put it back down.

It was time to take a risk and bounce this off someone who had more of a grasp of what was happening at the time than him. 'One thing's standing out. So far, it looks like most of the papers conserved from Martinford refer to a weapons project called Banshee. And they date to 1964.'

Gerry stilled. For several moments, he stared out of the window. 'Do you think Banshee could be PEREGRUZKA?'

'So far, it's unclear what Banshee was. It could just be coincidence.'

'Or synchronicity.'

The two men smiled.

Gerry relaxed back into his chair. 'Mark said I could trust you to take everything I said with a pinch of salt.'

Alex laughed. 'I'm a sceptic by nature. I prefer as much information as possible before I make a judgement.'

'What does your instinct say?' Gerry leant forward. 'You're an intelligence man. Intelligence is as much about instinct as information.'

'From everything you've said, Banshee could be PEREGRUZKA. That's what I feel is the truth.' Alex hesitated. 'The body discovered was male. But wearing expensive civilian clothes. Like a Savile Row suit.'

'Hmm. Well, the KGB were paying DOCTOR and GREY handsomely for their work. The figures are in there.' Gerry's eyes gleamed. 'I imagine your searches have turned up no candidates?'

Alex shook his head. 'Neither us nor Warwickshire Police have found anyone. Our man appears to have come from nowhere.'

Gerry tilted his head to one side. 'Any missing officers?'

Alex stroked his chin. Technically… 'None recorded, though we're still compiling a list of officers serving at Martinford at that time. We've found some discrepancies, but some of them could just be clerical errors.'

Gerry nodded, pondering.

Alex continued, 'My gut reaction, if I'm honest, is a lot of people already wish this had stayed buried. Certainly, I think Braxton regret digging.'

'Tread carefully. That's my feeling.' Gerry gave Alex a serious look. 'If it's more convenient for all that this… disappears, be wary.'

Alex smiled ruefully. He already had that feeling.

'My friend told me MI5 are on the case. He said the chap in question is quite a political animal. Not a compliment.'

That must be Mr Ponsonby. Alex held back a groan, but Gerry caught his change in expression.

'I see I'm teaching granny to suck eggs,' he observed with a wry grin. 'You've already encountered the man?'

'Yes. But only briefly.' And Alex couldn't disagree with that assessment. He took a deep breath. Every investigation was a challenge, but this seemed to be growing by the day, like some sort of Japanese Knotweed.

Gerry coughed. 'My friend said that in his last posting, this man's colleagues referred to him behind his back as Brutus. Watch yours, dear boy, else you may find a knife in it.'

That evening, Quentin pushed through the revolving doors into the subtly lit, thickly carpeted building. As always, the doormen, sharp black suits not disguising their thick frames, let him pass with a nod. He was known here.

Though this was a Saturday night ritual he'd repeated countless times on both sides of the Atlantic, it never failed to send an anticipatory tingle down his spine. It wasn't just the lure of winning. It was the test, the experience – the challenge. This had an immediacy, an intimacy, that playing the same game via his computer or smartphone lacked. Not that this stopped him, during his quieter evenings, but he always longed for the personal touch of the tables.

As usual, the casino buzzed with people: the convivial atmosphere in the gaming rooms made this feel more like home than his actual flat. He made his way to his usual spot.

Some faces he recognised, some he didn't. Much to his surprise – and pleasure – Valentin was already seated. He gave Quentin a broad grin across the table and rubbed his hands with glee.

'You made it,' said Quentin.

'I did. When you told me about this place, how could I refuse?' Valentin spread his hands wide, like the grin still splitting his face. 'I must enjoy before Katya stops me, yes?'

Quentin laughed. 'Would she stop you doing something you loved?'

'Perhaps, if I love it more than her.' Valentin surveyed the green baize. Quentin recognised the glint in his eye from years before. Many an unwary player took Valentin's genial, expressive countenance at face value, much to their cost.

Quentin made a contemptuous noise. 'This table doesn't care if I play elsewhere.'

The glint in Valentin's eyes cooled. 'But do you screw it, or it screw you?'

'We screw each other.' Quentin pushed a sardonic sneer onto his lips. 'Isn't that the way? Sometimes one gives, sometimes one takes. The circle of life.'

Valentin quirked an eyebrow. 'That is true, my friend. Someone, somewhere, is always getting screwed.'

The game went well; it was poker, his preferred choice. Quentin kept a discreet eye on Val: though he was out of practice, he did well, outlasting most of the others on the table before throwing in his chips and admitting defeat.

Eventually, it was Quentin and one other man at the table.

Quentin had seen the man around but couldn't remember playing him before – at least, not at this stage of a game.

The dealer flicked the cards in front of them: Quentin slid them in amongst the others, careful to keep his face perfectly expressionless. Not the best hand, but salvageable, nonetheless.

The man slid a pile of chips in for his bid.

Electricity pulsed down Quentin's spine: that was the equivalent of £4,000, on top of what was already bid. A bold move.

Without hesitation, Quentin matched it. There was no way he was dropping out now. Not when he was so close.

He caught the tiniest flicker of the man's eyebrow; a bead of sweat glistened at his temple. His opponent blinked, as if to clear his head.

Quentin merely waited.

The man shook his head and threw his cards down: a full house.

Quentin stared, dumbfounded, at the hand in front of him. His full house was of a lower value. He had lost.

Only the merest tremble of his fingers as he laid his cards on the baize betrayed his emotions.

ONCE THE CONGRATULATIONS were over, Quentin excused himself from the table.

Safely in the elegantly tiled and mirrored lavatory, his facade cracked. He squeezed his eyes shut and ran his fingers through his hair, being careful to avoid catching his reflection's eyes while his conscience raged at him.

Fool. Bloody fool. Another debt to pay off – and with what?

Instincts warred: to retreat and lick his wounds, to march back in and play again to wrestle back some semblance of self-respect, to attempt to lessen his losses… but for the first time in a long time, he wasn't certain what to do. That in itself stung.

He felt on the lip of a precipice. One wrong move, and down he would tumble…

Come on, man. Pull yourself together, he told himself, *and get back out there.*

He washed his hands under the cold tap, dried them, then straightened his hair and collar. Hard-pressed he may be, but he refused to appear so.

When he walked back into the quiet corridor, Valentin was waiting for him. 'Are you all right?' he said in a low voice.

Quentin pushed a smile on his face. 'Of course. A temporary set-back.'

Valentin dropped his voice to a harsh whisper, only just audible above the hiss of the air conditioning. 'My friend, you lost five grand. That is not—'

'What of it?' rasped Quentin.

'That is not all you have lost this month. Is it?'

Quentin stared at Valentin, but all he could detect in his friend's eyes was concern.

Valentin sighed. 'I think we should move on from here tonight, yes?'

'Bored of the tables, are you?'

Valentin's jaw moved; he glanced down the corridor. When he met Quentin's eyes again, something grim flickered in his expression.

For several seconds, neither man spoke.

'Let me help. Tonight. I came prepared, but I have lost my edge.' Valentin held out a bag of chips.

'I can't—'

'Katya would not want to hear of me being near this place. Even if I won. So.'

Various responses travelled through Quentin's mind. Eventually, he said, 'Are you sure?'

Valentin nodded. He dropped the bag into Quentin's hand. 'Blame me and my lack of practice.'

'Only if you're sure.'

Valentin smiled, then ducked into the lavatory.

Quentin glanced into the small bag. A couple of rolls of chips, each labelled 100, glinted up at him, nestled among some loose 50s and 25s. A not inconsiderable amount. He tried to ignore the tiny voice in the back of his mind reminding him this would be yet another debt to repay.

The eternal dilemma: to save, or to spend…

He shook himself. After all, didn't one have to speculate to accumulate?

Sunday 30 October 2022

AT HOME THE next afternoon, Alex fished out Gerry's notes from his motorbike panniers. Though it was a Sunday, and in theory he shouldn't be working, there was no way he wasn't going to read them now. He'd be wondering about them, and Martinford, anyway.

He poured himself a large black coffee and suppressed a yawn. It'd been a good, though late night at Mark and Claire's, catching up over dinner, even if he no longer drank as much as he used to. Besides, riding a motorbike as tall and heavy as the GSA with even a small hangover wasn't his idea of fun. Still, the leisurely cooked breakfast he'd enjoyed before leaving took the rough edges off, although India asked if he'd come again soon, as Mummy never cooked *her* bacon and eggs.

It turned out many of Gerry's papers were photocopies of Mitrokhin's summations in Cyrillic. Fortunately, Gerry had marked up the appropriate passages and scribbled English translations.

He sighed and rubbed his temples. Trying to read handwritten Cyrillic was akin to deciphering the trails left by tens, if not hundreds, of drunken spiders.

Curious, he flicked through the notes till he found what each agent was being paid.

DOCTOR's payments were regular: anything up to £50, every four to six weeks for over three years, with an occasional bonus of £500 for information the Soviets particularly valued. Overall, GREY had been given £4,000, in a series of lump sums through 1963 and 1964.

What would that be today, though?

A few rough calculations later, Alex sat back, stunned. It couldn't be that much, surely? He double-checked both his numbers and the calculation to account for inflation. The numbers were correct.

He stared at the screen in shock.

In modern day terms, DOCTOR had taken home over £100,000 over the course of his betrayal. GREY's payments would be worth over £60,000 today.

Whatever PEREGRUZKA was, the Russians wanted it. No matter the cost.

IRRITATED, QUENTIN PUSHED the cafe door open and barged through the afternoon crowd. This was the last thing he needed, but Valentin's message said it was serious. Besides, Valentin was a friend. A friend who'd got him out of a big hole.

With bad grace, Quentin dropped into the comfy seat opposite Valentin. The place buzzed with people and conversation. For once, wine was absent, but Valentin had been kind enough to order a cafetière of coffee; that and two porcelain cups sat on the glossy black tabletop.

'Val,' he acknowledged.

Valentin leant forward. 'Thank you for coming. You are very busy, I know.'

'Aren't you?'

Valentin just smiled and poured them both some coffee. Its rich aroma filled the air.

Quentin ran a hand through his hair. 'You said you needed my help.'

Valentin nodded. When he met Quentin's gaze, his normally friendly eyes had a cold edge. 'I need to know if you will assist.'

Quentin took off his glasses and rubbed his eyes. 'Get to the point. Of course I will. What do you need?'

'I hear you are involved with an investigation of a death. At an old military base.'

Quentin went cold. 'Excuse me?' MI5's involvement was meant to be kept quiet.

Valentin ignored his question. 'You see, a long time ago, a countryman of mine disappeared while... on a job, you might say.'

Quentin stared at Valentin. Various thoughts ran through his head. Was he implying he knew who the body was? That amounted to an admission that the Soviets spied on the RAF – which they knew, but still... In lieu of speaking, he raised an eyebrow and replaced his glasses.

Valentin continued. 'This... job... involved a dangerous thing. Very dangerous. A threat to the continued security and prosperity of the whole world.' He sipped his coffee as nonchalantly as if they were discussing football. 'Me and my friends, we are concerned.'

Quentin held himself still. 'When was all of this?'

'The 1960s.'

Somehow, Quentin doubted he needed to tell Valentin the police had dated the body to that era. 'That's over fifty years ago. You're not seriously telling me that the... that you're worried about, shall we say, atomic developments?'

Valentin leant forward. 'My friends. They wish to know what happened to our countryman, if he is the body in the bunker. And if your country will renew this technology.'

Quentin scoffed. 'We all have nuclear—'

'This is not nuclear,' hissed Valentin.

'Is it biological? Chemical? What? What can be scarier than so-called mutually assured destruction?'

Valentin hesitated. 'We are not sure. But we do not want any such information to fall into unfriendly hands.'

Quentin leant forward too, so close that he and Valentin were virtually nose to nose. 'And what are you, Valentin Aleksandrovich? Friend or foe?'

Valentin blinked, seemingly taken aback. A grin oozed across his face. 'Friend, of course.'

'And you expect me to provide this information out of the goodness of my heart?'

Valentin's grin turned crooked, but he didn't reply.

'You know exactly what you're asking, don't you?' Quentin breathed. Adrenaline pulsed through his body.

'Then you also know that I know you have money troubles. Not just because of Saturday night. You made your last mortgage payment and car payment, but your five credit cards are all maxed out.' Valentin glanced at the ceiling, and his lips moved for a moment. 'You have loans. Your overdraft—'

'Get to the point.' Quentin loosened his suddenly too-tight tie and unbuttoned his shirt collar. He shot a fierce glare at Valentin.

'As for your – our – hobby…' This time, there was no mistaking Valentin's wolfish smile. 'This would compromise your career, yes? Is that not why you are back here?'

Quentin cursed himself. Valentin had him over a barrel. They both knew there was no point in him replying. Not that gambling was frowned upon, per se, any more than having an occasional drink, but others saw his pastime as an addiction. A problem.

'What do you propose?'

Valentin smiled – this time, more genuinely. 'If you help me, I help you. I ask for information, to know what you know, nothing more.' He reached into his pocket and retrieved a brown envelope. 'And my friends will show their appreciation.' With that, he slid the envelope across the table to Quentin. 'A token, in advance.'

Peculiar heat rushed over Quentin: an odd mixture of fury at being so ensnared so humiliatingly by one of the few people he'd deigned to trust, yet relief that no-one around seemed to notice.

He slid the thick envelope into his jacket pocket without opening it.

Valentin nodded approvingly. 'I do not want to see you in trouble, my friend.'

Quentin cleared his throat. 'You will keep my name out of this?'

Valentin nodded. Abruptly, his face softened, and something like his usual warmth came back to his features. 'I would not do this, but we are desperate. We do not want a return to the old days. Thank you.'

QUENTIN SAT IN his Audi A7 in the secure car park under his apartment building for he had no idea how long.

£2000 in crisp £20 notes still sat in the brown envelope in his jacket, close to his chest.

£2000 would go some way to clearing one of his credit cards. Or wipe out a significant portion of his overdraft. Assuming the cash was real, of course.

He pulled out his mobile and stared at it. Though he'd agreed in the coffee shop, now he was uneasy. If Valentin expected to know everything he knew… well, even his subordinates didn't know everything he knew about Martinford. There was much more he didn't know himself, or was under the remit of Flt Lt Farnsworth.

Part of his mind insisted he should call Valentin back and tell him he wished to return the cash. That he'd made an error of judgement. The same part urged him to report this as an attempt at bribery and corruption and remove himself from the case.

The rest of him knew the truth. He was over a barrel.

Even if he reported this in good faith, it would bring unwanted attention. Certainly, he knew of others who'd made similar reports, and no-one had ever looked at them the same way again. He was damned if he did and oh-so-damned if he didn't.

Valentin and his friends had to have been watching him, and fool that he was, he hadn't noticed. Clearly, he'd been careless. That would have to change. He'd been so consumed by it all, he'd dropped his guard. He wouldn't do so again.

Saturday night flashed through his mind; his conscience kicked him, hard. Of course. Valentin had bought him then. He should have known no favour ever came for free.

Unable to sit still, Quentin climbed out of his A7 and headed away from his apartment; anywhere for some fresh air, devoid of reminders of his failings.

A long Thameside walk served as a distraction to his thoughts. Much as he ached to visit his usual casinos, distract himself that way, he knew he couldn't afford it – literally or figuratively.

Only as daylight faded and streetlights blinked on did he return home.

When he opened his flat door, he spotted an unmarked brown envelope lying on the mat. Uneasy, he nudged it with his shoe, then picked it up by the corners.

It appeared almost untouched by human hands. A gentle squeeze told him it was filled with a few pages of folded paper.

He retrieved his paper knife, then sat at the table. Carefully, he slit open the envelope. A few folded A4 sheets slid onto the glass.

Typed text on one said: *This is the information you require.*

Nothing to confirm the sender's identity.

Yet the sheets gave details of the missing Russian. Colonel Oleg Vladimirovich Kuryakov, last contact with the KGB August 1964, aged 41. A printed copy of a black and white passport photograph was paperclipped to the page: the man was stocky and unsmiling, but otherwise unremarkable.

To Quentin's surprise, the man had multiple cover names: Paul Johnson, Walter Carr, and Michael Davies. The files didn't hint which names he used where. He camouflaged his work in Britain by being a radio salesman, which gave him plausible cover for travelling the country.

Could he be the body in the bunker?

Quentin stared at the ceiling, considering.

If Valentin had given him this information, there must be evidence to suggest Colonel Kuryakov had contacts within RAF Martinford – and that he'd disappeared in the area.

Memory nudged him. Farnsworth said documents recovered from Braxton related to RAF Martinford up to August 1964. Dare he think that date a coincidence?

Could the KGB really have infiltrated the heart of Britain's nuclear deterrent?

Quentin blew out a long breath and pushed the papers away. Braxton's bungling had revealed a nest of vipers, never mind a can of worms.

A photograph caught his eye. It hadn't come out with the others…

It was an excellent quality image of himself and Valentin in the cafe.

As if he needed reminding of his position. He flipped the image around, but the back was blank. Without a second thought, he slid the print through his shredder.

Now he was in this situation, he had to manage it. Luckily, managing unpleasant situations happened to be his forte.

An evil and entirely humourless smile creased his face.

If he was bought and sold, there had to be a way to turn the situation to his advantage.

Monday 3 August 1964

GORDON SHUFFLED THROUGH the papers on his desk. He glanced at his watch; it was almost ten o'clock.

Fli-Tek would be in shortly to refit the Banshee control units to XL447 and XM568.

So far, the feedback from the crew chiefs from the last four days was that while there were some minor snags, besides the issues already found, all the aircraft were physically fine. The worst snag, '47's dodgy wiring, they already knew about. That said, neither Chief Morton nor Andrews were impressed by the quality of Fli-Tek's installation; Morton commented that some of the shielding attachments and wiring joins looked like they'd been done by badly trained monkeys. Having had a look himself, Gordon couldn't disagree.

If the aircraft were fully functional and as specification, that meant Banshee had to be the cause of '47 and '68's issues. There were still several areas that could be the problem, though. It could be that the Banshee device generated a much greater electromagnetic pulse than expected; it could be shielding was inadequate, in the wrong places, or both; perhaps Banshee's designers hadn't properly mapped the extent of the pulse generated once the system was in an aircraft. It could easily be all of the above.

Would Fli-Tek bring any answers? He doubted it.

Stuff it. He couldn't just sit and wait. Restless, he pushed himself up and went to pace around the edge of the hangar.

XL447 and XM568 filled opposite corners of the huge, rectangular space: sunshine from the high windows dazzled off their shiny paint and reflected on the cool, white walls. A pungent mix of hydraulic fluid, avtur and oil scented the air. Platforms waited nearby, ready to be pushed underneath by whoever wanted to tinker.

Somewhere in the distance, at least one Olympus turbine whined in a steady idle. It had to be one of the OCU aircraft; XL433 was outside on the dispersal.

The engine shut off and spooled down; the silence rang.

The door creaked open and shut again with a bump. Footsteps and voices echoed: Hunt, and others he didn't recognise. A trolley rattled. Watson's grumbling tones undercut the echoing chatter and clatter.

Of course. Fli-Tek wanted their own men to reinstall the control units.

Resentment poked him. The trouble was, it had been agreed by Merrick and Burroughs that he could watch, but that was it. Burroughs hinted earlier Watson didn't even want him anywhere near the building but had been told to like it or lump it.

Gordon took a deep breath. All he needed was the results of the control unit testing, then he could leave everyone to it. He headed towards the centre of the hangar.

A group of men in bright orange coveralls pushed a large trolley stacked with cardboard boxes of various sizes. Watson and Kelly walked behind. Kelly carried a folder full of paperwork; he caught Gordon's eye and nodded. Watson scowled and looked the other way.

Irritation flared, but he held it back. Fraser was right about that man. Not that he needed telling.

The party split. Watson, and the group of men, headed towards '47. Kelly, and his buff cardboard folder, headed for Gordon.

'Good morning,' said Kelly, handing the folder to Gordon. 'Here are the test reports for both units.'

'Thanks.' Gordon tried to return Kelly's smile, but his gaze drifted back towards Watson. What was that man going to do to those aircraft?

Kelly glanced over his shoulder. 'A lot of the tests are for our internal benefit, but the conclusions are what you'll be interested in. Any questions, just ask me.'

Before Gordon could respond, Kelly walked over to join the cluster of men by '47. Already, Chief Morton stood by her, scowling at the back of Watson's head. Gordon smiled to himself. He might not be there, but he knew and trusted the men who were. That would be enough.

SOME TIME LATER, Gordon flipped the folder closed. He sighed and rubbed his eyes. On autopilot, he lit a cigarette, then leant back in his chair to think.

In the background, muffled voices and clinking echoed in the hangar as Fli-Tek and the other techs worked to refit Banshee to the Vulcans.

He hated to admit it, but there was a lot in those reports he didn't understand. Talk of signal gains and frequency ranges. Pages and pages of graphs, showing pulse waveforms, signals and response times, and other arcane things that seemed a world away from the practical reality of flying an aircraft.

Their complexity rendered the conclusions of the test reports harder to believe.

Apparently, the control units functioned according to specifications, and no issues had been found.

And Gordon was a monkey's uncle.

What could he do, though? Realistically, all he could do was what was planned anyway: get Banshee back on the aircraft and start testing again.

With that thought, he stubbed out his cigarette and pushed himself away from his desk. Time to see how things were going in the hangar.

He could hear the raised voices echoing down the corridor before he even arrived. *Oh, great.* He paused, took a deep breath, and steeled himself.

When he opened the door, a red-faced Watson argued nose to nose with Chief Morton. Kelly stood back, motionless, lips bit into a thin line; his wide eyes were fixed on the wall on the opposite side of the hangar. A group of RAF techs and Fli-Tek men huddled under the bomb bay. The RAF techs watched with interest; the Fli-Tek team shuffled their feet and looked down at the floor.

Kelly turned at Gordon's movement. Relief flickered across his face. 'Ah—'

Watson's head spun around; his mouth flapped. Without another word to Morton, he practically pushed him out of the way and marched straight for Gordon.

'What the hell are you doing here?!' Watson waved at XL447. 'I specifically said—'

Gordon held up his hands.

Kelly interrupted. 'George, he's not touching the Vulcans or Banshee, is he.' He sounded like he was talking to a child.

Morton barged his way towards Gordon. He pointed an accusing finger at Watson. 'You—'

'Stop. Everyone, stop!' Gordon took a deep breath. Why did he feel like he was in a sandpit dealing with squabbling children? 'I came in here to see how things were progressing. That's all,' he said to Watson. Then he turned to Morton. 'What's happened?'

'Well—' began Morton.

'I said—' interjected Watson.

'One at a time, please!' yelled Gordon.

Even Morton took a step back. Watson glowered, but he didn't flinch.

'Mr Watson. What is the problem?' Gordon snapped. There was no point asking Morton first; Watson would talk over him, anyway.

'You,' spat Watson, 'have interfered with Banshee.'

Morton opened his mouth; Gordon held up a hand, and he closed it again. 'What makes you say that?'

'He—' Watson pointed at Morton, '—told me so.'

Morton reddened and scowled; his jaw worked.

Gordon put his hands on his hips. 'Define *interfere*.' He tried to keep a lid on his temper. 'We inspected all the aircraft systems while the control units were removed. We did not change any part of the Banshee system that was left.'

'Ha.' Watson scoffed in triumph. 'Inspect.' He spat the word. 'We all know what that means. You—' he jabbed a shaking finger at Gordon, '—you—'

'Asked the crew chiefs to take charge of inspecting the aircraft and to let me know the results.'

'That's what I said!' protested Morton.

Watson snorted in derision.

Kelly rolled his eyes, still avoiding everyone's gazes.

Gordon struggled to keep calm. 'What physical evidence do you have that things aren't right?'

Watson opened his mouth, but Kelly spoke, with a disparaging look at his colleague. 'Personally, I haven't seen anything significant.'

Not for the first time, Gordon wished he was able to record the almost comedic outrage that overtook Watson's face. The man flushed so red, he stiffened so abruptly, Gordon half wondered if he'd need to call the medics. Without another word, Watson stomped away. His right hand delved into a jacket pocket, though he didn't look down at what he was doing.

Kelly blinked. He took off his glasses and rubbed his eyes. 'I'm sorry. I've no idea what to say,' he mumbled.

'Join the club.' Gordon watched Watson, now at the far side of the hangar. Was it his imagination, or did Watson swig from a hip flask? Something small and metal glinted in his hand.

Kelly looked in the same direction; his expression hinted he saw just what Gordon did, and he'd seen it before. The men shared an uneasy glance.

'Are you happy to take over with Chief Morton?' asked Gordon. 'Assuming you're OK with things?'

Kelly nodded. He cast yet another frown in Watson's direction; the man was now pacing up and down.

'Would you like me to send down my CO, or H-S?' Better they hear this now, than later from a grumpy Watson, he reflected.

'Um…' Kelly pressed his lips together. He glanced at Morton, then in Watson's direction. 'It might be wise.'

Gordon caught his meaning. Sarcasm coloured his smile. 'I'll see what I can do.'

He went back to his office, called Burroughs, and let him spread the news around. Discretion was the better part of valour, so he stayed at his desk for the rest of the day. He re-read the Banshee unit reports and scribbled various notes and questions. Then he turned his attention to the updated test plan.

Some time later, Hunt knocked on his door.

'How's it going out there?' asked Gordon.

Hunt pulled a face and sat down. Gordon suppressed a chuckle.

'Well. Given SEngO had to go and get Wingco Merrick…'

'You're joking.' Hunt's face said otherwise. Gordon winced. 'Good grief…'

'The Wingco took him to the mess for lunch. Since then, the chaps have managed to get quite a bit done.'

'That's good. I've read the reports. The conclusions say everything is as per spec, but…'

Hunt nodded.

'Want a read?' Gordon pushed his notes over. 'Second opinions are always good.'

Hunt read through the first few pages, his brows knitting occasionally. 'I wonder if we need to run this past some of the ECM boys. They might have some comments.'

'We could, but…'

'Fli-Tek.' Hunt sighed. 'Yeah.'

'That's why all the ECM units are out by the tail.' It was the furthest they could be away from the rest of the aircraft. Gordon shook his head. 'I hate to say it, but I think all we can do is just carry on with the testing, as planned.'

'I think you're right.' Hunt stood up. 'Cuppa?'

'That's the best idea I've heard all day.'

XM568 LOOMED OVER him. XL447 lurked behind her, with XL433 squeezed in by the doors, packing out the cramped hangar.

This afternoon had been interesting. Merrick had stomped out of his office, swearing under his breath about Watson. He returned much later, having spent a large part of the afternoon in the mess. Watson apparently got through a significant quantity of gin; though his demeanour hardly changed, he calmed down somewhat. Perhaps that made sense of the tiny hand tremors he'd observed when Watson, along with the rest of Fli-Tek's group, walked to the hangar this morning…

Merrick wasn't impressed at having to babysit Watson for the afternoon, but equally, Thompson had done exactly the right thing in passing the buck upwards. Either Thompson had better political sense than he gave him credit for, or he, too, was just tired of Watson's grandstanding.

Try as he might, he couldn't quite make sense of Watson's behaviour. The man was ever more fidgety, nervous, and evasive; something that both annoyed and concerned Command. It hardly inspired confidence in the crews, either. Even Kelly seemed to merely tolerate his superior's increasingly paranoid and tetchy outbursts.

Unless…

Realisation dawned.

Could Watson be the other agent his controller mentioned?

On one hand, it seemed ridiculous. On the other…

Watson behaved like a man close to breaking point.

If the grapevine was to be believed, many within the Air Ministry and upper echelons of government were unhappy at the time and money Banshee was taking. Every complication and delay brought the risk of cancellation closer.

The question was, what had Watson done? What was he saying to his Russian controllers about all this?

He deliberately derailed that train of thought. Whatever was said, how Watson conducted himself – if, indeed, Watson was a Russian agent – was out of his control. But the strain of that, on top of the strain of Banshee itself, would certainly explain a few things.

He had to send a signal to Peter. Tonight.

He stared up at '68. Her closed bomb bay doors betrayed nothing. '33 and '47 sat, equally mute and still. All three aircraft were like silent sentinels, watching and waiting for his next move.

The thought crossed his mind that in the event of nuclear war, they'd all be sent out, probably never to return. Certainly, there'd be little to return to. No country left to speak of.

His mind hissed that they were at war; clandestine, undeclared, but fighting nonetheless. Otherwise, what was he doing here?

Trying to stop open warfare, part of him whispered. If they ever were sent out in anger… he'd failed. The nuclear deterrent would have failed.

And millions of innocents throughout Europe, Russia, probably North America too, would die.

Involuntarily, he shuddered.

It was what he was trained to do. He would do it, without question or hesitation, if required.

He just prayed Watson and his interference hadn't brought that day closer.

Tuesday 4 August 1964

ALL THREE VULCANS now had a clean bill of health. Gordon wanted to do a quick ground test of Banshee on all the aircraft before they restarted flight testing, but Burroughs – well, Merrick – vetoed that. Flight testing had to restart as soon as possible.

The rejigged plan meant '68 was due to fly up to Scotland this lunchtime, while '33 flew over Wales mid-afternoon and '47 repeated a couple of ground tests tomorrow. He didn't miss the relief flash across Tony's face at that; he couldn't blame him, either.

There was a tap on his door.

'Good morning, Mr Thompson.' Fraser strode in. Despite his smile, there was an edge to his voice. 'What's the verdict?'

'All aircraft are ready to make sure no-one can listen to the BBC Light Programme in a hundred-mile radius.'

Fraser chuckled. 'Radio Caroline, surely.'

Gordon considered. Doubt didn't visit him often, but... 'D'you reckon Banshee will work?'

'As in, right now, or ever?'

'In anger. I mean, the hope is that this will wipe out every early warning radar and more to give others a clear path in...' Gordon trailed off.

Fraser's expression didn't change. 'It's basically replicating the electromagnetic effects of a bucket of sunshine without the nuclear tan. Whether it will take out defences, radar, communications and such...' Uncharacteristic uncertainty flickered across his features before he schooled his face into a humourless smile. 'Ours is not to reason why.'

'Hmm.' Gordon couldn't argue with that. 'That's assuming it even works in the first place.'

'A big if.'

'You around later?'

Fraser shook his head. A more genuine smile creased his face. 'No. I'm taking Sophie to dinner this evening. Somewhere special.' He paused, as if to say something else, then seemed to shake his head at himself.

'Oh, lovely.' Gordon couldn't blame him. Given the choice, he'd plump for dinner with a beautiful woman over his own company, too. 'Well, think of poor me in the mess while you're eating haute cuisine.'

Fraser scoffed, though he grinned widely. 'Not a chance.'

XM568 CLIMBED OUT of Martinford and turned north.

Fraser frowned at the Vulcan's dials. Something wasn't right. She climbed slowly, like she was lined with lead, though her engines clamoured to raise her skywards. An electric sizzle popped in his ear; the flight controls momentarily sagged, so briefly he almost thought he'd imagined it. Worry tingled through him. 'Mike, what's going on?'

Over the intercom came a muffled curse from his AEO. 'Skip,' Mike snapped, 'I don't know what Banshee's doing, and I'm fucked if I know how to fix it.'

Fraser caught his breath: Mike *never* swore when they were airborne. Things were bad. He swallowed.

'The readings are all over the place,' Mike continued. 'I can't disengage it from the alternators. If the readings are right, it's fully charged but still charging itself. That makes no sense.'

'It's interfering with the radar,' said Ken. 'Hard to make out the image.'

'Should we try to discharge it?' asked Brian. He added, 'We could drop to the weeds. Minimise it, at least. Maybe?' He rubbed the patch of cheek above his oxygen mask.

None of them were sure what would happen if they tried that. Fraser for one didn't want to try. 'And risk taking out most of Warwickshire?'

He shook his head. 'No. We can't.' Just the thought of what might happen chilled his bones.

'At the moment it's sucking every bit of juice the engines are putting out,' said Mike, frustration obvious in his clipped tones. 'I can't make head nor tail of what these gauges are telling me.'

Unease gnawed. This was bad. 'Nearest base?'

Jim coughed. 'Tie. Martinford or Gaydon. Seven minutes flying time to either.'

Once more, the dials jumped and spun; the controls went limp then snapped back to life. Her engines seemed to groan.

'Radar screen's just static now,' said Ken, incredulous. 'Nothing's working. We're flying blind.'

'Shit.' Brian pointed at the readouts in front of him. 'Bomb bay temperatures.'

The temperature inside the bomb bay was climbing to danger levels. Fast. *Shit* didn't cover it.

Training kicked in, overriding the fear clenching Fraser's insides. 'Declare an emergency. Start bomb bay venting procedures. We've got to get down ASAP. Ken, do your best to get us pointing back to Martinford.'

'Roger.' Brian busied himself with cutting airflow from the engines and other measures to reduce the temperatures.

Adrenaline quickened. Fraser swallowed to try to moisten his suddenly dry mouth. The temperature continued to rise. The leaden feeling in his gut solidified.

He pushed the Transmit button. 'Mayday, Mayday—'

BANG!

XM568 shuddered violently. Warning lights flashed: engine number two was on fire.

Fraser yanked the slack control column; nothing happened. They'd lost flight controls. Shock and panic prickled the back of his neck.

XM568's whole airframe vibrated and convulsed under him, unresponsive in her death throes. *No, no, this isn't happening*, sang a voice in the back of his mind.

Reflex pushed terror out of the way. 'Get out, get out, get out!' Fraser hit the 'ABANDON AIRCRAFT' switch.

GORDON, AT HIS desk at the back of Hangar 3, frowned at his clock. '68 wasn't due back for a couple of hours; Hesketh-Shaw hadn't taken '33 up yet. Perhaps he should—

There was an echoing *boom*, like a distant explosion.

The hangar fell silent.

Dread filled him like ice cold water.

Klaxons split the air.

The crash alarm.

Oh, God, no.

That was when he knew he'd replay this moment, in his nightmares as well as memories, for as long as he lived.

He grabbed his hat and ran out of the hangar to where men streamed towards one of the buses. Their grim faces told him all he needed to know. Foreboding congealed: that noise, and the crash alarm, meant only one thing.

XM568 had gone down.

What made it worse was there was nothing he could do; he wasn't part of the crash team. In fact, as one of the engineering officers for 449 Squadron, everything he'd done on that aircraft would now be under the microscope.

Then again, so would Banshee. At least, it would if he had anything to do with it.

What about Fraser? The rest of the crew? Had they escaped? If she was at altitude, they had a chance, but... Gordon closed his eyes and tried not to think about it. He couldn't change the outcome, much as he wished.

Shock, fear, horror swirled impotently in his system. He felt stuck to the spot.

John strode towards him, looking worried. 'OCU crew binned it?'

All Gordon could do was shake his head.

'But... Fraser? No. What about H-S?'

Gordon kept shaking his head, still unable to speak.

John stared at Gordon; the colour drained from his face.

Behind him, the crash vehicles and Land Rovers growled off in a cloud of diesel fumes, leaving desolate silence in their wake.

WALKING AROUND THE thin curtain to Fraser's hospital bedside an hour or so later, Gordon wasn't sure what to expect. The crash team who'd told him where to go hadn't given him any other news; the nurse who'd directed him here just said he was in intensive care.

From the chest up, Fraser was bruised, battered, but recognisable, attached to all kinds of drips and medical equipment. From the chest down? Better not to dwell on it.

Gordon swallowed. He tried to plaster on a brave face. 'Look at the mess you've made of yourself, eh?'

To Gordon's surprise, Fraser's eyelids cracked open. The ghost of a half-smile flickered across his face. His lips moved, as if to speak, but his eyes closed again. Despite the bruising, his face was pale. Fraser wouldn't want to live if he couldn't fly, but that didn't mean Gordon wanted to stand there and watch him die. He wanted him to live. Not just for himself, but for Sophie.

Fraser mouthed what looked like *Gordy*; the fingers on his right hand beckoned him close.

'I'm not kissing you,' said Gordon. 'You're not bloody Nelson.'

Fraser smiled. A brief shudder of his chest was a laugh. His eyes fluttered open again.

Nervous, Gordon leant close. He grabbed Fraser's hand and was somewhat reassured when Fraser held his back; his skin was clammy, his grasp a shadow of its former self.

'Thanks…' Fraser's voice was barely audible. His chest heaved as he fought for breath.

'What for?'

'This…' Fraser's eyes closed again.

'What else was I going to do, eh?'

'Sophie… seven… thirty…' Fraser rasped. 'Regent… Hotel… Leam…'

'Don't worry. I'll tell her.' Gordon forced a smile. 'Then she can come here and nurse you.'

A weak smile briefly creased Fraser's face. He frowned, mustering the strength for another sentence. 'Banshee… failed…'

'I guessed. I'll sort Watson out; you can count on it.'

Fraser almost nodded. What was left of the colour in his cheeks faded.

'I mean it,' continued Gordon. 'He's not going to get away with this.'

Fraser just managed to speak. 'H… S… I… he…'

Gordon was dimly aware of footsteps behind him: a nurse.

But it was too late.

Fraser's white face stilled; his grip loosened.

Gordon squeezed Fraser's hand harder, but there was no response. The tiny spark of hope he hadn't even realised he was kindling faded. His heart sank.

'Come on, chap,' he managed. He didn't care that his voice cracked. 'We need you.'

Nothing.

In a daze, Gordon let the nurse shepherd him away. The rattle of the curtain being drawn behind them had an awful finality.

GORDON RAMMED THE helmet on his head. He charged to the Bonnie and barely let it get running properly on the choke before he hared off down the road to Leamington.

He had an important mission.

What felt like mere moments later, he squeezed his motorbike into a small space in the row of parked cars that lined The Parade, the main road through the centre of Leamington Spa. He spotted a large, elegant Regency building rendered in gleaming white, with large golden letters proclaiming its name.

The Regent Hotel.

Wow. Fraser really had gone all out to impress her.

That thought caught in his throat; he swallowed it and stared in awe at the impressive facade. He squared his shoulders and headed through the portico.

The maître d' was effortlessly polite, despite a raised eyebrow glance at Gordon's working uniform, and he informed him that Flt Lt Campbell's table was over there. Gordon thanked the man and walked in. Suddenly, he wished he wasn't doing this, but what else could he do? He'd promised.

It took him a few moments to realise the stunning woman seated at a table on her own, anxiously searching each face that approached, was Sophie. The enormity of what he had to tell her squeezed his guts.

He hesitated mid-step as she scanned him; her expression changed from recognition to confusion. As he neared her table, she looked him up and down. She frowned.

'Gordon?' She stood, and glanced at her watch, brows wrinkled in bewilderment. 'Where... where's Fraser? What... you're in uniform, aren't you? But—'

Gordon took a deep breath. His insides turned to jelly. Ignoring other diners' curious glances, he sat, and gestured that she should, too.

'I am, yes. I... I'm sorry. Fraser was involved in an accident today. He—'

Sophie gripped her chair and swallowed, hard. She stared at the tablecloth for a few moments, before looking back at Gordon, eyes bright with tears. 'He sent you?' she asked, voice wobbling.

Gordon faltered. How could he answer that? His throat wouldn't let him speak.

Her eyes widened. Horrified, she covered her mouth with her hand. 'What happened?' she whispered. 'Is... is this to do with the plane that crashed? I heard on the radio something had happened.'

Gordon nodded. He braced himself to deliver the news. 'He... he made it out, but... but he was too injured. I'm... I'm sorry.'

Tears spilled down her cheeks; her wide blue eyes implored him to laugh, smile, do anything to make this not be real, to be some kind of cruel joke.

Instead, his own tears welled and he brushed them away, not trusting himself to speak.

GORDON MADE EXCUSES for Sophie – and Fraser – to the maître d', and gently guided her out to the street. They walked slowly down the gentle hill, minds elsewhere, with no real destination in mind. Though plenty of people were out on this late summer evening, passers-by gave them a wide berth, as if kept away by their sadness.

After a few moments, he realised Sophie was trembling. 'Are you cold? Would you like my jumper?'

She shook her head. 'No. I… I don't know. I just…'

'I'm sorry if you'd been waiting a long time. I… came straight here from the hospital.'

She stopped. 'You… were you… were you with him?'

He nodded. His throat constricted; even if he knew what to say, he couldn't speak.

Despite her tears, she gave a thin smile. When she spoke, her voice cracked and shattered into tiny, pained pieces. 'Thank you. I mean it. I… I couldn't bear it if… if he'd been all alone.'

They restarted walking as if on automatic: their feet moved without any input from their brains.

'Please,' said Gordon, 'don't ask me more. I don't know. I don't know what happened, but I do know Fraser wouldn't have let go – of anything – without a bloody big fight.' He took a deep breath. 'He asked me to come tonight. I couldn't have done anything else.'

Her cold, quaking hand held his for a few seconds; though she didn't say anything, her eyes shone their gratitude.

Without a word, Gordon yanked off his jumper and handed it to her: she hesitated, then smiled shyly and pulled it over her head. He offered her his hanky; too late, he noticed muck where he'd wiped something on the Bonnie, but she dabbed her eyes before he could say anything. Black mascara joined the oily smears.

Still in silence, they walked slowly down the hill; past the bright flowerbeds, the parade of small shops, until they reached what looked like a pair of small white gatehouses, one either side of a large wrought iron gate that guarded the entrance to Jephson Gardens.

The gate was locked.

Sophie sighed. 'Shall we walk around the Pump Room gardens?'

Gordon could only nod.

They crossed the road to the large expanse of trees and grass that sprawled to the right of the impressive sandstone Regency building. Golden capitals along the plinth above the elegant colonnade proclaimed it to be the Royal Pump Room & Baths. In silence, they walked around the wide paths, and even circled the ornate bandstand that stood proudly in the middle.

Not that Gordon was really paying any attention; his feet moved without any kind of active thought.

Fraser's last words nagged at him. Now, it wasn't a surprise he'd mentioned Banshee, but Sqn Ldr Hesketh-Shaw? While they hadn't been best friends, Fraser respected him. Or at least, he had as far as Gordon knew. But whatever it was would forever remain unsaid.

While he was here, a team would be working through the night, recovering what they could of the Vulcan and its crew. As he was so closely involved, Gordon was barred from taking part in the investigation, but he knew enough people on the base to be able to find out something.

He was 90% certain that the aircraft's crash was no failure on the part of Fraser. Or his crew, come to think of it. Oh, he knew most crashes were down to human error, but—

Sophie pulled Gordon's jumper tighter around herself. 'I wonder if I should go home.' Her voice was thick with tears.

With a start, Gordon realised they must have circled the park at least twice. The air had a bit of a chill, now. 'Would you like a lift?'

'If… if you don't mind.' Sophie gave him a guilty smile. 'I'm sorry to put you to the trouble.'

'Not at all.'

They walked silently back to the Triumph, parked just outside the Regent Hotel. There were gaps in the lines of parked cars; fewer people were around.

Gordon started the bike with a bit more care this time, though her exhaust barked and echoed off all the buildings just as loudly anyway. He could imagine Fraser smiling at it shattering the evening peace; the thought stabbed him, hard.

He picked up his white helmet and handed it to Sophie. 'I've only got the one,' he said. 'I'd rather protect your head than mine.'

'Are you sure?' She eyed the helmet, then the bike. She bit her lip, nervous, and looked back at him.

'Fraser would kill me if anything happened to you.' The words were out before he could stop them; he winced.

Tears glimmered in her eyes, but she nodded.

After putting the helmet on, Sophie perched behind him; she held on so tightly he could feel her shivering.

Gordon rode the Bonnie with more care than he'd ever remembered, acutely aware that Sophie clung onto him for dear life. By the time they reached her house in Lillington, the edge of the horizon was darkening to purple as dusk fell.

Sophie climbed off the Bonnie with surprising grace. She hesitated, and touched Gordon's shoulder. 'Thank you. For everything.'

'What else could I do?' He could hardly have left her, drained and tear-stained, by herself.

'Please… you will call, won't you? To let me know the… the funeral details. And… and do stay in touch.'

'Of course I will.'

She smiled. As if on impulse, she leant forward and kissed his cheek. Her perfume still lingered in the evening air. 'Thank you.'

He stayed and watched until she was safely inside her house. As she turned to close the door, she gave him a sad smile and a wave.

The traitorous thought ran across his mind that Fraser really didn't know how lucky he'd been with her.

He shut and locked his office door and leant against it, panting. Desperate, he closed his eyes. Sweat beaded on his forehead, and he rubbed it away with a clammy hand. His shirt felt damp. The consequences of what had unfolded today were just too terrible to contemplate.

Had he wanted this? Well, yes, but not like this. He wanted to stop this madness. Escape. Settle a score into the bargain, maybe. But not like this.

The gallows flickered across his mind's eye; he shuddered.

Not like this!

When he opened his eyes, Fraser stood behind the desk. He was even wearing his flight suit. To all intents and purposes, he looked just like he would've done this morning, before… *before*—

'Hello, George.'

His skin prickled. The sweat down his spine turned to ice. What was left of his hair tried to stand on end. Was it just the light in here, or was Fraser translucent? He screwed his eyes up. *What on earth?* 'Fraser? Bu… wha… how did you get in here?'

Fraser smiled, though there was no friendliness to it. 'Oh, quite easily.' He walked straight *through* George's desk, straight through the mess of papers and drawings. Straight towards him.

George tried to speak, but all that came out was a strangled squeak. Before his eyes, Fraser was becoming more and more transparent the closer he got. He stopped at what would've been nose-to-nose if he hadn't been see-through, though his eyes burned with an unnatural intensity. George's arms tingled as if invisible needles pricked him; his skin crawled.

'I know all about you now…' Fraser's voice – and his body – faded into nothing.

George slid to the floor, shivering uncontrollably. This had to be a nightmare. Yes, a nightmare. Figment of an overwrought imagination. He dug his bitten nails into the palms of his hands and hissed as they scratched the tender skin. All right, a hallucination, then. It had to be. *Come on man*, he told himself, *stand up and pull yourself together; don't be so weak.* He groaned and squeezed his eyelids together. Moisture trickled down his quivering cheeks. Fear clenched his stomach and pushed a whimper between his dry lips.

Fraser's words once more sent a tingle down his spine. *I know all about you now…* He stopped himself. No, he didn't. Ghosts did not exist. He was just – under pressure. Upset, perhaps. That's all. He didn't want to even admit to himself that he felt the slightest bit of guilt or remorse for what had happened. That would make it all too real.

He'd already heard from the head of the RAF Board of Inquiry. The Accidents Investigation Branch would be here soon enough. He didn't doubt they'd be involved. As the primary representative of Fli-Tek for Banshee, he'd be a key witness.

George's throat felt like he'd swallowed the Sahara. *Oh, God…*

Thompson was too scrupulous an engineer not to investigate every avenue of potential failure. More than anyone else, he would want to know why XM568 had gone down. He would dig, and dig, until he found the truth.

What have you got yourself into, George? What have you done? The voice of his conscience sounded uncannily like Maureen, his late beloved wife. He shook himself, trying to ignore its prickling.

Even so, he didn't dare answer that question.

Wednesday 5 August 1964

THAT MORNING, GORDON walked out of his boss's office and headed towards the hangar and the briefing room. Time to officially pass on the news.

On his way back from Sophie's, he'd hammered the Bonnie through various Warwickshire lanes, only turning towards Martinford when she coughed and spluttered, letting him know her main tank was on fumes.

On returning to Martinford, he'd tried to sleep, without much success. Eventually, he gave up, had a cold shower, and got dressed. He'd like to say he was ready to face the day, but in truth, nothing could make him feel ready to face what today held.

As he walked in, all conversation stopped. All heads turned to him: sadness, and unanswered questions, etched on their faces.

'Good morning, everybody.' Gordon cleared his throat. 'The morning briefing for today is XM568 crashed yesterday, and all 449 Squadron activities are suspended. No work is to happen on any 449 Squadron aircraft; no flying for us today.'

A low buzz of chatter filled the room, but he carried on. 'As for tomorrow? We'll find out then. The Board of Inquiry will be here at some point. You may be called as witnesses, you may not, but if you are, just answer their questions honestly.' At some point, he'd be interviewed by the RAF Board of Inquiry. It looked like it'd be made up of officers from nearby RAF Gaydon; it was a rule that officers from the affected station couldn't run an accident investigation. He'd be surprised if they didn't call in Avro – well, Hawker Siddeley – as well, and maybe even the civilian Accidents Investigation Branch.

Gordon paused and scanned the room: the grapevine had no doubt worked overtime overnight, but he didn't relish what he had to say next.

'My boss told me this morning they've found all the crew.' His throat tightened, but he managed to keep his voice level. 'Flight Lieutenants Markham, Farrell, and Duffy, and Flying Officer Grice were confirmed dead at the scene. Flight Lieutenant Campbell passed away in hospital last night.' Apparently, Brian had been found still strapped to his ejector seat; Burroughs hadn't mentioned anything about the others.

Judging by the shock on some of their faces, not all of them had heard that.

'We don't know what happened yet,' he added, 'but we're to support the investigation however we can. For today, though...' He sighed. 'Time to do all the jobs we don't normally get to do. I hear stores needs a tidy and the toilets need a mop.'

There was a faint chuckle and groan.

'That's all.' Gordon gave a sad half-smile. 'Dismissed.'

Hunt, at the front, caught Gordon's eye and stepped forward as the ranks began to spread out. 'Are you all right, boss?' he asked, so quietly Gordon almost didn't hear him.

Gordon blew out a long breath and shrugged. 'Didn't sleep last night. Saw Fraser in hospital. At the end.'

Hunt nodded. Sadness shadowed his eyes. 'I'm sorry. Where did she go down?'

'Less than ten minutes flying time from here. The other side of Long Itchington.' That stung; he hadn't expected them to be lost within reach of safety. He hadn't expected this at all.

Hunt closed his eyes and gave a short, sharp exhalation from his nose. 'So close.'

'I know.'

Hunt frowned. 'I'll keep the chaps busy. Heaven knows what trouble they'll get into otherwise.'

Gordon smiled. 'Thanks, Bob.' He repressed a sigh. Now he just had to keep himself out of trouble. That would be easier said than done.

AFTER LEAVING THE hangar, Gordon argued with himself for all of about a minute before giving in and finding a spare Land Rover to take him to the crash scene. Then he ferreted around to find a map and worked out how to get there.

The spot was a good few minutes' walk from the road, along footpaths that seemed obvious on the map but weren't in reality. Sparse raindrops pattered on the ground. He glared at the grey sky, daring it to start pouring down. Then again, to come here and have it all bright sunshine just wouldn't seem right. Despite the dull day, vibrant green hedgerows bordered the golden fields.

As he got closer, the scent of burning drifted in the air; he was almost in the right place. He hesitated for a split second. Was he doing the right thing? Somehow, he couldn't face just walking back to the Landy. He squared his shoulders and carried on.

RAF policemen, their white hats clear, stood around the edge of the field. He braced himself for a confrontation as he approached the nearest.

'Sir.' The man saluted.

Gordon returned it. 'I'm Flight Lieutenant Thompson. I've come to—'

The policeman glanced at him; faint recognition crossed his face. He waved Gordon past. 'Through you go, sir.'

He was sure he recognised the policeman, too, but he couldn't place from where. Twenty years in the RAF meant he'd been around the block a few times, so to speak. Either way, he wasn't about to argue. He carried on.

Even now, almost twenty-four hours since the crash, the sticky-sweet smell of burnt avtur clung greasily to the ground. It was several seconds before he realised the crumpled, torn chunks littering the battered earth were, in fact, parts of an aircraft.

Parts of XM568.

Some were scorched and unrecognisable; others, he knew what they were but didn't want to think about it. Twisted sheets of metal, the biggest roughly the size of a Mini, sat amongst scattered soil.

Firemen picked amongst the still smouldering wreckage.

Dear God. What happened?

'There's a question. Apparently people called the police reporting explosions,' said the nearest fireman.

Gordon blinked; he must have spoken his thoughts aloud. 'From here?'

The fireman rubbed his face and left a sooty trail down his cheek. He stared up at the sky, considering, before he nodded. 'Think so. The first lot came from a few miles up the road – Ryton way.'

Interesting. Gordon frowned, trying to work out what that could mean.

The fireman added, seemingly as an afterthought, 'We had a call from a farmer up that way this morning, as it happens. Something landed in his field, and he also heard a bloody big bang. Another team's been sent up to search.' He scanned the scattered debris then gave Gordon an assessing glance, as if wondering who he was.

Gordon frowned. 'I only heard one explosion at Martinford.' That was thirteen miles away.

The fireman glanced at Gordon's uniform, then said, 'Should you be here? Sir?'

Gordon stared at the wreckage strewn over the churned soil, trying not to think about what it really was.

Another RAF officer in working uniform, with Flt Lt stripes, trod his way carefully towards them. He glanced at Gordon. 'You see how each fragment's made its own crater?'

'Thrown from impact?' asked Gordon.

'Well…' The officer gestured around him. 'We've been searching since yesterday evening, but we've not yet found a single impact point. We haven't found all the engines yet, and we're still missing the vertical stabiliser and the port wingtip. Two of the rear crew—'

The fireman coughed pointedly. Unease needled Gordon's spine: his brain asked him if he really, really wanted to hear this. But he had to know.

The officer frowned and shot Gordon a look.

Gordon steeled himself. Hopefully none of his emotion showed on his face; his voice, when it came out, was as level and dispassionate as could be. 'What about the crew?'

The officer met Gordon's eyes. 'We're waiting for the aerial photography to confirm. However, my best guess right now, from the… ah… evidence, is that the aircraft broke up mid-air.'

Shock tingled through him; his blood froze. That airframe was solid – he knew her inside out. He'd seen enough of it, after everything. How could she—

The officer glanced at the fireman, then frowned at Gordon. 'I say, you're not on the Banshee recovery team, are you? We're expecting them shortly.'

'I knew the crew,' Gordon managed.

'Then you shouldn't be here.' Despite the harshness of his words, the man put a kindly hand on Gordon's shoulder.

Head spinning with the implications of what he'd learned, Gordon let the man lead him away.

'I do understand,' the officer said quietly. 'It's happened to me. More than once. It is hard, but—'

'You'll find the truth?'

The man nodded. 'It's our job.'

In a daze, Gordon plodded his way through the fields and climbed back into the Landy. He sat, unseeing, his hands on the steering wheel, for he had no idea how long, just staring in the direction of the scarred field. Rain pattered rhythmically on the Landy's canvas tilt.

Part of his brain reminded him he didn't have confirmation of anything; what he'd heard were surmises, guesses. Shaped by evidence, yes, but still not conclusive.

Explosions.

And a Vulcan breaking up in flight.

He didn't want to ask how you could tell with the bodies, but he could guess. It didn't take a genius to work it out—

He stopped. They weren't just bodies he was thinking of.

It was Fraser, Brian, Mike, Jim, and Ken.

Fraser had ejected; Brian had, too, but hadn't made it: injured after ejection. From what the boss said, his 'chute had deployed, everything had done what it was supposed to, but he was a goner before he reached the ground.

Fraser's injuries looked like they happened after ejection, too.

What could injure men in the air?

Flying debris.

What would make debris fly?

An explosion.

He hadn't seen many crash sites, not for a long time, but he'd seen a few.

Memory stirred. In fact, there was one, over twenty years ago, that reminded him of this.

A Heinkel He-111 that had been mauled by fighters and disintegrated in flames as it fell to earth.

OK, that had left a much smaller spread of wreckage, as it hadn't been as high or as big. He'd found a body, the poor man's parachute tangled around him as he'd struggled with it in his final seconds. The suddenly fresh image of sooty, blood-spattered silk lingered in his mind's eye. He shuddered, trying not to think of Ken, Mike, and Jim meeting their end that way. Friend or enemy, both were human, and it wasn't a good way to go.

What had they missed? Was it possible he'd sent her up with some structural flaw, or some ticking time bomb in her electrical or propulsion systems? Could he have avoided this, if only he'd done something different?

Distantly, he knew this thinking was futile, but his thoughts travelled the track regardless.

There was one thing he wasn't sure of.

Just what would make a Vulcan disintegrate in mid-air?

HE DROVE BACK to Martinford, what he'd seen and heard still churning over in his mind.

As he parked the Landy back in its place outside the ops block, an admin corporal hurried over, looking harassed. 'Oh, sir, the Wingco was looking for you. Can you go to his office now?'

Gordon suppressed a sigh. What was he in for? Oh well. There was only one thing he could say. 'Yes, of course.'

'Ah. Mr Thompson. Sit down.' Merrick gestured at the chair in front of his desk, though he avoided looking up.

Gordon glared at the man. If he'd been allowed to do a ground check…

Merrick coughed. He looked up, though his eyes refused to meet Gordon's. 'On a personal level,' he said, 'I'm sorry. Fraser was a good man and an excellent pilot.'

For a moment, Gordon didn't know how to respond. He hadn't expected that. He settled for, 'Thank you. Sir.'

'I need to ask someone, and you're the only name that came to mind.' Merrick sucked his teeth and glanced back down at the glossy wood of his desk. A faint hint of polish drifted on the air. 'Would you be Fraser's Effects Officer? I need a man to make sure all his uniform is returned to stores, help clear his room for reallocation, all that. Are you up to the task?'

Gordon breathed in. Not that he'd want anyone else to do this – that wouldn't feel right – but he couldn't say it was a job he wanted, either. In the absence of a miracle, or this being a nightmare, there was only one response he could give. 'Of course.'

Much later that afternoon, Gordon had a list of items to retrieve, a borrowed copy of the Casualty Procedures AP 1922, and a key to Fraser's room. He couldn't quite believe this was really happening, that this was a job he had to do. Still, he knew Fraser would rather it was him than anyone else.

What jarred was that even if 449 Squadron was grounded, the rest of Martinford could hardly stop operations. As he walked to Fraser's room, the air resonated from a Vulcan landing: an OCU crew returning from a training flight.

With a deep sigh, he opened Fraser's door.

The sheer ordinariness of it punched him in the gut. It looked – well, it looked like Fraser could walk back in at any moment. To all intents and purposes, it was like every other room in the mess, his included: regulation furniture, cream walls, and those horrible curtains. The only trace of Fraser's personality was a couple of framed photographs on the bedside cabinet. One of Fraser and Sophie, that Gordon took just a few short weeks ago; the other from a Lone Ranger he and his crew had done the year before. Five young men smiling in front of their aircraft.

Five young men who were no more.

Four other poor souls would have to do this for Brian, Ken, Jim, and Mike. None of them left yesterday thinking for one moment they wouldn't be coming back. Their families would've expected them home. Maybe even had their dinners in the oven…

For a moment, he almost closed the door and locked it again. Should he leave this for another day? No. This would only get more difficult the longer he left it. Best to get it over and done with.

He swallowed the knot in his throat and forced himself over the threshold.

He went through the items of uniform and all the other boring bits of kit without much trouble. They were the common things, the things that were never really theirs. The easy bits to deal with.

The more personal things, though…

Pinned to the inside of the wardrobe door was a faded, creased black and white photo. A small boy – recognisably a young Fraser, maybe eight years old – stood by a teenage boy, with a stern-looking older man and woman, in front of some grand pile of stone. Was that Fraser's family? Fraser rarely talked about them; he hardly even acknowledged his Scottish roots, beyond his fondness for single malts. Fraser's parents had died when he was young, and as he and his brother had been sent to different boarding schools, family was something other people had. As far as he knew, Fraser's brother had been a fighter pilot, killed at some point during the war; not that Fraser ever really said much about that, either.

To Gordon, brought up in a crowded East End house, and then by his nan after the Blitz shattered his life, it was a strange glimpse into another world. Family was the one thing you should always be able to rely on.

The small bookcase next to the wardrobe held a collection of well-thumbed paperbacks. Even a couple of Ian Fleming's Bonds lurked in there.

A trunk at the bottom of the bed held some of Fraser's off-duty clothes – neatly folded, of course. It also hid an unopened bottle of scotch, wrapped in a paper bag. Even he could tell it was a very, very nice single malt; a cut above what Fraser would normally drink.

Gordon stared at it as a memory unfolded.

What was it Fraser had said a few months ago? That he'd train Gordon to appreciate whisky if it was the last thing he did?

It was his birthday in a few weeks. Not a big milestone, mind you, just nudging closer to that big 4-0.

Fraser, you bastard, he wanted to shout. He wanted to tell him he didn't have to do that. Not for him. Fraser should've been here to give it to him, drink it with him, tell him all about it…

Gordon scraped the dampness off his cheeks, then gently laid the bottle back amongst the clothes.

On the side, he found the keys to the Austin-Healey. Fraser no doubt had a will, but he had no idea who'd be graced with the beautiful red machine. Still, he'd keep the keys safe for the time being. Next to them, he spotted an unexpectedly small box. A box he'd never seen before.

A jewellery box.

His fingers trembled as he lifted the plush, navy velvet cube. It was surprisingly heavy for such a small thing. Gingerly, he opened it.

A ring glittered in the light: a large central square diamond, flanked by small rectangular diamonds. For a moment, he thought it was silver, then the weight and colour registered. It was platinum.

Dumbfounded, he stared at it, then, slowly, closed the box.

Had Fraser been planning to ask Sophie to marry him last night? Certainly, he'd been hinting that he wanted their relationship to be something more than just courting. And that restaurant, well… it wasn't somewhere he'd take a girl every night. Even a girl as special as she was.

The ring had to be worth several months' salary, if not more: it was no cheap trinket. Gordon ran his fingers across the plush box. On impulse, he opened it again, transfixed by the jewel inside. Not that he was an expert, but it looked Art Deco. Perhaps it was an heirloom, kept close in case the right girl turned up? Now, he'd never know. Sorrow squeezed his heart.

One thing he knew beyond doubt was that Sophie deserved such a beautiful ring.

He wondered how she was. He'd see if he could call on her later and make sure she was OK. Even if he didn't have any news about anything else.

There was one thing he wondered. Had Fraser done it? He checked the last drawer.

Sure enough, there was an envelope with enough money to keep 449 Squadron, and its ground crew, supplied with beer for an evening. If the rest of the crew had done the same, no flying would be done by 449 Squadron for a good long while.

Right now, that didn't seem like such a bad idea.

PETER SAT ON the bench, nonchalantly reading The Times. The unobtrusive grey trilby and camel coat were a clear signal: it was safe to talk.

He took his time strolling around Jephson Gardens, to all intents and purposes just enjoying the evening sunshine, while Peter flapped the paper's pages. In reality, this was the final precaution of counter-surveillance: although no-one had followed him during the afternoon's merry-go-round of shops, public transport and other public places the Americans called "dry cleaning", he couldn't afford to relax. Flowers bloomed; their colourful heads bobbed above the green lawns in the cool, lazy breeze.

Finally, he sat at the other end of the bench.

Peter looked up and nodded. He said blandly, 'Marvellous weather, isn't it?'

'Isn't it? Though autumn will be with us soon.'

Mundane though it sounded, those words verified this meeting was safe. Time to get down to business.

'I passed your information regarding Dogberry's possible identity on,' said Peter. 'Thank you.' An eyebrow twitched as he surveyed his charge. 'Any news of yesterday's incident?'

Incident. One way to describe XM568's loss. He put his elbows on his knees and rubbed his forehead, groaning. 'No.'

'I'm sorry.'

'Thank you.' He straightened up. No need to tell Peter about the trips to married quarters, to tell wives their husbands wouldn't be returning. Or how tightly his own wife hugged him as soon as he'd set foot in the door.

'You said your suspect is erratic?' prompted Peter.

'To say the least.' He stared blankly into the middle distance. 'The day before yesterday, our unit CO had to babysit him in the mess to stop him interfering. He's inconsistent. Unreliable.' Probably an alcoholic. 'In my opinion, he's a risk.'

Peter smoothed his paper and deftly folded it to the crossword. 'Is he the only risk?'

He took a deep breath. There were so many risks. Where did he start? Should he mention Thompson? Instinct and experience told him Thompson was a man of integrity and honour, and not a direct threat to him.

He continued, 'I've been summoned to meet Cassius.' A red ribbon had been tied around a fence post on the way out of Martinford village: their agreed signal for an out-of-the-ordinary, face to face meeting in three days' time, in their usual place. At least he wouldn't have to worry about Campbell spotting him now, he thought ruefully. What a waste…

Peter's pen hesitated above the paper. Concern flashed in his eyes. 'When?'

'Saturday evening.'

Peter pursed his lips and clicked the pen. 'Dangerous.'

'I imagine Cassius has put two and two together regarding the… incident…' he said.

Peter nodded, as if to himself, and scribbled a word on the paper. Then he looked up. For the first time, worry lined his face. 'We've intercepted a number of transmissions in the last few days that can only refer to Chancer. They don't fit the prearranged pattern. As yet, we've not managed to decrypt them. I'm pushing for us to remove you.'

Relief and surprise straightened his back. He looked directly at Peter; the man met his gaze and nodded.

'Chancer's time is running out,' said Peter. 'Your service won't be forgotten.'

'You remember what I asked for?'

Peter smiled. 'I believe your Canadian colleagues will welcome someone with your experience with open arms.'

A new start. Away from all of this. It was almost within reach. 'Thank you.' Without realising, he breathed out a long sigh of relief. Soon this – Banshee, Chancer, whatever – would be over.

Monday 7 November 2022

QUENTIN STEELED HIMSELF and picked up the phone. It had been a good few days since he'd heard anything from anyone about Martinford. True, the dead could wait; but the living wanted answers. Preferably this afternoon.

Sure enough, after a few rings, Farnsworth answered. 'Farnsworth.'

'Ah, Flight Lieutenant—'

'Mr Ponsonby,' said Farnsworth. 'And to what do I owe this pleasure?'

Quentin ground his teeth. 'Excuse me?'

'I passed Warwickshire Police's updated report to your team last week. I understand—'

'Yes, yes, thank you.' Quentin couldn't resist adding, 'And the situation regarding the, ah, paperwork is still being discussed.'

'Should any clarification be needed, I'm more than happy to discuss it.' There was no mistaking Farnsworth's amused tone.

Quentin forced a laugh; the man's enjoyment of this rankled. 'Oh, that shouldn't be required. No, I'm calling regarding the report. I see no more progress has been made towards identifying our man.'

Farnsworth chuckled. 'That depends how you define progress. We've ruled out a number of possibilities.'

Colonel Kuryakov's chunky, unsmiling countenance flashed across Quentin's mind. If the body really was this KGB spy, how on earth could he explain the British state effectively covering up his murder? He shuddered. 'Still nothing?'

Farnsworth paused. 'Only the apparent disappearance of Squadron Leader Hesketh-Shaw. I say apparent; he isn't reported missing, but he disappears from the face of the earth when 449 Squadron disbands.'

'Do we know anything about him?'

Papers rustled in the background. Farnsworth coughed. 'He was 449 Squadron's flight commander. Previously, he'd been a flight commander on 83 Squadron at Waddington and a Qualified Flight Instructor with 230 OCU at Finningley. He was a very experienced, and well regarded, Vulcan captain.'

'Just what were 449 Squadron doing?'

'You mean our friends at the JIC haven't told you?'

Quentin just suppressed a growl.

Farnsworth continued, without missing a beat. 'They were evaluating something called Banshee. What that meant, I hope to find out shortly.'

Something about how he said it hinted he knew more than he let on. Quentin frowned. That must be the mysterious project to which Cavendish – and Valentin – alluded. 'This was almost sixty years ago. Surely it can't be that complex?'

'Nuclear weapons were developed almost seventy years ago. They're rather complex as well as still very sensitive.' Farnsworth paused. 'Nothing so far indicates Banshee had any nuclear components, but… it was highly secretive.'

Both men were silent for a few moments.

'I see our man died from a nine-millimetre bullet to the head,' said Quentin. 'Clearly not self-inflicted.'

'His probable time of death stacks up with the papers found around him,' said Farnsworth. 'The two were more than likely hidden at the same time. The latest documents discovered so far date to August 1964. They may not be linked, but it's hard to imagine they wouldn't be.'

'It would be something of a coincidence.' Quentin tapped his pen on his notepad. 'As it would be coincidence the weapon used appears to have been similar to those issued to RAF aircrew at the time.'

Farnsworth hesitated. 'I know.'

That was as good as an admission. 'Can you trace the weapon used?'

'Only if we find it, to attempt to match it to the spent ammunition. And after fifty years…'

It would be like trying to find a fraction of a needle in a multitude of haystacks. Quentin grimaced.

Farnsworth continued, 'By this time, I'd guess it's either been destroyed or deactivated and sold on. I don't know if many ex-forces Brownings are in private hands, but barrel markings and even the firing pin change over time with subsequent firings.'

'So even if we found the smoking gun, aha, there's no guarantee they could be matched?'

'Precisely.' Farnsworth sighed. 'We may be able to construct a list of Martinford personnel who were issued weapons, but it's not likely to narrow our search much further. And, of course, that presumes our shooter didn't simply steal another's.'

'I trust you're already building a list of former Martinford residents?'

'Of course. Some we've made progress on tracing; however, it seems some of them did their best to erase 449 Squadron from their records.'

'If we can offer you any assistance in this—'

'We have our own sources. Thank you.'

Quentin scowled but kept his voice level. 'You're already aware that certain aspects of 449 Squadron were highly sensitive. Well, so are we. You're concerned for the military aspects; I'm concerned for the security aspects; the police are investigating the criminal aspects. No man is an island.'

Silence echoed down the line for a few moments. Quentin let it linger.

'In which case,' said Farnsworth eventually, 'you're admitting there is a security aspect to this investigation.'

Quentin replayed his words. Yes, he had. Was the man always so stolid? 'I would have thought my involvement gave it away.'

'I think we need to have a chat. In person.'

Quentin thought fast. An idea occurred to him. 'Can you get to central London tomorrow evening?'

There was a pause. 'Probably.'

'Then let's have dinner and discuss things. Offline, as it were.'

ONCE OFF THE phone, Alex scanned the various updates he'd received.

Despite what he'd hinted to Ponsonby, records were scant on the crews who'd served at Martinford.

Relatives of the crew of XM568 were scattered far and wide. Flt Lt Markham's widow had remarried and emigrated to Canada by 1968; Flt Lt Farrell's widow never remarried and died in 1979; Fg Off Grice was engaged but Alex couldn't find any information about the lady concerned; and Flt Lt Duffy had only just got married – his widow remarried but was killed in a car accident in 1984.

As for the other two Vulcans…

Woods had set up an appointment tomorrow for Alex to meet then Flt Lt, now retired Wing Cdr John Miller, the former co-pilot of Vulcan XL447. Flt Lt Tony Brookes, XL447's captain, moved into an instructional role and was killed in a motorbike accident in 1972; his nav radar, Flt Lt Dave Gregory, went on to be an instructor and died of cancer in 1991; Flt Lt Bob White, the nav plotter, went on to become Sqn Ldr White and head of navigation training, dying in 2012; and Flt Lt Neil McGoldrick, the AEO, moved to France in the 1980s.

The crew of XL433 were older than their counterparts: all of them had already passed away. Flt Lt Trevor Marshall had captained his own Vulcan on his next tour, after moving to 617 Sqn. XL433's nav radar, Sqn Ldr Ted Radcliffe, had been a Mosquito navigator during WW2; the nav plotter, Flt Lt Reg Mitchell, started on Canberras.

But no matter how or where they searched, no trace of Sqn Ldr Hesketh-Shaw, or his wife, could be found. It was as if they'd disappeared into thin air; he wasn't recorded as leaving the RAF, yet neither was his onward posting listed, as it was with the others. Warwickshire Police confirmed he hadn't been recorded missing. Neither had they found any sign of a death certificate. He simply vanished.

Gerry's words from Saturday rang in his mind.

Information gleaned from Mitrokhin's archive hinted PEREGRUZKA was electronic; Braxton's recovered archive implied Banshee was, too. Certainly, the timeframes matched.

The very fact Mitrokhin referred to an officer involved in modifying the RAF's strategic bomber fleet to accommodate this weapon… He shuddered.

Could an RAF officer really have been working for the KGB? Alongside a civilian? And then both of them – and their KGB controller – simply vanish from the face of the earth?

What he needed was evidence. Something hard and concrete, something to grasp and wrestle with.

Instead, all he had were shadows, suspicions, and his gut feeling.

Suddenly weary, he rubbed his face and closed his eyes.

It was a long shot, but maybe Wing Cdr Miller would have some answers for him tomorrow.

Tuesday 8 November 2022

MRS MILLER WAS a petite, elegant elderly lady who reminded Alex of his paternal grandmother. She ushered Alex through the furniture polish-scented immaculate hallway into a cluttered, cramped study. 'I expect he'll see you in here.'

Crammed bookshelves crowded the walls and bordered the window. What wall space wasn't taken up with shelves was filled with pictures of aircraft and people. Books and papers filled every available flat surface. They piled around the computer, the desk, the chairs – even on the chairs – and overflowed onto the once-plush green carpet.

Mrs Miller sighed but still found a polite smile. 'He'll be down in a moment,' she said. 'Would you like a drink?'

'Please. Black coffee, no sugar. Thank you.'

Left to his own devices, Alex studied the framed photographs clustered on the wall by the door. One caught his eye.

A white Vulcan. With five men in front of it, holding some sort of trophy.

A voice, with a faintly northern tinge, interrupted his thoughts. 'Ah. That was 1963. The year we won the Navigation and Bombing Competition.'

Alex turned. Wing Cdr John Miller was about his height and probably used to be lean until middle age finally spread. He still had a full head of salt and pepper hair, a proud smile, and sharp, inquisitive eyes. Though he had to be in his eighties, he looked fit and robust. 'Flight Lieutenant Farnsworth, I presume?'

'Yes.'

They shook hands.

'Call me John,' said Wing Cdr Miller. Then he laughed. 'Or Wingco. The kids at ATC called me that.'

Soundlessly, Mrs Miller appeared behind him in the doorway, carrying a tray laden with drinks and biscuits. She smiled warmly at Alex but gave John a distinctly disapproving look. John rolled his eyes, then picked a towering pile of books off a spare chair.

'Just leave the drinks on the desk, please, dear,' said John.

'On top of the books?' she asked. Though her words were sharp, humour softened her face with a ready smile.

'The flattest ones, yes.' John looked around, grunted, then lowered the pile he held on top of another pile. 'Thank you, dear. Please, sit, Flight Lieutenant.'

'Call me Alex, please.'

John settled into the chair in front of the computer, while Alex carefully lowered himself into the now-free chair. From this vantage point, he could see that even the space under the desk was filled with books.

John peered into the mugs. 'Ah, this must be yours.' He handed Alex the black coffee. 'So, how can I help you?'

'You've heard about the body found under former RAF Martinford?'

'Of course. A curious business.' John glanced into his own mug and took a sip, before adding, 'I was stationed there, briefly.'

'In 1964.'

John blinked, then nodded. 'Yes. 449 Squadron,' he said, slowly.

'Electronic Warfare Test and Evaluation Unit.'

John's eyes narrowed, and he frowned at Alex. Several seconds passed in silence.

'Quite a large part of 449 Squadron's operational archive was discovered alongside the body,' said Alex. 'Which makes up for the fact very little was officially recorded.'

John blew out a long breath. 'As far as I'm aware, nothing is meant to have happened. Officially.'

Alex couldn't help a wry half-smile. 'Officially.'

John gave Alex a sharp, assessing look. 'I was a co-pilot then. That photo – well, after that competition, I'd wanted to captain my own

Vulcan, but our crew was… selected, you could say, for 449 Squadron. They wanted the best flyers, the best crews, you see.' John stared reflectively into his mug. 'Not that that occurred to me at the time. I was more annoyed I hadn't got that captaincy. Looking back, of course…'

'I understand from the recovered papers there were three crews attached to 449 Squadron.'

'Yes.' John's eyes flicked across the piles of paper and books: his brows drew together, and he leant across to a tottering stack. 'Hold on.' He ran a careful finger down the edge, reached a point about a third of the way down, and eased something out. 'Here's a photo of all of us. In case we were about to cover ourselves in glory.' He handed the small rectangular black and white print to Alex.

'What did you cover yourselves in?' Alex asked.

'Mess, to put it politely. If you've got the archives, then you know the project.'

'Banshee? Some of it, yes.' Alex studied the traditional squadron photo. 'And the accident.'

John pointed to a group at the front, in the middle. His voice was quiet. 'That was the crew of XM568.'

Alex studied the young men; younger than him, at any rate. After a moment, he said, 'We've uncovered some data regarding that crash. You knew them?'

'Yes. I knew Fraser Campbell, the pilot, well. He was a good friend. We were both on 101 Squadron at Scampton for a while. He lent me his car – he'd got an Austin-Healey – when I was courting Miranda. She saw through that straight away,' added John with a nostalgic smile.

'What we've found hints that the squadron disbanded shortly after the accident.'

'It ended the project.' John's blue eyes, still direct, pinned Alex to his seat. 'And I've never spoken about it. Until now.' He sighed, his expression somewhere between regret and anger. 'It was a bloody mess. All of it.'

'The archives we've recovered reveal some of the truth.' Alex handed the photograph back.

'Ha.' John peered at the photograph, then gave Alex a pointed look. 'But not all.'

'There are a lot of gaps. Both in what we've recovered and what can only loosely be termed the official version of events.' Alex cleared his throat. 'As I'm sure you can understand, it's taking my team quite some time to track down anyone stationed at Martinford with 449 Squadron at the time.'

'I can imagine.' John carefully laid the photograph on top of its original stack. 'The whole thing was... well, the brass hats couldn't wait to shed it, tell the truth. About the only advantage was we were posted on with no questions asked, or at least answered.' He drummed his fingers on the edge of the desk; the only free space.

'I'm not interested in the details of the project,' said Alex carefully. 'I'm more interested in those you served with.'

John's eyes narrowed. 'So it's true you haven't been able to identify the body?'

Alex quirked an eyebrow. 'Currently, all we know for certain is he was an adult male, and he was hidden along with 449 Squadron and Banshee.'

'I've never been superstitious, but that project felt doomed from the start. At least Tony, our captain then, thought so, and after a while, I was inclined to agree.' John shook himself. 'So, your assumption is he must have died around the same time as 449 Squadron, ah, disbanded.'

'That's our starting point.'

'In which case, I can give you a possible name straight away. Many of us bumped into each other again in the years afterward, but none of us ever saw our flight commander again. Nor did we ever find out where he got to. It was as if he disappeared into thin air.'

'Really?' Though Alex already knew the name, at least this would be independent corroboration.

'Yes. Squadron Leader Charles Hesketh-Shaw.' John shifted in his seat. 'And let me tell you, whenever his name was mentioned to anyone senior afterwards, it was like we'd said something unspeakable. Worse than a curse. Worse even than the project itself.' John avoided Alex's gaze and studied a pile of books intensely. 'And I'm afraid I'm not willing to talk more about it. Not with Miranda in the house. She knows nothing, and I want to keep it that way.'

Alex nodded slowly. Not that he liked it, but he had to respect John's wishes, at least until he had more evidence to force his hand. 'Do you have a picture of him?'

John grunted and turned to another unsteady pile of papers. After a couple of false starts, he pulled out another print. 'Here's a better image of us. I'm there—' he pointed to a still-recognisable figure, then planted his finger on the image, '—and there's H-S. As we called him.'

Alex studied the man. Even in his formal Number 1 uniform, his build appeared leaner than Alex's: he also looked a bit older, and he wore a half-smile that bordered on the sardonic. Though at first glance his eyes were smiling, a closer look showed a hint of wariness.

Somehow, he couldn't imagine a man that slender expanding to fill the size of the suit they'd found on the body, but he needed hard evidence to prove it, one way or the other.

'Can you tell me more about him?' he asked.

John narrowed his eyes and inspected Alex for several seconds. 'Have you ever been in a fix?' he asked eventually. 'Been told to do something you didn't like, or agree with, or think was right?'

'Yes.' Alex leant forward. 'It was a few years ago, now. Being young and principled, I dug my heels in over what I thought was right.' Even with the benefit of hindsight, and several years more experience, he could honestly say he'd still do the same. 'It didn't go down too well with some.'

A grin cracked John's face, and he nodded. 'Who did you upset?'

'The Americans.'

'Oh, well done. What did you do?'

Alex grinned. 'You could say I obeyed the spirit of the order while disobeying the letter. I was lucky my immediate superior backed me. That probably saved me.' So did the fact that as time went on, he was proven right.

'Ha. The more the world changes, the more some things stay the same.' John picked up his mug and sipped his tea. 'It wasn't quite like that for me, but Tony knew he'd burned his bridges.' He nodded to himself. 'Well, I don't know if that was what happened to H-S.'

'Encouraged into another post?'

'The end of the project was… well, it was utter chaos. The… there was a civilian company working with us. There was a big bust up on site, I remember; the civilian liaison man stomped off in a huff. Not long after that – I can't remember if it was the same day, or a few days later – we were all called into the ops room to be told officially that 449 Squadron had never existed. We'd be posted onwards, but in the meantime, we were ordered to pack up our stuff and take a month's leave. Starting immediately.'

Alex whistled. That was highly unusual.

'I know,' said John. He continued, 'Well, we were told this by our Wingco, Merrick, his name was. H-S's crew were there and his co-pilot, Trevor, asked point blank where the man himself was, as they'd not seen hide nor hair of him for a few days. Tony piped up that he'd seen him leaving site in an awful hurry the other evening.

'Wingco interrupted him and said as far as we were all concerned, Hesketh-Shaw had been removed from command, effective immediately, and that was that. No discussion and no debate. It was none of our business why. Tony wouldn't drop it, and he was essentially told to shut up or resign his commission.'

'Why did Tony feel so strongly?'

John paused. His jaw worked for a few seconds. 'It was all rather personal. We'd had an in-flight, ah, incident. Initially H-S and this civilian thought it was pilot error on our parts, until Fraser suffered a similar issue, and Tony never forgot that. He always felt… well, Fraser was the squadron golden boy. Tony put a friendly face on, but Fraser was a better flyer and he made sure we all knew it.'

'The civilian manager?'

'A chap called Watson. Rather odd fellow. He never really inspired confidence in anything. Mind, he and Fraser didn't get on at all. Hated each other on sight.'

Alex waited.

'You know, the loss of Fraser and his crew hit us all hard. But we just had to swallow it and carry on. That was how it was done in those days. Though without all this "keep calm and carry on" nonsense. We didn't need to be told to do it. It was expected. That said, this was…' John pursed his lips and scanned Alex. 'Are you married?'

Alex hesitated. 'No.'

'I was – well, still am. Miranda was pregnant with our son, not that we knew that till a few weeks later. Fraser's nav radar, Ken Markham, had a little boy, and he never saw his daughter.' John looked away, pensive. 'We knew the risks, of course, but…'

'Was Fraser married?'

'No. Although…' John trailed off. 'He was seeing a lovely girl that summer, and it was definitely serious. We made quite the foursome, for a while. Mind, he was thick as thieves with our integration JEngO at the time.'

'Your JEngO?' JEngO, or Junior Engineering Officer, was one of those in charge of the ground crews and the technical side of keeping the aircraft functioning and flying.

'Oh yes. We had a specific flight of ground crew and avionics techs, too. The OCU was a bit pissed off, as we took over one of their hangars to hide our Vulcans in. Plus, we escaped the centralised aircraft servicing coming in at that time. Our Vulcans were ours alone. But yes, he was solely for us. Flight Lieutenant Gordon Thompson.' John smiled wistfully. 'Good chap, actually. He…' He stopped.

Alex recognised the glint in John's eye as that of someone who'd said rather more than they were intending.

Before he could respond, John nodded slowly. 'I think I've taken up enough of your time.'

Alex swallowed a reply and instead nodded politely.

'I see you've learnt the tricks of the trade in getting people to talk.'

Alex couldn't help a smile. 'It's my job, sir. But I'll leave you. For now. I'm afraid you've still been very helpful.'

QUENTIN PUSHED THE door open and strode in, the deliberate tap-tap of his shoes on the floor the only sound. Cavendish's words rang in his mind: to consider the *appearance* of following procedure…

It'd been a long, long time since his last visit to the archives, though things rarely changed in this world of paper so old it was virtually ossified.

Strictly speaking, he should have requested assistance from the archive staff, but that could lead to questions. Inconvenient, though not incriminating. Not that this was wrong, per se; he just preferred to limit the traceability of his actions.

Shelves stretched in front of him, contents hidden in anonymous cardboard files. Prior knowledge told him they were arranged by year: arcane codes on discreet labels shed no light on their contents to the uninitiated, but he knew their secrets.

A quick scan of the codes told him he was in roughly the right place and the right departments: he slipped out a file and began his search.

Several files later, he groaned and stretched his aching neck and back.

His suspicions were confirmed. Despite the almost surgical excision of 449 Squadron and the mysterious Banshee from the records, some lingering traces remained like scar tissue, even in these ostensibly irrelevant files.

Of course, they were heavily redacted, even for internal consumption – and in some cases, not present at all – but there were crumbs. Pieces of the puzzle.

An RAF Squadron. Testing something not identified or even hinted at.

And evidence the programme was infiltrated by at least one, and potentially another, enemy agent.

Quentin blew out a long breath and tried to ignore the shiver that ran down his spine.

Damn Valentin. Damn the KGB and their modern brethren.

Much as he searched, the files immediately afterwards were suspiciously empty of references to what had to be 449 Squadron and Banshee.

MI5 would no doubt have tried to identify the extent of enemy intervention; Colonel Kuryakov was an organ grinder, not a monkey, and so his agent had to be much closer to the programme itself. Had this agent been unmasked? Had he subsequently betrayed Colonel Kuryakov? Had he been turned, persuaded to bluff the KGB with MI5's blessing? Or was it vice versa; had he fed false comfort to MI5 and the RAF for the KGB?

Looking back, it seemed the establishment at that time was riddled with spies and intrigue. Scandals and shocks abounded. The Portland Spy Ring, George Blake, John Vassall, Kim Philby's defection in 1963, along with the complications and embarrassment of the Profumo affair... All rather mortifying for those in power.

How far would MI5 have gone to prevent further treachery?

Quentin pinched the bridge of his nose and closed his eyes.

Treachery. One way to describe such actions.

Was it for ideology? That unshakeable belief that communism was for the benefit of the people? Perhaps ironic, from such a product of the British class system as Philby. Or was it more prosaic? Plenty betrayed their country not for high ideals, but simply for cash, and lots of it.

Were morals ever not negotiable for money?

A quick glance at his watch told him he'd spent far too long down here: it was time to leave.

He eased the files into their folders, then back in their places, and slipped out.

THOUGH IT WAS dark and damp, it was still unseasonably mild for the time of year; Quentin shrugged off his light jacket and sat down. From there, he could look over heads through the windows and survey the evening passers-by. A gaggle of busy commuters, heads down, sheltering under hoods and umbrellas, either staring at their phones or listening to whatever their headphones broadcast; a gang of teen boys swaggering rather amusingly; a harassed mother with a plastic-wrapped pram trying to negotiate her way through the traffic...

He glanced across the restaurant: his companion for dinner had arrived.

Part of him hadn't expected Farnsworth to agree to this meeting or to this venue, Noble Rot, snuggled in Bloomsbury. Then again, perhaps he, too, was angling for leads.

Farnsworth approached. To Quentin's surprise, he'd dressed well, and appropriately, for the evening: navy chinos in a fashionably slim fit, brown deck shoes, and a grey and blue checked shirt, open at the neck.

A dark navy tweed jacket nestled in the crook of his arm. He looked younger out of uniform, though he still carried the same serious air. Some of Quentin's surprise must have shown; a mischievous grin flitted across Farnsworth's face.

'Ah, good evening.' Quentin stood.

'Good evening.' Farnsworth shook Quentin's hand. 'I suppose we can dispense with the formalities this evening. Call me Alex, please.'

'Quentin.'

Farnsworth carefully arranged his jacket over the back of the chair then eased himself in.

'Thanks for coming,' said Quentin. 'I thought a little relationship building would be worthwhile.'

Farnsworth nodded, though his expression was wary. 'Indeed. I doubt I'll surprise you by saying our, ah, task, isn't what either of us was expecting.' Farnsworth glanced at the twin rows of framed magazine covers on the wall behind Quentin, their bright colours an antidote to the dark ceiling and furniture.

Quentin had to agree with that. 'I don't think anyone expected it to take this particular course.'

A wry smile touched Farnsworth's lips. 'No.'

'I took the liberty of ordering wine. You do drink, don't you?' Not that he'd found anything about Farnsworth's bad habits; surely the man had some?

Farnsworth shrugged. 'I do, but… not as much as I used to.' He scanned the extensive wine list. 'The older I get, the longer the hangover seems to last, and that's not fun any more.'

Quentin couldn't help a nod. That was true for him, too; not that he'd say so much. 'However, in this place, not ordering wine would be a crime.'

Farnsworth smiled, but it didn't reach his eyes. 'I've heard good things about here – the food and the wine.'

'I've been coming here since I moved back to London. I practically count it my second home.'

'I have to admit I'm a country cousin in that respect. I come here for meetings, and that's it.' Again, his gaze flicked around, then out of the window; Quentin found himself glancing around, wondering what he was seeing.

'I'm not used to busy places these days,' said Farnsworth, with a hint of apology.

'The mess, surely?'

'Oh, the mess is different. Especially at Dining-In.' Farnsworth grinned. 'Have you served in the military?'

'Oh, no, no. I chose the way of the bureaucrat. Still bitter fighting, but our weapons are paper and print. And our wits, of course.' Quentin glanced out of the window. 'My father was in the Army. My older brother is a lieutenant colonel in the Royal Artillery.'

Farnsworth nodded. 'You could say the RAF's in my blood. My grandfather flew Beaufighters in Coastal Command during World War Two, and my father flew Buccaneers in the Gulf.' At this, he smiled, lopsided. 'I'm not quite sure he's forgiven me for being chairborne.'

Quentin laughed. 'My father viewed the civil service as at least being a better option than the clergy.'

Farnsworth's face split into a genuine grin; he chuckled.

Quentin continued, 'And to be fair, I'm hardly suitable for the religious life.'

A waiter arrived with the wine: a Premier Cru Burgundy Quentin had been eager to try for some time. He sampled the bottle and proclaimed it suitable; it was exquisite. While the waiter poured them both generous glasses, Quentin handed Farnsworth a menu.

'This evening is on me. Call it… extending courtesy.'

Farnsworth blinked, taken aback. 'If you're sure.'

'I insist.'

Farnsworth surveyed Quentin; caution filled his eyes, even if his face remained amiable. 'Thank you. That's very kind.' He scanned the menu. Only a practised face watcher would have caught the moment his eyes briefly widened at the prices. As if to distract himself, he reached for the wine; to his credit, he savoured its aroma before taking a leisurely sip. 'Mm. This is superb, isn't it?'

Quentin wondered if he was going to have to revise his opinion of the man. Perhaps he wasn't the cold, strait-laced flatfoot he appeared.

Before Quentin could respond, the waiter arrived to take their food orders. Quentin chose the roast Yorkshire mallard with quince; Farnsworth plumped for the roast pork loin with pearl barley and mustard.

As the waiter left, Quentin cleared his throat. He picked up his glass and took a sip. It was obvious Farnsworth's guard remained firmly up; despite the wine's allure, he'd barely drunk a drop. He'd need to be careful tonight.

'Have you been back in London long?' asked Farnsworth.

'Ah.' He couldn't avoid this. 'Around six months. I was stationed in Washington for many years.'

Farnsworth stilled. If Quentin thought his guard had been up before, that was nothing compared to his face now: it was as if steel shutters surrounded the man's soul.

Watchful, Farnsworth put his wine glass down. 'In which case,' he said, slowly, 'I presume you've heard plenty about me over the years from my American counterparts.'

It was pointless pretending he knew nothing. Quentin waved his hand magnanimously. 'Not directly, but yes, I'm aware of the incident.'

Just a hint of discomfort flickered in Farnsworth's eyes.

'And we considered that overall, your intervention was a good thing,' Quentin soothed. Even if it had been done with the delicacy of a tapdancing rhino.

Farnsworth took a larger sip of his wine and acknowledged Quentin's words with a nod. He leant forward and lowered his voice. 'I found a USAF Captain nose to nose with one of our analysts – an exceptionally capable NCO – telling her she should have stayed home having children, and how dare she, a mere girl, question what he said. Even though the evidence clearly contradicted him. He didn't take it well when I said I agreed with her, my CO agreed with us both, and if he was going to use that sort of language again I was going to throw him out. He persisted in being abusive, so I dragged him out. Literally.' He paused before adding, 'Oddly, he didn't take up my invitation to air our grievances more fully later.'

That was part of the story Quentin hadn't heard. 'Ah. The officer concerned's father is a senior Marine Corps general.'

'I wondered if he had friends in higher places.'

Quentin nodded ruefully. Said Major General made rather a lot of noise about the insults to his son and was offensive himself about the RAF and their behaviour. However, to stand up to such bullying took strength of character; assuming, of course, this was an unembellished version of events.

'I imagine that part of the story wasn't broadcast,' said Farnsworth. He smiled, though there was no humour in it.

'No. What a surprise.'

Both men stared contemplatively into their wine glasses; Quentin drank, while Farnsworth seemed reluctant to drink his.

'I suppose I should apologise for the fuss I caused,' he said.

Quentin blinked. For the first time, it seemed Farnsworth's shields were lowered; there was a new earnestness to his gaze.

'Even if I wasn't aware of the full consequences of my actions,' Farnsworth continued, 'any embarrassment I might cause elsewhere was the last thing on my mind.'

Farnsworth's expression hinted the awkwardness was genuine. Quentin considered how to respond. He could hardly admit he'd favoured a hardline approach to try to keep the United States Air Force onside, and had been furious at having to relay the news that the officer concerned wasn't even under investigation. He settled for, 'A battlefield is a fast-changing place. Home politics were far from your thoughts.'

Farnsworth drank some wine; he savoured the mouthful before carefully setting the glass down. 'Indeed.'

'And our coalition allies admit you prevented an embarrassing and potentially costly error.' Which was true. Although by that time, more senior officers on both sides had stepped in to smooth ruffled feathers.

'Hmm.' Farnsworth stared at his wine glass, lost in thought.

They were saved from further discussion by the arrival of the food.

Conversation lulled while they ate, but it was blatant that Farnsworth was avoiding anything remotely related to the Braxton investigation. His shields might have lowered discussing his actions in Afghanistan some years ago, but they were firmly back in place now.

Once the superb meal had been despatched and desserts ordered, Farnsworth reached for his glass. 'What made you come back to England?'

Quentin hesitated. He should have known that question was coming. 'Well, the right offer simply came at the right time. It was time to explore new opportunities, as the phrase goes. America has many advantages, but… it's good to be back.'

Before Farnsworth could continue that thought, Quentin emptied the dregs of his glass and gestured with the bottle. Farnsworth, uncertain, frowned at the dribble left in his glass.

'Are you driving?' asked Quentin. 'You've drunk with food, so you should be fine. And a single glass barely counts.'

The way Farnsworth's mouth moved, he wasn't sure about that, but he said, 'A half glass, please.'

'I may make a wine aficionado of you yet.'

Farnsworth smiled, but it didn't ring true.

Quentin signalled to the waiter then tipped a generous measure into Farnsworth's glass. He emptied the rest into his own. 'Are you travelling back tonight?'

'Yes, train from Marylebone. Although it's not a long drive home from Aylesbury.' He stared beyond Quentin's head, idly tracing a finger around the stem of the wine glass. 'I'm finding this case needs everything I can throw at it.'

Quentin grinned. 'It is something of a challenge, isn't it?'

The merest twitch of Farnsworth's mouth may have been amusement. 'That's one way of putting it.'

A waiter arrived with a second bottle of the Burgundy and topped up Quentin's glass. Another followed with the desserts: a cheese plate for Quentin and gianduja mousse for Farnsworth.

Quentin delicately placed some Camembert on a Bath Oliver. 'That's what I hoped to discuss with you.'

Farnsworth, savouring a mouthful of chocolate-hazelnut mousse, raised an eyebrow and leant forward. He swallowed. 'I'm listening.'

'It seems, as often happens, our masters have given us complementary tasks yet forbidden us from sharing helpful information.'

'I don't believe you've ever clarified what your task is,' Farnsworth murmured.

'As I'm sure you've found, Martinford during the time frame concerned is rather a sensitive subject.' Quentin gently swirled the wine in his glass. 'Hence my involvement. Rather more may have been happening there than first meets the eye; at least, that's what the JIC seem to believe.'

'Really.' Farnsworth's tone was flat: not a question, more a statement. He frowned and cast a quick glance around; the place was busy and fairly noisy. Quentin recognised the impulse. Yes, this was potentially dynamite; neither wanted to be overheard.

'I presume you wonder if we've a present-day risk on our hands,' said Farnsworth.

Quentin nodded. 'It can't be denied this whole scenario is highly unusual.'

'Understatement.' Farnsworth took a deep draught from his glass. 'It also can't be denied that everything put under Martinford was never meant to see the light of day again.'

'The question is, why?'

'I suspect there's more than one answer to that question.' Farnsworth's gaze drifted off into the middle distance.

'I appreciate the police are concerned with our gentleman's suspicious end, but we still have a number of unanswered, even unasked, questions regarding the site itself.'

Farnsworth frowned, considering. 'I don't think we can yet separate out our initial mystery, if you like, from his location and surroundings,' he said eventually. 'Archaeologists talk about "context"; where and how you find something can tell you as much as the object itself, like each layer of soil on a dig. They may not be related, but all must be interrogated to make sure.'

'Yet we're forced to separate this out, aren't we?' Quentin sipped his wine. 'The police tackle the criminal; you tackle the military; I tackle the security. Each in our own little bubble.'

Farnsworth's eyes narrowed, but he didn't respond.

'This doesn't strike me as the best use of all our time or resources,' said Quentin. 'We're busy men. Our superiors want results – fast. Yet we're bound by convention and procedure.'

Farnsworth slowly nodded. He rubbed his chin.

Encouraged, Quentin continued, 'I'm aware we need practices in place to safeguard investigative integrity, but surely how we are at the moment can be improved.'

'There's always room for improvement,' Farnsworth conceded.

'Perhaps we can develop a way between us. Smooth relations. Ensure our practice works, then we can make recommendations. Based on experience, of course.'

The corner of Farnsworth's mouth lifted in a sardonic half-smile. 'I imagine this means me telling you everything I'm doing?'

'Oh, no, no,' Quentin demurred, 'merely keep me informed as to your progress, and I will of course do the same as to mine. Exchanging information. Privately. Quid pro quo.'

Farnsworth studied the rich, dark liquid in the bottom of his glass for a moment then looked up, his steel-blue eyes meeting Quentin's, who almost flinched. He had the awful feeling Farnsworth could read his mind.

It was a good few moments before Farnsworth spoke. 'Off the record, no doubt?'

'That's a rather binary view, isn't it? Who's to say what should be on record and what shouldn't? We all have sources. Some must be protected, some cultivated—'

'And some wined and dined?' There was no mistaking Farnsworth's disdain, though his expression hadn't changed.

'I merely wish to extend a hand of friendship,' said Quentin smoothly, 'to demonstrate my willingness to co-operate – officially or unofficially – as best to allow us both to fulfil our duties.'

'You want us to circumvent protocol.'

'Not as such—'

'An unofficial information sharing arrangement?'

'When you put it like that—'

Farnsworth interrupted; though his voice was low and calm, it was underscored with anger. 'Your colleagues would've hung me out to dry in Afghanistan if it kept the Americans happy. Forgive me if I'm not willing to sacrifice myself on your altar.' He downed the last of his wine and set the glass down with a deliberate clink. 'Anything I have to share with you, I'll do so via established channels. I trust you and your team will do the same.'

Quentin's mouth opened, but for once, he was lost for words.

Farnsworth stood and picked up his jacket. Disgust flashed in his eyes when he met Quentin's gaze, until the shutters slammed down and hid it from view. 'Thank you very much for this evening. I'll no doubt talk to you soon.' With that, he walked purposefully away.

Wednesday 9 November 2022

IN THE COLD light of Wednesday morning, the previous evening played on Alex's mind. What the hell was Ponsonby playing at? Several times, he'd opened his mouth to tell Burden what had happened; every time the words had dried up. How did he even begin to explain? Especially as, depending on your opinion, it could hardly look good for him, either. He wasn't surprised news of him upsetting the Americans all those years ago had almost become legend: he'd heard so many different versions of what he was supposed to have done, now, he found it paid to get the truth in first.

What was clear was that like him, Ponsonby was desperate for information – however he had to get it.

There was a rat-a-tat on Alex's office door.

Woods opened it and peered around. 'Sir? Are you busy right now?' His eyes gleamed with excitement. 'I've just had a call from the Air Historical Branch. They've found something.'

A couple of hours later, Woods and Alex arrived at RAF Northolt. After the initial reviews with Ball, the police had opted to hand everything recovered over to the RAF Air Historical Branch. Given the quantity recovered, DI Parkins considered the best people to interpret it all were those who were surrounded by similar paperwork all day. Alex couldn't argue with that.

'I've been in touch with a Natalie Booth, one of the civilian archivists,' said Woods. 'She called this morning to say we'd better come and have a look at what we've got.'

Sure enough, within a few moments, Booth emerged. She was tall, like Woods, with curly brown hair forced back into an attempt at a bun. Freckles dotted her nose and cheeks. After the introductions, she gestured for them to follow her. 'I think you'll find this very interesting,' she said.

Their feet padded on the carpet as they followed her down the corridor. She led them into a medium sized room full of papers piled on tables.

'So, you've found something?' asked Alex.

'Oh, have we.' Her eyes sparkled. 'This is fascinating. What we have here, in 449 Squadron's documents, is evidence the RAF and MOD were looking beyond a physical, or nuclear, explosive-based offensive role for the Vulcan.'

Woods blinked. 'Like what?'

Alex immediately recognised the common thread. 'Banshee?'

'Yes.'

'So…' began Woods.

'We've found out what Banshee is.' Booth switched her gaze between the two men. 'Are you ready for this?'

Woods frowned. Alex exchanged a glance with him. 'As we'll ever be.'

'It's a weapon. In today's terms, we'd call it an e-bomb.'

Alex blinked. 'A what?'

'An electronic bomb. Electromagnetic pulse discharge, according to what we've got here. Not just a defensive electronic countermeasure, but an offensive weapon in its own right.'

Alex's mind raced. Of all the possibilities, he hadn't expected this. 'Rather than camouflage the aircraft from radar and deflect weapons, it would disrupt enemy radar?'

Booth nodded. 'More than. Several documents state Banshee was meant to target anything electrical and electronic in the vicinity.'

'Was it an air-to-air weapon?' asked Woods.

Booth rocked a hand in the air. 'We don't think so. There's nothing in any of this that mentions targeting aircraft. Mostly ground based radars and communications. One step beyond jamming.'

'Have you anything about the aircraft themselves?' said Alex.

'Three Vulcans were modified specifically for this programme. A lot of documents refer to them as B.2.Bs.' She flicked through the papers. 'XM568 was built with more powerful Olympus 301 engines, but XL433 and XL447 actually underwent works to retrofit these engines as well. Quite a few reports detail repeated upgrades to their electrical and electronics systems. It seems like they had a few problems.'

'Wouldn't surprise me,' muttered Woods.

'We've got schematics, specifications, all kinds of technical documentation,' said Booth. She grinned at Alex. 'I assumed you'd want copies of as much as possible, so I've gone ahead and done them.'

Alex returned her grin. 'Thanks. That's very helpful.'

She bustled off to the back of the room, then returned carrying a bundle of folders. 'Here you are.' She handed the pile to Alex. 'I've done my best to organise it by subject, as well as chronologically.' Eyes bright, she looked at them both. 'Do you know what happened to the Vulcans that didn't crash?'

'It seems XL433 and XL447 were scrapped soon after 449 Squadron disbanded,' Alex said.

'Interesting.' Booth's brow creased. 'We've come across a few things about XM568. After the crash.' She looked between Alex and Woods. 'Have you looked that up in official records, at all?'

Alex noted her choice of words. 'Not yet.'

'Hmm. Well. I know it's not the focus of your investigation, but I personally would bump looking at the official crash investigation report higher up my priority list.' Abruptly, all humour disappeared from her face; she met Alex's eyes with a serious, intent gaze. 'I don't believe the body is all that was hidden. Not by a long shot.'

Alex finally managed to tell Woods Gerry's information about the potential espionage connection once they were in the car, heading back to Halton.

Woods absorbed it, staring through the windscreen in silence for some time as he drove.

'Hmm. Did you believe it?' he asked, eventually.

'I'm not sure. At the moment, we don't have any physical evidence,' said Alex. 'Plus, he's not exactly an official source I can quote. But it would be a massive coincidence, given so much of what he told me seems to match.'

'Bloody hell.' Woods sucked his teeth. 'Might explain why MI5 have been sniffing around, then.'

'More than likely.' It would certainly explain a lot.

Woods sniffed, then scratched his cheek. 'Funny, though. I don't think they know much more than us about it. Why would they be asking us if they already had the information?'

Alex reflected. Going by his interactions with Ponsonby, that was true; the man constantly seemed to be fishing for something. 'Good point. You'd think if whoever was under Martinford was ours, they'd know about it.'

Woods drove in silence for a few moments, brow furrowed. 'Unless,' he said slowly, 'our mystery man was actually KGB.'

Alex blinked. 'My source said they lost contact with the agents *and* the controller…'

Woods shot him a brief, shocked, glance, then turned his eyes back to the road. His fingers flexed around the steering wheel.

'So far,' said Alex, 'we don't have any conclusive evidence our body is Squadron Leader Hesketh-Shaw, apart from him seeming to disappear off the face of the earth around the right time. If anything, the body's build hints he wasn't.'

'Have you got a photo of him?'

'Wing Commander Miller showed me one of him when they were all with 449 Squadron. I'd say he was average to lean, build-wise. And as Miller didn't mention him suddenly gaining several stone…'

Woods chewed his lip but kept his eyes on the road. 'Does this mean someone smuggled a KGB agent onto an active V-bomber base, executed him, and hid the body?'

Alex stared out at the darkening skies, not sure he wanted to consider what Woods suggested. However…

'I think that's a possibility.'

BACK AT HALTON that evening, Alex sent a message to the archivists requesting a copy of XM568's official crash investigation report, then read the careful copies of original documents Booth gave him.

If his understanding was correct, then Banshee was definitely an air-to-ground electro-magnetic pulse device. Nothing in the documents mentioned effects against other aircraft; only impact on electrical and electronic ground-based infrastructure.

Uneasy, he arranged to see some former colleagues at Waddington. He needed some independent verification of the facts, and Waddington housed specialists in the dark art of electronic warfare, as part of the Air Warfare Centre, or AWC.

After a while, he pushed the documents away and stared at the ceiling, deep in thought.

If their body wasn't Sqn Ldr Hesketh-Shaw, then who was he?

Was it really possible he could be this KGB agent? If so, where had Hesketh-Shaw gone?

Wing Cdr Miller had said 449 Squadron's men were posted on with no questions asked, let alone answered: presumably that applied to those in command, too. Perhaps Hesketh-Shaw had just gone overseas: overseas postings were comparatively plentiful at that time, just before Britain really started withdrawing from the Empire, but even so, there should be some sort of paper trail.

XM568's accident was a complication. He wasn't all that surprised by Booth's assertion that the official records would differ from those retrieved from the bunker, but what was the difference? Had critical information been redacted, or was it something more creative?

Pensive, he tapped the edge of his desk.

Could the crash, the body, and the hidden archive be linked in more ways than one?

Friday 11 November 2022

'WHAT DO YOU make of these?' Alex slid the copied documents across Flt Lt Jasbir Mann's desk. Their paths had crossed a few years ago; Alex was lucky Mann remembered his name and was happy to help. Mann had since moved into an operational analysis role as part of the Joint Electronic Warfare Operational Support Centre at RAF Waddington; Alex hoped he could shed some light on the subject. Even the tiniest crumb of information might make the three-hour drive up the A1 this morning worthwhile. Woods confirmed yesterday that the National Archives held XM568's crash report, and he'd already made arrangements for Alex to go and see it next week. Neither of them needed to voice the fact that despite the frustrations, untangling this mystery was far more enjoyable than anything else they were tasked with.

Mann studied them, then gave Alex a quizzical look. 'What are they?'

'They're copies of documents retrieved from the site of former RAF Martinford in Warwickshire.'

'Ah.' Mann's face lit up with curiosity. 'The body in the bunker case?'

'Yes. These were found alongside the body.'

Mann read in silence for a few minutes, his brow furrowed. 'Has the date of these been verified?'

Alex nodded. 'They tie up with the known history of the squadron concerned. 449 Squadron, Electronic Warfare Test and Evaluation.'

'Haven't heard of that one.' Mann frowned.

'The EW part seems to have got lost as time's gone by.' Alex snorted. 'For some reason.'

Mann stared off into the distance, pondering. Then his dark eyes focussed on Alex. 'And these are exact copies of genuine documents?'

'Yes.'

'Electronic warfare as we know it today was in its infancy then…' Mann trailed off.

'I'm not an expert. Which is why I'd like your opinion.'

Mann leafed through the documents again. After another few minutes, he gave Alex a sharp look. 'You are serious? This isn't some kind of joke?'

'No. I don't think I've ever been so serious.' Alex leant forward. 'Is what it says plausible?'

Mann nodded. 'Can I show this to one of my team?'

'Yes, but I'd rather they came in here. I don't want to be leaving copies of this, if I can help it.'

Mann picked up his phone and dialled a number from memory. 'Morning. Can you come to my office as soon as possible? Yes… that's fine. Thanks.' He hung up, then looked back at Alex. 'Flight Sergeant Thorpe is an expert on this type of thing. She'll be here shortly.'

'Thanks.'

Barely moments later, Thorpe arrived. After the introductions, Mann handed her the papers. 'What's your opinion on these?'

Thorpe scanned them, then gave Mann and Alex a sceptical look. At Mann's nod, she carried on reading. After a few minutes, she blew out a long breath. 'Well…'

'Before you ask,' said Alex, 'we've no reason so far to doubt that these documents, and their dates, aren't genuine.'

Thorpe's eyes widened. 'Right. Well, first thoughts are if this is real, it's dynamite. Almost literally. This would work. It's a very clever arrangement of the kind of technology I'd expect in the sixties.' Thorpe pursed her lips and considered as she carried on reading. 'Shielding on key aircraft wiring and systems, I see.'

'Shielding?'

Thorpe flicked the paper around so Alex could see. 'Here. This looks like a Faraday cage type arrangement on part of the… flight controls?' Thorpe turned it back around, frowning.

'That would make sense,' said Alex.

Thorpe read on, still frowning. 'This was fitted to Vulcans?'

'Three. As a trial,' said Alex.

Thorpe was silent for a moment. 'Any losses?'

'One. I'm waiting to see the crash investigation report.'

'Do we know why it was lost?' asked Mann.

'Not exactly,' Alex said. 'All we've found so far is it suffered a systems failure.'

'Ha.' Thorpe smiled, with no humour. 'It would have. That's what EMP's meant to do.'

Mann and Alex exchanged a look.

Thorpe continued, 'This system would generate a non-nuclear electromagnetic pulse – EMP – sufficient to overload most electrical and electronic systems within a radius of about twenty-five miles, when flying at a thousand feet. Fry them, basically. And they wanted to increase that radius.' She studied a sheet closely. 'Hmm. This would emit a fairly broad spectrum of reasonable power.'

'Meaning?' asked Mann.

'EMP doesn't discriminate between civil and military technology. Anything unshielded would be damaged beyond use and probably beyond repair. And when I say anything, I mean anything. A pulse of this spec could potentially take out a power substation and more besides. Ground-based early warning radars, radio and TV broadcasts, telephones…'

Mann's eyes widened. He leant back in his chair.

Alex whistled. He wasn't sure what he'd expected, but it wasn't *that*.

'This is targeting infrastructure,' said Thorpe. 'On a very ambitious scale.' She kept reading. 'Oh. Interesting.'

'What?' asked Alex.

'This isn't a munition. It's not dropped by the aircraft.' Thorpe frowned. 'Can I put these on the table?'

'Sure.' Mann cleared his desk. Alex moved out of the way.

Thorpe spread a couple of sheets, dense with diagrams, across the tabletop.

'If I'm understanding these right, this isn't any kind of stand-off weapon or missile. It's not dropped like a conventional munition, either.' Wide-eyed, Thorpe scanned the text. She pointed to a diagram.

'This was carried and operated entirely within the Vulcan. Looks like they did a lot of work to beef up the electrical system and engine generators to supply it.'

That would explain the B.2.B designation. Alex studied the drawings.

The blueprints made the technology look deceptively simple.

Banshee took up the middle third of the Vulcan's huge bomb bay. The front and rear thirds were occupied by additional, removable, fuel tanks of a standard design already in use, by the looks of it. All of this fitted with the bomb bay doors closed. A new antenna spanned each wingtip, from leading edge to trailing edge.

When the bomb bay doors opened, an antenna spread across the aperture; it didn't protrude underneath the aircraft, but dotted lines hinted at some ability to direct it.

'Why the extra fuel tanks?' murmured Mann.

'Did you say this was powered by the Vulcan?' asked Alex.

Thorpe nodded.

Realisation dawned. 'This isn't a one-time use weapon,' said Alex. 'If you've got fuel, you can keep flying, recharge it, and…'

Mann looked down at the diagrams. 'And knock out enemy infrastructure in a massive area.'

'That must have been the plan,' said Alex.

The three of them looked at each other in silence for several moments. A chill travelled down Alex's spine: he shuddered. No wonder Banshee and 449 Squadron had been hidden.

Alex thought he knew the answer to this, though he had to ask anyway. 'If it took out a power station then, what would it do now?'

Thorpe's expression darkened. 'It'd be quicker for me to list what it wouldn't damage.' She paused. 'That said, if it was that easy or simple, we'd all have been doing this for years.'

'This would be pushing the boundaries, now,' said Mann. Disbelief edged his voice.

'To say the least,' said Thorpe. 'To try to overload everything beyond repair.'

Overload.

Alex went cold.

This had to be PEREGRUZKA.

… But if it was, then the Russians already knew all about it.

WALKING OUT OF the Air Warfare Centre, Alex's mind whirled.

No wonder Banshee and 449 Squadron had been erased from the records.

This was Gerry's PEREGRUZKA all right. What better way to describe it than overload?

And now MI5's involvement made even more sense. If this became public knowledge…

He groaned.

He had proof of a top-secret weapons programme; evidence it was infiltrated by the Soviets; and indications there may have been a British agent on board too. Once cancelled, the whole project was deliberately concealed.

He rubbed his forehead. This case was turning into a real headache.

He glanced at his watch: almost time for his next meeting.

Right on cue came an 'Alex?' in faintly Brummie tones. He recognised the voice instantly; its owner was just the man he wanted to see. Shorter, stockier, and some years older than him, with a sprinkling of dark hair, and he still looked like he wore a shirt under sufferance.

'Smeghead. Good to see you.' In reality, the man's name was Steve, but with Rimmer as his surname, there was no way he was going to escape any reference to the character from *Red Dwarf.*

Flt Lt Steve Rimmer grinned back. 'And you. Been a while.'

Alex stuck his hand out. 'Hasn't it?'

Steve shook it heartily. 'You're looking well, though.'

'So are you. What are you up to here?' asked Alex as they walked across to Steve's office.

'Just moved into ops support. Bit quieter than Kandahar,' said Steve, with a wry smile. He opened his office door, gestured Alex to the single spare seat in a corner, and went off to get a drink. After a few minutes, he came back with two mugs.

Alex was not at all surprised that Steve remembered he had black coffee; he took it with a smile. 'Cheers.'

'Cheers.' Steve held up his mug in a mock toast: still builder's tea, from the looks of it. He leant forward in his chair and fixed Alex with a look that combined appraisal with sympathy. 'How's it going? Everything else, I mean? I know we've had a couple of chats the last few months, but…'

Alex slid the mug onto the top of the desk, sat back in his chair, and let out a long sigh. How did he answer this? 'Where do I start?'

Steve smiled, understanding. 'You know we've got your back. Anytime.'

Alex returned the smile. 'I know. I just…' He rubbed his face.

'You glad you moved?'

Alex nodded. He picked up his coffee again and cradled the mug in his hands. His throat closed up. He hadn't broached this with anyone, not even his family. 'I had to.'

Years ago, he and Steve had once been in the back of a Chinook, skimming Afghan mountain ranges, expecting enemy fire at any moment; he'd take that journey, every time, over the threat of bumping into Anna again. The wounds she'd inflicted cut deep into his soul.

'There's not an in-person equivalent to blocking yet, is there?' Alex forced a bitter chuckle. 'Anna – once I pulled the plug on us, she didn't stalk me, as such, but…' he swallowed, '…I'd see her, her friends, around. At the shops. At the petrol station. Not so often I could say they were following me, but…' Words failed him.

'You felt like you were being watched.' Compassion tinted Steve's voice. 'You never said.'

'I felt like a paranoid idiot for even thinking it,' admitted Alex. For weeks, he'd felt like he was seeing things. It had taken him months to realise just how much the whole thing unsettled him. One more reason for a clean break.

Steve gave him a sympathetic look. 'It's the sort of trick she'd pull, though. Lisa said she saw her around a few times, but she ignored her.'

The men shared a glance. Anna had tried to speak to Steve's wife Lisa, to spin another web of lies around Alex: she made the mistake of lying about things they already knew to be true.

'You did the right thing, moving.' Steve glanced into his mug. 'If you were here, I think she'd still be needling at you like that.'

Alex tried not to roll his eyes.

'My opinion,' said Steve, 'is she wanted to have her cake and eat it. She didn't count on you finding out, and I don't think she counted on you kicking her out.'

Alex smirked, though it was tinged with sadness. When the first rumours of her affairs leaked out, he didn't confront her straight away. Instead, he carefully collected evidence, bit by bit.

At first, that had been because he didn't want to believe it, but the harsh truth soon became clear. She'd used the cover of Covid restrictions, and her nursing job, to live a double life.

His friends helped him out in so many ways. In particular, Steve and Lisa had kept their ears to the ground and helped him collate more evidence. Not only that, they'd offered Alex their spare room for as long as he needed; so had Mark and Claire, though the distance meant their support was more moral than practical.

At least he and Anna had only been renting; he'd handed over the tenancy of their flat, and all the furniture, to her when they separated. Some thought he was being generous, but to be honest, he just didn't want any reminders of her around. And he didn't want to give her any more excuses to try to screw him over.

Then Phil Redfern, from his course at Cranwell, had let him know about the role he'd moved into…

'She didn't count on you, either.'

Steve grinned.

'I'm not sure I'd be here without all of you,' said Alex, quietly. He meant it.

'Like I said,' said Steve, 'we've got your back.' He drained his tea and sighed. 'Dan would've had my arse if we didn't.'

'He'd have seen her coming a mile away,' murmured Alex.

'No, he wouldn't. None of us did. You've nothing to be ashamed of, there.'

Alex snorted but couldn't look at Steve. He stared at the floor, his cheeks burning. That was exactly how he felt: ashamed. Ashamed at being taken for a ride, gaslit even. Ashamed at almost being beaten down. Ashamed of the fact that his wife cheated on him. Ashamed that his marriage hadn't worked. Ashamed that he'd run away.

'Only an idiot hangs around where he knows there'll be trouble. Unless he wants the trouble,' added Steve, quietly. 'Which most of us don't.'

Alex lifted his eyes. 'Fine line between bravery and stupidity, is that it?'

Steve shook his head. 'Sometimes it takes more balls to walk away.'

'One day I might believe that.'

'You should.' Steve stood. 'Another drink?'

Both men picked up their mugs and walked to the small kitchen area.

'How's Lisa?' asked Alex. If he remembered correctly, Lisa had recently increased her hours at work; she taught maths part-time at a local comprehensive.

'She's good, thanks, apart from when she has to teach our Maisie.' Steve chuckled; their daughter, Maisie, was fourteen. Steve rinsed his cup then plonked another teabag in it. 'They both said hello, by the way. I meant to ask before but forgot: you stopping up here tonight?'

Alex hesitated. He hadn't planned on it, although he had his go-bag with a couple of days' clothes in the car anyway, just in case. Not that he had any firm weekend plans. All he'd thought about was a trip to IKEA, to finally replace a bookcase he'd let Anna have, and possibly a solo trip out somewhere on the motorbike.

'Spare room's free, if you want. Lisa's doing pulled pork and beans in the slow cooker.' Steve grinned. Lisa's cooking was legendary. 'I mean, it'll go in the freezer or get hoovered up by Maisie and her mates if you're busy, but y'know, the offer's there. And if you've got your laptop, there's space in my office this afternoon. Saves you battling Friday night traffic.'

Alex dumped some instant coffee into his mug. His smile was bittersweet. Sometimes, the distance cut hard. 'You're going to make me wish I hadn't moved, now.'

Steve scoffed. 'You wouldn't be getting this every night, you know. I don't.'

'If you're sure, I'd love to.'

Steve nodded, satisfied. 'We're sure.'

After the rigmarole of filling their cups with hot water, and in Steve's case a token drop of milk, they walked back to his office.

Steve sat down. 'Now, then. You said you were having a bit of fun with a certain chap at MI5…'

Alex grinned. 'What have you got for me?'

'I've had some fun with this one.' Mischief lit up Steve's face and made him look about ten years younger. 'Quentin Ambrose Ponsonby. Came back to England six months ago and moved across into counter terrorism and MI5 from the Foreign Office. The interesting thing is, he was one of the attachés at our embassy in America right about the time you… how can I put it…'

'Did my bit for international relations?'

Steve chuckled. 'Yeah. Word on the street is he—' He paused. 'He was brownnosing the high-ups, shall we say. Seemed to be doing all right, but there was a bit of unpleasantness on a trip to Las Vegas that got him sent back early. I dunno exactly what, but it doesn't take a genius to guess what it might be if it was Vegas, does it. Involved a tidy sum of money. Upset someone he shouldn't have.'

Interesting. Alex sipped some coffee, considering what that could mean.

'There are a few waiting to see what he does. Sounds like he's had, if not a demotion in name, one in practice. If you know what I mean.'

'That'd make sense.'

'The interesting thing is,' said Steve, 'my mate who knows people who know people, if you get my drift, he says this guy's lifestyle doesn't match his income. And one of them, who does security for a couple of very high-class places in London, is sure he's seen him with a, how did he phrase it? A person of interest, given the situation between Russia and Ukraine, and our stance on it.' Steve raised his eyebrows meaningfully and drank some tea.

'A person of interest?' Alex frowned.

Steve put his mug down. 'A rich Russian ex-pat. Living the high life in Chelsea the last few years, by the sounds of it.'

Alex groaned. Another Russian connection? Really?

Steve paused. 'But this is just between you and me.'

'What is?' said Alex innocently.

'Exactly.' Steve grinned.

For a split second, Alex longed for the days when it was him, Steve, and Dan in a hot, dusty tent of an office, disturbed by the roar of fast jets and the frequent *wokka-wokka* of Chinooks…

Steve had a rare talent: not only did he have an easy manner that endeared him to most ranks, but he was also a good talker and an even better listener who earned and kept confidences. Despite that, he kept his counsel to those few he trusted: if he told you something, you needed to know it, and he expected you to use it with discretion. The man had many fingers in multiple pies, more connections in more places than seemed possible – and, not for the first time, Alex was grateful.

'From what I've heard, this Ponsonby seems to be a slippery character,' said Steve.

'Hmm.' Alex had to agree. 'What's making me uncomfortable here is it looks like there's a Russian connection to what was under Martinford.'

Steve, halfway through taking a sip of tea, blinked over the rim of the mug. 'Really?'

Alex summarised what Gerry had told him about PEREGRUZKA and what he'd found out from Flt Lt Mann. 'If it's not connected, it would be one hell of a coincidence…'

'Wouldn't it?' Steve drank his tea. 'Got to wonder why he's involved.'

'All I know is, he's been sent from on high.' Alex swirled his coffee in his mug. 'So, it's official. If you know what I mean.'

Steve nodded. 'You've been given a good one here, haven't you?' he said, drily.

'Maybe my reputation precedes me.'

Steve laughed. 'Everyone knows you tell it as it is. Whether people want to hear it or not.' He paused, looking thoughtful. 'Be careful around this chap, though.'

Alex groaned. 'It might be too late.' He told Steve all about Tuesday evening and Ponsonby's abortive attempt to get information out of him.

When he'd finished, Steve stared up at the ceiling, thinking. 'You reported it?'

'You think I should?' Alex paused. 'I've been in two minds about it.'

Steve nodded. When he spoke, his tone was serious. 'Cover your arse. I mean it.'

Tuesday 15 November 2022

ALEX WALKED UP to the National Archives building in Kew. The sharp, grey, brutalist concrete was a stark contrast against the autumnal beauty of the surrounding grounds. Once inside, he found his way to the reading rooms and signed in. Midweek, the place was quiet, but still numerous heads were silently bent at desks, studying.

He found the folder he wanted in a locker, the number of which corresponded to his allocated desk. It was a stack of papers, encased in a dog-eared blue cardboard file some three inches thick. He picked up the pile and, after a moment's thought, fetched some protective foam wedges to support the file on the plywood desk.

Finally, he took his seat and studied the papers.

Text on the front stated that it was the RAF copy of the Board of Inquiry into an aircraft accident. The cover gave sketchy details: 4 August 1964, at Long Itchington, Warwickshire, Vulcan B.2.B XM568 from RAF Martinford, flown by Flt Lt F. J. Campbell. All five crew were killed.

Even though the file had been released, the aged bundle still had TOP SECRET writ large across the top. Someone had written, at one point, "Review in 1994" and highlighted it green; a further hand had added in black biro, "Hold until 2014".

Tentatively, he balanced the file on the supporting foam wedges and unfastened the loose string that held the stack together. With care, he lifted the cover. The pile held handwritten pages, typed transcripts and other text, plus numerous clear plastic folders containing multiple black and white photographs. An index was helpfully tagged to the folder's inside cover. The dusty scent of old paper drifted in the air.

He turned to the first page: a memo from the RAF liaison officer to the chief investigator. The dense, handwritten sheet apologised for the lack of forthcoming technical details of the prototype TL.772 weapon system fitted to XM568, and in particular the absence of information as to how said system may have influenced aircraft behaviour. However, though security requirements dictated this severe clampdown, both Hawker Siddeley Aviation and Fli-Tek, the company responsible, were reviewing the data thoroughly to ensure all lessons could be learned. Airworthiness and reliability of the UK's airborne deterrent was, of course, the utmost priority.

A sarcastic half-smile crossed his face. Over fifty years had passed, but the language of bureaucracy never changed.

He slipped on white cotton gloves and eased the first group of photographs from their folder. They were large, perhaps six by eight inches, on glossy paper so thick it was almost card. The pin-sharp black and white images looked as if they could have been printed yesterday. Careful capitals in black biro on the white border identified some prints, some had a description written on the back, and a few were unlabelled.

This first batch showed the crash site from various angles in stark, unremitting detail.

Crumpled, tattered chunks of twisted metal lay scattered over a huge area, surrounding scarred and burnt earth. One fragment was recognisably a wingtip and a length of trailing edge. A triangular shape in the foreground was once part of the landing gear; somehow, the wheels were still attached.

In one, firemen and others in uniform stood around still-smoking wreckage, by a fire engine splattered with the detritus of fire extinguishing foam. Their body language hinted a search was about to take place.

Suddenly, he felt both ghoulish and voyeuristic. The dead crew's remains were probably somewhere in that image. No-one could have survived something that tore a Vulcan to shreds. Those facing that grim task may well have known those they were searching for.

With a sigh, he refocused his gaze on the photographs.

Macabre it might be, but ultimately, he wanted to uncover the truth. That was the least he owed the dead.

He finished studying the photographs and carefully returned them to their places. Time to examine the written evidence.

As he worked his way through the interviews and summaries, making careful notes, his unease grew. Frowning, he retrieved the photographs once more.

It wasn't just that there were gaps in the information here. Something about these images didn't stack up with this official report.

The recorded narrative was that XM568 lost all electrical systems then plunged to the ground, but the debris didn't look right. A Vulcan was large; if one hit the ground at any speed, surely it would leave some kind of crater. Not to mention the force of impact would shatter it into tiny pieces. Instead, it appeared a series of impacts had occurred. As if sections of airframe had fallen from height.

Had XM568 actually broken up in flight?

Another thing struck him: Vulcans had suffered similar electrical failures before. In fact, the Vulcan B.2 had a redesigned, more robust, AC generating system, which was supposed to prevent that kind of systems malfunction bringing down an aircraft. Not only that, but while the three rear crew's chances weren't great, if failure occurred at altitude there could have been sufficient time for them to bail out and the pilots to eject. Instead, all of XM568's crew were lost. Why would they choose to stay with an uncontrollable aircraft they knew was doomed?

Had something more catastrophic occurred?

One of the sheets was a diagram of XM568's flight plan, showing her intended route over the country. A dot marked the point where radio contact was lost. An irregular shape around it indicated the debris field; it was almost teardrop-shaped, but it started just behind where contact was lost and stretched forwards. A handwritten addition noted that most of the Vulcan fragments had been found in an area stretching over three miles by two.

Much to his irritation, an actual map of debris scatter, showing what had been found where, didn't seem to be in the file. Neither were any eyewitness statements regarding the impact.

Stop, he told himself; he was getting distracted. He wasn't an air crash investigator, and there was no way he was going to figure this out by himself right now.

The best thing to do was request a copy of this whole file, photographs and all. Once they had that, he and Woods could compare it to whatever was recovered from Braxton.

No matter how he thought about it, though, it was hard to imagine how a single ground impact would result in a debris field over six square miles in area.

'Back again, Flight Lieutenant?' Mrs Miller frowned.

'I did call, however—'

'I'm not sure I want to talk to you,' interjected Wing Cdr Miller. He glared at Alex but put a gentle hand on his wife's shoulder. They exchanged a look; she pulled a face but nodded.

'Excuse me,' she murmured. John guided her out of the way.

Only when she was out of earshot did he speak. 'Well?' he snapped.

'Can we talk inside?'

John scowled as he gestured Alex through to his cluttered study then shut the door firmly. He made no move to sit down, nor offer Alex the spare chair.

'Fraser's crash,' he said. 'Why are you dredging that up now?'

Alex took a deep breath. He'd known coming straight here after the archives was a risk, but he had to try. 'Evidence shows what was officially recorded wasn't what actually happened.'

John scoffed. 'I could've told you that.'

'So why didn't you?'

There was a pause. John's eyes narrowed. 'Why does this matter now?'

'Shall we say it seems some didn't want the full truth to be known? I want to find out why.'

John's expression seemed to set. He stared at Alex, assessing, for several seconds; Alex returned his gaze, unwavering.

Finally, John sighed. He waved to the spare chair and sat down himself. 'We were never told officially what happened, beyond "systems failure".' He marked the words with air quotation marks. 'Unofficially, though…'

'The evidence is no systems failure occurred. At least, not the systems meant.'

'We all suspected—' John stopped.

'Banshee.'

John hesitated, then nodded. He gave Alex a sharp look.

'That's what the evidence so far hints,' said Alex.

'Gordon – Flight Lieutenant Thompson – obviously couldn't take part in the investigation, but he supplied all the info he had, and I know he didn't mince his words. He shouldn't have told us what he did, but he felt safety was at risk. And even then, he didn't tell us much. Just enough to get the flight test programme stopped.' John stared at his desk, brow furrowed in thought. 'Not that Tony wanted to fly, anyway,' he said eventually. 'Can't say as I was keen, but I felt I had to get back in the saddle, as it were.'

'But the MOD put a stop to all testing before you could get airborne again.'

John blinked; something softened in his expression, but suspicion lingered. He straightened up and gestured Alex closer. 'You really are telling the truth, aren't you?'

'There are still files I haven't read, or understood. I'm not an avionics expert, and neither do I know much about Vulcans,' admitted Alex. 'But it's clear to me that Banshee was deliberately hidden and the reason for XM568's crash, and her crew's loss, manipulated accordingly.'

'So what happened?'

'I'm trying to find out.' Alex gave a rueful smile. 'All I'm sure of so far is the official reports bear little resemblance to what actually happened. There's no corroborating evidence I'd expect to see, such as witness statements or interviews. What evidence has been left in contradicts the official conclusion.'

'What do you mean?'

'The official conclusion was electronic systems failure left XM568 uncontrollable, leading to the crash. Is that correct?'

'Yes.'

'Someone left a map in the file, showing where XM568 was when contact was lost. It refers to a debris field that totalled more than six square miles.'

'That'd be one hell of a systems failure, all right,' growled John. A hint of respect glimmered in his eyes. 'Gordon said he thought she was disabled and in bits before she hit the ground. Fraser would've kept her flying as long as possible, and he wouldn't have wanted the others to hang around, either.'

'You were there. You knew the project, the people, the place.' Alex took a deep breath. 'Will you help me piece this together?'

John sat in silence. Various expressions flitted across his face, but eventually he looked up and nodded. 'All right. You win. I'll tell you what I remember.'

Friday 7 August 1964

GORDON SCOWLED AT the test plans strewn across his desk. Bloody Merrick.

In spite of everything, Merrick insisted testing had to restart next week, seven days after Fraser's crash; those orders had been passed down from Burroughs this lunchtime. This meant Gordon had to rejig the test plans to make sure the remaining two aircraft were fully utilised. In other words, both aircraft flying as much as possible, with minimal time for maintenance or checks…

He growled to himself.

Personally, he didn't want XL447 or XL433 to fly anywhere until they'd had a bloody good look at every single part of them both. What he wanted to do was rip each aircraft down to her bare bolts. Dismantle Banshee into its constituent components. Make certain that each Vulcan, each system, was—

Well, wasn't going to repeat what happened to Fraser and XM568.

He rubbed his forehead. Burroughs was sympathetic, but ultimately, the whole thing was Merrick's call. He had to do what he could, which felt like precious little.

There was a knock on his door. Hunt came in, carrying two cups of tea.

Gordon smiled. 'Thanks.'

Hunt grinned. 'Not a problem. How's the test plan looking?'

Gordon spun the sheets around. 'Like I'm trying to fit two pound of lard into a pound bag.'

'Maybe we can find Doctor Who to lend us the TARDIS or something.'

Gordon humphed. 'I can think of more I'd do with that than get this blasted plan to work.'

The two men stared at the text.

Abruptly, the staccato trill of his telephone broke their thoughts.

Gordon picked it up; the person on the other end spoke before he could get a word in. 'Can you come to Wing Commander Merrick's office? As soon as possible.'

Gordon just about withheld his sigh. 'Of course.'

The line went dead. Gordon dropped the handset into the slot with a clank. He glanced down at the scribbles and dates. 'D'you think you can work miracles? Or shall I just tell him the truth now?'

Hunt pulled a face. 'Depends how much you want to keep your job, I suppose.'

Gordon paused. Realisation dawned with a rush of anger. 'You know what? If keeping my job means endangering crews unnecessarily, then they can shove it.' With that, he strode out.

When he got there, Merrick's door was ajar; Gordon tapped on it.

'Enter.'

'You asked to see me, sir.' Gordon closed the door behind him then stood in front of Merrick's desk. The man himself, seated, scanned a number of documents on his tabletop; he briskly signed one then pushed it to one side. Only then did he look up.

Much as Merrick's face didn't change, Gordon caught the surprise flash in his eyes; maybe his face betrayed his thoughts. Good.

'Sit down,' said Merrick.

Gordon sat. He never took his eyes off Merrick.

Merrick's expression stayed still. It was like the man was set in concrete. 'I heard from the crash investigation team that you visited the main crash site.'

'I did. The day after.'

'Why?'

'Why wouldn't I?' Gordon retorted.

'Protocol, man!' barked Merrick. He stood, leant forward, and put his hands on top of his desk. 'You know damn well that as the crashed unit—'

'So does that explain the teams you sent out scouring the countryside for bits of Banshee, then?' snapped Gordon. Rage – hot, almost comforting – filled him. 'Oh, I heard about them all right. How's that different? I looked; I didn't touch. You were removing evidence!' Rumours of those men were all over Martinford, never mind 449 Squadron; he'd seen the black Bedford CAs and Morris Minors filled with sombre men, driving in and out of the gatehouse. Even without it being broadcast, it was blatant these men had a job to do that was separate to the usual business of crash investigation.

'Do you have any understanding of this project?'

'Only that you want it to go ahead, no matter what the cost.' Gordon stood, too; he leant his hands on the table and pushed his face nose to nose with Merrick. 'Tell me, what makes a Vulcan disintegrate at five thousand feet?'

Merrick's eyes briefly widened before the steel in them cooled again.

'I'm not an idiot,' snapped Gordon. 'I've seen crashes before. I know when something's hit the ground. I also know when it hit the ground in bits.'

Merrick slowly straightened up and looked away. 'You're emotional, Mr Thompson,' he said, levelly. 'Too emotional.' Still, he didn't look back at Gordon.

'And you're not emotional enough.' Gordon stood back; he put his hands on his hips. 'Besides. Think of the other consequences. What if this was because Banshee triggered itself? We're lucky it was low power and over open countryside. Can you imagine if this happens when we're at full power, flying over western Europe, running into target? Or training in this country? Or if we use it when we play war games with the Yanks? Do *you* want to tell the president we broke their power stations and telephones?'

Merrick, face set, stared out of his office window, almost as if Gordon wasn't there at all.

'Do I want to stop the project?' Gordon took a deep breath. 'I don't know. I do want to pause it. The whole point of Banshee is it gives us an advantage without obliterating everything under the sun first. I don't see why we should obliterate ourselves rushing it. Besides, you talk about time and money. If we have to keep replacing Vulcans and crews, that's not quick and they're not cheap. Neither will be compensating anyone who ends up with bits of aircraft on their land.'

Behind Gordon, the door whispered open and closed. Someone coughed.

'Time isn't on our side,' came Hesketh-Shaw's voice.

'Is it ever?' snapped Gordon. 'You know what? Remove me from this project. I'll go and see SEngO—'

'You'll do no such thing,' interjected Hesketh-Shaw.

Merrick blinked. For the first time, his facade cracked; shock opened his mouth, but no words came out.

Hesketh-Shaw stood next to Gordon, though his gaze was fixed on Merrick.

'Your test plan is worth nothing if we refuse to fly,' said Hesketh-Shaw. 'And I agree with Mr Thompson.'

What? Gordon blinked, taken aback. Had H-S really just said that?

Hesketh-Shaw continued, 'I do not believe Fli-Tek have been open and honest with us.'

Gordon folded his arms. 'Neither do I.'

Merrick avoided both their gazes; he stared intently at the letters on his desk.

'Give me two weeks,' said Gordon. 'I want to tear those aircraft down. With or without Fli-Tek. Then, and only then, do I think we should restart flight testing.'

Hesketh-Shaw nodded. 'At minimum.' He looked questioningly at Gordon. 'Did I overhear something about Campbell's crash?'

'I visited the crash site,' said Gordon. 'I'd swear XM568 disintegrated in mid-air.'

Merrick stood unmoving, like a statue.

'I've heard similar things. You can't stop rumours,' murmured Hesketh-Shaw.

'Indeed not,' said Merrick, slowly. His face rearranged itself into a grim rictus as he switched his cold gaze between the two men. 'But a lie can travel halfway around the world while the truth is still putting on its shoes. You should both consider fully what that means.'

Gordon gaped. Was that a threat?

Hesketh-Shaw laughed; a full, hearty sound. Merrick goggled, mouth hanging open; Gordon felt like that himself. What the hell?

'Oh, sir,' said Hesketh-Shaw, still chuckling. 'Is that a promise, or a threat? Because the first isn't attractive, and the second doesn't scare me. Not one bit.'

Disconcerted, Merrick's jaw flapped up and down; no words came out. Instead, he blankly watched them.

Hesketh-Shaw clapped Gordon on the shoulder. 'Mr Thompson. Let's go and see SEngO Burroughs.'

HALF AN HOUR later, Gordon opened his office door and walked back in.

Hunt, head still bowed over the mess of papers spread across the desk, shook his head. 'Sorry. I can't—'

'Don't.' Gordon wondered how best to sum up everything that had just happened. 'I wouldn't.'

Hunt looked up, puzzled. The frown only deepened when he saw Gordon's face. 'What's up?'

Gordon couldn't help a laugh. Where to start? There was one good place to begin. 'Go and get us each a cuppa. Then I'll tell you.'

Over tea, Gordon expanded on what had just occurred, and the outcome. 'Instead of updating the flight test plan, we're to come up with a detailed aircraft teardown, inspection, and functional check plan. Both Vulcans at once.' He drained his mug and set it on his desk with an appreciative sigh. How lovely it was to enjoy a nice, hot cup of tea for a change. It almost made the afternoon bearable. 'Not Banshee, yet, but...'

Hunt supped his tea. He nodded in approval. 'About time, too.'

'Burroughs agreed we can have two weeks.' He'd also agreed, off the record, to push for them to disassemble the Banshee system, too.

'Merrick wanted it signed off by the end of next week, didn't he?'

'Yeah, well…' Gordon wondered about Hesketh-Shaw. Obviously, the man wasn't stupid, but even so, something nagged at Gordon's brain about him. 'If his crews refuse to fly anyway, that's still put the tin lid on it. I don't think Tony's itching to get airborne.'

'He could overrule them, though.'

Gordon pondered. 'True.' The whole exchange still repeated itself in his mind. 'But I don't think H-S would care.'

'Blimey.' Hunt bit his lip. 'Comes to something when that happens.'

'Doesn't it.' Gordon repeated Merrick's threat and Hesketh-Shaw's response.

Hunt just stared, open-mouthed. 'That's…' He scratched his head. 'I don't even know what to say. To any of that.'

'Join the club.' Much as part of his brain felt he could relax, deep down unease stirred Gordon's guts. More was going on here than he knew, far beyond just politics; if Merrick was so inclined, he could do both Gordon and Hesketh-Shaw, maybe even Burroughs, for insubordination. Would he, though? Gordon didn't think so. The way Merrick reacted to Hesketh-Shaw's cool rebuttal… it was almost like he was unnerved and cowed by the younger man. Not that Gordon could blame him.

THAT EVENING, GORDON hesitated outside the mess. Should he go in? While he'd got an invite to dinner tomorrow with John and Miranda, he didn't feel like being sociable tonight. Neither did he feel like sitting in his room, though.

There was always one thing he could do.

He made his way to where his white and orange Triumph lived, under a tin roof along with a black Matchless and a well-used grey BSA Bantam that belonged to one of the OCU's co-pilots. His Bonnie hadn't moved since the night of Fraser's crash. That thought felt as peculiarly painful now as it did three days ago.

Aware he was trying not to think, he buckled his helmet, climbed on, and kicked her into life.

At a loss, Gordon just rode. He didn't have a destination in mind; he just went whichever direction felt right at each junction and roundabout. Somehow, his surroundings felt more and more familiar…

With a jolt, he realised why he recognised the semi-detached houses. His subconscious had routed him straight to Sophie's.

For a moment he sat outside her house, Bonnie idling, before he keyed off. Not that he had any idea what he was going to say, but his presence was pretty obvious. Already, net curtains twitched at a few windows.

Oh well, time to give them something to really talk about.

He jumped off, unfastened his helmet, and headed towards the front door. He rapped on the wood.

The door cracked open, barely enough for him to see inside. 'Hello? Can I help you?' an older, female voice demanded.

'Erm… Mrs Baxter? Sorry. I'm Gordon. Flight Lieutenant Thompson. I, er, dropped your daughter home the other night—'

'Oh, I remember now. Yes?' Her voice relaxed. The door swung open to reveal Mrs Baxter. She was recognisably Sophie's mother; a little shorter and a little rounder but evidently the source of her daughter's beauty.

'I was just calling to see how she is,' Gordon finished, feeling it was somewhat lame. He glanced over his shoulder at the Triumph. Just what did this look like? Awkward, to say the least. 'I was only passing. Um. I'm sorry. It's a bit late. I didn't think—'

Inside the house, he thought he heard Sophie, but he couldn't tell what she said. Mrs Baxter glanced over her shoulder, then looked Gordon up and down. 'You'd better come in.'

She ushered him through into a formal sitting room, which smelled of beeswax furniture polish; an oak sideboard, nice and modern, gleamed underneath the brightly coloured knick-knacks that crowded the surface. By the time he'd lowered himself carefully onto the sleek velour eau-de-nil settee, she'd disappeared.

Somewhere, crockery clanked and a kettle whistled. Voices murmured on the other side of the door; from somewhere drifted the sounds of what even he recognised as the Coronation Street theme.

Sophie pushed the door open. 'Oh, Gordon… it… it's so good to see you—'

Without realising, he rose to his feet. Sophie flung her arms around him and pulled him close. He fumbled his arms around her, somewhat gingerly, before letting himself hold her as tightly as she clung to him.

She trembled against him, her face buried against his neck.

He stroked her hair. 'It's OK. I'm sorry. I didn't mean—'

She loosened her grip and moved away a little, though her arms still encircled him. She shook her head and swallowed back a sob. Tear tracks glistened on her cheeks. 'No, no, please, don't worry. Thank you so much for coming. And for Tuesday night. It… it means a lot.' A smile edged bravely onto her face, though her eyes welled with tears. 'I heard about the crash on the radio. They said all the crew were killed. Is… is that true?'

Gordon nodded. He didn't trust himself to speak.

'You knew them, too?'

'Not as well as Fraser, but… yeah…'

Sympathy shone in her eyes. She stroked his arm. 'I'm so sorry,' she whispered.

All he could do was shrug. What could he say, anyway? 'How are you? I know I promised to call—'

There was a tap on the door, and it swung open.

Sophie let go of him, her cheeks pink. She sat, gesturing for Gordon to sit next to her. Mrs Baxter edged in, carrying a packed tray. 'Would you like some tea? Gordon, didn't you say?'

Gordon glanced at Sophie: she smiled and nodded. 'Oh, yes please. That'd be lovely. Thank you.'

Mrs Baxter carefully laid the tray down. It was laden with delicate, pastel floral china cups and a decorative teapot, as well as a silver milk jug and sugar bowl; clearly their best set.

'I understand you're a friend of Fraser's,' said Mrs Baxter. She started pouring the tea.

'Yes.' Gordon cleared his throat. 'I've known him for years. Sorry if I caused any, er, alarm with my visit.'

Mrs Baxter set the teapot down, then looked at her daughter. 'Not at all. It was just a surprise.'

Sophie coughed. 'Can… can you tell us anything? About the crash?'

Mrs Baxter tutted. 'I'm sure they're investigating,' she said, sternly.

Gordon took a deep breath. How did he say this? 'There is an investigation, yes. But I don't know any more than that. Because of my role, I'm not part of the team. And we won't know any findings for some time.'

Sophie's face fell, but Mrs Baxter nodded sagely.

'I do know my colleagues will be doing all they can,' he added. That felt like a hollow platitude, but both women nodded, seemingly comforted.

'Of course.' Mrs Baxter gave Gordon a nod. 'I'll leave you to enjoy your tea.' With that, she retreated and gently closed the door behind her.

Sophie let out a long sigh. 'I love my parents, really, but…'

'She's just worried about you. As a mum should be.' Gordon shuffled around to face Sophie. 'How are you? I was just passing, and… and I thought I'd drop in.'

Her eyes searched his, as if inspecting his soul to find the truth. An eyebrow arched. 'Really?'

Oh well, if he had to admit it… He smiled, sheepish. 'I've had what you could call an interesting day. I thought I'd take the Bonnie for a bit of a ride, and… I ended up here.' With that, he looked down. To distract himself, he reached for the milk jug and tipped a tiny bit of milk into his tea.

Sophie touched his hand. 'You're very kind.' She added milk to her tea, then returned her gaze to his. 'I'm… numb, I suppose. It's so hard to believe.'

'I keep expecting him to walk in and say it's all a joke, or a mistake, but—' Gordon stopped. His throat tightened. It wasn't. He knew that, in all its finality. But part of him still didn't want to accept it.

Sophie squeezed his hand; he squeezed back.

'He always said he didn't really have family,' said Sophie sadly. 'He said to me last weekend I was his family, now.'

That ring flashed across Gordon's mind's eye: he swallowed and closed his eyes. He was a man, a Cockney at heart, and he didn't do crying. But dampness squeezed out between his eyelids, nonetheless. Maybe there was a bit of grit in his eye, or something.

'Gordon? Are you all right?'

He started to nod, then gave in and shook his head. Could he tell her? Should he tell her that, now? And break her heart again? He had to tell her, maybe even give her the ring – but not yet. No. That would be too cruel.

Something touched his knees; a hand shoved something soft into his.

He opened his eyes to see her, knee to knee with him, holding a box of tissues. She dabbed her eyes.

'I don't think I've ever cried so much,' she murmured.

He wiped his eyes. He didn't trust himself to speak.

'He said you two went back years, but he never told me how you met.' She forced a smile. 'Could you tell me? Please?'

What could he say without telling her all about the V-Force? He tried. He explained about his stint as air crew, with Fraser as a junior co-pilot, though he skipped the more sensitive details. But he told her all about a year or so after that, when Gordon went back to engineering where Fraser was now a pilot on the same squadron – and they kept in touch, breaking the usual separation between ground crews and air crews. So that when the Martinford posting had come up, each had recommended the other as being suitable. Even their commanding officers noted how well they worked together.

Sophie dried her eyes and listened, eyes wide; a few times she smiled, remembering the man she knew, too.

When he'd done, they sat in silence for a while, drinking their tea.

'You know what he'd say,' she said eventually. Her voice was so quiet he thought for a moment she hadn't spoken. 'Life goes on.'

That much was true. 'Yeah,' he said. 'We carry on, but…' Fraser wouldn't want them to mourn forever; he wouldn't want them to stop living. Yet neither would he want them to pretend they wouldn't miss him. He closed his eyes. Why did it have to be so complicated?

She cleared her throat and dabbed at her eyes. 'Can you promise me something?'

Gordon couldn't tear his gaze from her earnest blue eyes; there was a depth, a seriousness in them he hadn't seen before. 'Of course.'

'You will find out what happened, won't you?'

'You can count on it.' He nodded, solemn. 'I promised Fraser I would.'

GEORGE FIDDLED WITH his tie and played with the buttons of his jacket. His palms itched; he absent-mindedly rubbed them together. *Calm down*, his brain whispered. *Look casual.*

Still, the Royal Shakespeare Company's theatre in Stratford-upon-Avon was a public place. This evening's performance was Henry IV, Part 2: not that he knew when Part 1 had been shown, or even if it would make any difference. Theatregoers swarmed through the austere Art Deco foyer: a low hubbub of conversation filled his ears as he made his way to his destination.

Johnson said to meet by the stalls bar. The man was seated at a bistro table by one of the floor-to-ceiling windows overlooking the canal and the river. Waist-high troughs of exotic greenery broke up the space, including some impressive Swiss Cheese plants. Neither the plants nor Johnson's tailored brown suit camouflaged his stockiness.

Johnson gave a smile that, from a distance, looked pleased. He raised a glass tumbler filled with whisky and water. 'Ah. You made it.' He scanned the room, his eyes narrowed.

Uneasy, George looked over his shoulder to see where Johnson looked.

He had to have messed up. Why else would Johnson have bothered to come all the way here, from the safety of London?

The crash, reminded that still, small voice in the back of his mind.

XM568's spectacular end caught everyone off guard. Even he'd been astonished by the destruction. Although he hadn't contacted Johnson explicitly about what happened, the national newspapers reported the crash of one of Martinford's Vulcans with the barest of details. The man was no fool; he must have put two and two together.

George's conscience demanded again and again: was this what he wanted?

All he knew was, he wanted this to end.

He snapped back to his surroundings. In the general hubbub, it was hard to hear just what Johnson was saying. Even if he'd been listening.

Johnson rolled his eyes; disdain wrinkled his mouth.

George winced. 'Sorry,' he said lamely.

'Shall we get a drink?' Johnson stood. His expression hinted it would be the first of many they'd both need to get them through the evening.

'That sounds like an excellent idea.' George followed Johnson across to the busy bar area. His fingers stroked his hip flask through his jacket pocket. Before he could stop himself, he pulled it out, unscrewed the top – but he managed to mime taking a drink, just in time. He'd filled it with what you could call a more potent mix than usual, in case Johnson fancied a snifter during the interval or something. The last thing he wanted was to drink the cocktail himself; the harsh taste lingered on the small part of his mouth that made contact with the liquid.

He carefully ignored the voice in the back of his mind that hissed, over and over again, *Are you sure you want to do this? Do you really know what you're doing?*

Of course I do, he told himself. *I'm working my way out of this.* One way, or the other.

And desperate times called for desperate measures.

MUCH AS GEORGE wasn't a theatrical man, he could appreciate the work and effort put in by the cast and crew. Johnson, on the other hand, seemed spellbound by the performance.

When the play ended and the cast took their curtain call, the crowd spilled out into the night. George recalled that just down the road, overlooking the river, was a pub. Though its formal name was the Black Swan, it lived in legend as the Dirty Duck; whether it got that name from the thespians who frequented it, or somewhere else, was lost in the mists of time.

It was conveniently located, both for a drink and for his plan. He checked his watch and sighed in relief. 'Shall we go to the pub?' he asked. 'We should have time for one before closing.'

'Sounds perfect,' murmured Johnson.

A few moments' walk later, they arrived at their destination. A wide white building, large, black-lined windows glowing in the dusk, sat above the road as if on top of the almost head-height red brick wall that bordered the pavement. Blooming shrubberies under the lamppost scented the night air. Judging from the buzz, quite a few theatregoers were already refreshing themselves. Perfect cover for what would happen next.

'This is it.' George smiled. 'Come on. The first round is on me.' He trotted up the steps that curved from the gap in the wall, past the tree that seemed to lean away from the entrance.

While Johnson found them a seat somewhere, he pushed his way to the bar and ordered one large gin and tonic and one tonic. In the press of people, it was the work of a moment to hide topping up Johnson's glass from his hip flask…

George's conscience sang a tremolo; he ignored it. Time to wait for the cocktail to take effect. Soon, this would be over.

Saturday 8 August 1964

GEORGE WALKED ALONG the pavement, trying to enjoy the late summer evening. He hadn't explored Leamington Spa much up till now, but it was a lovely little town. The wide main road through the centre, The Parade, was lined on both sides with shops and parked cars; off various side roads were pubs, cafes, more shops, and other places to eat and drink. Even at this time in the evening, the place bustled with life.

He swallowed to try to ease the dryness in his throat. For what felt like the umpteenth time, he deliberately slowed his steps; he wedged his hands in his pockets and looked around.

Much as the play itself had slipped out of his memory, last night's post-theatre discussion with Johnson still rolled around his mind. Their drinks at the Dirty Duck, and the riverside walk afterwards, had been… illuminating.

If he'd thought things were bad before, it didn't compare to the trouble he was in now.

Whether he'd meant to or not, Johnson had let something slip before he went.

He was due to meet another agent. At a coffee bar. At seven o'clock. Tonight.

As he walked, his subconscious nagged at him: *you can't talk your way out of this one, George. You can't do what you did yesterday…*

He paused by a crossroads and took a swig from his new hip flask.

Almost empty. *Drat.*

At least he had another bottle in the Rover's glovebox; that was parked behind him at the top of The Parade, nestled between a dusty black Austin A35 and a pale blue Ford Anglia. He hesitated, then turned back to get it.

Even knowing what dirty money purchased it, he did love his pale green Rover 2000. She was sleek, modern, and shiny; a world away from the ancient old Standard he had before. He'd even paid extra for the soft, supple, beige leather interior, whose rich scent bathed him every time he opened the door. Small consolation, and a bit of comfort the rest of his life sorely lacked.

He retrieved the small bottle of gin and topped up his flask, though he still took a quick nip from the bottle before he put it back.

Johnson's slurred words echoed in his mind, again and again: *one of you is working for the British…*

Once the Rover was locked, he started back on his way.

One of you is working for the British…

What was worse? The shock of realising he wasn't on his own, reporting on Banshee? Or that the Soviets suspected one of them of being a double agent?

George wasn't sure exactly where this coffee bar was. Neither was he sure who this other agent could be. His palms sweated just thinking about it.

He reached a crossroads with – he glanced at the sign – Regent Street. A Midland Red single decker bus grumbled uphill past the parked cars, swirling diesel fumes in its wake. There were so many places it could be…

What was the name Johnson mumbled? Cobema?

The large place towards the bottom of the hill caught his eye: a Cadena Cafe. Ah ha. That must be it.

Even now, he wasn't sure what to do when he got there. Should he walk in? Or sidle past, as if searching for something else? If he walked in, would he approach – whoever it was? Would he even recognise him? It was highly unlikely the place would only have the one customer, he thought with a sinking feeling. He knew his colleagues, of course, but there were a fair few air force men he didn't.

Still. He was here, now. It was worth a look.

Perhaps after this he'd find a pub for a meal and a drink to set him up for the drive home.

Assuming he wanted to eat, of course. Even the thought of food turned his stomach. The near-permanent adrenaline that had pulsed around his system ever since seeing Johnson off had shrunk his appetite for everything but liquids.

The Parade curved to the left down the slight hill. Shops and cafes lined the road to his right, and in front of the grandiose, brick and sandstone Victorian town hall to his left was a tall, ornate statue of Queen Victoria; closer to him, still on the left, was the elegant white Regent Hotel. Stone-edged beds full of bright flowers lined the wide pavement on that side of the road. Virtually opposite that, on his side of the road, was the Cadena Cafe.

Unconsciously, he pulled the flask from his pocket and took a sip.

First things first. Walk past, peer in, then have a look in the window of neighbouring Burton, a few doors down. Then go back for another look.

The sharp-suited slender mannequins in Burton's window made him feel old. And fat. With a sigh, he went to retrace his steps. And stopped.

An all too familiar figure moved towards him.

His heart thudded in his chest. No! Not him. Surely not!

Some primal instinct pushed him back towards Burton, close to the window, to peer at the suits. And watch the reflections behind.

Sure enough, the man, casually dressed in a tweed sports jacket and trousers, walked purposefully past. Out of the corner of his eye, George watched him head into the Cadena; he showed no signs of seeing, let alone recognising, anyone around him.

George checked his watch; his fingers trembled. It was just before seven o' clock.

Realisation tickled his backbone.

Of all the possibilities, he hadn't even considered it could be *him*. Someone lower down the pecking order, maybe. A rigger. A fitter, perhaps. An NCO at the absolute limits. Not someone of *his* rank.

It couldn't be coincidence. Could it?

His heart thumped against his chest.

No wonder testing had stopped. No wonder that second aircraft hadn't gone up for her flight.

How on earth could he get out of this mess? Everything he did just seemed to make things worse! He was trapped in a nightmare of his own making.

He fought to take a deep breath. His watch told him it was past seven now. No-one else had gone in.

That had to mean—

Panic rose. Vomit touched his tonsils. He couldn't go in there. He'd be recognised. Worse than that, he'd give the game away; he lived in Bromsgrove, he had no reason to be here, did he? At least, no innocent reason.

Oh, God. What was he going to do?

He'd heard from Kelly that the Air Ministry had commanded a teardown of the Vulcans. How quickly would Thompson's men—?

Thompson wanted to vindicate Campbell; that wasn't in doubt. How far would he go?

All the way, George realised. Thompson might not be able to poke around what little was left of XM568, but he sure as hell would pick over every last nut and bolt of XL433 and XL447. George shuddered.

What was he going to do?

Everything he'd worked for was going to crumble around him.

And it was all his own fault.

GORDON MENTALLY TICKED off the houses as he walked down the road towards the Millers' married quarter. Wellington Avenue was lined on both sides with reasonably sized, virtually identical semi-detached houses; he was sure he'd heard John mention theirs was three-bedroomed. Still, the houses were fairly modern, the lawns tidy enough.

He'd passed the accommodation blocks for airmen and women and the terraces for married NCOs; somewhere there'd be larger, semi-detached and detached houses for more senior ranks. House size was allocated by rank, not number of children; probably another reason Tony agitated for promotion.

The Millers' blue Ford Zephyr sat on the road outside.

Just as he went to knock on the door, John opened it. A mouthwatering aroma of roast beef wafted out. 'Come on in,' he said, with a grin.

John ushered him through the hallway into the open-plan living and dining room. Already, there was an open bottle of red wine on the table, with four filled glasses.

Four?

Before Gordon could ask, Miranda bustled through from the kitchen, resplendent in a bright striped and floral apron. 'Lovely to see you. It's been a funny old week.' She pulled him into a hug.

Unsure what to say, Gordon just returned her embrace.

'Help yourself to a glass.' She pointed to the dining table. 'I'll be back in a bit.' She gave John a look he couldn't quite read before disappearing in the direction of the scent of cooking food. Another voice murmured in the background.

John heaved a sigh. He grabbed two glasses and passed one to Gordon.

Gordon cursed. He knew he'd forgotten something. 'I was meant to bring another bottle, wasn't I?'

John drained his glass. 'Yes, but we've got one or two in, so we shan't be short tonight.' He gave Gordon a glance that somehow managed to combine anger, grief, and guilt.

'Isn't a roast more appropriate for a Sunday?' Gordon drank some wine.

John shrugged. 'Miranda ordered this in for... for a meal we'd planned. With Fraser. Tonight.'

'Ah.' Gordon inspected the deep red liquid sloshing around the crystal bowl. 'Waste not, want not. That's what he'd say, anyway.'

John smiled, sadly. 'Isn't it?'

'Gordon?'

He turned at the familiar voice.

Sophie came through the doorway, wearing a navy long-sleeved shift dress with a white Peter Pan collar. At least, that's what he thought it was called. Despite the sad cast to her face, her smile was broad and genuine.

'It's lovely to see you,' said Gordon, and meant it. It was the most natural thing in the world to give her a hug; she kissed his cheek.

'Miranda said to still come over, but I didn't know you were coming, too,' she said. 'I'm glad you're here.' Her arm lingered around his back; she seemed in no hurry to move away.

'John bumped into me yesterday,' said Gordon. 'He asked me then.'

John shrugged. He refilled his glass. 'Well, I hope you don't feel as if you're second choice.'

Gordon laughed. How could he put this without sounding callous? 'That's OK. I'm sure Fraser wouldn't begrudge me eating his dinner, given the situation.'

Sophie chuckled but looked down. She sipped her wine.

'John?' Miranda called from the kitchen. 'Darling? Can you come and help me, please?'

John emptied his glass, again. 'Excuse me.'

After a few moments, Sophie moved away from Gordon. Her cheeks were pink.

'I'm sorry,' said Gordon. 'I know I'm not—'

'Oh, stop it.' Sophie gave him a brave smile. She pulled a handkerchief from her sleeve and dabbed her eyes. 'As you said last night, life goes on. And I can't think of a better place to be than... than with our friends. His friends.'

Miranda's roast beef was absolutely superb. She'd done all the trimmings, too: crisp roast potatoes, tender carrots, and even the cabbage wasn't boiled into mush. As for her Yorkshire puddings... perfection.

Gordon lost track of how much wine they drank. All he knew was he was glad he could walk back to his room. If he could move, between all that food and the alcohol.

'That was delicious,' he managed.

John almost, but not quite, suppressed a belch. 'Compliments to the chef.'

Miranda beamed. She reached for her glass. 'You're welcome.'

'You may have to roll me out of here,' Gordon admitted.

'I'm glad I'm staying here tonight,' murmured Sophie. She covered her mouth as she yawned. 'I don't think I can move far.'

'Shall we swap to the comfy seats?' Miranda eased herself from her chair. 'Leave the dishes. They won't go anywhere.'

Gordon sat on one end of the burnt orange sofa; Sophie nestled on the other. Miranda curled up in a chair.

John shared the remains of the wine between their glasses, still at the dining table. 'Might as well finish it,' he muttered. One by one, he transferred their glasses to the teak coffee table, with all the exaggerated care of the inebriated. Then he perched in the one remaining easy chair.

'I wonder what next week will bring,' murmured Miranda, half to herself.

John froze.

'No flying,' said Gordon, before he could stop himself.

All eyes turned to him.

'I had a bit of a, well, chat with the Wingco.' To distract himself, Gordon picked up his glass. He already knew he'd regret this much wine tomorrow, but what the hell. He finished the last dregs. 'I told him I wanted some time to properly have a look at all the aircraft.'

Miranda exhaled slowly.

John closed his eyes for a long moment, his shoulders dropping.

'And I wish—' Gordon stopped. His throat closed up.

'I know,' said Sophie and John, simultaneously. They looked at each other and exchanged a sheepish smile.

'Whatever happened,' said John, 'it's not your fault.'

Sophie nodded. She suppressed another yawn but still managed to reach across and pat Gordon's hand. 'Please. Don't blame yourself.'

Unable to look at anyone, Gordon stared at his knees. What could he say, anyway? The room seemed to spin around him; the wine finally seeped through the meal, he supposed.

Miranda cleared her throat. When Gordon raised his head, she looked straight at him with a gaze that combined sympathy and, for some reason, admiration. 'We all know there's nothing on this earth that will stop you finding out what happened. And neither do any of us think what happened is your fault.' She clapped her hands together. 'Now, I think I could do with some coffee. Anyone else?'

Monday 10 August 1964

A FTER A FITFUL night, Gordon wearily threw on his uniform. Yesterday's hangover was only just receding. It was Monday, and a new week. Time to get going.

He went through his usual morning rituals on autopilot. His cooked breakfast in the mess was little more than texture, eaten out of habit rather than any real hunger. He was hungry, yes, but it only occurred to him as an afterthought.

As he headed to the engineering offices, his mind was elsewhere. What was he going to do this morning?

Put the finishing touches to the teardown plan, get Burroughs' approval, then start the long, slow, painstaking process of inspecting Banshee and every system or component interaction on '47 and '33.

And find out what happened to '68.

It couldn't have been pilot error. Fraser was the best pilot he knew. Even Hesketh-Shaw acknowledged that, and he was the boss. Gordon couldn't imagine the rest of them making such a huge mistake, either.

But something had gone wrong – whether it was human or aircraft.

'Oh, there you are,' said a voice behind him. It was Burroughs.

'Morning, sir,' said Gordon.

Judging by the bags under Burroughs' eyes, he'd slept about as well as Gordon had. He cleared his throat. 'We've had clearance this morning from the Air Ministry to disassemble Banshee ourselves, along with our teardown. Hawker Siddeley are keen to know how this thing—'

'Went wrong,' said Gordon flatly.

Burroughs nodded.

'What about Fli-Tek?'

Burroughs looked away. 'Screw Fli-Tek,' he muttered, so low Gordon almost didn't hear him. 'We've been ordered not to wait for them,' he said, louder. 'Just do it.'

HUNT RAISED HIS eyebrows when Gordon walked in. He pointed wordlessly to the cup of tea that already sat, steaming, on Gordon's desk.

'You're a lifesaver,' Gordon groaned. Then he grinned. 'Have you heard? We've got Air Ministry approval to take Banshee to bits.'

Hunt returned the grin. 'Oh ho. This will be fun.'

'Let's have a look at the aircraft and work out the sequence.' Gordon picked up his tea, blew on it, then took a sip. 'We've got one chance to get this right, and I don't want to waste it.' He owed it to Fraser and the rest of the crew of XM568. Whatever Fli-Tek were up to, he wanted to find out. Equally, if it wasn't down to Fli-Tek, he also wanted to know. That thought almost stopped him in his tracks, but it was true. Blaming innocent people wouldn't bring Fraser back. Neither would confronting the guilty, to be fair, but it would at least set his conscience at rest that he'd done all he could.

That meant doing things, as far as possible, by the book. If they found nothing, no-one would care how they'd done it; but if they found something, how they'd done it would be put under the microscope. There'd be something they'd miss, undoubtedly, but as far as possible, he wanted to minimise it.

'I spoke to the crew chiefs,' said Hunt. 'They're more than happy to help.'

'If they – or whoever they say can help – are around this morning, then let's get the plan nailed down.' Gordon smiled. 'If Fli-Tek have been taking us for fools, I bloody well want to prove it.'

Hunt returned the grin. 'Believe me, sir,' he said, 'we all do.'

BACK IN HIS room that evening, Gordon wondered what to do. On impulse, he reached for the bottle he'd found in Fraser's room. He'd brought a few things back for safekeeping; Fraser's room would now be cleared and ready for its next occupant. An odd thought. The alluring amber contents glistened as the whisky sloshed, tempting him to crack the bottle open and drain it dry.

With a sigh, he set it down on the bedside table. After a moment's thought, he grabbed it and hid it at the back of his wardrobe. Out of sight, out of mind, as his mum used to say.

If he didn't see it, he didn't have to think about it. Or where it came from.

Anger and grief tightened his throat again. Maybe he should go down the mess. Take his mind off things.

The trouble was, drinking wouldn't take his problems away. Even if it probably was the time-honoured way a man dealt with this kind of thing. Lost your best friend? Why not drink yourself into a stupor?

Except he wanted to know *why* he'd lost his best friend. However much he drank, it wouldn't help him answer that.

With a groan, he flung himself back on his bed and stared at the ceiling. Again. Every crack, every splodge, was etched on his memory, probably for eternity.

It was that or his wan face reflected in the mirror every morning as he tried to remove the stubble from his chin, though he usually ended up looking into his own bloodshot, drained, and empty brown eyes, wondering if the bags under them could possibly get any bigger.

Maybe a bit of a drink would help him sleep. Slow his mind down a bit.

Still, it hadn't been as bad a day as it could've been. Hunt and the others had come up with a workable sequence for inspecting the Vulcans and Banshee and then dismantling key parts. He'd spent the day flitting between them and chasing up the remaining paperwork the accident investigators required for the inquiry into '68.

Then there was Sqn Ldr Hesketh-Shaw…

It didn't escape comment by the others that they'd been scheduled to take '33 up for her flight the same day as Fraser's crash; John had muttered something about Trevor getting all uppity about the fact he felt they'd cheated death, and H-S just ignoring it.

Given some of his crew had served with distinction in the second world war, that felt a bit rich: Sqn Ldr Ted Radcliffe, his nav radar, first served on 109 Squadron as a Mosquito navigator and even had a Distinguished Flying Cross. You didn't disregard all that experience as if it were nothing. Yet that was what H-S was doing, if the mutterings were to be believed. Would their flight commander really be so dismissive?

In those dim and distant days of youth when he'd been the lowest of the low as Lancaster ground crew, death was… not different, as such, but…

Maybe he'd been different. It's easy to be blasé about risk when you're young and invincible. Not so easy when you're closing on – though some would say already in – middle age and looking ahead to an eventual future outside the service you'd known all your working life. Maybe he'd just grown up. Others hadn't been so lucky, but that was the way it was. If you dwelled on it, you'd never get on with things.

Fraser wasn't the first pilot he'd known die in an accident, but he was the first for a fair few years.

The question was, would the truth ever come out?

He groaned involuntarily.

Watson and his sidekick, Kelly, were due in tomorrow, and he had to be there. No doubt they'd have heard the news from the Air Ministry, and Watson was unlikely to be happy about it. Bundles of fun to look forward to.

What would be worse: dealing with Watson with a hangover or without a decent night's sleep?

With a grunt, he rolled off the bed and headed to the door. Right now, a hangover seemed the lesser of two evils.

Even considering it was a weeknight, the officers' mess was unusually subdued. The atmosphere crystallised as he walked up to the bar. He could feel the weight of people watching him; silence seemed to spread from him.

A quiet group in the corner turned: it was John, with a couple of H-S's flight crew – but not, he realised, the man himself. Tony was also absent. John waved a hand in welcome and gestured for him to join them.

Gordon ordered a pint of mild then walked over. 'Evening.'

Various mutters of welcome echoed.

Gordon felt at home with H-S's crew; even though they'd not been on the same squadrons or done the same roles, there was that common thread of the war between some of them. He might once have been a lowly erk, but Ted used to be an NCO, too.

'Not seen you in here much recently,' said John.

'No.' Gordon supped some beer.

'We were just comparing notes.' John drained his glass. 'On our aircraft.'

'Complete bloody farce, this project,' muttered Reg, H-S's nav plotter.

'How that Watson man is running this show I have no idea,' declared Ted. 'I asked him the other day about some HF system interference we saw on the ground, and he mumbled some utter tripe then walked away before I could challenge him. And as for whether this system is actually airworthy…'

'All you get is "it's development",' sneered Reg. 'As if that justifies anything.'

Trevor leant forward. 'H-S says—'

'H-S should know better. I know he does,' said Ted. 'But—'

They all stopped and glanced over their shoulders.

Reg held up a hand. 'Shush, now. Walls have ears, you know. And I'd like my pension in a few years.'

'Going back to Cyprus?' retorted Trevor.

'That bar in Luqa, more like,' muttered Ted.

Raucous laughter ensued. Gordon chuckled. He remembered that bar in The Gut all right; he'd spent many a happy, if drunken, night there on various detachments. There was that one time, when he was lucky enough to be on his tour as aircrew and an AEO, he'd had to rescue a certain now-Flt Lt who was then a junior co-pilot who'd got himself into a bit of a fix…

A good swig of beer loosened his constricting throat. Fraser – and the others at the time – swore him to absolute secrecy, but the tale had still got around. Albeit with a few minor, but amusing, modifications.

None of them ever looked at exotic dancers the same way again, that was for sure.

Reg headed to the bar and came back with a tray full of beers. He handed them around.

Gordon found he'd already emptied his first one without really noticing. With an internal sigh, he took the offered drink.

Ted leant close and murmured, 'Any news about…'

Gordon drank some beer. 'Not much I can repeat. You know we've got permission to take Banshee to bits, now?'

The men exchanged glances. Some nodded.

'About time,' said Reg.

'The chaps have done the preliminary tests and what-have-you today, so we're going to start properly tomorrow.'

'Aren't Fli-Tek coming in tomorrow?' asked John.

'Yeah.' Gordon scowled.

'Oooh.' Ted grimaced, but there was no doubting the mischievous glint in his eyes. 'That'll be fun.'

Gordon snorted. 'Won't it.'

'Can we watch?' asked Trevor, smirking.

'If it's anything like last time, I'll end up calling the Wingco to come and deal with him.'

'I heard he got down a week's worth of gin,' said John.

'What, the Wingco?' Ted grinned.

'I would, if I had to babysit Watson,' grunted Reg.

John's face grew serious. 'Is it true there are big differences between our aircraft?'

Gordon sighed again. He rocked a hand. 'I mean, every Vulcan is unique to a point. But… so far, we're seeing more significant differences than I'd expect. Particularly where Banshee interfaces with things. And we've not really started the teardown yet.'

John exchanged a sombre glance with Gordon. He picked up the full pint Reg had stuck in front of him.

'I'm not sure if it's good or bad our aircraft are all different,' murmured Reg.

'Maybe we'll just blow up in a different way,' said Trevor.

There were a few moments of uncomfortable silence.

Trevor cleared his throat. He stared into his pint and didn't look up as he said, 'H-S is being odd, though.'

Ted and Reg nodded.

'Last time he was like this, it was Offutt the other year,' said Reg. 'We pasted the Yanks that time, though.'

'Their beer's a bit weak. Didn't stop us sampling plenty just to make sure,' added Trevor.

'Oh, that bar. That girl took a real shine to him, didn't she?' said Reg.

'I reckon he must've—' began Trevor.

Ted coughed pointedly.

'But—' tried Trevor again.

'Remember Lola?' snapped Ted.

Trevor glowered but shut up.

Gordon recalled the unspoken rule of "Ten Degrees West"; that what happened on Western Rangers stayed on Western Rangers, between the crews. It was a matter of confidentiality. He'd never misbehaved that much, but some of the men took advantage of a bit of freedom and got themselves into some potentially sticky situations. It sounded like H-S's crew had certainly done that.

Ted eyed Gordon over his pint but didn't drink. Instead, he said, 'You look like you're thinking.'

'I'm thinking lots of things,' admitted Gordon. 'Top of the list is trying to get a straight answer out of Watson about what's going on with these systems.'

'When do you think you'll get that?' asked Ted.

Gordon drained his pint. 'When hell freezes over.'

Wednesday 12 August 1964

AFTER A MORNING check of his admin, Gordon buried himself in the bomb bay of XL447. Of the two surviving aircraft, this had had the most issues up till now, and he wanted to know what was going on. SEngO was happy with the plan they'd drawn up; various techs were already hard at work on both aircraft.

Hangar 3 was quiet and solemn. No-one spoke in anything more than a whisper. Tools clinked as he poked around '47. Another team worked on '33. Even the abrasive rattle of a ratchet seemed subdued.

Strictly speaking, as an officer, he shouldn't be anywhere near the oily bits, but he didn't care. Right now, he itched to be doing something constructive – well, de-constructive, in this case – and if he'd finally got the permission he wanted to strip these units down, he wasn't going to waste it.

Gordon looked over his shoulder to see West approaching; he looked positively bewildered to see his CO, sleeves rolled up and tools in hand.

'Morning,' said Gordon. 'Fancy stripping down a Banshee unit with me?'

Gordon rapidly conceded that West and the chaps were much quicker at unfastening nuts and bolts than him, and turned his attention to the bomb bay doors. He trailed his hands over the riveted inner panels. Shards of broken paint and tiny bits of swarf pricked his fingers where dings and dents gouged the metal; more, and deeper, than he remembered from the last time he'd been up close. The marks were just underneath where Banshee sat. He reached up and yanked the lowest part of the mechanism; it clanked and wobbled on its mountings.

'He… hey! Leave that alone!' Shoes slapped on the concrete floor. Gordon ducked out from under the bomb bay to see Watson, red and sweating profusely, waving his hands in outrage.

He savoured the moment. 'Actually, Mr Watson, we can. We've had orders to.'

'Bu… bu…' Watson gasped. His pudgy fingers planted on '47's bomb bay door to steady himself.

'Squadron Leader Burroughs told us yesterday morning. Orders from the Air Ministry.' Gordon glanced at his men; though their faces were still focused on their work, their heads tilted to listen. 'Avro, well, Hawker Siddeley—'

'Have nothing to do with this!'

'Really?'

Spittle flicked from the corners of Watson's mouth; his face reddened. 'It's not their technology!'

'But it is their aircraft.' Gordon drew himself up. 'And our colleagues were killed.'

Watson blinked, then flung himself under the Vulcan, arms flailing—

Gordon yanked the man's shoulder backwards. 'You so much as attempt to interfere with my team, and I'll have you thrown offsite.' He hadn't meant to shout, but his voice echoed around the suddenly silent hangar.

'You can't do this!' protested Watson.

Gordon picked up a spanner and waved it in Watson's face. 'Watch me.'

Watson slapped the spanner out of Gordon's hand. It clanked off the bomb bay door then hit the floor, ringing like a bell.

Without another word, Gordon pushed Watson away; taken by surprise, the man stumbled. Gordon clamped a hand around Watson's wrist and yanked his arm up behind his back. Watson's shoes squealed on the concrete as he struggled; Gordon planted him unceremoniously belly-down on the floor.

'Show your face in here again without my permission, and I'll—' Gordon began.

'What the hell is going on here?' Hesketh-Shaw glared at them as if they were scuffling schoolboys.

Gordon let go and stood up. He'd not even heard the man walk in. He unconsciously wiped his hands on his trousers. Watson staggered upright, tie skew-whiff and shirt untucked. Damp patches darkened under his armpits.

Watson opened his mouth, but Hesketh-Shaw held up a hand. 'Mr Thompson,' he snapped. 'Explain.'

Gordon took a deep breath. 'He came running in here as if he owns the place, ordering me and my men to leave Banshee alone. As you know, sir, we've had orders to take Banshee and these aircraft apart regardless. I don't appreciate some civilian pushing me and smacking tools out of my hands, either. Never mind the Vulcans, it could have hit someone like he hit me.'

Hesketh-Shaw's eyebrow lifted. 'Mr Watson, is this true?'

'W… well… I didn't know about the orders…'

'Did you strike Mr Thompson?'

In the hushed hangar, even Gordon felt the weight of his men glaring at Watson.

Suddenly aware he was in a hostile environment, Watson shrank back a little. 'Um… in the heat of the moment I may have overreacted…'

Hesketh-Shaw gave Gordon a look that said they'd discuss this later; inwardly, Gordon groaned.

'Mr Watson, you and I shall continue our conversation outside. Mr Thompson, carry on.'

'Sir.'

Gordon watched Hesketh-Shaw tow a still-reluctant Watson out of the hangar. Once the door thudded closed behind them, he rubbed his eyes and pinched the bridge of his nose. Barely ten thirty in the morning, and his temples throbbed with what was going to be a humdinger of a headache in an hour's time.

He turned.

His men, who had been watching the show in silence, snapped back to their tasks, avoiding his gaze.

Despite himself, he half-smiled. 'You heard him. Let's crack on.'

MUCH AS HE itched to take Banshee apart himself, there was one task he had to do that he hadn't been looking forward to: chasing up the remnants of XM568's paperwork for the Accident Investigations Branch, who were investigating alongside the RAF Board of Inquiry. They were due to retrieve the relevant documents tomorrow.

Papers sorted, Gordon was about to check on progress in the hangar when there was a knock on his door. It opened before he could speak.

Hesketh-Shaw strode in and sat down.

Gordon swallowed his first, sarcastic, response. Hesketh-Shaw could potentially make his life very difficult, given what happened. 'Afternoon, sir.'

'Good afternoon. What have your men found?'

Gordon waved at the piles. 'I was about to check. I've just got things in order for the investigators, sir.'

Hesketh-Shaw surveyed the stacks. 'Thank you. I wish ops were as organised as you.'

'I try.' Gordon shut his mouth and waited.

Hesketh-Shaw studied the desk for several seconds before finally looking up. 'I've had Mr Watson's side of the story from this morning. Tell me yours. Please.'

With a sigh, Gordon related exactly what had happened. Hesketh-Shaw listened, impassive, though there was a hint of a smile when he described planting Watson on the floor.

'And I could ask any of your men about this?' he asked.

'Feel free.' Gordon shrugged. 'Go out there now, if you like.'

Hesketh-Shaw shook his head. 'I don't think that's necessary.'

Gordon's eyebrows shot up in surprise.

'Do you know, he claimed he hadn't hit you at first?'

Gordon snorted in derision. 'Of course he would.'

'Funnily enough, he changed his tune when I reminded him how many witnesses there were.'

'Why would he come running at me like that? What was I supposed to do? I didn't have time to do much else. I just had to make sure he wasn't a threat to me, my team, or the aircraft.'

'So far as I'm concerned, you did the right thing. Perhaps a little roughly, but we can't have men going off half-cocked like that. Even civilians.' Hesketh-Shaw glanced away. 'Especially with the accident investigation ongoing.'

'How much of an investigation is it going to be, though?'

Hesketh-Shaw pursed his lips. 'Hawker Siddeley have asked us to determine the exact nature of the interactions between Banshee and the Vulcan's systems. I reminded Mr Watson of this.' He met Gordon's eyes with a disconcertingly direct stare. 'I see you were taking charge of dismantling Banshee on '47.'

Gordon dropped his gaze, unable to look anywhere but at the documents waiting for review. 'I just wish I'd done the same on '68 last week,' he murmured.

'I know.' Hesketh-Shaw stared down, reflective. 'I've made it clear to Mr Watson that as a visitor to our site, he must abide by our rules. If there's any further misbehaviour on his part, he'll be banned.'

'Thank you, sir.'

Hesketh-Shaw paused. 'Tell me, were you ever in the wrestling team?'

Gordon blinked, confused. 'Er… no?'

A rare, genuine smile creased Hesketh-Shaw's face. 'Pity. I think we'd win if you were.'

Friday 14 August 1964

GORDON TRIED TO pull his stomach in but failed. It had been a while since he'd worn his formal Number Ones; the trousers were a bit snugger around the middle than he remembered. Perhaps the cleaners shrunk them, or something.

Funerals for XM568's crew were taking place over the next couple of weeks. Fg Off Brian Grice was being buried by his family, back in Sheffield; Flt Lt Mike Duffy's funeral would be in Tonbridge, Kent; Flt Lt Ken Markham would be interred next to his father, he'd heard, somewhere near Peterborough. Flt Lt Jim Farrell's family were all in Northern Ireland; he didn't know what would be happening, yet.

And in his will, Flt Lt Fraser Campbell had left express wishes to be buried in the place nearest where he served.

Gordon couldn't believe the Campbell family actually had a private mausoleum, up near St Andrews. It shocked him even more to realise Fraser wanted no part in it. Fraser had a will, and the old family firm of lawyers would be executors… but that was as far as it went.

To be fair, there didn't seem to be any living relatives left, sad as that was. While Gordon's parents and grandparents had long since passed, his sister still lived in Hackney with her kids, and he saw them every few months. Various cousins were dotted all around Essex, and he saw them most Christmases. It seemed Fraser never had that; whether he wanted it was another matter. Everyone was different.

Martinford itself was a little hamlet that must have been sleepy until the RAF moved in next door. The village centre clustered around a small green just off the main road, where the quaint half-timbered butcher, baker, and grocer faced off against the Victorian post office and pub. The bright white and blue petrol station sat a few hundred yards further down the main road towards Stratford; opposite it was the village school. A few neat 1930s bay-windowed bungalows stood out like sore thumbs, interspersed between thatched cottages and tiny Victorian terraces.

The buff stone church of St John's nestled amongst several tall trees. It sat on a patch of raised ground, encircled by a low, grey stone wall. The tall square tower, buttressed at the bottom and matched in height by a magnificent old yew tree, rose to a top that reminded him of medieval castles, but with an arched window high on each wall. About a third of the way down the front face of the tower, a faded blue clock with burnished gold numerals glinted in the late summer sunshine.

On a neatly manicured lawn in front of the church itself was a white granite obelisk, perhaps five feet tall: Martinford's war memorial. Names, harsh in black capitals, stood out on the plinths around its base. Bright, colourful flowers surrounded it. Clearly, someone took pride in keeping it tidy.

Would there ever be a Cold War memorial? For as sure as anything, men were dying, even though active, hot combat wasn't happening.

If it ever did, memorials would be pointless. Turned to ash like everything else in a nuclear holocaust.

Gordon shook himself. Thinking like that didn't help anything. What was he doing, if he didn't believe he was helping to stop such a thing from ever happening?

'Gordon?'

He turned. It was Sophie. She wore a black shift dress and a wide-brimmed black hat. Already, bits of eyeliner and mascara dotted under her eyes; she swallowed and tried a brave smile. 'I'm glad to see you.' She rushed forward and flung her arms around him.

Without thinking, he wrapped his arms around her and held her close. Her floral scent drifted in the air. 'It's good to see you, too,' he said.

'Sophie, dear!' John's wife, Miranda, hurried over, also clad from head to foot in black. John, stiff in his Number One uniform and hat firmly on his head, exchanged a nod with Gordon as he joined the group.

'Miranda. I'm still not sure this feels real.' Sophie moved out of Gordon's embrace, though her fingers still brushed his hand.

'I know. I was just thinking about that party, eh?' Miranda shot a slightly mischievous glance at her husband, who struggled to look innocent.

'Flight crews only,' John murmured to Gordon. 'At ours a few weeks ago.'

'Even Tony?' quipped Gordon.

'Shh!' John hissed. He glanced around.

Miranda chuckled. 'And June. Bless her. Tony's like another kid sometimes.'

Sophie's brow wrinkled till memory dawned. 'Ah, I remember. He's got curly hair, hasn't he?'

'Yes. That's the only time you've had the pleasure, isn't it?'

Sophie nodded. She looked at Gordon, as if expecting him to add to the conversation.

He didn't bother hiding his confusion. 'Have I missed something?'

Miranda raised her eyebrows meaningfully; John searched the faces nearby, then nodded. He sighed.

'Didn't Fraser tell you?' asked Sophie.

Gordon shook his head.

'There was a bit of a ding dong,' said John. His voice was low, and his eyes scanned the gathering blue crowd. 'Between Fraser and Tony. H-S and Sophie here dragged Fraser one way, June dragged Tony the other. Outside.'

Gordon whistled.

'Tony started it,' said Sophie, somewhat defensively.

'That I can believe,' said Gordon.

Miranda and John exchanged a glance and a sad half-smile.

Silence spread, flowing like a river. Ripples of conversation stilled.

From somewhere, Gordon had no idea where, appeared Padre Dick in flowing white robes. They should go in.

St John's was much bigger inside than it looked on the outside. Bright colours streamed through the stained-glass windows, warm on the tiled floor. Most pews were taken, and he knew the majority of those in them.

What he had to do next weighed on him. He fingered the notes in his pocket. He couldn't do it. But he had to.

The organist at the back of the church began to play. Measured, even footsteps approached. He didn't need to turn to know these were the pallbearers, shouldering their sombre cargo. Chief Andrews had volunteered; so had Hunt and a couple of the others.

Gordon stared straight ahead as the coffin processed past. Strange to think that oak box, with shiny brass fittings, held what was left of his friend—

No. Don't think about that. Not now.

He was dimly aware of Sophie next to him dabbing her eyes, fighting her own tears.

What happened to that aircraft? This shouldn't be happening. Fraser shouldn't be in that box.

Automatically, his gaze found Watson; seated near the front, next to Wing Cdr Merrick.

He must have made a noise, or something; Sophie squeezed his hand, tightly. He didn't even know she'd taken hold of him. He blinked. The sudden wetness on his cheeks surprised him.

After the hymn, and the reading given by John, it was his turn.

Hesketh-Shaw asked him a few days ago if he would give the eulogy. Of everyone in the squadron, he knew Fraser the best; and again, Gordon admitted to himself Fraser probably wouldn't want anyone else to do it, either.

Gordon steeled himself as he headed up to the lectern. Padre Dick gave him a sympathetic smile and touched him reassuringly on the shoulder. 'You can do this,' he whispered.

Gordon raised his eyes to the gilded crucifix above the altar, in a silent prayer for help.

He took a deep breath. Turned to face the congregation. Unfolded his notes. And began.

'I first met Fraser when he was a junior co-pilot, fresh out of the OCU…'

He described Fraser. His keenness to learn. His desire to be the best pilot he could be. How he felt that was his duty – and should be everyone else's. How much he sometimes annoyed the rest of his crew; a few people chuckled at that. But also, how they'd forged a friendship that transcended normal trade barriers as they learned their roles together.

Much as he tried not to look at faces, or make eye contact as he talked, he couldn't help it.

Tony stared fixedly at the back of the pew in front of him, head bowed and wetness glistening on his cheeks; his wife, bright blonde hair hidden under a geometric black and white scarf, looked at the coffin with glassy eyes and an expression somewhere between relief, guilt, and fear.

Hesketh-Shaw sat next to a willowy brunette, elegant despite her sombre clothes; she held his hand tightly but kept her eyes firmly downcast. Hesketh-Shaw's gaze met Gordon's; grief contorted his face for a split second before he regained control and looked away, frowning.

John stared, wet-eyed, up at the crucifix; he blinked, slowly, and half shook his head. Miranda gently wiped tears from the corners of her eyes.

Tears poured down Sophie's face, though she made nearly no sound.

Merrick's face betrayed no emotion whatsoever, though he looked alternately at Fraser's coffin and the cross. His gloved hands were folded neatly on his lap. A middle-aged woman who had to be Mrs Merrick sat next to him; her blue-rinsed hair peeked out of a black turban-style hat. She, too, held her hands primly on her lap, but her eyes glistened with sadness.

Watson looked anywhere but at the coffin or Gordon; his hands constantly twisted a handkerchief around and around as his gaze shifted from place to place.

'Old Man Turnbull – who I know some of you knew, too – had his work cut out with us to start with, but by the end of our tour, he said we were a team to scare the Ivans witless.' He paused. 'Because we sure as hell scared him.'

The church erupted in laughter.

Gordon finally allowed himself a look at the coffin. The church quieted.

'Goodbye, old friend.' His voice cracked. 'Till we meet again.'

All he could focus on, as he returned to his seat, was Sophie's smile. Despite her tears, she almost looked happy. 'You were wonderful,' she whispered brokenly. 'Fraser might even forgive you for that last line.'

That did it. He screwed up his eyes, but her shuddering in grief next to him shattered the dam of his emotions. Tears wouldn't stop running down his cheeks. As they fell, anger rose. It simmered within, underscoring the hymns that followed. His mouth moved, sound came out, but it all seemed disconnected from reality.

All he could think, and feel, was that this should not be happening. He should have done something; what, he didn't know, but he should have stopped this from happening. Somehow. It would not happen again, if he had the slightest thing to do with it. Not on his watch. He owed it to Fraser.

Fury and guilt bubbled through his veins as they headed out to the quiet churchyard, a few hundred yards from the church itself.

The late summer afternoon was almost idyllic. Birds twittered in the distant trees; the grass was lush and neatly trimmed, all the graves well-kept. Some had flowers.

The hole destined to contain the mortal remains of Flt Lt Fraser Campbell, though, didn't yet. The coffin lay by the dark cut in the earth, flowers on the top.

A familiar rumble echoed in the air. It swelled; the ground trembled.

All heads turned to see a brilliant white Vulcan roar a few hundred feet over the church. Even the air vibrated from the sheer force of thrust. Her wings dipped right, then left, then she howled skyward, soaring in a spiral climb. Soon, she was barely a spec among the clouds, her corkscrew tracks lined with exhaust smoke. The noise faded, leaving a faint scent of burnt avtur.

'That howl,' murmured John.

Gordon nodded; no aircraft announced itself quite like the Vulcan. It was good of the OCU to fly and pay their respects.

Sophie wiped tears away and gave Gordon a smile.

THE REST OF the day passed in a blur. Everyone had been invited back to the officers' mess for the wake. Sophie was staying with John and Miranda for the night, a small thing that Gordon was thankful for.

Alcohol flowed freely, but for once, he didn't feel like drinking. Everyone else seemed to be making up for him, though; the air echoed with boisterous chatter and swirled with cigarette smoke.

Sophie sat next to Miranda, and John stood by her; June, Tony's wife, was nearby, as was the woman who had to be Mrs Hesketh-Shaw. Tony himself was with the Wingco.

Hesketh-Shaw eased his way through the crowd to join them. He exchanged a nod with Gordon. 'I should've realised you flew with Old Man Turnbull.'

'Ha. Yeah. I think a lot of us did.'

'He expected a lot from us, but… it did us good.'

'Yeah.' Gordon inspected his glass of orange juice.

'Fraser kept that bit quiet, though.' Hesketh-Shaw gave a lopsided smile.

Gordon chuckled. 'There are a few stories I could tell he wouldn't thank me for.'

'Old Man Turnbull has stories like that about most of us.'

'Yeah, well. We've all got skeletons in the closet.'

Hesketh-Shaw stilled; he frowned at Gordon and opened his mouth as if to say something else.

'Well,' interrupted Miranda, 'I think me and Sophie here are going to call it a day.'

Sophie looked exhausted, and that wasn't just down to the smeared traces of mascara surrounding her red, teary eyes; she trembled slightly as she stood, despite holding onto Miranda's arm. 'Thank you so much for today. It… it means a lot. If you'll excuse me?'

'Of course,' said Hesketh-Shaw, smoothly. He exchanged a look with his wife; she murmured something into Miranda's ear before Miranda gently guided Sophie away.

Gordon's conscience poked him as he watched the two women carefully make their way through the crowd to the door. Today's tasks hadn't been the only thing weighing on him. He made his excuses to

H-S and made it outside just as Miranda and Sophie stepped onto the path.

Gordon reached into a pocket. 'Um. Sophie. Before you go…'

She turned. Miranda glanced over her shoulder, confused. Both women stopped.

He thrust the small navy velvet cube out in front of him and pushed the words out before his throat refused to let him speak. 'Um. I found this. By Fraser's car keys. I'd never seen it before. I suppose he was going to, er, bring it with him, that night. And whatever happens, I know Fraser would want you to have this.'

Sophie's brow wrinkled, but she gingerly picked the box from his fingers. At his encouraging nod, she cracked it open.

For several long moments, she stared at the ring inside. Her face, her body, was still as a statue.

Tears filled her eyes. Her hand trembled as she closed the box.

Without another word, she bolted down the path. Miranda frowned at Gordon then ran to follow her.

Gordon stared after them. His heart plummeted to the floor. Somehow, he couldn't move.

Friday 18 November 2022

THAT LUNCHTIME, QUENTIN swapped his usual snatched sandwich at his desk for something else; he had an important rendezvous. Despite the rain and grey skies, he weaved his way through the busy city streets and found the cafe Valentin had recommended. It was small but bustling: a board outside proudly proclaimed various baked delights. A welcome refuge from the dreary, mild damp.

Valentin had ordered a cafetière of coffee and was seated at a corner table. Quentin briskly ordered a cream cheese and salmon bagel then went to join him.

'My friend.' Valentin grinned broadly as Quentin sat. He poured some coffee while Quentin shrugged off his jacket.

'Val.' Quentin picked up a small cup of steaming coffee and sighed. 'You're having problems?'

Quentin rocked a hand. 'One or two. Some I can ameliorate, others… no.' He sipped his drink; the coffee was good and flavourful. 'But I do have some news.'

'Good? Bad?' Valentin sat forward, eager.

'Awkward.'

Quentin had spent the morning re-reading the post-mortem report; as Farnsworth said, it was impossible to separate out their man from where and how he was found. He still hadn't quite recovered from the brusqueness with which Farnsworth had rejected his offer. Perhaps he'd underestimated the man.

He'd certainly underestimated the challenges Martinford brought…

One thing stood out with brutal clarity.

Quentin cleared his throat, leaned closer, and lowered his voice. 'Reading between the lines, our mystery man was executed.'

Valentin's eyes widened, but he didn't speak.

'The post-mortem obviously doesn't go so far as to say directly, but our man was likely to have been sitting on the floor when he was shot in the head by a person standing in front of him.' Quentin paused while a waitress brought him his lunch. He delicately picked up half of his bagel. 'It also appears there wasn't that much of a struggle beforehand.'

Valentin sat back. Uncharacteristic seriousness lined his face; he nodded as he absorbed the news.

Quentin took a bite of his bagel and chewed, considering his words. 'The RAF have confirmed one of their officers, stationed at Martinford at the time, disappeared off the face of the earth around the same time as our man died. A Vulcan pilot as well. Squadron Leader Charles Hesketh-Shaw.'

'Is he the man?' Valentin sipped his coffee.

Quentin chuckled. 'It would be nice and neat if he was.'

'You think he isn't?'

'Even the RAF think he isn't.'

Valentin frowned, taken aback.

Quentin finished another bite of bagel. He wasn't looking forward to admitting this. 'Having seen the photo of… your gentleman in question… I would say his build and age is not dissimilar to the body found.'

Valentin slowly nodded. 'I see.'

'One could argue whether he should have been in this country, doing the job he was doing. However, there are ways of dealing with such things. You recall the case of Gordon Lonsdale and the Portland Spy Ring in 1961, I think?'

Valentin nodded. 'He was arrested, charged, put on trial and then imprisoned for spying, yes?'

'Yes.' Quentin idly tapped his fingers on his coffee cup. 'All without revealing his true identity. He was exchanged in a spy-swap for Greville Wynne a few years later. Still, it shows there were ways and means of dealing with such cases that were all above board. By the book.'

Farnsworth's comments from Tuesday night flashed through his head. He ignored their sting.

Valentin stared into his cup, as if shocked. 'This cannot be right,' he murmured.

'I know. It hardly seems possible.' Quentin considered. Yes, Colonel Oleg Kuryakov should not have been in the country. Neither should he have been participating in espionage, under a false identity. But he was, and he was certainly not the only one ever to have done so, before or since.

They sat in silence, drinking coffee, for several moments.

Quentin cleared his throat. 'I suppose we have to consider others he may have been working with. Perhaps they had their own careers, their own reputations to be concerned with. Doing things by the book invariably means bringing one's own misdeeds to light. Whichever way you wish to look at this, they certainly hid things for a while.'

'I don't recognise the name Hesketh-Shaw.' Valentin pulled out his mobile phone and tapped away. 'I will ask my friends to check.'

'Thank you.' Quentin paused. 'Do you know much more about the job he was doing? Any specifics?'

Valentin gave an exaggerated and insincere shrug. 'Not much.'

'We seem to have wiped everything from our archives,' Quentin muttered.

'It does not exist?'

'Officially? No. Nothing happened at Martinford. Ever. It was all rather dull. No secret projects or anything of that sort. Even the squadron concerned barely merits a mention in the histories.'

'Someone knew something, then.'

Quentin nodded. 'It certainly looks that way.' There was no other way to think about it; not that he wanted to speak the words aloud.

That the British state had, if not actively directed, then indirectly sanctioned the murder of a foreign espionage agent, without any kind of trial or due process being followed. Whatever the truth, it was increasingly evident there was a subsequent cover-up.

Valentin met Quentin's gaze; the set of his eyes, and the nod he gave, said it all.

ALEX LISTENED TO the recordings he'd taken, with permission, during his last chat with Wing Cdr Miller, and made notes. As co-pilot on the junior crew, Miller's perspective on life in 449 Sqn was possibly skewed, and time would no doubt have smoothed the bumpiest memories, but… it was all he had.

Miller didn't camouflage his dislike of his captain, Flt Lt Brookes. He made no effort to paint him in a positive light, either; the best you could say, with the passage of the years, was neutral.

Hesketh-Shaw was an interesting character; slightly older, and not one for all the fun and games some younger officers enjoyed in the mess. His crew of seniors, as Miller put it, were generally widely respected throughout Martinford, not just 449 Sqn; with a couple of World War Two veterans among them, they had valuable experience.

Campbell, on the other hand, came across as a bit of a Marmite character. Some, like Miller and Flt Lt Thompson, got on well with him. Others, like Brookes, repeatedly clashed. Hesketh-Shaw acknowledged Campbell's flying ability but seemed to be on the fence about everything else.

Miller had asked outright if he thought the body was Hesketh-Shaw; Alex had pulled a face. Much as he considered his words carefully, there was no way to avoid saying he doubted it.

That begged the question of just where did Sqn Ldr Hesketh-Shaw go?

Miller wasn't sure. Wingco Merrick retired: whether he chose to or not, who knew, but that's what the men were told. He saw some of the others around, in passing, but…

Miller had paused, considering.

'There was one time,' he said eventually, 'where I was sure I'd seen H-S. Or at least, his double. I was on an exchange posting some fifteen years or so later, out in the US, and some Canadian air force officers joined my USAF colleagues for a different event. There was a lieutenant-colonel around the right age who could've been his spitting image. Not that I got a chance to speak to him.' Miller had sniffed and stared out into the middle distance for a few moments. 'Still. Some people have doppelgängers, don't they? My sister was always being mistaken for another girl in her class at school. And the mind can play tricks.'

As for the mysterious Banshee... Alex shared a bit of detail about what they'd found under Martinford alongside the body.

Miller explained it was common knowledge at the time that Martinford, as a former WW2 airfield, had numerous hidden buildings and crevices; gun emplacements, defences... and the bunker. They were mostly left to rot as curiosities and remnants of a not-so-distant past.

The Banshee project ended around the time Works and Bricks announced the bunker area was dangerous, and no-one should go near it. A number of bulldozers and tipper lorries full of earth arrived on site a few days after that, apparently to make the area safe.

By then, though, Miller, along with the rest of 449 Sqn, waited to be re-posted. It didn't need to be said that their time at Martinford was something to be glossed over; truth be told, most of them were happy to forget it and move on.

'There's one other thing that always bothered me,' said Miller. 'The company that developed Banshee – Fli-Tek. I don't think they got off scot-free, but I think they went under after this. It served them right, frankly, for putting such underdeveloped and dangerous equipment on our aircraft.' He paused. 'Gordon had such battles with them, and the brass hats. One of their engineers, he wasn't so bad, but George Watson was the absolute worst. Fraser knew him from previous flying, and disliked him, and the feeling was mutual. Gordon didn't think much of him, either.' Miller blew out a long breath. 'Gordon pushed for the squadron to stop all flying after Fraser's crash, and somehow – I don't know how – got permission to dismantle and examine every part of Banshee and the two remaining aircraft.'

'What happened then?'

Miller paused. 'All hell broke loose.'

Monday 24 August 1964

ORDON GLANCED AT his watch. This morning, at nine o'clock sharp, Fli-Tek and others more senior than him were meeting with the Accidents Investigation Branch; he'd been told to be ready to be called but also that he might not be required.

That didn't mean he was capable of doing anything remotely resembling work while he waited, though. Instead, he stared blankly into space, unable to shift the leaden dread that sat in his gut.

Put simply, he didn't trust Watson as far as he could throw him – well, not even that far.

There was a knock on his door.

One of the admin NCOs stuck his head in. 'Sorry to bother you, sir, but the Accidents Investigation Branch would like to see you. Now.'

THE NCO USHERED Gordon into the ops room that had been commandeered for the inquiry.

A few men were seated around the table: Hesketh-Shaw, Wing Cdr Merrick, Watson, Kelly, and another two men in sober black suits.

Merrick stood; a pretence of a smile crossed his face. 'Ah, Mr Thompson. Take a seat.'

'Thank you, sir.' Gordon took the one remaining spare chair, next to the Wingco. Watson whispered something to his colleague, then gave Gordon a shiny, smug smile.

Unease prickled the back of his neck. Unbidden, Fraser's words ran across his mind: '*Watson's a vindictive bastard. You might not even know why you pissed him off, but he won't have forgotten it. And he'll get you back when you least expect it, at the worst possible time. He likes to make sure you know he's got the better of you.*'

Gordon's heart sank. What had he done that Watson could—

Oh.

'Mr Thompson, you're the Officer Commanding Avionics and Integration for this project, is that correct?' said one of the black-suited men. He wore thick, square horn-rimmed glasses.

'Yes, sir.'

'I understand from these documents and from Mr Watson and Mr Kelly here that you allowed your team to perform an unauthorised inspection and partial disassembly of Banshee on XM568 on the twentieth of July of this year.'

No point denying it. 'Yes, sir.'

Watson blinked, but momentary surprise didn't dent his smugness. Kelly raised his eyebrows.

'And why did you do that?' The investigator asked smoothly.

'As I explained in my report, which should be in that pack, the arrays had detached from the main body of the unit without any other interference.'

The investigator nodded. Peering through his glasses, he shuffled one of the stacks of paper until he found what he was looking for.

'You'll also see we performed the same operation on XL447, for the same reason.' Gordon tried not to bite his lip. He was conscious of his terseness, but he didn't want to walk into whatever trap Watson had set. It was all too easy to talk himself into trouble he couldn't talk his way back out of.

Watson leant as far forward as his gut allowed. 'You allowed untrained personnel – without even informing us—'

The investigator coughed. 'You were aware of the arrangement, were you not, Mr Thompson?'

Gordon swallowed. 'Yes, sir.'

The investigator made a note. 'But you didn't inform Fli-Tek, nor request their permission or assistance?'

'I knew Mr Watson was due onsite that morning. I took the decision he could be informed then.' At that, Watson looked so full of his own self-importance Gordon was amazed the man didn't explode.

'Even though your men aren't trained by Fli-Tek in handling these delicate electronics and components?' asked the investigator.

'A Vulcan *is* a collection of delicate electronics and components,' said Gordon. 'She contains some of the most sophisticated jamming and radar equipment in the world as it is. She's a cutting-edge aircraft. My men know how to treat her, sir.'

'Nonetheless,' said Merrick, 'this was unauthorised action on your part.' Ice could've formed on the edges of his words.

Part of Gordon whispered that he should just shut up and take the kicking, but most of him was determined to go down fighting. He'd promised his men he'd take the flak for what he knew was the right decision, but that didn't mean he had to roll over straight away. 'So, should this happen again, I'm to order my men to let the expensive pieces of trial system just fall to the ground or bounce off the interior of the aircraft until Fli-Tek can be with us?'

The investigator took off his glasses. Merrick gave Gordon a distinctly cold stare. To Gordon's surprise, Hesketh-Shaw met his gaze: a smile shadowed his lips for a second.

A memory nudged him. 'Fli-Tek were immediately granted access to our hangar, the parts, and the aircraft, as soon as they were onsite. I didn't want to hide what we'd done. It isn't in anyone's interests to develop an "us and them" attitude.'

Watson sniffed.

Hesketh-Shaw cleared his throat. 'I wish to add that I then asked Mr Thompson to perform a similar inspection on XL433, also without Fli-Tek's pre-agreement, prior to the trial I performed on the twenty-first of July.'

At that, Watson shot a surprised, furious glare at Hesketh-Shaw.

Gordon realised his mouth was open, and closed it.

'By that time, we were present,' Watson managed. 'That's not part of what we're discussing here.' With an air of triumph, he pointed at Gordon. 'The point is this man and those under his command were messing about with my system. I raised this at the highest level afterwards, too. They assured us nothing had been altered on either aircraft, but how do we know?'

'Are you accusing me of damaging it?' snapped Gordon.

'Are you saying you know exactly what you removed, adjusted, or refitted?' retorted Watson.

'Well, as one of your colleagues signed off the reinstallation—'

'Actually,' said Kelly hurriedly, 'we didn't.'

'What?' Gordon couldn't believe his ears. 'But—'

Watson's smug face could probably be viewed from outer space.

'We only signed to acknowledge we were there,' continued Kelly. 'At no point did we agree…'

Gordon bit his tongue. So, that was the game, was it?

'So, procedures are unclear and not fully understood by all sides,' said the investigator. He slid his glasses back on and stared at Gordon.

Gordon knew it was time to fold. 'Sir.'

Watson, puffed up like a pigeon, opened his mouth to speak.

Hesketh-Shaw interrupted. 'Hawker Siddeley now wish to be more involved with the remaining aircraft.'

Watson, frowning, ran a hand over his balding pate, but it was Kelly who spoke. 'We know. The request came via yourselves. We can't permit it until they've signed a further confidentiality agreement.' He glanced at the investigators. 'This is absolutely top secret, gentlemen. We're not being deliberately obstructive. We're trying to act in the best interests of the air force and the country as well.'

Gordon wanted to ask how on earth they were meant to operate this weapon when they weren't allowed to know how it worked, but silence was definitely the best idea right now.

'Mr Thompson,' said the investigator, 'can you guarantee that your men did nothing to adversely affect the operation of this system?'

Various responses flitted through Gordon's head, none of which were helpful. He settled for, 'My understanding was Fli-Tek had inspected our reinstallation prior to flight.'

'So you were placing the burden of airworthiness checks onto them?' The investigator raised an eyebrow.

Gordon fought the urge to flip the table and then punch Watson. 'Only for Banshee. As Fli-Tek keep telling us—'

'Hmm.' The investigator made a couple of brief notes. The only sound in the room was the scratching of his pen. There was no mistaking the victorious sneer twisting Watson's face; Gordon hoped the anger itching his fists didn't show.

'The rest of those aircraft and their systems were airworthy,' added Gordon.

'But you cannot guarantee no defects were introduced,' said Kelly.

The investigator cleared his throat. 'We will discuss this with you further at a later date, Mr Thompson. Once we've reviewed the data.'

Gordon swallowed and nodded. 'Of course.'

'However, there were several failures in communication. Unclear procedures. Many opportunities for something to have been missed.' The investigator fixed Gordon with as stern a stare as he could manage through the goldfish bowl lenses; his watery brown eyes blinked owlishly. 'Rest assured; we will be examining the remains of the airframe in minute detail. Mr Kelly, I believe you will be assisting?'

'Actually,' interjected Watson, 'I will be taking on this task. As senior engineering manager.'

'Excellent. Then Mr Kelly can assist the team reviewing XM568's documentation and procedures.'

Gordon suppressed a smirk; Watson suddenly looked like a boy who'd lost his favourite toy.

'Thank you, Mr Thompson,' said the investigator. 'That will be all for now.'

Left to his own devices, Gordon closed his office door behind him and sank into his chair. In the silence, he put his elbows on his desk and rested his head in his hands, eyes closed.

Since when had Fli-Tek moved the goalposts? Not that there was any point him protesting; Watson would deny the sky was blue at this point in time. Watson wanted to hang him out to dry.

And Watson was going to be looking at what was left of the airframe.

Up till now, he was sure he'd complied with every order, every requirement and done everything by the book. What if he'd been working to the wrong book? What if he'd missed something? What if he'd unknowingly handed Chief Andrews a time bomb that neither of them had the knowledge to fix? What if the chaps had damaged XM568? What if they had damaged Banshee? Or both?

One thing was for sure. Watson was going to pin every little bit of evidence he could onto the RAF. Specifically, him.

About the only consolation was that it wouldn't be Watson picking through the paper trail, it would be Kelly. Gordon held out little hope the man wouldn't be jaundiced by Watson's prejudices, though.

He'd done everything he thought was best; followed what he'd been told were the procedures, mostly to the letter.

But then, since when was "I was just following orders" any kind of defence? It didn't excuse him from actually thinking about what he was doing or ordering his men to do. Or considering the consequences.

A long, low groan slipped out. He rested his head on the cool wood of his desk.

Had he made a mistake? Had his oversight effectively sent Fraser and the rest out to die?

A tiny spark of defiance reminded him there were others in the chain, others who were closer to the action than him, who also had a say on whether a Vulcan was fit to fly. Fraser, for one, had to sign to take the plane over from the ground crews; he and Brian had to do a pre-flight inspection. Chief Andrews, too.

But then, none of them knew what on Banshee would class as a no-go.

Neither did he, for that matter.

That was why he'd requested—

He growled and pushed everything off his desk in one sweeping motion in sheer frustration.

If Fli-Tek were going to deny everything, what hope did he have?

His door opened. 'Boss—' began Hunt, '—Oh.' He stopped in the doorway, nervous, and eyed the mess of papers, pens, and spilt tea.

Gordon raised his head off the desk, ignoring the furious embarrassment threatening to turn his face red. 'What is it?' he managed.

'We… we heard you had to speak to the investigators,' Hunt mumbled.

'Yeah. That was a barrel of laughs.' Gordon pulled himself upright: his chair's wheels squeaked. 'What's the procedure for clearing Banshee post any inspection?'

Hunt blinked. 'We ask Fli-Tek to inspect and sign off as compliant.'

'We got that in writing?'

'Somewhere. We're—'

'We're about to have the book thrown at us for not following procedure. I had Watson and Kelly damn near accusing us of sabotaging that blasted system, accidentally or not!' Gordon slammed his fist on his desk. 'Now, I know you chaps wouldn't be so stupid, but my word isn't going to be enough.'

'But, sir—'

'But nothing. Hell, stop all actions on '47 and '33.'

'But we've got Banshee out of both aircraft.'

This time, Gordon blinked.

Hunt continued, 'We've made sure we've recorded every last detail. And—'

'What, both of them?'

'Yes—'

'Are they the same? Same system, same components?'

Hunt snorted. 'They're not even mounted with the same bolts.'

'And you've recorded this?'

'Absolutely everything. About the only thing we've not included is what we had for lunch.' Hunt paused. 'I thought Fli-Tek might do something like this. Especially after last week's, er, visit. That's why I didn't let the lads stop until we'd got them out. They can't tell us to stop if we've already finished.'

For the first time in ages, Gordon felt a genuine smile start.

'And I thought you might want to see what we've found,' said Hunt.

IT TOOK HOURS. Gordon dismissed the airmen, thanked them, and made a mental note to put some money behind the mess bar for them on Friday. They deserved to let their hair down after this week. Hunt, however, stayed.

The two of them pored over the meticulous notes, inspected what components had been removed, and generally went through as much as they could with the proverbial fine-toothed comb.

For all Watson's reassurances that the systems differed just in fine detail, the installations on XL447 and XL433 were only superficially similar. About the only major assembly that looked the same was the main PGU, or pulse generator unit, and even then, the ancillaries bolted on the outside varied in position.

There was one thing that was more than a little worrying.

It was a dull metal box, perhaps four by six inches and two inches deep. A stamped metal label on the side included various serial numbers and the acronym C.A.C.U. A handwritten addition across the top in chinagraph pencil was "XM568"; that had been crossed out and "XL433" written underneath in a different hand. Fixing lugs where the box mounted to Banshee were scuffed and worn, but that wasn't the only cause for concern. Electrical tape held the box lid on; three of the six small screws that should have held it were missing. Hunt gingerly peeled the tape off; the box split apart.

Both Hunt and Gordon stared at the pieces inside.

'I'm not an expert,' said Hunt, 'but that looks deliberately damaged.'

On autopilot, Gordon reached for the packet of cigarettes in his pocket then stopped; he'd had the last one that afternoon. He sighed. 'It does.'

Lost for words, they stared at the mess of electronics within the box.

Gordon's stomach sank. All he knew was this circuit shouldn't look like that, but as for what it did, or what had been done to it… 'Where was it?'

'Right up next to Banshee's batteries and capacitors. It was wired into them and took power from the aircraft via the fuse board.'

'Probably the charging controls.' Gordon frowned.

'We took a picture of this in situ before we unbolted it. Especially because…' Hunt trailed off and gestured at the numbers.

Gordon nodded. 'Do we know who touched these bits last on '68?'

'Isn't that—'

'In what I sent to the BOI and the Accidents Investigation Branch the other day. Yeah.' Gordon cursed under his breath. He racked his brains, trying to think.

'H-S last looked at this airframe,' said Hunt eventually. 'I think. But I don't think he went near Banshee.'

'Are we sure Watson—' Gordon stopped. 'Watson didn't want us near '33, either.'

The two of them stared at each other, confused.

'Wait a minute,' said Hunt. He rubbed his eyes. 'Where that was in the aircraft, you'd have a heck of a job getting to it, never mind opening it. So I don't know how that could've happened here.'

Gordon glanced at his watch; it was so late it was more like early. He ran a hand through his hair and suppressed a yawn. 'Come on. Let's make sure all this is secure, and we can think about it later. Because we're sure as hell not going to figure this out now.'

Tuesday 25 August 1964

THE FIRST THING Gordon did that morning was leave a message for both Sqn Ldr Burroughs and Sqn Ldr Hesketh-Shaw, requesting they visit the hangar at nine o'clock.

Burroughs and Hesketh-Shaw arrived at the hangar together, right on the dot.

Without any preamble, Gordon led them through to where he, Hunt and the chaps had worked early into the morning. Much as he hadn't expected to sleep, sheer exhaustion had pulled his eyes closed for a couple of hours. If only he felt better for it.

'The chaps have made progress with the teardown. We've already found so many variations between the aircraft, it's ridiculous.' He took a deep breath. 'We can run through them in detail with you, if you need. Everything is being recorded. But we wanted to flag this up to you both now.'

'Good. Thank you.' Burroughs frowned at the scatter of parts.

Hesketh-Shaw pointed at the metal box. 'What's that?'

'We believe that's part of the charging controls,' said Gordon. 'It was located by the input wiring for the chargers on '33. '47 had a similar box in the same position.'

'That says XM568.' Burroughs' voice was flat.

'And XL433.' Hesketh-Shaw frowned.

'You never got to take her up for your flight on the Wednesday, did you, sir?' asked Gordon.

Still frowning, Hesketh-Shaw shook his head.

'Is that really held together with electrical tape?' The disbelief in Burroughs' voice was clear.

'Yes. We have a photograph of it like that on the aircraft.' Gordon wanted that to be remembered. He wasn't going to be accused of whatever had been done to this. He picked it up and showed it to them both. 'But this is what it looks like inside.'

The tape was even less sticky now than it had been last night.

The state of the circuit board, however, was just as bad.

Hesketh-Shaw paled, like he'd been dunked in white paint. He stared, wide-eyed, at the box.

Burroughs gasped, then swallowed. He glanced at Hesketh-Shaw.

'Given Fli-Tek's secrecy,' said Gordon, 'we can't say for certain what this would do to Banshee's operation. But—'

Hesketh-Shaw took a deep breath. 'It wouldn't be good.' He shook his head in disbelief.

'That isn't in-flight or fitting damage, is it,' said Burroughs flatly.

Gordon shook his head. 'We don't think so, sir.'

'Bloody hell,' Hesketh-Shaw murmured. He rubbed the back of his neck.

For several moments, they all stared at the mess of electronics.

'I'm going to see the Wingco. Fli-Tek must not be allowed anywhere near '68's remains any longer.' Burroughs met Gordon's gaze, determination in the set of his eyes. 'Thanks, Gordon. Do you have the data ready?'

Gordon picked up one of the piles of paper that sat on the table nearby. 'Here, sir. We've got copies as well. Sergeant Hunt is off developing the photographs as we speak. The chaps are continuing the teardown.'

'Get those to me ASAP. I assume you're happy I share all this with the Board of Inquiry?'

Gordon nodded.

'Good.' Burroughs took the papers from Gordon with a grim smile. 'I'll see you later.' With that, he strode off.

Hesketh-Shaw's gaze was fixed firmly on the damaged control unit. He spoke so quietly, Gordon wasn't sure he'd heard him. 'Thank you.'

'Just doing my job.'

Hesketh-Shaw sighed. He shook himself and finally looked at Gordon. Sadness and regret etched his face. For a moment, he looked as if he was about to say something else, but he nodded, then followed Burroughs.

GORDON WENT TO the airmen's mess and the sergeants' mess and made sure his men, as well as the crew chiefs and their techs, would be able to enjoy several drinks on him. Whatever the outcome, they'd worked bloody hard, and he owed them.

When he got back to his office, Hunt was waiting for him. He held three large paper envelopes. 'I've got the first batch of photos so far. One set is for us, and two others.'

'Excellent. Thanks.'

'How did it go?' said Hunt.

Gordon considered his response. 'Burroughs is going to demand Fli-Tek stop all involvement with investigating '68.'

Hunt whistled. Satisfaction twisted his smile. 'Assuming it's not too late.'

'There is that.' Gordon sighed. 'Can I have a set? And make sure the others are somewhere safe, please.'

WHEN GORDON REACHED Burroughs' office, the door was closed. From within, he was pretty sure he could hear Merrick's abrasive tones, and the man did not sound at all happy.

Oh well. Gordon grinned to himself. Time to make things worse.

He rapped sharply on the door.

The voices stopped.

'Come in,' called Burroughs.

Gordon opened the door. Sure enough, Burroughs stood one side of the desk and Merrick the other; both turned to face him. Pages of the report lay across the desk between them.

'Sorry to interrupt—' began Gordon.

'Are those the photos?' interjected Merrick.

'Yes, sir.'

Merrick strode towards him and snatched them from his hand. 'You can go now—'

'Actually, sir,' said Burroughs firmly, 'I'd like Mr Thompson to stay.'

Merrick glowered. 'He's hardly unbiased.'

Stung, Gordon opened his mouth.

Burroughs spoke first, almost snarling. 'Are you saying my men haven't done their jobs properly?'

'The data and these photos were all taken by the techs,' snapped Gordon. 'Not me.' He folded his arms.

Merrick's jaw tensed. Anger seethed in his voice. 'What evidence do we have that this control unit was damaged prior to removal by YOUR men?'

Gordon glared. 'It's not possible to remove the top while it's bolted to the aircraft.'

'Prove to me it was damaged before it was fitted. Before you opened it.'

'Call Flight Sergeant Hunt. Go on. Ask him what the sequence of events was.' Gordon clenched his fists in an attempt to contain his temper. 'Either you believe us, sir, or you don't. If you don't believe me, why am I even here? If you don't believe my men, why are we working on your Vulcans?'

'You're asking me to believe Fli-Tek—'

'So, you believe Fli-Tek over me?' Gordon consciously lowered his voice. It wasn't done to be shouting at senior officers. He spread his hands. 'I don't know why they'd do this, either. It doesn't make sense.'

'You're right there,' muttered Burroughs.

'It's by the grace of God '33 didn't go up for her flight the same day,' said Gordon. 'With that fitted.'

Even Merrick paled then. *Good.* About time reality hit.

'Banshee's hardly a frozen system. Going by this, it's still being developed,' said Gordon. 'What I don't like is Fli-Tek not being upfront with us about any of this. Is this why they won't let us so much as breathe on it?'

'Hang on. Fli-Tek installed those units, didn't they?' said Burroughs.

'Yes, sir. That was when—'

'I entertained Watson in the mess,' growled Merrick. He closed his eyes and pinched the bridge of his nose. 'Yes. I recall.'

'And I stayed out of the way. Even Mr Kelly can verify that,' added Gordon.

Merrick stared into space. Gordon exchanged a raised-eyebrow glance with Burroughs.

'I was in my office reviewing all the test paperwork that said the units functioned as per spec,' said Gordon. 'That was why you—'

'I recall,' muttered Merrick. Something seemed to leach out of his stance; his usual ramrod straight posture sagged a little before he dragged himself firmly upright again.

'Someone did this. I don't know who. But I do know it's not possible to do this on the aircraft,' insisted Gordon.

'Why?' murmured Burroughs. 'That would make it premeditated.'

The three men looked at each other in silence for several moments.

Burroughs opened the envelope. He pulled out the prints and flicked through them until he came to the images of the damaged control unit. He spread them on the desk, on top of the report.

There was a moment's shocked silence.

Merrick exhaled through his nose. He shook his head. 'I never thought I'd see the day,' he murmured, as if to himself.

Gordon gestured to the photographs. 'May I?'

Burroughs passed the remaining images to him. Gordon rummaged through them until he found the ones of the unit fixed in the aircraft. 'Here you are, sir. This is where it was.'

Merrick studied them carefully. He pursed his lips, and finally nodded. He met Gordon's eyes; though the man's expression didn't change, there was a hint of contrition in his voice. 'I see what you mean, Mr Thompson.'

'We need to take this to the Board of Inquiry,' insisted Burroughs.

'We do.' Merrick breathed out. 'There's only one word for this, gentlemen. Sabotage.'

Sabotage.

As he walked back to the offices, Gordon couldn't stop thinking about that word.

Or its implications.

Merrick and Burroughs had gone to see the senior investigating RAF officer on the Board of Inquiry, a Wing Cdr Jenkins. Then the information would flow from there: definitely to the Accidents Investigation Branch, and more than likely to the Air Ministry. From there… who knew.

Hunt came out of the crew room; chatter spilled out into the corridor then silenced as the door swung shut again.

Before he could say anything, Gordon spoke. 'It's going to the investigators.'

'Yes.' Hunt punched the air.

'Tell the lads happy hour is on me. And the next few hours after that.' Gordon paused. 'And it is for you, too.'

Hunt smiled, but there was a tinge of sadness in it. 'We'd have done it anyway.'

'I know. Thank you.' Gordon bit his lip. 'Have you had a look at the same unit on '47 yet?'

'Yep.' Hunt's face darkened. 'While you were out. Exactly the same sort of damage as '33's. We've recorded it all.' Before Gordon could respond, he added, 'We found out what that unit is. I had a read of the test reports and documentation we were given before – well.' He paused, and swallowed. 'It's the Charge Accumulator Control Unit. If I understood it right, it's what tells the aircraft generators to charge, or stop charging, Banshee's accumulators and batteries.'

'A pretty fundamental part of the system.'

Hunt shook his head. 'I can't see how that sort of damage could be accidental.'

'Neither can I. And nor can SEngO or the Wingco.'

Hunt nodded, satisfied. 'The next shift are busy continuing to dismantle the smaller subassemblies. We'll need to get some sparkies in to tackle the wiring.'

'Call whoever you need to. I'm sure Command will say yes.' Gordon fought a yawn. Now he knew they were being taken seriously, tiredness was catching up with him. 'I'll be in my office if you need anything.'

GEORGE'S MORNING WAS not going well.

First of all, the Rover had refused to start. Last night, it appeared he'd forgotten to switch its headlights off when he got home, so the battery had gone flat. Anxiousness pushed him to carefully inspect as much of the car as he could, just in case someone, perhaps an unknown friend of Johnson's, had added some kind of explosive or other unpleasant surprise. Fortunately, there was nothing obvious, and one of his neighbours helped jump start it.

Then he'd been stuck in traffic, as a lorry had collided with a lamppost on the main road.

He'd finally arrived at the office to be met by a delegation of officers from the RAF Board of Inquiry as well as a representative from the Accidents Investigation Branch.

'Mr Watson,' said the most senior officer there, a Wing Cdr Jenkins, 'I'm here to inform you personally that as of now, the physical remains of Vulcan XM568 and your Banshee device will be inspected only by experts in all systems based at the Accidents Investigation Branch at Farnborough. Anyone associated with Fli-Tek, or working on Fli-Tek's behalf, is to stop any and all actions associated with this investigation, unless specifically requested to do otherwise.'

George swallowed in a futile attempt to stop his throat closing up. 'W… Well… What? Why?'

Some of the RAF men behind Jenkins exchanged glances. One shot a look of suspicion and contempt George's way that made his insides shrivel in shame.

They know, his conscience hissed.

'But what if you need to—'

'We will come and ask questions, where we feel the need,' said Jenkins coldly. 'Your representative at Martinford was informed when he arrived earlier. He's offered his full support.'

Kelly. Kelly was meant to be reviewing procedures…

Astonishment froze his vocal cords. His mouth flapped open and closed. What the—? What could he do? There was nothing he could say.

'We'll be in touch,' said Jenkins. The men turned to leave.

George was already opening his bottom desk drawer by the time the door clicked shut. His questing fingers retrieved a hexagonal glass bottle and fumbled the lid off, all without him needing to look. Then he closed his eyes and drained it. Glugged the gin like it was water, until there was no more. He wiped his mouth and set the empty bottle on his desk with a grimace.

Pity he'd only had half a bottle left of the Booths. It was good stuff.

What was he going to do? What could he do, for goodness' sake? Every day brought another challenge, another unexpected result…

Another obstacle you put in your own way, his memory reminded him.

Should he go to Martinford and see Kelly? No, that would raise suspicions. Besides, Kelly would probably be on his way back to the office; if there was nothing he could do, what was the point of him being there?

What was *he* going to do?

No matter how much he drank, it didn't shut out the constant singing of that small voice in the back of his mind.

Time is running out, George.

GORDON STARED AT the documents in front of him, but the text blurred and swam. He yawned, stretched, and grunted.

Much as he didn't want to admit it, he was exhausted.

Besides, what could he do, right now? The lads were busy; they knew their tasks, and he didn't need to keep reminding them. He'd already ensured all XM568's paperwork was collated and submitted.

Short of keeping his boss up to date with things, there wasn't much to do.

Maybe a walk would help clear his head.

He made his way out from the hangar, considering his options. Perhaps a circuit of the site, and he'd call in at the mess on his way back for a cup of tea. And possibly a snack, if any were being served. Something to tide him over.

An unfamiliar white Mini parked outside the ops building poked him from his thoughts. A man sat in the driver's seat.

With a start, he realised the man was Mr Kelly, of Fli-Tek.

Before he worked out if he should approach or not, Kelly glanced up and immediately opened his car door.

Uh oh.

'Mr Kelly,' said Gordon. He tried to sound brighter than he felt. 'How can I help you?'

'What… what's happened?' Kelly glared at him. 'I got here, right on the dot, and I was told – well, to sit and wait here, and they'd call me if I was needed!'

'Who said that?' Gordon frowned.

'Oh, I don't know. Some admin WAAF, from the Inquiry. Wing Commander's orders, she said.' Kelly bounced on his feet. He practically vibrated with irritation. 'I was expecting George – Mr Watson – to join me, but he hasn't shown up.'

'Has anyone said anything to you about why?' Gordon did his best to keep his tone curious. He knew why, all right; he just wanted to know if Kelly did.

Kelly shook his head. He ran a smoothing hand over his brylcreemed hair. 'I… I don't understand.'

Gordon glanced at his watch; it was after lunchtime. No wonder his stomach grumbled. An idea occurred to him. 'Tell you what. How about I take you to the officers' mess, we get some lunch, and we'll take it from there?'

While Kelly devoured a sandwich, Gordon called his boss and let him know what was happening. Then he, too, joined Kelly for lunch.

Even if they hadn't been busy eating, the atmosphere was hardly convivial. Gordon couldn't think of anything to say, and Kelly was unwilling to volunteer anything beyond his thanks for the food.

As he'd promised, Sqn Ldr Burroughs arrived; a quick, tight smile scuttled across his face. 'Ah. Mr Kelly—'

'What's going on?' Suspicion furrowed Kelly's brow as he looked back and forth between them.

'As a matter of fact, we do have something we need your help with. On XL433's Banshee unit.' Burroughs enunciated each word as clearly and carefully as if it were crystal.

Gordon blinked. He'd never heard that deliberate tone of voice before. 'Has something cropped up, sir?'

Burroughs raised an eyebrow, then looked pointedly at Kelly. 'You could say that. Follow me, please. Both of you.'

The walk across site felt long and awkward. Kelly occasionally glowered at Gordon; all Gordon could do was ignore it. What had the team found now?

Another good question was why did it look as if all 449 Sqn's techs were milling around outside?

And why were they going that way, instead of to the engineering offices?

Burroughs caught Gordon's puzzled glance and gave him a look as if to say "just wait".

Kelly didn't seem to see the men, nor register their significance.

A strange feeling buried itself in the bottom of Gordon's gut, and it wasn't his lunch. Had the chaps found something else? Already? If they had, it couldn't be good.

'I appreciate you're meant to be here to review procedures,' said Burroughs as they entered the hangar, 'however, as you're here, we'd like to ask you a question.' Still, his voice had an edge.

Kelly swallowed. He gave Gordon a nervous look. 'Well, I'll help as much as I can.'

The hangar was quiet. Too quiet. Only a few men gathered around the top half of the Banshee mechanism on the benches by XL433—

Confused, Gordon exclaimed, 'Why are the armourers here?'

'Why do you think, Mr Thompson?' Burroughs' tight smile became brittle. Gordon sensed that strange feeling twist into a knot. There was only one reason they'd call in the armourers...

Kelly stared at the men and the partly disassembled unit, his face somewhere between worry and frustration.

'Mr Kelly,' said Burroughs evenly, 'why did your firm not think to tell us that the Banshee system incorporated explosives?'

'What the hell?!' Gordon interrupted. 'Where are they, then?'

Kelly licked his lips. 'Um—'

Burroughs continued, his voice sharp, 'Are we right to presume the same components will be in place on XL447?'

'Um—'

'And that similar was fitted to XM568?'

Gordon froze. Images of the crash site filled his mind's eye.

Explosives. On Banshee.

That would make a Vulcan break apart in mid-air, all right.

'It's… it's the emergency Banshee power source!' bleated Kelly. 'I… I thought we needed to tell you, but Mr Watson—'

'Mr Watson has a lot of explaining to do,' snapped Gordon. He looked across to the armourers, then to Kelly. 'Where does this explosive sit?'

'It's towards the middle of the device, and close to the top. So it would sit near the roof of the bomb bay, almost in the centre of the aircraft. It… but… it shouldn't…' Kelly trailed off.

'Shouldn't? Shouldn't what?' demanded Gordon.

Kelly swallowed. 'It should only… er… trigger, in the event of the aircraft's own power failing. And… and we did studies, we—'

'Put a lump of bloody dynamite or whatever right where it would snap a Vulcan in half!' His voice echoed around the hangar. Gordon clamped his mouth shut before he said something he'd regret.

Kelly stared down at the floor, face ashen. 'It… it shouldn't have done anything,' he mumbled.

Burroughs raised an eyebrow. 'What would happen if anything were to interfere with the charging controls?'

'It… well… it depends…' Kelly coughed. 'There should be a failsafe circuit in there to prevent—'

'Should,' said Gordon flatly.

Burroughs gave him a meaningful look, then turned to Kelly. 'Mr Kelly. Can you accompany me to my office, please? Gordon, are you happy to supervise the men here?'

'Of course, sir.'

Gordon watched as Burroughs strode towards the door, Kelly almost scurrying to keep up.

Two armourers stood by '33's Banshee unit. One peered at the charge. The other looked up at Gordon.

'Excuse me, sir, but I think you'd better leave, too,' he said. 'Better safe than sorry.'

Gordon laughed bitterly. 'You're the first ones to worry about that with those parts for a while.'

MUCH LATER THAT evening, Gordon nursed a pint of mild in the corner of the mess, staring blankly at the paper in front of him. Not that he was reading it.

Today had been… how could he sum it up?

Already buzzing with rumours, Martinford was a hotbed of gossip. Even more than usual, he'd felt the looks, heard the sudden hush as he walked in; for once, he genuinely didn't care.

The fallout from today's revelations spread far and wide. Wingco Merrick stalked the base all afternoon, brow increasingly furrowed as he travelled to and fro, before disappearing off in a staff car to urgent meetings somewhere.

Burroughs had ordered him and his men to leave the aircraft and Banshee well alone. A group of crash investigators had visited the hangar that afternoon; neither Kelly nor Watson were anywhere to be seen.

As far as he knew, Burroughs went through the results of '33's and '47's teardowns with the investigators. Gordon wished he'd been there to see Kelly's face when he was presented with the wrecked control units. If, indeed, he was shown them; he could understand if that information was kept to those who needed to know it.

What a bloody mess.

A slurred voice broke his reverie. 'Hey, what's the news?' It added, with a sneer, 'Flash?'

Gordon rocketed to his feet; the paper clattered to the floor. Before his brain intervened, he pinned the speaker roughly to the wall by his neck.

Tony.

Wide-eyed, his hair a mess despite the Brylcreem, Tony's jaw worked, but no sounds came out.

In the ringing silence, Gordon growled, 'Only one person in this squadron had the right to call me that, and it sure as hell wasn't you.'

Abruptly, he realised Tony's pulse pushed against his thumb. He let go: Tony sagged, gasping, and avoided Gordon's gaze.

'Would you rather I let you make a smoking hole in a field somewhere?' Gordon snapped.

Still refusing to look up, Tony rubbed his neck. In a low voice, he said levelly, 'No need to make a scene.'

Anger rushed Gordon: he couldn't even speak. His fists clenched—

'Bad form,' interjected John.

Gordon hadn't even registered him strolling over. He shook himself and forced his hands to open.

Tony momentarily wobbled on his feet. Gordon's fists itched, but he fought to ignore it.

John jabbed a finger at his captain. 'No, you.'

Tony blinked; his nose wrinkled. 'Why—'

'Just because you're not sorry to have seen the back of Fraser doesn't give you the right to be such a child.' John folded his arms and raised his chin.

Hands on hips, Tony looked down his nose at his co-pilot. He shot a poisonous glance at Gordon. 'He assaulted me.'

'I didn't see anything.' John turned, eyebrow raised, and scanned the room. Most men focused intently on their pints.

From a nearby table, Ted cleared his throat. 'Well, I didn't see anything. Or hear anything.'

Realising he wasn't going to get any support, Tony huffed. He pointedly barged Gordon's shoulder as he left – or, more accurately, flounced – and cast a withering glance his co-pilot's way.

The door slammed.

Tension leached out of the room: there was an almost audible sigh of relief. Now the drama was over, the drinking could continue.

Before John could speak, Gordon cut him off. 'Thanks. I mean it. But I think it's time I got out of here and left the rest of you in peace.'

He gestured to the remnants of the paper still littering the floor. 'You can even have the paper. There's not much in it, to be honest.'

Outside, Gordon leant against the wall and took several deep breaths. Just what was happening to him? OK, he didn't exactly like Tony, but he'd been able to be civil and grown-up with him, no matter how uncivil and childish Tony was.

A cold, lumpy engine coughed into life then complained as it was revved hard; Tony's green Vauxhall Victor saloon juddered and whined down the road. If he carried on at that speed, someone would be bound to tell him off. At least, he hoped so.

Anger faded. This vindictiveness wasn't him at all.

He needed a break. Someone to drink this through with. What he wanted to do was find Fraser—

Loss punched him in the stomach once again.

There wouldn't be another finding Fraser. Or at least, he knew where Fraser was, and that was no place to have a drink.

Why did it have to be XM568? Why did it have to be Fraser? Why did five families have to be robbed of their sons, husbands, fathers? Why did he have to lose his best friend? And why did he have to try and be nice to smug bastards like Tony and Watson while they got away with it?

That sudden thought chilled him to the bone. He froze, waiting for his hindbrain to continue.

Got away with what?

It still felt unthinkable, incredible even, but evidence was growing that what happened to XM568 was deliberate.

But why? Who stood to gain if it was?

Not Watson, surely? After all, this was his company's technology. He'd want to make sure he kept his job. But… he was more and more erratic. And he hated the thought of people taking *his* aircraft and system to pieces with a passion that was more than just him wanting to protect his company's equipment.

No, it wasn't passion, Gordon realised. It was fear.

Fear of what, though?

Tony, on the other hand…

'You still here?' Ted, pipe clamped between his teeth, frowned at Gordon, though not unkindly.

Gordon shrugged. 'Not for much longer, if I keep doing that.'

'Doing what?' Ted winked.

Despite himself, Gordon gave a weak smile.

Ted stepped closer and lowered his voice. 'Between you and me, I'd have landed a few on him while he was there. He's insufferable.'

If even the rest of the crews felt that… Gordon chuckled.

Ted gestured back towards the building with his pipe. 'I had a word. Nothing happened.'

'But I might want to make sure there's a bit behind the bar?'

Ted grinned. 'Could be wise. Right, I'd best get home to the wife…'

As Ted strolled away, Gordon headed back to his room, his mind whirring.

Too many questions, not enough answers. And nothing like enough sleep.

Monday 21 November 2022

'How's it going, sir?' asked Woods, mid-morning. 'Anything useful from your interviews?'

Alex scanned his notes. How did he sum up how he felt? 'Miller's been helpful, but…' He sighed. 'I can't help but doubt we're going to get much further in identifying our man.' Then he registered Woods' smile. 'You've found something?'

Woods waggled a hand. He sat down at Alex's gesture. 'Maybe. I don't know. Natalie's team have been tracking down some more of the names on the paperwork, and we might have a lead. Tenuous, though.'

Alex raised his eyebrows.

'They've found contact details for a Mrs Sophie Thompson. Widow of Flight Lieutenant Gordon Thompson.'

'Ah.' Alex sat forward, eager. Given how frequently Thompson cropped up in Miller's recollections, perhaps a breakthrough was closer than he thought.

Half an hour later, Alex pulled the phone towards him and dialled the number from the details Woods had sent through.

After several rings, it went to answering machine. He left a brief message stating his identity, that he called regarding Flt Lt Thompson and RAF Martinford during the 1960s, and could she call back as soon as was convenient. He dictated his office number, then hung up.

Barely five minutes later, his phone rang.

'Good afternoon—'

'Is that Flight Lieutenant Farnsworth?'

'Speaking.'

'This is Chris Thompson. You asked to speak to my mother.'

'I did, yes.'

'I'm afraid you can't,' he snapped. 'She passed away nearly three weeks ago.'

Alex winced. He closed his eyes and cursed his ignorance. 'Ah. I must apologise. I had no idea. I'm so sorry for your loss.'

'Thank you.' There was a pause and a sound like a man trying to take a deep breath. 'I must say, you've amazing timing. I don't think we've had anything to do with the air force since Dad died, and that was a long time ago.'

1998, according to the sparse details in Woods' email. Alex didn't know how old Flt Lt Thompson's sons were, but how much of life at Martinford would they have known? Little, if anything.

Mr Thompson cleared his throat. 'Why did you want to speak to my mum?'

Alex braced himself. 'You might have seen on the news that unidentified human remains were discovered some weeks ago at Braxton Sports Cars, which was once RAF Martinford. Your father served there in the 1960s. I was calling to ask if your mother recalled anything of Martinford at the time.'

'Ha, yeah, I have. Crumbs.' Mr Thompson made a noise like air being sucked through his teeth. 'I never knew he was there, though. Mind, it was like anything before they got married didn't exist for us kids.'

Disappointment, though not surprise, pushed at Alex, but he kept it at arm's length. This was something Mr Thompson couldn't have controlled. 'You must be very busy. I'm sorry for intruding at such a difficult time.'

'You weren't to know. Besides, it's a distraction, and anything distracting is, well…' Mr Thompson trailed off. He coughed. 'Anyway. This body at Braxton, the former RAF base. Why did you think Mum could help?'

'We're trying to speak to those connected with the squadrons that once served there to build up a picture of what life was like and if any incidents stood out. Obviously, it was many years ago, but…'

'It's all you've got.'

'Yes,' Alex conceded.

'Well, I don't remember anything off the top of my head that either of them said, but I'll ask my brother if he remembers anything. You never know, we might find something.'

'If you do, even if you're not sure it's relevant, please, let me know.'

'No problem. This number, again?'

After a few more minutes, Alex tactfully drew the conversation to a close and passed on his condolences once more. Mr Thompson seemed to welcome the interruption, but pressing him for answers at such a difficult time was distasteful. Besides, grief did odd things to the brain.

Alex wasn't expecting a call back. Even if one occurred, he doubted he'd glean much useful information. Second or third-hand recollections, fogged through time and Chinese whispers, might be even less use than nothing at all.

Frustration pulled a groan from him. He stood up. A walk to update Woods on the situation might help distract him for a while.

Monday 31 August 1964

GORDON PUSHED OPEN the doors to Hangar 3.

Since the discovery of the explosives and the sabotage last week, 449 Sqn had stopped. No flying, no maintenance; no anything.

Gordon had been sure it wouldn't be long before a bullish and stubborn Watson appeared, determined to tell everyone it was the RAF's fault. But he hadn't. Neither had Kelly returned. Instead, Burroughs told him to wait to be called – and not to breathe a word of what was happening to anyone.

Almost a week had passed. Days where he and his men were virtually pushed out of their own hangar. Experts from Farnborough, Hawker Siddeley, and the Board of Inquiry pored over both '33 and '47 and scrutinised what Gordon's men had found.

Fli-Tek had been notable by their absence.

He'd spent the first few days giving the Bonnie a thorough clean and service. Then he'd turned his attention to some of the unread books on his bookshelf. The other day, John asked his help to fettle the Zephyr's brakes, then the three of them ventured to Stratford-upon-Avon for an explore.

Every now and again, Sophie crossed his mind; he kicked himself for how he'd given her the ring. Both John and Miranda pointed out that there'd hardly be a good time to hand it over, but more than ever, he wished he could travel back in time…

He'd considered calling on her. A couple of times, he'd ridden the Bonnie towards Leamington and then thought better of it. She probably wouldn't be glad to see him, and the last thing he wanted was to cause her even more pain.

Now, though, he was bored and wondering what was going on.

His boss wasn't around. Neither was Wingco Merrick.

As far as he could tell, none of the personnel who'd been busy during the last week were here this morning. It was uncharacteristically silent.

The door bumped closed behind him.

For several moments he just stood there.

At last, that new paint smell was going: avtur, hydraulic fluid and oil finally edged out the pear drops. Unsurprising, considering it appeared both Vulcans had been disembowelled.

Inspection panels on each Vulcan's wings and fuselage were removed, leaving the aircraft's innards visible. Components in varying stages of disassembly were everywhere. Only a token pathway around and between each aircraft remained clear.

Despite the outward chaos, he recognised the inner order.

The door creaked open. 'Should you be here?' came a voice behind him. Burroughs.

Gordon turned and saluted. A sheepish smile crossed his face. 'Probably not, sir.'

A smile passed across Burroughs' face. 'I thought I'd have seen you in here earlier.'

'I didn't want to prejudice things.'

Burroughs nodded in appreciation.

'Have Fli-Tek been told any of this?' said Gordon.

Unusual mischief flashed in Burroughs' eyes before he composed himself. 'Mr Watson and Mr Kelly are coming here shortly. I don't believe they know any details beyond us uncovering the hazardous material last week.' He stared off into the distance for a moment. 'Direction from the BOI was not to inform them of anything else until the teardowns were completed.'

That sounded sensible. Gordon cleared his throat, itching to ask a question.

Burroughs pre-empted him. 'As your men uncovered key evidence, I think you should be present, too.'

Gordon grinned. Burroughs had read his mind. 'Thank you, sir.'

Burroughs asked Gordon to wait outside until he returned, presumably with the Wingco and Fli-Tek. Fortunately, the late summer day was pleasantly warm and sunny.

Sqn Ldr Hesketh-Shaw strode across the road towards Gordon. 'Mr Watson will be here soon.'

'Apparently so, sir.'

Hesketh-Shaw grinned. 'And I hear you'll be joining us.'

Gordon didn't bother pretending to hide his smile. 'I will.'

'Excellent.' Hesketh-Shaw put his hands on his hips. 'I understand we'll be informed of some of the findings. We haven't been told anything, so far.' He glanced over his shoulder; a gaggle of men headed their way from ops. Even at a distance, Watson's figure was more than recognisable. 'Let's go and wait by the aircraft. I believe we're starting there.'

Gordon followed H-S back into the main hangar. The man whistled through his teeth when he saw the extent of the teardown.

Footsteps and voices echoed down the corridor. Gordon unconsciously braced himself.

The doors swung open, and the men walked in; two RAF officers and three civilians. He guessed, after Burroughs, the other officer was part of the Board of Inquiry; one of the civilians he'd seen walking around the hangar, so he presumed he was part of the Accidents Investigation Branch; and then there was Watson and Kelly.

Kelly was pale, jiggling from one foot to the other in nervousness. He saw Gordon and gave half a nod of acknowledgement before seeming to remember himself.

Watson was red, scowling and sweating. His eyes zeroed in on Gordon. He glowered, opened his mouth as if to speak, then shut it. He cast a suspicious sideways glance at the Board of Inquiry officer. All the while, he twisted and rubbed his hands together as if trying to wash them.

'I understand the wing commanders are elsewhere this morning,' said the officer. He glanced at Gordon; recognition glimmered on his face, but he didn't speak. Gordon swallowed. He was the officer he'd spoken to at the crash site.

Burroughs cleared his throat. 'Yes. Wing Commander Merrick is being briefed by Wing Commander Jenkins as we speak. If you could go ahead?'

'Thank you, sir. I'm Flight Lieutenant Warner,' said the officer. He looked at the Fli-Tek men. 'I'm the primary airframe investigations officer for this incident. Mr Davison is my civilian counterpart from the Accidents Investigation Branch.' The man raised his hand; he was probably a bit older than Gordon, with neat greying hair and a tidy goatee.

'I don't understand why we've had to get civilians involved with this,' snapped Watson. He mopped his forehead with a handkerchief.

'Because we asked them,' said Warner, calmly.

Watson frowned. Kelly nodded absently.

Warner continued, 'Evidence is clear. XM568 broke apart in the air, due to an explosive decompression.'

Gordon resisted the urge to punch the air in triumph. He knew it!

Kelly went white.

Watson's eyes bulged. His cheeks flushed. 'But—'

'We've recovered enough of the airframe structure to confirm,' said Davison.

'What do you know?' spluttered Watson, indignant.

'Perhaps I should say,' said Davison sharply, 'I'm an accident investigator of many years standing. I spent several years at the RAE, and I assisted with the testing of Comet Yoke-Uncle. That experience has been most useful.'

Gordon raised his eyebrows. Three De Havilland Comets were lost during the early days of jet passenger aircraft in the 1950s; to start with, no obvious cause could be found for them breaking apart in flight. A long and complex investigation, involving testing the fuselage of Comet G-ALYU, determined the root cause to be metal fatigue, due to the repeated pressurisation and depressurisation of the cabin. Much as De Havilland re-engineered the Comet to eliminate the risks, its reputation never recovered.

Watson shrank back.

Warner eyed the Fli-Tek men. 'Investigations are still ongoing, but Mr Thompson's team uncovered a critical piece of evidence last week.'

Watson pointed a trembling hand at Gordon. 'You! It's always you, isn't it? I bet you planted it,' he spat in fury.

What the hell? Where had Watson got that from? Gordon fought to keep his mouth shut.

Warner gave Gordon a curious look. 'Why would you say that, Mr Watson?'

'He's always been nitpicking, fault-finding, undermining everything we're working towards!' Watson's head swivelled around as he looked, wild-eyed, at his mostly impassive audience. 'He tried to get the testing stopped before. He tried—'

'Are you referring to the incident with Brookes and '47?' asked Hesketh-Shaw.

'Yes! His men found problems that definitely weren't there when she left us!'

Gordon opened his mouth, caught Burroughs' eye, and closed it again.

Warner held up a clipboard Gordon hadn't realised the man carried. He scanned a few pages before finding the section he wanted. 'Indeed. And I have evidence here that you suggested these issues were linked to your trial weapon system, and Thompson's men followed your advice.'

Some colour returned to Kelly's cheeks, but he still looked as if he'd rather be anywhere else.

'Much about this system is unknown,' said Warner evenly. 'The documentation you have supplied, Mr Watson, falls far short of the reality of what's been installed on these aircraft. I took the liberty of discussing things with Hawker Siddeley, and it seems you misled them on certain aspects, too.'

'W… well… I absolutely did not,' insisted Watson.

Kelly took off his glasses and rubbed his eyes. 'George,' he muttered, in warning tones. 'The—'

Watson whirled around. He jabbed a furious finger at Kelly. 'You as well, now?'

'Decisions were made,' said Kelly, in a louder voice. He put his glasses back on and did his best not to look at Watson. 'I was told it was on security grounds.'

'We can't tell every man and his dog how this works!' shouted Watson. Spittle flicked from the corners of his mouth; his cheeks glowed so red that Gordon wondered if the man was entirely well.

Kelly fidgeted, uncomfortable. 'The emergency triggering system. We—'

Watson's eyes bulged. 'You shouldn't have said anything!' he roared. Once more, he waved a shaking hand at Gordon. 'I told you; he'd find any excuse—'

'The emergency triggering system,' interrupted Warner. He spoke in tones that brooked no argument. 'How does that work, exactly?'

'It—' began Kelly.

Watson pointed at Kelly. 'Shut up, or you're sacked,' he snarled.

Stunned silence spread in the echo of his words.

Kelly closed his eyes for a moment. He took a deep breath. 'It uses an explosive to force—'

'SHUT UP!' screamed Watson.

Gordon realised his mouth was hanging open.

Kelly looked at Watson. He blinked, once. Then he turned to Warner. 'It uses an explosive—'

'We… you can't just give away our secrets!' interjected Watson. His redness quickly shaded to a pallor. His forehead was beaded with sweat. A hand dived into a pocket and seemed to fidget around of its own accord, searching fruitlessly for something; not once did he look down to try to find what he wanted. Instead, his gaze refused to stay still; his eyes wouldn't stay on one person for more than a split second.

'They're not secret any more,' said Kelly. Defeat filled his voice. He spread his hands at the dismantled aircraft around them. 'Look.'

Watson refused to throw even the merest glance in their direction. 'There's been a… a conspiracy to stop us developing this. To get this taken off us. And I'm not having it. I'm not!' He stamped his foot like a child.

Burroughs raised a bemused eyebrow at Gordon. Gordon shrugged. He'd never seen anything like this.

'I'm not having you tell me that… that we brought down that aircraft,' babbled Watson. He swept a crumpled hanky across his brow. 'I refuse to accept—'

'Why would you think you brought down XM568?' asked Warner. He exchanged a look with Davison.

Gordon clenched his fists. He knew it. Judging by their expressions, Warner and Davison did, too.

Watson backpedalled furiously. 'I don't! But he—' he aimed a wavering finger at Gordon, '—does! He's trying to pin this on me, I know it!'

'Like you have me?' Gordon retorted before he could stop himself.

Burroughs shook his head.

'Sorry, sir,' Gordon mumbled.

Warner frowned at Watson. 'I understand there was a discussion with my colleagues about sign-off procedures and inspections of this system. We found contradictory statements from Fli-Tek in the paperwork supplied regarding who had responsibility for final approvals. I understand you stated you were not responsible for approving reinstallations, following flight trials?'

'Er… well…' spluttered George.

Kelly blushed, but he nodded. He looked at the floor.

'I found a report written some months previously that stated each unit should be checked by Fli-Tek personnel pre and post-test, if any issues were encountered. And that a signature on behalf of Fli-Tek marked approval to continue. Written by yourself, Mr Kelly.'

Gordon gritted his teeth. So he hadn't imagined that, then.

Warner continued, his voice sharp. 'So why did you state in the meeting that this was not the case, that you were merely acknowledging your company's presence?'

Shame tinged Kelly's cheeks. 'I—'

'We modified our procedures!' snapped Watson. He glared at Gordon.

'So it seems,' said Warner.

'It's development—'

'It's uncontrolled,' said Davison. 'From my point of view, Fli-Tek do not have robust engineering practices.'

'How dare you!' yelled Watson.

Kelly looked like a man who would shortly be handing in his resignation, regardless of whether Watson followed through with his threat to have him sacked. If only the man had found his backbone earlier.

'You have not supplied us with half the data requested,' said Warner. 'What data we have is incomplete. For example, we've a sheet to say that prior to the accident, the Banshee units were refitted to the aircraft, but—'

'I refitted them.'

'But you did not accurately record which serial numbers were fitted to which aircraft,' said Davison.

Watson's mouth flapped open and closed. 'I don't have to listen to this… this nonsense!'

'Pity.' Warner folded his arms. 'The Air Ministry are very keen to hear us out.'

Watson rushed forward; Gordon didn't have time to react as Watson's face loomed large in front of him. His words cut Gordon to the bone.

'Just because you can't believe Campbell could make a mistake,' he hissed. 'Oh, he made plenty. Believe me. Just like you, with this. You'll see. You will.' Malicious triumph gleamed in his eyes.

Was that alcohol on Watson's breath? Focus on that. Not the words, Gordon told himself. Anything to avoid reacting to Watson – though his hands ached with the effort of not punching Watson, hard. Oh, he'd lay the man out—

A strange, maddened half-giggle slipped out of Watson's mouth. His wild, staring eyes roved around the hangar, not focusing on anyone. 'It's too late.'

With that, he turned on his heel and almost skipped out of the hangar.

Dumbfounded silence reigned in his wake.

What the hell was that all about?

'I wish I knew,' said Burroughs, bewildered. 'Er, H-S, would you—?'

Without saying more, Hesketh-Shaw hurried after Watson.

Gordon realised he must have said his thoughts aloud. Again. That wasn't a habit he wanted to get into.

Kelly cleared his throat. 'Um. Excuse me, gentlemen. I… now I seem to be, er, no longer employed by Fli-Tek—'

Warner interrupted. 'We'd still like to talk to you, Mr Kelly.'

Kelly glanced around. There was no sign of Watson or Hesketh-Shaw returning. He looked at Gordon; awkwardness flickered across his face. 'I was under considerable pressure. I'm not now.'

'We have a lot to discuss,' said Warner. 'Thank you, Mr Thompson, for your time this morning.' A slight smile crossed his face, matching the genuine appreciation in his voice. 'You may not think it, but you've been very helpful.'

Gordon walked slowly out of the hangar, trying to process what had just happened. Perhaps that had been the plan. After all, it was common knowledge he and Watson weren't exactly friends; how better to provoke some kind of reaction from him, if the investigators suspected something?

Maybe fifteen feet ahead, H-S seemed to be deep in discussion with Watson as they slowly walked towards the road; he couldn't hear anything. Much as he wanted to eavesdrop, staying out of the way was probably wiser. There was only so much drama he could take in a day.

Did this mean Watson—?

OK, it was unlikely anyone else had either the access, knowledge, or opportunity. But why would Watson damage his own company's system? Was getting one over on Fraser really that important to him? It didn't make sense. None of it made sense.

Watson heard Gordon's footsteps and turned; H-S did the same, a split second later. His expression hinted Gordon should just keep walking.

'Excuse me—' Gordon went to walk past.

Watson thrust out a hand and shoved Gordon in the chest. 'I will not excuse you a thing,' he snapped.

'Mr Watson—' began H-S.

Gordon forced himself to take a deep breath and stay calm. 'Let me past. Please.'

Watson grabbed a handful of Gordon's jumper, right over his heart, and tried to drag him closer. 'How does it feel, knowing Fraser couldn't fly his way out of something for once?' Watson's eyes blazed in the grim rictus of his face. The madness in them shook Gordon; here was a man who was quite a long way from reality. 'He wasn't so superior after all, was he?'

Gordon gritted his teeth, desperate not to react. He wasn't going to listen to Watson's poison. The man was trying to get a rise out of him, and he wouldn't give him the satisfaction.

H-S pushed at Watson's hand. 'Mr Watson, please…'

Watson let go.

Without another word, Gordon hurried on.

IN THE ABSENCE of any other orders, Gordon climbed on the Bonnie. A good few hours riding around Warwickshire country lanes helped clear his mind; it was hard to dwell on things like Watson when he had to concentrate on – well, staying shiny side up. Besides, it kept him away from Martinford and anyone else who'd be likely to see him.

Maybe one blessing was that Watson had lost it in the presence of others, without anything Gordon would call provocation. Not that it made any of this make any more sense, but…

Could Fraser's accident have been avoided? Possibly.

But they'd trusted Fli-Tek, and Watson, and…

What could they have done differently? Presumably that was what the investigators would look at, too.

Eventually, he rolled back onto the base and parked her up in the usual spot.

As he took his helmet off, someone walked closer.

'Ah.' It was Hesketh-Shaw. 'Glad I caught you. Don't bother saluting,' he added.

Oh, what now? Gordon grasped his helmet in one hand and tried not to groan. 'Sir?'

'Well done, earlier.' Hesketh-Shaw flashed his teeth in a brief smile. 'Mr Davison and Flight Lieutenant Warner asked me to pass on their thanks. I believe Squadron Leader Burroughs is waiting for you in the mess.'

Sure enough, his boss sat at the bar in the mess, a whisky in front of him. He looked up, saw Gordon, and waved to the seat next to him. 'What are you having? This is on me.'

Gordon hesitated. Normally, he'd go for a pint of mild, but this evening… 'I'll have a Glenfiddich, please.' Somehow, that seemed appropriate.

The white-coated steward slid a crystal glass across the bar to Gordon; he nodded a thanks.

Only then did Burroughs speak. 'That's for this morning.'

'You thought me being there might push Watson a bit, didn't you?' said Gordon, bluntly. He sipped the whisky.

Burroughs had the grace to look away. 'Yes.'

'Well, it worked.' Gordon inspected the glass: rainbows shimmered in its cut-glass facets.

'H-S told me what happened afterwards, too.' Burroughs sipped his own drink, sympathy in his eyes.

Gordon drank some more. 'I didn't want to give Watson the satisfaction.'

'People underestimate the power of stubbornness,' murmured Burroughs.

'Are the investigators happy?'

'I'm not sure happy's the right word,' admitted Burroughs. He finished his whisky with an appreciative sigh. 'They haven't shared many details, but they agree with your assessment of the other control units as sabotaged. Likely by someone who knew what they were doing.'

'I don't understand.' Gordon drained his glass. 'Why?'

'That's the question.' Burroughs nodded at the steward; a second glass of whisky appeared in front of Gordon, as well as a refill for Burroughs. 'Personally, I think we'll go mad trying to understand.'

Watson's wild eyes lingered in Gordon's mind. He shuddered involuntarily. 'Watson's mad already.'

Both men stilled. Gordon met Burroughs' eyes; the man nodded, silently acknowledging the revelation.

'We need proof,' said Burroughs. He picked up his whisky and swirled it gently. 'And the investigators are looking.'

Gordon stroked the sides of his glass.

'And I hear,' added Burroughs, 'that Mr Kelly is now very keen to help the investigators with their enquiries.'

'If only he'd been more helpful earlier,' grumbled Gordon.

Burroughs nodded. He tilted his glass towards him but didn't drink. He seemed to be weighing something up.

The doors swung open, and both men glanced over their shoulders. John, along with H-S's co-pilot Trevor, and a few others of their crews, ambled in.

Burroughs finished his whisky and stood up. 'I'll see you tomorrow. Ten o'clock, my office?'

Tuesday 1 September 1964

GORDON NURSED HIS hangover as he walked to Burroughs' office. It had been a good night in the mess. Tony didn't show his face, and the rest of them drank and put the world to rights until they were finally turfed out and told to go home.

He was getting too old for this. Every step made his too-tender brain bounce off the inside of his skull.

Even worse, Hunt and the rest of them were still officially off-duty, so he had to make his own cup of tea when he got to his office that morning. He cushioned that particular blow by adding an extra spoonful of sugar to the strong brew; it almost helped.

What he thought was a gentle tap on Burroughs' door felt more like smacking a hammer against his head. He winced.

At Burroughs' call, he opened the door and stepped in with what even he knew was a slightly sloppy salute.

'Thank you for coming,' said Burroughs. 'Make yourself comfortable.'

Gordon gingerly lowered himself into a chair. 'Thank you, sir.' He took his hat off.

'Good night last night?'

'Possibly a bit too good,' Gordon conceded, with as much of a smile as he could manage.

'Well. This will certainly sober you up.' Burroughs straightened up and laced his hands on top of his desk; his face became serious. 'Wingco Merrick met with us execs this morning. It's still to be confirmed, so don't spread this around, but it's probable 449 Squadron will be disbanding. Personally, I expect we'll be stood down before the end of September.'

Gordon leant back in his chair. He blew out a long breath, trying to think. He couldn't work out if he was surprised or not. After all, once those in charge heard about what happened yesterday, you'd have to be a pretty special kind of deluded to carry on full steam ahead. Watson's manic face flashed before his mind's eye; probably that level of deluded, all right. But that didn't stop him wondering what would happen next.

Burroughs forestalled his question. 'I understand the Air Ministry are terminating the Banshee integration programme. Certainly, I can't see why they'd continue it.'

'What does that mean for us right now?' Gordon tried to switch his mind to more practical matters. They had a hangar full of dismantled Vulcans, for a start.

Burroughs cleared his throat. He glanced down at the table. 'Ask Sergeant Hunt and his team to package up all Banshee components and our related test equipment and move it all to one side ready for disposal. The others will restore as much as is needed to make those aircraft airworthy, without reinstalling any Banshee components.' He paused. His expression seemed to go blank. 'And you are to collate every single scrap of 449 Squadron documentation and paperwork in your possession, with a view to, ah, permanently archiving it.'

'Permanently archiving?' Gordon frowned. 'Where?'

Burroughs hesitated. 'It seems there's a suitable facility onsite.'

'What?' Gordon scratched his moustache. Where could Burroughs mean?

'Apparently there are some disused underground works.' Burroughs coughed. He laced and unlaced his fingers together. 'From the war.'

The penny dropped. 'Oh. The bunker—' Gordon stopped. 'But that's… that's not procedure. Well. I can't say as I've ever been in this exact position before, but…'

'None of us has,' murmured Burroughs. 'However, they're our orders.'

Gordon couldn't help a bitter smile. 'And ours is not to reason why, is it, sir?'

AFTER CALLING HUNT and ensuring he called the rest of the men in, Gordon set to his office.

So, Merrick wanted all Banshee's paperwork hidden, eh?

For a moment, he almost considered not complying. Everything in him screamed that hiding the papers in the abandoned WW2 bunker was wrong.

Undoubtedly, what really happened to XM568 would end up in there, too.

It was a cover-up. Of the highest order.

His temples throbbed, and it wasn't all due to last night's beer.

Yes, he knew the value of discretion. Of security. Of keeping certain information under lock and key. But… men had died. Surely their families deserved the truth?

What if the truth was dangerous, though? He grasped the edge of his desk and lowered himself deliberately into his chair. What would the families, the public, the world think if it came out that a V-bomber had crashed because it had been sabotaged?

Not that he knew that for certain, but he felt in his bones it was the truth.

He took a deep breath and held it for a few moments. Then he let it out in a resigned sigh.

It wouldn't look good. You didn't need to be a genius to realise that. Not only that, but it could also potentially endanger England, the RAF, or even the world; it was a sign of weakness. A sign the Soviets would no doubt exploit.

Let's face it, the Americans would pounce on it as well. They were already busy trying to flog their aircraft to the RAF and the Fleet Air Arm; this would be another excuse they could use. Besides, they were keeping Banshee completely under the radar, so to speak; no-one knew they'd been working on this technology. To declare what had happened risked blowing Banshee's cover, too.

It would be stupid to allow even the merest chink in their armour to show. More was at stake here than just Fraser's honour.

He groaned and reached for the nearest stack of papers.

He might have to do this. He might even agree with the reasons why. That didn't mean he had to like it.

Everything about this bloody project was wrong. It had been from the start. Nothing good ever came of being volunteered, or chosen, for anything... Maybe when Group Captain Marwell had told him those setting up 449 Sqn wanted him to transfer, he should've said no. But then... Fraser had mentioned him, too.

Would all this still have happened? Who knew.

If nothing else, at least he'd had one final chance to fly with Fraser again.

The truth of what happened to XM568, whatever it was, was bound to be awkward, inconvenient, and embarrassing. Much as he hated to admit it, perhaps it needed to be camouflaged: if not by outright lies, then a web of uncertainty. For the sake of the air force, the nuclear deterrent, and all of that.

'I'm sorry, chap,' Gordon murmured under his breath. 'Needs must.'

Wednesday 23 November 2022

A LEX, MORNING COFFEE in hand, hung up his jacket and pulled out his chair. He reached across to switch his laptop on.

His desk phone rang.

Startled, he almost dropped his coffee. Somehow, he managed to fumble the mug down and answer the call.

'Farnsworth.'

'Oh, good morning. Um, it's Chris Thompson.' He coughed. 'I know we only spoke the other day, but, well, we've found something you might want to take a look at…'

CHRIS THOMPSON USHERED Alex into the 1960s semi-detached house situated in a quiet suburban cul-de-sac in a village near Southend. It had the sad air of an unlived-in home: faint shapes on the red and cream striped wallpaper in the hall hinted pictures had been taken down. Dark wear lines in the beige carpet weaved around plush patches where furniture once stood. Scuffs and holes on the stairs marked where a stairlift had been removed. Cardboard boxes and filled black bin liners dotted the stairs and filled what he could see of the landing.

All the furniture that remained in the living room was a careworn floral three-piece suite and a rectangular mahogany coffee table. Tufts of bubble wrap peeked out of another cardboard box by one of the chairs; yet more boxes, sealed with parcel tape, were lined up against a wall. If the air smelled of anything, it was disturbed dust.

Chris introduced his brother, Fraser. Both men were tall and dark haired; Fraser looked to be in his late forties to early fifties, Chris a few years younger.

Fraser waited till Alex was seated on the sofa before speaking. 'Thanks for coming. I have to say, I hope we're not wasting your time with this.'

Chris interjected, 'But you said to call if we found anything. Even if we weren't sure.'

Fraser shot his brother an exasperated glance.

Alex cleared his throat. 'I did, yes. And thank you. At this stage, anything that can shed even a tiny bit of light on RAF Martinford could be useful.'

The brothers exchanged a look.

Chris went to a battered and dusty black fake leather chest that languished in the corner behind the chair; he dragged it over and lifted the lid. Patterns on the surface looked like someone had tried cleaning it but given up. 'We found this – locked – in the loft yesterday morning. We're going to sell up, so…'

'We're clearing the whole house,' said Fraser.

'We busted the lock off it, and inside…' Chris took a deep breath, but words seemed to fail him. He looked at Fraser.

'We found these.' Fraser reached into the chest; he brought out a handful of notebooks of varying sizes. All looked old, some more dog-eared than others. 'We've had a flick through, and they look like diaries. There's more in there.'

'It's definitely Dad's handwriting,' added Chris.

Fraser gently handed the top quarter of the pile to Alex.

The cover of the top notebook was clearly marked with Thompson's name, rank, number, and the year: 1965. Underneath, he'd scribbled RAF Scampton, 27 Sqn, Avionics.

'They go all the way back to 1943,' said Fraser. 'Not every year, but most years till the mid-sixties…'

Alex blinked, stunned. 'Have you read them?'

The brothers shook their heads.

'Not all of them,' said Fraser.

'We've had a flick through the later ones,' added Chris. 'And the earliest. But to be honest, it's all so new to us, we don't know what to think.'

Alex carefully leafed through the pile: just as he hoped, a couple had RAF Martinford scribbled on the front. As he eased one out, impatient to see what it said, Fraser coughed. 'This is what's really puzzling us, though.'

Before Alex could respond, Fraser picked up another stack of papers and thrust them into his hand. 'It looks like a crash report. I googled it, and… and it's a real accident, but…'

'But what's online isn't what's said here, if you know what I mean,' added Chris.

Alex stared, open-mouthed. The faded blue cardboard cover, soft with age, gave details he already knew: 4 August 1964, at Long Itchington, Warwickshire, Vulcan B.2.B XM568 from RAF Martinford, flown by Flt Lt F. J. Campbell.

This time, NOT FOR DISTRIBUTION was stamped across the top in stern black lettering that had lost none of its force over time: underneath ran TOP SECRET.

What on earth?

'As far as we can work out, Dad shouldn't have had this,' said Chris.

'No. No, he shouldn't,' said Alex, puzzled. What was the file he'd read at the National Archives, then? He flicked through the gently browned pages; a map caught his eye.

The missing debris field map.

A tingle coursed down his spine. Could this be true? Unconsciously, he whistled under his breath.

'I take it we haven't wasted your time, then?' said Fraser.

'Not at all.' Alex looked up, and grinned. 'Not at all.'

SOME HOURS LATER, Alex arrived back in the office, having returned the pool car to its parking space. Fraser and Chris Thompson had insisted he take the crash report, as well as the diaries dating from 1964 that mentioned Martinford. They'd also insisted he take a couple of black and white photographs that at first glance appeared to be of the same date. One showed a dark-haired man with an attractive woman, standing by an Austin-Healey 3000; the man seemed to be rolling his eyes at the photographer, but the woman looked as if she was laughing. The Thompsons thought she was their mother but didn't know who the man was; it wasn't their father. Another was a squadron photo; the same as the one Wing Cdr Miller had, if he wasn't mistaken.

The Thompsons were shocked at their father's hidden past. By all accounts he'd glossed over his previous career, hardly mentioning it except in passing, to tell Fraser he was named after an old friend. Both seemed keen to uncover a life story they'd never known, and they had plenty of material to research.

He suppressed a yawn and stretched. Over five hours behind the wheel, plus two hours with the Thompsons, hadn't featured in his mental plan of the day. His phone buzzed with calls on and off as he drove back, but he'd been far too busy processing the potential implications of the piles of paperwork to answer.

To his dismay, he'd got four separate voicemails. One was from Steve Rimmer, so it had to be something important.

Grumbling under his breath, he glanced at the clock. It was already nudging six o'clock. His stomach rumbled at the reminder.

Stuff it. He could catch up with his messages, and read, at home.

ALEX FINISHED EATING his pasta, then set out the paperwork on his dining table.

It made sense to start with this new copy of the crash report; it would no doubt raise yet more questions. Thompson's diaries, if that's indeed what they were, might provide interesting context, but would make more sense once he was back in the office and could refer to the documents Booth had supplied previously. In fact, he should probably pass them on to her.

Should he be reading this at home? Probably not, but as he'd barely stopped in the office all day, he could argue the case.

An hour or so later, he straightened up and rubbed his eyes. With a long breath, he closed the cover. He stared into space, deep in thought.

Without a doubt, the crash report was genuine – and uncensored. No surprises this version of the document hadn't made it to the National Archives. He re-read the conclusions and shivered. No wonder the project, and 449 Squadron, had disappeared.

Now they had the full story of what really happened to XM568. This document had maps, witness statements, technical details, and discussions of the scarred and torn wreckage. All of which had been notable by their absence from the "official" report.

Now he had another question: how had Flt Lt Thompson got hold of this?

Thursday 24 November 2022

THE NEXT MORNING, Alex left a message for Woods as soon as he got in.

Yesterday's answerphone messages, left while he was driving back from the Thompsons, still needed his attention. One was from Sqn Ldr Burden; he'd update him shortly at their planned 0930 meeting. One was from Ponsonby, whose sneering arrogance and impatience oozed down the line; he'd figure out how to handle that later. The third was from DI Parkins, letting him know the facial imaging of their man was almost complete. Steve's, which he'd listened to last night, was very interesting indeed…

Woods tapped on his door. 'Morning, sir. Did you say you've got something?'

Alex grinned. He pointed to the pile on his desk. 'I had a call from Flight Lieutenant Thompson's family yesterday. They found a few things that might help.'

Woods blinked, then frowned. He went to pick up the first document. 'Holy sh—' he stopped himself. He looked at Alex with wide, incredulous eyes. 'Does that say what I think it does?'

Alex nodded. 'It does. Natalie was right about '568's crash.'

'Not for distribution,' read Woods. 'Blimey.'

Alex lifted the folder off the top to reveal the notebooks underneath. 'And these look like Thompson's diaries.' He itched to get these to Booth: she and her team were best placed to stitch everything together.

'So we can find out what happened?' Excitement shone in Woods' eyes.

'I hope so.' Alex tried to keep a lid on his own eagerness to find out. 'Let's get these to Natalie as soon as we can.'

Woods nodded. 'Makes sense.' He hesitated. 'D'you think we might actually have some answers here, after all?'

'Some, maybe.' Alex eyed the diaries. He didn't want to get his hopes up, but a solution felt tantalisingly close.

WHILE WOODS WENT off to arrange things with Booth, Alex went to see Sqn Ldr Burden.

What a surprise. Ponsonby was there, too.

Alex withheld his sigh and rapidly re-thought how he was going to handle this. Truth be told, he didn't want Ponsonby to know all about yesterday's discoveries, but it seemed his hand was forced. Fortunately, he had other, interesting, information of his own…

'We wondered if you had some news,' said Burden. He cast a slight glower Ponsonby's way. Ponsonby's mouth curled, but he didn't speak.

'Some,' admitted Alex. He sat down. 'I must apologise for not returning your calls yesterday. I was travelling with respect to some information that may help us solve this case.'

Ponsonby scoffed. 'Really?'

'The family of one of 449 Squadron's engineering officers found some documents. They called me to have a look.'

Burden frowned.

Ponsonby looked almost contemptuous. 'Do you believe the dead can tell us anything?'

'The dead can tell us plenty,' said Alex, with a smile. 'It's up to us if we want to listen.'

'Did they have anything useful to share?' prodded Burden.

'Yes, sir. Including what appears to be an official, uncensored crash investigation report into what truly happened to Vulcan XM568.'

Both men stared.

'Why would that be so?' managed Ponsonby.

Alex braced himself. Time to blow the lid off things. 'Perhaps something to do with the fact unrelated, separate sources state that there were foreign agents entrenched within the programme.'

Ponsonby scoffed. 'Really—'

'So, the name Colonel Oleg Kuryakov means nothing to you?'

Burden gaped. Alex shot him a look to say he'd explain later; Burden's brow wrinkled, though he nodded, unconvinced.

Ponsonby stiffened.

'Of course,' said Alex, 'he had other names. Paul Johnson may be more familiar. At least, those are the names Vasili Mitrokhin refers to, in his archive of KGB papers.'

Ponsonby simply blinked; no other part of him moved.

'Alex,' said Burden, 'this is—'

'Mitrokhin also referred to a 1960s British weapons project, codenamed PEREGRUZKA by the Soviets. Where one agent was an engineer, another an RAF officer, and both were in contact with Colonel Kuryakov. Both agents and controller disappeared, along with the project. By coincidence, around the same time as Banshee and 449 Squadron.' Alex smirked. 'I'm afraid, Mr Ponsonby, that even I have sources.'

Burden took off his glasses and rubbed his face. Then he registered Ponsonby's lack of reaction. 'And another mystery reveals itself.'

'That's not entirely why you're here, though, is it, Mr Ponsonby?' Alex paused. Much as he tried not to take pleasure in another's misfortune, he was going to enjoy this. 'I understand a friend of yours is rather curious about our investigation. He's taken quite an interest, I gather.'

While Ponsonby remained motionless, what colour he had slowly drained from his cheeks.

Thank you, Steve; the man's myriad connections had once again paid off. A few carefully worded questions had yielded very interesting answers in his voicemail. Obviously, Alex made sure to repay information in kind when he'd returned the call earlier; the flow of intelligence travelled both ways.

'You're not telling me we found a Russian under Martinford, are you?' managed Burden.

Now for the awkward part. Alex cleared his throat. 'This is it. We don't know, sir. Circumstantial evidence is that three men connected with PEREGRUZKA ceased all contact with the KGB at around the same time. The only name we know for certain is Kuryakov's. We haven't identified the others. And we've only one body.'

'You must admit,' drawled Ponsonby, 'that even in the present climate, it would not look good for us to admit any of this.'

Pensive, Burden replaced his glasses, but he didn't speak.

'Admit what to whom?' Alex raised an eyebrow.

Ponsonby spread his hands. 'Come, now, even you can read between the lines—'

'—And wonder why an old Russian friend of yours is so curious about an anomalous discovery at a base which was, to be honest, regarded as a bit of a dull posting at the time.'

Shocked, Burden leant back in his seat.

Ponsonby swallowed, stunned. For the first time, his facade cracked; fear flashed in his eyes as he fidgeted with the knot of his lilac silk tie. 'I don't know what you mean,' he managed, but his voice held none of its usual confidence.

'I'm sure the staff at Aspinalls will be more than happy to explain a few things to me.'

Ponsonby gasped; he turned it into an attempt at a cough. 'I must protest—'

'Similarly, I wonder if I should call the manager at Caesar's Palace in Las Vegas?'

'Alex, what are you talking about?' interjected Burden sharply.

Music shattered the tension: Ponsonby's mobile phone.

Stiff with fury, he pulled it from his pocket and scanned the display, hissing a breath out between clenched teeth. He flicked it onto silent with a flourish but cradled it in his hand. 'My friend, as you refer to him, is in fact a British citizen—'

'Who still has contacts, friends of friends, within those referred to as Putin's *siloviki*. Or did you not think to check that?'

Silence spread. Ponsonby refused to look at either Burden or Alex.

With a groan, Burden put his elbows on his desk and rubbed his forehead with both hands. 'Whichever way you want to paint it, Alex,

Mr Ponsonby has a point. Do we want to give Russia any excuse for escalating any aspect of the conflict in Ukraine?'

'Of course not.' Alex cleared his throat. 'Which is why we should continue our investigations as thoroughly as we have been. Once we have our findings, we can consider what we do with them.'

Ponsonby's phone buzzed again. Much as he tried to glare at the screen, his expression faltered as he scanned the text.

Alex continued. 'DI Parkins left a message to say the forensic artist's facial impression of our man is almost complete. I suggest showing it to Wing Commander Miller, who flew one of 449 Squadron's Vulcans. If he can identify the man, all well and good. If not…'

'We'll take it from there,' finished Burden. He frowned at Ponsonby, who sat motionless, staring at nothing.

Alex hid a smirk. Perhaps others already acting on the information Steve had passed around. 'Yes, sir. If there's nothing else, I'd like to carry on examining the documents we were given yesterday.'

Ponsonby held his phone limply on his lap.

Burden scrutinised Ponsonby, then nodded at Alex. 'Perhaps you can find more pieces of this puzzle.'

Alex looked at his watch; it was time to examine the rest of what the Thompsons had given him. He was looking forward to this. He said with a grin, 'Frankly, I hope the next few pieces are something other than just the background. I'd like to fill this in.'

WHILE THE AUDI'S stereo whispered Classic FM in the background, Quentin drove back to London. It felt as if he left his innards behind him.

Cavendish wanted to see him. Urgently.

How – just how had Farnsworth come to know about Valentin? It wasn't like their paths crossed regularly. He thought – he'd tried…

Not hard enough. His unhealthy bank balance testified to that.

He growled and slammed the wheel.

Clearly, the man had connections. Perhaps one reason why he hadn't been censured more strongly for his clash with Major van Allen all those years ago.

The matter was irrelevant, now.

He parked up and walked through the quiet office. Cavendish's PA gave him a blank smile. 'He's waiting for you,' she said. 'Just go in.'

Quentin swallowed the sudden knot that closed his throat. That was code for the man's displeasure at being kept waiting beyond what he considered reasonable. Banalities about delaying traffic weren't even to be considered. He acknowledged her words with a nod.

Despite the tension threatening to seize him, he briskly tapped on the door then opened it.

Cavendish frowned up from his seat. He simply pointed to the soft leather chair in front of his desk. 'We've come across some information that is concerning, to say the least.'

'I see.' Quentin sat down.

'Some time ago we were made aware of a potential foreign agent, residing here in London.' Cavendish met Quentin's gaze with a directness that unnerved him. 'While he's been resident in this country for some time, electronic and other surveillance over the last few weeks has proven he's in regular contact with persons connected to a foreign intelligence gathering organisation.'

'I'm sure there are several such individuals,' managed Quentin, with an airiness he didn't feel.

Cavendish's face didn't change. 'Hmm.'

Uncomfortable silence seemed to echo. Even if he could think of a response, Quentin wasn't sure he could speak.

'I'm disappointed,' said Cavendish. His tone hinted that was the truth.

'Excuse me?'

'Do you not appreciate several of us took a risk – personally, as well as professionally – to find you a welcoming role here?' Cavendish folded his arms and glared. 'You assured us the contretemps in Las Vegas was a temporary lapse of judgement, nothing more. Yet I've been given absolute proof that is not the worst you have done. Lessons have gone unlearned.'

Quentin's mouth dried up. No words came to mind.

'I have contacts in the, shall I say, hospitality and entertainment industry,' said Cavendish. 'I won't go into details, but… I've been informed you have quite exclusive tastes. And exclusivity has a price. A price that would seem to be a stretch for you.'

Didn't it just. Quentin winced.

Cavendish sighed. 'Must I spell this out?'

'I'm afraid I don't understand.' Quentin was amazed the lie made it out of his mouth.

Cavendish was not convinced but had clearly had enough. 'Your gambling friend, Valentin Zhilin. He's SVR. We have proof of you meeting him. And evidence you were passing information in return for payment.'

Quentin closed his eyes. The words rang around his mind. Val? An SVR agent? No, surely not. Yet who did he think wanted the information? Why else would Val even care what happened at Martinford? 'He… no. We went to Oxford…'

Cavendish raised a disdainful eyebrow. 'Unfortunately, an Oxbridge degree is no guarantee of good or honourable character.'

'We're friends—'

'It also appears you attempted to manipulate the Martinford investigation.'

Quentin scoffed. 'Really?'

'Flight Lieutenant Farnsworth volunteered the information to his CO of his own accord. The staff at Noble Rot were most helpful assisting with inquiries.'

'It was nothing more than relationship-building,' spluttered Quentin.

Cavendish's question was sharp. 'For what end? I've seen no evidence of you using other, more conventional, methods.'

Quentin opened his mouth. He closed it again. Normally, he prided himself on being able to counter any argument. Verbal sparring was his forte. But today, his wits drew a blank.

Cavendish's desk phone rang. 'Yes? Ah… good. Send them in.' He dropped the handset back into its cradle, but his hard, dark eyes were fixed on Quentin.

'I'm afraid this is one indiscretion too far,' Cavendish murmured.

'Am I to be…' Quentin couldn't even say the word. Sacked?

The door opened; Quentin glanced over his shoulder. Two gentlemen entered, clad in average suits.

Cavendish merely nodded.

'Quentin Ambrose Ponsonby?' said the shorter, stockier man of the two.

Quentin turned. 'Yes?'

He held up his identity card. 'I'm DS Roberts, Metropolitan Police. I am arresting you on suspicion of passing confidential information, in breach of the Official Secrets Act…'

The police officer carried on with the rest of the official caution, but the words washed over Quentin. Arrested? Him? Surely not.

Yet the taller, skinner man gestured for him to stand.

The shorter one opened the door. 'Through you go. Sir.'

All his mind could do, as he followed the men out through the office, was whisper that this couldn't be happening. It couldn't. Neither could the curious stares of those in the office.

The thought began to percolate through his mind that for once, he wouldn't be able to charm his way out of this problem.

In his office that lunchtime, Alex considered going to grab some food. Woods was with Natalie Booth at the Air Historical Branch, going through 449 Sqn's archive and Flt Lt Thompson's diaries; they'd let him know once they knew more. Much as he wanted to go over and read for himself, realistically he'd just be in the way. Woods would be in touch once they knew anything. There was nothing to gain by him annoying them.

Virtually as soon as he stood up to leave, his phone rang. For a split second, he debated leaving it, but curiosity got the better of him.

'Farnsworth.'

'Ah, glad I caught you.' It was DI Parkins. 'I wanted to let you know we've completed our man's electronic facial reconstruction. Did you say you've someone you'd like to show it to?'

'Great. Yes,' said Alex. He explained about Miller. 'Are you happy I show it to him first?'

'More than.' He could hear Parkins' smile over the phone. 'Shall I email it to you?'

'Please.'

There was a knock on his door. Just as he put the phone down, Burden walked in.

Before he could speak, Alex held up a hand. 'I know, sir. There's a lot I need to fill you in on.'

'There is. I appreciate not having to micromanage you,' said Burden evenly, 'but do not drop bombshells like that on me again. Especially not in front of others.'

Alex swallowed. To be honest, he'd expected far more of a dressing down and Burden to be much more annoyed at how this morning unfolded. 'Sorry, sir. I was rather hoping I'd be able to update you separately, first.'

'How did you find out about Mr Ponsonby's acquaintance?' Burden's eyes glinted with curiosity. 'I literally had the phone call half an hour ago to tell me.'

'I… have some friends from my time in Afghanistan who also have friends in various places.'

'That wouldn't be, oh, what's his nickname? Smeghead? I believe he knows the Staish as well.'

Alex chuckled. 'It would. And I think he knows almost everyone.'

'Well. I was informed that Mr Ponsonby has been arrested on suspicion of passing classified information in breach of the Official Secrets Act. We'll see how that goes.'

Alex whistled.

'On the subject of Russians, what on earth is this PEREGRUZKA? Are there really three missing men? And why am I only just finding out about it?'

Alex sighed. 'You'd better sit down, sir. This will take some explaining…'

IT TOOK A while to go through things with Burden. Fortunately, Alex still had the copies Gerry Fletcher made of Mitrokhin's notes. Burden conceded that Alex had been sensible in not immediately broadcasting the espionage connection but warned him to bring it up sooner next time. Not that he hoped there was a next time.

Meanwhile, the mugshot arrived in his inbox. Alex printed it out in as high a resolution as he could, then called Wing Cdr Miller and asked if he'd be willing to have a look at the image. Miller readily agreed.

Fortunately, their home on the outskirts of Henley-on-Thames was only an hour away from the office. He pulled up outside the neat, detached house. The mild autumn this far south hadn't yet stripped the wisteria above the door of its leaves; they clung in varying shades of brown and green to the spreading, sinuous branches.

Mrs Miller opened the door and ushered him in. 'Oh, hello. John said you were visiting.'

'Yes, again.' Alex smiled ruefully. 'I hope I can leave you alone soon.'

She laughed. 'Between you and me, I rather think he's enjoyed having someone to talk to about the past.'

John's voice echoed down the corridor. 'Are you talking about me, dear?'

'About you, not to you,' she retorted, grinning widely. 'I'll get the kettle on. Black coffee, wasn't it?'

'Please.' Alex smiled. The Millers' relationship was certainly in rude health.

John gestured for Alex to go into his study, though he didn't close the door behind them.

'So,' said John, 'a facial reconstruction, eh? Is that like one of those sketch things?'

Alex nodded. 'Yes, the same as ones they do for unidentified bodies.' A sudden thought poked him. They'd been looking for missing persons; perhaps they needed to look for a body that remained unidentified. He carried on. 'It's an approximation, using skeletal data and extrapolating from his clothing size.'

'This is a best guess at what our man in the bunker may have looked like, then,' stated John. Eagerness and uncertainty flickered across his face. He rubbed his hands together. 'No time like the present, eh?'

Alex handed the greyscale image to John. 'Here you are.'

John's eyes widened. His mouth opened and closed a couple of times. 'Well,' he managed.

A tingle coursed down Alex's spine: could they really have a name for their man?

Mrs Miller bustled in with a tray of drinks. Her eye caught the face on the paper, and she hesitated. 'John?'

'Bloody hell,' John murmured. He wiped his face, then blew out a long breath. The sheet trembled. He lifted his gaze to Alex. 'This – this is the man, is it?'

'It is. Do you recognise him?'

'Yes. They've not done a bad job. Made him a bit younger and not so fat, but I remember that face, all right.' John snorted and shook his head, as if in disbelief. 'George Watson.'

'The Fli-Tek engineering manager?'

'Oh yes. They've given him more hair as well. He was thin on top when I last saw him. But it's him. Without a doubt.'

Mrs Miller frowned over her husband's shoulder. 'Should I recognise him?'

'No, dear,' said John. 'You didn't get the pleasure of working with him.' He stared contemplatively into the distance.

'Would you be willing to confirm this to the police?'

John handed the sheet back to Alex. 'Of course.' He hesitated, the question clear on his face. He exchanged a glance with Mrs Miller. 'We always wondered… what about Squadron Leader Hesketh-Shaw, then?'

Alex pulled a face. 'That's something we'd all like to know.'

'Well, I don't remember any more bunkers under Martinford.' John smiled wryly. 'So, one mystery reveals another.'

ALEX ENJOYED HIS coffee with the Millers, then excused himself to ring DI Parkins. She spoke to Wing Cdr Miller, who repeated his identification of the body as George Watson. Then she asked to speak to Alex again.

Just as they were wrapping things up, Alex cleared his throat. 'It's occurred to me we might have been looking in the wrong places.'

'Excuse me?'

He chewed his lip. How could he explain this? 'It might be better if I come to Leamington to discuss it in person at some point. We haven't found any trace of Squadron Leader Hesketh-Shaw in even Martinford's archive, and…'

'Are you thinking we should look at any unidentified deaths from that time?'

'I can't imagine there'll be many,' admitted Alex. 'But yes.'

'We can try.' Parkins paused. 'I don't know what our chances are. But if we don't look, we don't know.'

'If it comes down to finances, let me know,' said Alex. 'As we've an apparently missing officer, we've got an incentive to help.'

'Of course.' Rustling paper echoed down the line. 'Mr Watson hadn't cropped up as a missing person in our search, so I'll see what we have on record for him, too. Out of interest.'

Alex grinned. It would indeed be interesting to see what the police found.

Thursday 3 September 1964

H E GLANCED AT his watch and grunted. It was almost time.

He'd had a discreet word with the RAF police on guard at the gate: it helped that Martinford buzzed with all kinds of fantastic rumours about what, exactly, 449 Squadron had been doing. A few crumbs of info there, a refusal to comment here, and he'd ensured Watson's name wouldn't be added to the records for "operational reasons".

No doubt someone higher up the chain would be down here later to make sure that page of the records got lost, just to be on the safe side. Whether that someone was RAF, Air Ministry, or the Security Service was no concern of his now.

Blood had been on his hands ever since XM568 was lost: Campbell and his crew shouldn't have died. By rights, he should have taken her sister aircraft up later that day. He'd wanted to avoid deaths, minimise collateral damage…

He sighed.

Earlier, he'd met with Wing Cdr Jenkins of the Board of Inquiry and Wing Cdr Merrick. The Board of Inquiry had their preliminary findings.

What could only loosely be termed the official crash investigation report, for external consumption, murmured vaguely about a catastrophic electrical systems failure. Purely a sop to interested external parties, it existed simply to camouflage the truth.

The uncensored, internal-only report was damning and conclusive.

XM568 was indeed sabotaged.

The explosives discovered by Thompson's men were a sizeable charge, intended to force-generate an electromagnetic pulse in the event of aircraft power not being sufficient. As it was envisaged this would only be used in the event of serious damage to the Vulcan, it disabled Banshee in the process. Unfortunately, neither Fli-Tek nor Hawker Siddeley had verified what would happen if an uncommanded detonation occurred; particularly as this charge lay close to the front internal fuel tank and virtually at the top of the Vulcan's spine. The presumption was the explosive could not self-trigger.

Someone, and it could only have been someone at Fli-Tek, butchered the control units: the carnage was targeted and deliberate. Testing of the same units recovered from '33 and '47 showed the battery charge circuits were damaged so that recharge time was drastically reduced, and the link that stopped charging once capacity was reached, severed. At the same time, the feedback controls to cut off electrical power in the event of this happening were disabled.

Careful examination of the recovered remnants of XM568 showed that Banshee's overheated and electrically overloaded batteries had exploded. That sent parts of the mechanism through the bomb bay walls and severed the Vulcan's powered flight controls, rendering it uncontrollable. Fire had erupted as hot fragments of Banshee slashed fuel lines and peppered engine number two. It was sheer luck that Banshee didn't properly discharge before destroying itself.

At this point, the Vulcan still had sufficient height for the crew to escape: the post-mortem of the aircraft remains showed the Abandon Aircraft switch was hit. But time had run out.

Triggered by the electrical overload and the sudden increase in temperature, the explosive detonated. It blew apart the bomb bay, ruptured the auxiliary fuel tanks – and destroyed the aircraft in a huge fireball.

The official investigation was coming to a close; no doubt there'd be a secret hunt for the saboteur. Although he, and clearly the investigators, had suspicions there…

Whatever happened, 449 Squadron were finished.

The Wingco, he knew, had sent discreet messages to intelligence and HQ questioning the integrity of a couple of officers under his command. His name among them.

His career, as it stood, was over. Once that knowledge would've devastated him; now, it was liberating.

He'd had enough of this double, even triple, life: so much for promises he'd be kept safe. Or promises his wife would be kept out of things. After Campbell, Grice, and the crew, what grieved him more than anything was the fact he'd soon tear her life apart. She, who was innocent in all of this, would pay a high price for his deception. Yet still he could never, ever, come completely clean with her.

Lies tangled in his mind, suffocated his soul; he'd had enough. Enough for a lifetime.

He rubbed the back of his neck.

Soon, it would be over.

It wouldn't be soon enough.

PAPER RATTLED AND metal clinked as Watson shuffled through the stacks of papers. 'I think that's everything.' He rubbed his eyes and coughed. 'Including all your papers.'

'Good. These are the last ones.' Hesketh-Shaw dropped the last folder on the floor. Even Thompson had grudgingly passed over his documents to be "stored", as he'd sarcastically called it. He glanced up at the single light bulb glaring shadeless from the dank ceiling. How this place still had electricity was beyond him: would Works and Bricks ever get around to disconnecting it?

Tomorrow, these crumbling stairs would be capped by another concrete slab. At some point in the coming days, earth would be piled on top of that. Everything that could tell the world what really happened to XM568 and 449 Squadron would be deliberately concealed, forever out of reach.

Personally, he'd rather have burned all the papers, but Wingco Merrick thought a massive bonfire would bring too much attention. For once, he had a point.

Watson pushed a stack of papers to one side. 'As it's just you and me, here… I need to talk to you about something.'

Hesketh-Shaw straightened up. 'What do you mean?'

Watson licked his lips and ran a hand over his balding pate. 'I was wondering when the right time to talk to you about this would be, and there's no time like the present… I believe we've an acquaintance in common.'

Hesketh-Shaw shook his head slightly. 'I don't follow.'

At that, Watson's mouth curled into a smile and his eyes gleamed. 'Oh, I think you do. Why else were you going into the Cadena Cafe on your own that Saturday night?'

Hesketh-Shaw cursed. Adrenaline needled his spine. It hadn't been a trick of his mind, after all. 'So it was you by Burton,' he hissed.

A smug grin flitted across Watson's face before worry creased his brow again. 'I didn't expect to see you there, of all people. Gave me a start, I can tell you.' He fumbled in his pocket, then groaned to himself. Whatever he searched for clearly wasn't there.

Hesketh-Shaw breathed in. *Think, man, think*: he wasn't entirely surprised, but he had to tread carefully. 'What were you doing there?'

'Oh, I'd had a little… rendezvous with our friend the day before, you see. Mr Johnson.' Hesketh-Shaw's eyes widened in shock; Watson smirked. 'He told me all about this other agent, you know. Told me he was air force. Said he was sure one of us was playing him for a fool, working for the British as well.' Victorious scorn oozed from every pore. 'He mentioned where he meant to meet this chap, so I thought I'd take a look. And who should walk past but you?'

Play it cool, Hesketh-Shaw reminded himself. If Watson seriously wanted to hurt him with this, he'd had plenty of time to do so. 'So why have you sat on this until now?'

Watson almost preened. 'Knowledge is power, Squadron Leader. I'm prepared to bet good money none of your colleagues know the slightest thing about your activities. Nor your good lady wife. How would she react?'

'You leave her out of this,' snapped Hesketh-Shaw.

'Oh, a dirty conscience?' Watson sneered. 'Maybe Johnson's tale of a man who couldn't resist a pretty bit of skirt was true, after all.'

Hesketh-Shaw gritted his teeth. He didn't need reminding of his own selfish lust and stupidity.

'I'd have thought you were better than that,' said Watson.

'You know, we do have counter-intelligence officers?' Hesketh-Shaw put his hands on his hips. 'I reported my mistake straight away. I was persuaded that if the Soviets were going to infiltrate this programme, the best thing to do was line up alongside. Feed them misinformation. Manipulate. Control them. You know, I sometimes wonder if I should have gone into acting, rather than flying, but then I tell myself this way, I've made a difference. What's your excuse?'

Watson laughed. 'My excuse? It's not an excuse.' His tone sharpened. 'At least someone recognised I had value. More than anyone else in this blasted country has ever done for me, since Maureen. Of course,' he conceded, 'I didn't mean for them to get Banshee, but—'

'What did you think they wanted?' spat Hesketh-Shaw. 'The football scores?'

'I did my best!' Watson whined. 'I tried to muddle things. Send silly, pointless information. But… I could never keep track. I knew I'd said too much. Johnson said as much,' he added, bleakly.

Hesketh-Shaw had to ask. 'What have you done to Johnson? Where is he?'

Watson blinked rapidly before meeting Hesketh-Shaw's gaze with an unnerving smile. 'We had a little meeting by the river in Stratford. He liked a drink, did Johnson… pity the river is so close to the path. It's very easy to fall in. Particularly if you're three sheets to the wind. I… gave him a little something to help, some barbiturates I had, years ago. He thought I was the double agent, you know. Me!' Watson cried, as if offended.

Breathe, Hesketh-Shaw reminded himself. *Stay calm*. 'Why would he think that?'

Watson's mouth wobbled. 'Well… look—' He broke off and mopped his forehead with his handkerchief.

'Would it be the fact you've sent them contradictory information, over and over again?'

'I just… I didn't—'

'Or is it the fact you sabotaged your own system?' The accusation spilled out before he could stop it.

Watson blanched but didn't speak. All the confirmation he needed.

'You sabotaged all three units, didn't you?' Hesketh-Shaw snarled. Anger boiled within; he struggled to contain it. Anger at the loss of a crew. Anger at Watson's craven incompetence and selfish viciousness. Anger at ever being in this position. 'Why?'

'I needed this to stop,' said Watson, simply. He looked at Hesketh-Shaw, his gaze and demeanour the calm of someone well over the threshold of madness. 'All of it. If I tried to stop sending data, the Russians would just find me and threaten me all over again. But I've had enough. Enough of Russians, enough of Fli-Tek, and enough of Banshee. And I'd long ago had enough of Fraser bloody Campbell. Smug bastard. Did you know he once tried to get me sacked? Just because he and his chief pilot at the time happened to disagree with me on some report conclusions.' Watson sniffed in contempt.

Hesketh-Shaw blinked. Fury simmered down, replaced by incredulity. 'So, you decided to kill, because you weren't brave enough to hand yourself in?'

'Yes… no… what else could I have done?' Watson spread his hands, beseeching, before he turned defensive. 'You're not squeaky clean. Don't you dare tell me what I should or shouldn't have done.'

'You've burned your bridges in spectacular style,' snapped Hesketh-Shaw. 'You sabotaged the technology your company set its hopes on and interfered with the course of an accident investigation. Not to mention committing treason of the worst kind.'

'But you did it too!' Watson protested.

Hesketh-Shaw sighed, weary. He rubbed his forehead. 'Have you listened to anything I've just said? I fed our handlers just enough to render everything you sent totally useless. My trick was to get them to believe I was the reliable one.' His tone hardened. 'After all, I'm a married military officer, not a slipshod alcoholic widower.'

There was a plump, pregnant silence. Watson's brows raised and his mouth slowly opened. 'You set me up,' he gasped. 'You—'

'No. I just let you act as you wanted.'

'You bastard,' spat Watson.

'I let you hang yourself, yes,' said Hesketh-Shaw, contempt clear in his voice. 'But I had to. For the country. The country you betrayed.'

Watson sniffled. 'But… I never… I didn't…'

Hesketh-Shaw didn't bother hiding his bitterness. 'They say the road to Hell is paved with good intentions.'

'But… say I defect,' managed Watson, wretchedly. 'Well… sort of—'

'That's not an option.' Hesketh-Shaw sneered. 'You aren't seen as reliable. By either side.'

Fuelled by desperation, Watson lunged at Hesketh-Shaw: papers flapped and scattered in the scuffle. Though he was smaller, Hesketh-Shaw easily dodged Watson's thrusts and used the man's considerable weight to his own advantage. He spun around and landed a heavy blow to Watson's middle that sent the bigger man to the ground with a sound like a butcher slapping meat on a slab.

Watson groaned and curled in a foetal ball on the floor.

Realisation hardened. Only one of them could walk out of this bunker alive. Watson was unpredictable, unreliable, and utterly self-serving. There was no way he could let him go; Watson had killed six men in an attempt to save himself. What was to say he wouldn't erase the only other person who understood the reality of what he'd done?

Peter and his superiors hoped for a prosecution: that felt naive. There wouldn't be a trial, at least not on this earth, but Hesketh-Shaw could ensure this spy ring was broken for good.

Still, sadness washed over him: not so much at what he was about to do, but what it had cost to get here. His fingers brushed the leather holster where his service pistol lay. He didn't normally carry his weapon, but he'd deliberately hung onto it after practising at the range earlier. He'd known, deep down, it would come to this.

Watson, still wheezing, pulled himself into a sitting position up against the wall. He caught Hesketh-Shaw's movement and stiffened.

Hesketh-Shaw aimed the pistol directly at Watson's head. The metal felt cold but not alien in his grasp. The click as he flicked off the safety and cocked it echoed around the small room.

'Aren't you going to ask me if I have any last words?' Watson managed between panting breaths, sounding more resigned than defiant. 'Anything I want to get off my chest?'

'Is there?'

Watson's words spilled out. 'You don't know how much I wish I'd never gone to London for that event. How often I wished I'd never taken that first drink. But you know, it really goes all the way back to Farnborough, all those years ago. I should never have taken Maureen there, but she insisted. She was so proud of me. I shouldn't have left her to die when John Derry's DH110 disintegrated above us. I should have died with her, not run away. I hated how her loss never seemed to matter to anyone else. That they carried on the show. It hurt, you know. Still does.

'I'm sorry about the others, the rest of Campbell's crew. Really sorry. But I'm not sorry about Johnson. Or Campbell. He almost ended my career—'

'And you ended his life, yes. How poetic.' Hesketh-Shaw took a deep breath. He consciously relaxed his trigger finger. 'Do you feel better?'

Watson's silence said enough; he looked down at the floor.

'There's no way out,' said Hesketh-Shaw. 'I'm sorry, George.'

Watson looked up. 'But—'

BANG.

A single gunshot reverberated in the confined space.

Blood spread from where Watson sprawled.

Hesketh-Shaw lowered his weapon. His ears rang. He waited, motionless, for several moments; Watson didn't move. It was hard not to feel a tinge of pride at the accuracy of his shot, even if it had been at close range.

'Funny.' Hesketh-Shaw addressed Watson's corpse as he slid his weapon back into its holster. 'I wouldn't say I feel better, but I'm glad you can't destroy anything else, now. You've destroyed enough.'

There was something else he had to do before he'd finished. He rummaged through the piles till he found what he was looking for.

Now he could leave – and lock the door behind him.

Gordon lay on his bed fully clothed, staring up at the ceiling. It was only seven o'clock in the evening, but he didn't feel like doing much else. Too many thoughts whirled around his head.

The bunker would be sealed tomorrow morning.

Should he go and have one last look? Confirm what he already suspected, that Banshee brought down XM568? What good would it do, though? He wouldn't be able to tell anyone. Neither would he be able to do anything about it.

Watson's behaviour in the hangar the other day still played on his mind; he didn't appear to be sane or fully in control of himself. Neither was it the way someone innocent would behave.

Watson had done something to Banshee on XM568, just as he had the other control units. He knew it like he knew the sky was blue. He just couldn't prove it. And even if he could, what could he do?

There was a rat-a-tat on his door.

With a groan, he rolled off the bed and opened it. Hesketh-Shaw stood there, still in uniform. A bundle of papers in his hand. 'Can I come in?'

Nonplussed, Gordon stepped aside and waved him in.

'I'll get to the point,' said Hesketh-Shaw. He thrust the papers at Gordon. 'You'll want these.'

Gordon flicked through them. Recognition dawned. Open-mouthed, he stared at Hesketh-Shaw, who nodded. It was, very clearly, the uncensored crash report.

'I thought you needed to know,' said Hesketh-Shaw.

'Not that I can do anything with it.'

'Not that any of us can.'

'I wonder what Watson will do next,' said Gordon, half to himself. 'I mean—' He stopped and met Hesketh-Shaw's eyes.

'You were right,' said Hesketh-Shaw, simply.

'And the bastard gets away with it?' Gordon flung the papers down on his bed. 'That's just—'

'He hasn't.'

Suddenly, Gordon recognised the acrid scent of a recently fired gun wafting off Hesketh-Shaw; it might have been a while since he'd smelled it, but there was nothing else it could be. Not sure what to say, he just stared at him.

Hesketh-Shaw gave a nod and a humourless half-smile. 'I knew you were clever.'

Thoughts collided in Gordon's head; his mouth hung open. Surely that meant Watson...

'I can't tell you anything, officially,' said Hesketh-Shaw.

Gordon glanced at the papers across his bed. 'Just like I don't know what that is, right?'

Hesketh-Shaw raised an eyebrow. 'Like what is?'

Gordon snorted.

Hesketh-Shaw grinned. 'All I can tell you is that you and I were on the same side through all this. Watson wasn't.'

Gordon sighed. 'Fraser warned me about Watson, before...'

Genuine regret shadowed Hesketh-Shaw's face. 'I should have listened to you. I should have argued with the Wingco to stop the programme.'

'Yeah, well...' Gordon shrugged. 'I'm used to not being listened to. That's what engineering is for; management to ignore and then blame.'

'You won't be getting blamed for this. Not even officially.' Hesketh-Shaw took a deep breath. 'And officially, I haven't been here.'

'Where?' Gordon smiled.

A grin flitted across Hesketh-Shaw's face, but it faded. 'We won't see each other again. I'll be... reposted... come tomorrow.'

Gordon nodded, trying to absorb the news and its implications.

Hesketh-Shaw stuck his hand out. 'Goodbye. And thank you.'

Gordon shook his hand. Even after everything, the man's grip was firm and sure. 'Goodbye. Thank you, too.'

Before seeing Thompson, Hesketh-Shaw had dropped his weapon at the armoury. In an hour, he had an emergency meeting with Peter to discuss the arrangements for bringing Chancer to a close. Now, though, it was time to inform Merrick; even at this time, he'd still be at work. He went to the man's office and briskly knocked on the door.

'Enter.'

Hesketh-Shaw strode in. 'Sir. Everything has been placed in the bunker ready for tomorrow.'

'Everything?' Merrick raised an eyebrow.

'Everything that you identified as needing to be "specially archived"? Yes, sir.'

Merrick stared off into the distance. 'How was Mr Thompson about it?'

Hesketh-Shaw considered. 'Not entirely happy, but he understood. He complied fully with our orders.'

'Hmm. I half expected him to interrupt you and demand the report.'

'So what if he did?' Hesketh-Shaw met Merrick's cold grey gaze; for once, there was a hint of shame in it. The old man was close to retirement; even those with a generous cast of mind would find it hard to view 449 Squadron's story as anything other than disastrous. Not the way a man as proud as Merrick would like to end his career. 'You've said it yourself. This all ends here. Those who need to know, know. The rest of us…' He paused. How ironic to use a phrase he'd heard Fraser use, more than once. 'Ours is not to reason why. Is it, sir?'

Merrick sniffed. It was almost comical watching him react. Where Thompson very quickly cottoned on to what the faint scent that clung to him meant, Merrick's brow furrowed in confusion and disbelief for several seconds. When it cleared, there was no mistaking the fear in Merrick's eyes when he scanned his subordinate. Nor the relief when he realised Hesketh-Shaw was unarmed.

'Indeed,' said Merrick, in a strained voice. 'Ask no questions, tell no lies, is it not?'

Hesketh-Shaw grinned. 'I couldn't possibly comment.'

GORDON DIDN'T SLEEP that night. Instead, he scoured the official crash report.

It was there, in black and white. There was nothing he could have done to stop Fraser's death. Nothing he was allowed to have done.

He was right. Not that he wanted to be right, but it was a bittersweet vindication.

Did that confirmation help? In one way. In another, it just kicked him down a new track of things he should have done differently, in an ideal world. Even if this world was so far from ideal, it wasn't funny.

Though he didn't know for certain what Hesketh-Shaw was, and what had happened to Watson, he could guess: too much knowledge in this case was probably dangerous. Certainly, there was no other reason for H-S to have arrived smelling of a recently fired gun…

In some sort of acknowledgement of things being over, he cracked open the bottle of whisky Fraser had bought him and toasted his absent friends. Perhaps they understood – wherever they were, if some trace of them still remained. Hopefully, they felt Watson met the fate he deserved.

Peachy dawn kissed the sky, but the lingering chill hinted autumn was on its way.

He wrapped up warm, then made his way to the dispersal where a mostly-reassembled XL447 had been pushed outside. As far as he knew, XM568's remains were at Farnborough, and XL433 was in bits inside.

Still, this was the closest he could come to paying his respects to the airframes, and those caught up in them.

Even after years of not having gone to Mass, the memory of his Catholic nan made him cross himself and mutter a prayer under his breath. He'd wanted to know the truth, and now he did. The man responsible had paid the ultimate price. He'd known all along there'd be no public washing of this dirty laundry. And yet…

He found himself praying to the God he half hoped, half feared was real. All this felt so ridiculously unfair, unjust, even. Maybe one day, the record would be set straight. Even if he'd carry this on his conscience forever.

'Gordy,' said a voice behind him.

He turned to see John, also staring at XL447.

'John.'

'Come here for answers?' asked John.

Gordon snorted. 'No point.'

'Should see the cordon round the old bunker. Works and Bricks are doing well on the "safety" operation. Even dragged the snowdrops in.'

'Well, I'm sure they don't want us to hurt ourselves.'

'Squadron briefing at ten o' clock,' said John. 'Didn't know if you knew.'

Gordon almost nodded but turned it into a look of surprise. 'No.'

John frowned at him. 'You know something.'

'I know lots of things. Some of them are even useful.'

'You can't tell us, can you?'

Gordon glared. This was not a good start to keeping a secret for the rest of his natural life. 'This whole thing's been a… a… bloody mess. From start to finish. It started as one, and it's ending as one. It doesn't take a genius to work out what's going to happen.'

John kicked fitfully at the floor again. '449 Squadron disbands, we all get moved on, and none of this ever happened.'

'See? Even you can work it out,' said Gordon. 'You'll be a captain before you know it.'

'If anyone will touch us with a bargepole after this,' muttered John.

Gordon scowled. 'This whole bloody project's been too secret,' he added bitterly. 'I'll be glad to see the back of it.'

'You and me both.' John turned, started to walk away, then stopped. 'Oh. Are you seeing Sophie again?'

Gordon swallowed. 'I… er… maybe. If she's, er…'

'Miranda saw her in town the other day, that was all. She asked after you. Said she'd like to see you. If you were free.'

'Oh. Er. Right. Well…' Gordon smiled, bashful. That put a new slant on things.

John winked, then strolled away.

Gordon checked his watch. If he hurried, he'd be able to call on Sophie at home before she went to work. He jogged back towards the mess, his smile widening with every step.

Friday 25 November 2022

ALEX'S MORNING PASSED in many phone calls; much as their body's identification as George Watson solved one potential headache, it created a few more. Still, Sqn Ldr Burden sighed in relief at the news that their man was firmly British.

The last call cheered Alex up considerably.

Sgt Woods and Booth had worked their way through the relevant portions of Flt Lt Thompson's diaries; did he want to come over and go through things?

Nothing would stop him.

As SOON AS he walked through the door, Woods and Booth's broad smiles were evident.

'Morning,' said Booth.

'Did you say you've identified the body, sir?' asked Woods.

'Wing Commander Miller is sure the face belongs to a man called George Watson,' said Alex. 'He was an engineering manager at Fli-Tek, on the Banshee project.'

Woods and Booth exchanged a satisfied grin.

'Thompson's diaries corroborate that,' said Booth.

'Fantastic.' Alex grinned, relieved. A thought struck him. 'But how? And do they explain how he got the crash report?'

'It's all connected to our missing Squadron Leader Hesketh-Shaw,' said Woods.

'Thompson isn't certain what he was but reckons he must have had connections somewhere in the security services.' Booth picked up her notebook and flicked through it. She summarised the chain of events culminating in Sqn Ldr Hesketh-Shaw delivering said document to Thompson, then declaring they wouldn't meet again.

Alex blew out a breath. What a story.

'Obviously, Thompson doesn't know exactly what happened, but he says Hesketh-Shaw told him Watson had been dealt with. He didn't ask more.'

'You wouldn't,' added Woods.

'No, you wouldn't,' conceded Alex. Memory nudged him. 'Wing Commander Miller said he thought he saw someone who could've been Hesketh-Shaw years later, but he was a Canadian air force officer…' Alex trailed off.

'Thompson was sure Watson was behind what happened to XM568,' said Booth. 'He pushed to stop testing and investigate the two remaining aircraft. His team found evidence of sabotage on both.'

Alex whistled.

'Some of that is backed up by papers we recovered from the bunker,' added Woods.

All three of them exchanged glances.

'Let's pull this together,' said Alex. 'Watson is the man in the bunker. Circumstantial evidence from Thompson is that he was shot by Hesketh-Shaw. That same evidence explains how Thompson got the official crash report and gives the opinion Watson was the saboteur who was responsible for XM568's loss.'

'There's more than just a bit of evidence something was going on with Watson, at least in Thompson's diaries,' said Booth. 'He hasn't just pulled that opinion from thin air.'

Alex paused. 'OK.' He gathered his thoughts. 'It seems probable, then, that of our three agents Mitrokhin mentions, we've got two here.'

'And Squadron Leader Hesketh-Shaw is our double agent,' added Woods.

'Which explains why his disappearance is so neat,' said Alex.

'Obviously, Thompson had no idea of anything else going on,' said Woods, 'so we still don't know about that Russian – what was his name?'

'Paul Johnson. Or Colonel Oleg Kuryakov.' Alex scratched his head. 'I don't believe it's unheard of for KGB agents to lose contact with their home controllers. No doubt some decided they'd be better off by themselves in the West. But I've asked DI Parkins if her team can go through any unidentified bodies from that time. We might find something.'

Booth referred to her notes. 'It'd be helpful if Wing Commander Miller would be happy to corroborate a couple of things mentioned.'

Alex thought back to the photos. 'I'm sure he will.'

'AT THIS RATE,' muttered Wing Cdr Miller with a grin, 'I'll have to ask Miranda to make you dinner.'

Alex laughed.

'I don't mind,' came a shout from the kitchen.

'I've bothered you enough without eating all your food,' said Alex. Truthfully, he'd enjoyed talking with Miller: it was nice that the feeling was mutual.

'You said you had some things for me?' said Miller, as Alex followed him through to his study.

'Yes. I had a phone call from Flight Lieutenant Thompson's sons.'

At that, Miller frowned. He leant against the doorway, thinking. 'Gosh, I haven't heard from them – well, their mother, Sophie – for some years.'

Alex braced himself. There wasn't going to be a nice way to say this. 'I'm sorry. I'm afraid she passed away some weeks ago. I don't know much more than that.'

Sadness softened Miller's eyes. 'Ah. That's a shame, but… it comes for us all, eventually.' He pursed his lips, scanning the mess of papers and books that seemed to have moved around rather than be put away. 'I always tell my son clearing this will earn him his inheritance.'

Alex chuckled. That would be quite some task. 'I think that's part of what happened here. The Thompsons found some paperwork belonging to their father. That had been hidden for quite some time.'

'Oh?' Curiosity piqued, Miller's eyes lit up. He gestured for Alex to sit in his usual seat; he himself sat by the desk.

Alex reached into his messenger bag and retrieved a plastic wallet containing the Martinford diaries. 'It seems he kept diaries, intermittently, and these cover his time on 449 Squadron.' He showed the old, soft, cardboard-backed book to Miller. 'We'd appreciate it if you could corroborate a few things in here.'

Miller considered. 'OK.'

Alex ran through a few incidents mentioned in the diaries. Soon, Miller was happily sharing his recollections, and quickly Alex had more than enough to prove the diaries were accurate. That was a weight off his mind. Not that he thought the Thompsons would've lied about things, but every little helped.

Miller tapped his fingers on the edge of one of the piles of books, thinking. 'I always got the impression, afterwards, that Gordon had something weighing on him. Once 449 Squadron disappeared, if you know what I mean. I don't know if it was Fraser's accident, or something else, but... there was an awkwardness. Something he didn't even want to come close to.'

Alex nodded. That was one way of putting things. Should he tell Miller the full story? On one hand, he'd been there, and he deserved to know; on the other, if even Flt Lt Thompson hadn't told him, was it his place to break the decades-long silence?

'There's something, isn't there?' asked Miller.

'I'd never make an actor, would I?' Alex chuckled. He mulled over what to say. 'Yes. And I doubt it'd surprise you who it was connected to.'

'H-S,' said Miller, instantly.

Alex made a decision. Perhaps, half a century on, one of the men involved deserved the truth. 'I think, after so long, you should hear this...'

Monday 28 November 2022

DI Parkins met Alex in the reception of the Warwickshire Justice Centre. They walked through to her office, where they grabbed hot drinks and then sat in one of the smaller meeting rooms.

'I must say,' she began, 'I didn't think we'd get a name for our man. Nor such a definite identification.'

'Me neither,' admitted Alex. He sipped his black coffee. 'Did Flight Sergeant Woods send you the copies of the relevant pages of Flight Lieutenant Thompson's diaries?'

She nodded. 'They were quite interesting. I take it you've verified them?'

'Yes. Strictly speaking, Thompson shouldn't have kept a diary of any kind, but… we should be glad he did.' Alex sighed. 'Did you find anything out about this George Watson?'

Parkins nodded and raised her eyebrows. 'Yes. His death was covered up.'

Alex stared at her, wide-eyed. 'What?'

She grinned as if to say "wait till you hear this". 'He was recorded as presumed dead by suicide. His car, a Rover 2000, was found close to the Clifton Suspension Bridge in Bristol on the morning of Saturday fifth September 1964. Some of his belongings, including his wallet, were found nearby or washed up by the river over the next few days. It was assumed his body had gone out to sea. His colleagues confirmed he'd been increasingly agitated over the last few weeks of his life. The last time he was seen alive was Thursday third of September.'

'Which also matches the date in Thompson's diary,' said Alex.

Parkins looked at him, head on one side. 'Why would this man's death be covered up like this? And isn't it coincidence his probable murderer disappears?'

Alex tried to dodge the question. Coincidence was the last thing it was. 'You don't have any other unidentified bodies from that period?'

'Ah.' She held up a hand. 'Hold on a moment.' She got up and darted into the office; she returned a few moments later with a few sheets of paper. 'I'd forgotten about that. He's the only one in our area at any point during the 1960s.'

'Well, it'll be interesting to have the details, anyway,' said Alex.

'Here you are. Not many details, I'm afraid, but… an unidentified male, aged around 40 to 50 and wearing dark trousers and a shirt, found in the River Avon in Stratford-upon-Avon on the seventh September 1964. Pathologists at the time believed he'd been in the river a few weeks, so that rules him out as being the squadron leader. All they were able to tell at the post-mortem was he had water in his lungs and a lot of alcohol and barbiturates in his system. No-one close to his description was reported missing. Even dental records couldn't identify him.' She scanned the papers. 'He's described as heavy-set, about five foot nine or ten in height, and dark haired. Which also rules him out as being our squadron leader.'

'Hmm.' Alex wondered how likely it was that this death was unrelated to their investigation. He didn't want to jump to conclusions, but the timing would be yet another coincidence. 'If I could have the details anyway, for completeness, that would be helpful. Thank you.'

'Of course.' Parkins eyed him, curious. 'You still haven't answered my question.'

'Officially, it's very unusual indeed.' Alex hesitated. This felt like taking a step into a minefield. 'All I can really say is I now grasp why MI5 were so keen to get involved in the beginning.'

Understanding dawned. Parkins nodded, slowly. 'I see.' She half-smiled. 'That would explain the neatness of things.'

'You may find someone contacts you directly from them,' said Alex.

'I'll wait for the call, then.'

Alex nodded. 'What's the police position on this?'

She shrugged and blew out an uncertain breath. 'In theory, we've a murder on our hands. That said, the killer seems to be a man who disappears without a trace at the same time. Even if we could find him, he'd be in his eighties. Your diary writer passed away twenty-four years ago, so there's nothing else he can tell us.' Parkins heaved a sigh and ran a hand through her short, dark hair. 'None of this would stand up in court. If it even got that far.'

That was a very big if. Alex scratched his chin. If nothing else, he had to be pragmatic. 'I don't know what'll happen next. I expect we'll all be told to stop the investigation and leave it where it is.'

'Me too.' Parkins smiled. 'Well, it's been an interesting case. To say the least.'

ALEX SAID HIS goodbyes and headed out into the darkening evening. Already, traffic queued past the police station through Leamington. He glanced at his watch; it was 1600. Probably the wisest course of action was to stay put for a while, have a meal, then drive home once the worst of the traffic had gone.

Though he had no intention of driving anywhere, he opened up the Insignia and sat in it. Then he dialled Burden's number.

'How did it go?' asked Burden.

Alex quickly summed up Parkins' findings about Watson.

'That's… hmm…' Burden was silent for a good few moments.

'Isn't it?' Alex watched the cars file slowly past the end of his bonnet. Idly, he tapped his fingers on the steering wheel. 'The interesting news is, they did find records of a still-unidentified body, found in September 1964 in Stratford-upon-Avon, in the river. He'd apparently been there some weeks.'

'Our squadron leader?'

'Unlikely. The way he was described, he sounded closer to George Watson in build.'

'I've spoken to someone senior in MI5. Their records appear to have been destroyed.' There was no disguising the heavy sarcasm in Burden's voice.

'In which case, this Hesketh-Shaw must have gone… somewhere. To a new life.' Alex considered. 'Otherwise, why would someone go to the trouble of making Watson's death look like a suicide? Hesketh-Shaw clearly didn't do it by himself.'

Burden sighed.

Alex continued. 'We've nothing concrete, but I suspect we've got the three agents Mitrokhin mentioned. Not that we can prove the man in the river was Colonel Kuryakov. Watson was covered up, in part because anything else risked letting the cat out of the bag.'

'And everything stayed nice and hidden, until Braxton came along.'

'Exactly.' Alex pursed his lips. 'I told DI Parkins that I, ah, expected to be told to leave this case where it is. She agreed there'd be little to stand up in court. If it even got that far.'

'Perhaps that's the best-case scenario,' said Burden. His tone brightened. 'No point digging up the past.'

Alex chuckled at the choice of words. There was only one thing he could say. 'I think Braxton have done enough of that.'

Acknowledgements

FIRST, THANK YOU to all at Resolute Books. It's been an honour and a joy to work with such talented and passionate creators. This book is far better for the feedback and fettling it's received courtesy of my fellow authors. I can't thank Liz Carter enough for her superb editing.

I'm grateful to Fiona Veitch Smith, author of the Poppy Denby series and the Miss Clara Vale Mysteries; not only for her marvellous endorsement, but also her generous advice which made this book much stronger.

This is a work of fiction: all people and events are completely made up, and any resemblance to persons living or dead is purely coincidental.

There will no doubt be factual errors within this novel, either through unintentional omission, me mangling information, or committing the cardinal sin of invoking writer's prerogative. I can only apologise for any errors and claim them as mine.

Banshee, or TL.772, is a figment of my imagination. It's at the edges of the envelope in terms of technological feasibility today, never mind during the 1960s, but it has a seed of potential truth. Although I chose to make Banshee non-nuclear, EMP effects of nuclear weapons were known at the time; I recommend interested readers look up the American *Operation Fishbowl* series of high-altitude nuclear tests during 1962.

Avro Vulcan B.2s obviously exist, but XL433, XL447 and XM568 are imaginary, as is 449 Squadron.

Jaguar Land Rover and their Gaydon site, as it was circa 2001, inspired Braxton and RAF Martinford: however, there the resemblance ends. Wellesbourne Airfield, formerly RAF Wellesbourne Mountford, provided the idea for bunker in question, and Vulcan XM655 was herself an inspiration.

Martinford is also fictional; in my head, it's in south Warwickshire, within easy reach of Leamington Spa and Stratford-upon-Avon, and it borrows extensively from Whitnash, Kineton and Gaydon.

While the real Mitrokhin archives did lead to the identification of Melita Norwood as a KGB agent, I've taken liberties by adding my own agents. They, and their actions, are entirely fictional.

During my research, I made use of the National Archives, and also the archives of the Shakespeare Birthplace Trust in Stratford-upon-Avon: Henry IV Part 2 was indeed being performed at the RSC during August 1964, although on the 14th, not the 7th.

Many people have helped me with this book over several years. In particular, I'd like to thank: John Wood and Rod Holmes for information on Vulcans and the V-Force; Bryan Elwick, Kevin Prince and Martin Shepherd for their assistance with 1960s railways; Howard Heeley and Newark Air Museum for giving me access to, and many images of, Vulcan XM594, which were incredibly useful.

I also wish to thank Sqn Ldr Bill Turnill for his first hand testimony of what it was like captaining a Vulcan; he cast a sharp eye over the flying scenes in particular.

I owe a massive debt of gratitude to Phil Cain, who has seen this novel grow from an idea to what it is today; Gordon and Fraser wouldn't be who they are without his input, right at the start.

I also cannot thank my mother-in-law, Kerry, enough for giving the finished book a final check and read through.

Finally, there is one person for whom thank you isn't enough: my husband Dave. Without his patience, support, and willingness to listen to me talk about imaginary things and people as if they were real, this book really would not have happened. Few husbands are prepared to listen to their wives discuss how they've hidden the bodies – at least, not without calling the authorities afterwards.

About Resolute Books

We are an independent press representing a
consortium of experienced authors,
professional editors and talented designers
producing engaging and inspiring books of the
highest quality for readers everywhere. We
produce books in a number of genres including
historical fiction, crime suspense, young adult
dystopia, memoir, Cold War thrillers, and even
Jane Austen fan fiction!

Find out more at resolutebooks.co.uk

for the joy of reading

Milton Keynes UK
Ingram Content Group UK Ltd.
UKHW040110300824
447600UK00004B/63